Dead Town

Cal Noble

HAINT
- PRESS -

Dedication

To those who love and tolerate me.

CHAPTER 1

As a pre-engineering student, Chase Parker couldn't care less about literature, but since he needed an English class and Kenna-Grace said she was taking this one, he signed up for it, too. He sat at his desk, not listening to a thing Ms. Short said about Poe as she wrote on the white board. Instead, he did what he usually did in American Lit—doodled and stole glances of Kenna as she sat attentively at the desk to his right. Her long brown hair always flowed perfectly over her shoulders to the top of her seat back. It always had that slight golden glow to it, even on cloudy days like this. In his periphery he studied her long, lithe leg protruding from the bottom of her black skirt and bending down into the top of her black ankle boot. He looked over again. His eyes scanned up her leg to the bend at her hips. Up over her flat abs, hugged tightly by the black spaghetti strap top. Her thin tan left arm resting on her desktop as she took notes with her right hand. Her delicate shoulder. Her long neck and strong jaw.

Kenna looked at him, her bright blue eyes piercing his.

She mouthed, "What?"

Chase grinned and shrugged one shoulder.

Kenna whispered, "Pay attention." She pointed at him with her pen then her eyes followed the pen as it directed Chase toward the white board. She repeated the motions, smiled and lowered her head back to her note taking.

Chase tried to follow directions. He looked at the white board and listened to Ms. Short, but he really didn't care what the spindly woman had to say. His mind was on other things—mainly Kenna-Grace and the party tonight. Perhaps tonight would be the night he finally got the courage he had been trying to gather for six years since they first sat together in ninth-grade English.

After class, Chase and Kenna walked together to the parking lot.

"Ready for tonight?" he asked.

Dead Town

"When am I *not* ready for a good time?" Kenna said, almost giggling.

"We need a DD. There's supposed to be a couple kegs there and my cousin's picking me up some rum and vodka. You need him to get you anything?"

"You plan on sleeping 'til Sunday?"

"Alcohol poisoning. It's the only way to die."

Kenna rolled her eyes and flashed a bright white smile.

"Lunch?" Chase asked.

"Can't. Shit to do at home. The warden has been in a mood lately."

The warden was Kenna's disaffectionate term for her mother, a single mom with substance- and male-abuse problems since Kenna's father died in the early days of the War on Terror.

"Just come over when you're done," Chase said. "We'll figure out who the designated driver is and leave the cars at our place."

* * *

Kenna-Grace turned her '08 Hyundai onto the dirt driveway leading to the small prefab house paid for by her daddy's death money. As she rounded the curve, she saw a newer blue car parked in the yard next to her mother's white 2010 Crown Vic.

"Imagine that," she whispered out loud, rolling her eyes.

For a week or so, up until two days ago, there was a brand new 2019 Ford pick-up there.

Kenna parked in the grass on the other side of the warden's car and switched off the ignition. She took a deep breath, held it a second, and let it out. She could do this.

As soon as she started to open the front door, the warden said, "You're late."

"I'm right on time."

The warden stumbled out of the kitchen high or drunk or both again. Her dyed-red hair was fried and frazzled. She reached into the top of her oversized V-neck shirt and adjusted her breast and bra. Behind her walked a skinny man with three-days' worth of stubble on his face and a grungy white wife beater.

"Your dog shit in the hallway. Clean it up."

That wasn't like Pepe, her teacup Chihuahua. He was usually pretty good in the house. "Did you let him out at all today?"

The warden balled her fists. "Who the fuck do you think you are?" she asked. She relaxed her fists then reached over her right shoulder with both hands to cup the stranger's face behind her. "Poor Matthew stepped in it. Now clean it up."

Kenna rolled her eyes and huffed.

"I swear to God if you roll your eyes at me one more time, missy, I'll black both of 'em. You hear me?"

"Yes, ma'am."

"You're lucky I didn't kill that nasty little fucker," Matthew said, clearly trying to sound hard.

The warden turned around and laid a sloppy wet kiss on him. As they made out right there in the living room, Kenna walked to the bathroom.

"Pepe!" she called, but he didn't come. "Pepe, where you at?"

Pepe yipped somewhere down the hallway. She followed the sound to her room. He continued barking in the closet until she opened the door and let him out. Kenna cut her eyes toward the living room.

Assholes.

* * *

As Chase stuck the key into the lock to his apartment, the sweet oily aroma of weed filled his nostrils. He opened the door to a billowy cloud of smoke.

"Starting early, huh?" he asked, looking at Paul and Tanya sitting on the old sofa.

"Friday bake day," Paul said, passing a small red bong to Tanya. "Class over already?"

"Yeah. You missed it again."

Paul grinned. "Priorities, man."

"Flunking American Lit should be everyone's priority."

"Preach, Brother Parker."

Tanya giggled then took a hit off the bong.

Chase studied her for a second. He still couldn't decide what he thought about her. He guessed she was alright. She was a pretty girl with long blonde hair and bright blue eyes. Her chiseled, slightly up-turned nose looked almost like a flaw, though. As if the sculptor accidentally knocked off the tip at a forty-five degree angle. It was cute and odd at the same time. Despite her desirability, she just wasn't his type. But it wasn't her looks that made him wonder about her. In the three months she and Paul had been dating, she probably spent more nights at their place than her own home. But that wasn't it either. Paul always had a way of drawing girls in. He was like a black hole. They gravitated toward him and revolved around him, quickly getting sucked in. Then, fast as they appeared on his edges, they disappeared.

Probably what set him most at unease with Tanya were some of the tattoos that professed her fascination with witchcraft and the occult. It wasn't that Chase was overly religious. In fact, he didn't know *what* he believed. His parents dragged him to a strict holiness church until he was sixteen, then they let him decide for himself whether or not he wanted to go. He didn't. He loved the idea of the stories, but doubted them. Doubted that one man could atone for the sins of another, let alone the entire world and all generations before and after him. He was more logical than that. It was like that story they read in high school, *Everyman*. He always thought, *if* a hell exists, no one can save another from it.

So, while he didn't know if he believed in heaven, hell, God, the devil or any other set of gods or religion, he supposed he was still slightly uncomfortable with those things his parents' church always preached against. He chalked it up to superstition, and though he didn't consider himself superstitious, he still avoided walking under ladders and picking up pennies that were face down.

Paul took the bong from Tanya and pulled it to his lips. Before lighting it, he lowered it then thrust it toward Chase. "Want a hit?"

"I'm good."

As Paul placed it back against his lips, Chase watched.

The two had been friends since sixth grade when they played bas-ketball together. At that time, Paul was a forward and Chase was point guard. Somewhere during that summer, though, things changed. Paul seemed to stop growing and Chase grew like kudzu. By the time sev-enth grade started, Chase was six-one and Paul was still hovering around five-nine. Both added a couple more inches over the years, but

Paul remained a few inches shy of Chase's six-three. Width was another story. Paul got wider and more muscular. Chase, not so much. He remained lean. Not skinny. Not big. Just kind of there.

With his big build, dark blond fuck-boy haircut and bright green eyes, it was no wonder the girls loved Paul.

Chase walked through the cloud to the kitchen and poured a glass of sweet tea. As he reentered the living room, Tanya asked, "Want me to read your cards?"

She dug in her book bag and pulled out a purple Crown Royal bag.

"You carry those things around with you?" he asked.

"Never leave home without them." She smiled. "No telling when I might need them."

"I'm straight. Thanks." He sat on the mismatched recliner they pulled off the street one night. It was old, but in good shape. Definitely good enough for two fresh college kids who were just going to lounge on it and probably stain it with food, alcohol and bodily fluids if they were lucky.

"Suit yourself." She pulled the cards from the bag and started shuffling them. After a few seconds, she handed them to Paul. "You shuffle. I'll read *your* future."

"I *know* my future," Paul said. "I'm gonna get baked. Get lucky. Go to a party. Get wasted. Come home and get laid again."

Tanya's thin tweezed eyebrows arched up as a lascivious grin adorned her face. "Sure about that?"

"Never more certain." He pulled her close and gave her a quick peck on the lips. "And I don't need cards to tell me that."

As soon as he finished talking, she kissed him again, this time, though, she opened her lips and parted his with her tongue.

Chase stopped watching and looked at the television, which was on but muted. A few seconds later, Tanya began to deal out the deck in an odd pattern. That's where he took his leave. He could handle the making out. Hell, a couple times he and Paul had sex with girls in the same room or tent. That was no biggie. But the tarot bullshit set him on edge.

* * *

Dead Town

As the warden and her new beau stumbled out of the house, Kenna-Grace picked up the shit from the hallway then got a rag and washed and scrubbed at the carpet to get it out where Matthew had ground it in. Pepe stood beside her watching with a curious expression on his pointy face.

Once that mess was cleaned, she moved to the kitchen where the warden and her man-of-the-week managed to create a large pile of cups and plates. *How can two people use so many dishes in half a day?* She wondered. When they were washed, dried and set up, she moved to the living room to pick up her mother's shorts, thong, bra and t-shirt which were strewn around the room. Apparently, eating wasn't the only thing they did all day.

After vacuuming the carpet and mopping the kitchen floor, she picked up all the empty beer and whiskey bottles. The ashtray was full of cigarette butts and a couple of spent blunts.

Kenna shook her head.

Ninety minutes later, there was almost no evidence the warden even stayed at the small house. That was a great feeling.

Kenna pulled her cell phone from her back pocket and started texting Chase.

--WYD

--Nuthin WYD?

--Eat yet?

--Nah. Came home. Y?

--Done. Hungry now.

--Fuji's?

The truth was, she wasn't that hungry. She just wanted to get out of the house before the warden came home and fucked it up again. Sometimes, the woman was gone for days, high on meth or whatever. Other times, she went out and returned quickly in a mood and just started messing shit up so she could complain about what a horrible daughter Kenna was.

--Be there in 20.

Fifteen minutes later, Kenna-Grace stepped into the tiny Chinese restaurant geared more for take-out than dine-in. She took the table by the plate glass window up front and waited. She was always waiting on him.

* * *

"That's bullshit," Paul said, leaning back against the sofa and laughing.

"It's true," Tanya said. Then quickly added, "Or can be if you don't pay attention to the signs."

"Like stop signs and speed limits?" He giggled more.

"No, just pay attention to what's going on around you. The cards don't always tell you exactly what will happen. They tell you what is *going* to happen if you stay on the course you're on. Does that make sense?"

"I have no course," Paul said. "Other than bound for greatness, my life is an unwritten book. It's up to me to fill in the pages."

"That's what I'm saying." She grabbed her Newports off the coffee table and lit one. "Sort of. This reading tells you what will happen, one, five, twenty pages from now if you keep filling in the pages as they appear you will. You can throw in a twist or change something on page three and that will alter what happens on page four or eighty-four. Then again, maybe not. Some things are destined to happen, no matter what we do."

Paul grabbed his American Spirit cigarettes from the sofa's arm and popped one in his mouth. "I'm still calling bullshit."

"Well, for your sake, let's hope you're right or write something different."

Paul eyed her up and down. She was cute, but definitely gullible if she believed all this.

"That's a pretty convenient theory," he said just before lighting his cigarette. "You predict something is going to happen. If it happens, you say, 'See? Told ya so.' And if it doesn't happen, you say, 'See? Told ya so. Good thing you changed it.' You can never be wrong."

Tanya lowered her eyes and started to gather the cards from the table. Her face was blank as tomorrow's page.

If he wanted to get laid before going out and wanted to have a good night, he had to do something.

"Sorry," he said. "I just don't believe in all that."

Dead Town

Without looking up from the cards she was carefully stacking and sliding into the purple bag, she said, "Some things exist, whether you believe in them or not. A person who doesn't believe in gravity will still fall if he steps off a cliff."

"But that's different. *Everyone* believes in gravity. That guy is just an idiot."

Tanya took a drag off her cigarette and thought for a second. "Galileo said the earth revolved around the sun. No one believed him. *Everyone* believed we were the center of the universe. Did that make them right? Not believing in a truth doesn't make the lie more true or the truth less real."

Paul understood her logic, but still didn't agree. See. Hear. Feel. Taste. Smell. That's what he believed in. Nothing more. Nothing less.

CHAPTER 2

Kiara sat cross-legged on her bed and opened the oversized book she had on her lap to a random page. She had already read the book several times, but was testing herself to see how well she knew what each page was about based upon the first few lines or drawings. It wasn't enough just to read and repeat. She wanted every bit of knowledge to be woven into the fabric of her soul. She wanted it to be so much a part of her that when she exhaled, it was almost on her breath like the minty smell of fresh gum.

The drawing was of a talisman with the Pentacle of Venus and the Seal of Venus. That was an easy one. It was the same talisman she had dangling from a thin hemp strand around her neck. The talisman for success in love. So far, it hadn't exactly worked, but she knew it would. Some things were quick and easy. Some things required the universe to rearrange items and people. When it came to a true and lasting love, it wasn't as simple as plucking someone out of thin air or another state and dropping him or her in her living room. Bowling pins don't just automatically pop back into place on their own after being knocked down. There is a machinery behind the scenes, plucking, prepping, and setting them right. Love is no different.

Kiara was five for five. She closed the book, pleased with herself. This was her favorite book of spells, charms and talismans. It was short, simple, and—for the most part—contained many of the spells and ideas that first drew her to the craft. She looked at her dresser where many more books stood between large pink crystal bookends. Some were thick. Others thin. Most appealed to her, but the one she disliked was also the smallest book. Unlike the others on Runes, light magick, white magick, Wicca, Druidism and such, it was a dark book, aptly named *The Book of Darkness*. In it were various spells pertaining to the dead, summoning, and black rites. She never would have bought it for herself, but her friend Derek gave it to her as a birthday gift when she turned eighteen. A few months later, he was dead by his own hand. She kept it and read it for him, because he always claimed it was the most powerful shit he had ever witnessed. She read it alright, but there was no way she was ever going to try any of the shit in there. One mispronounced word or forgotten thing could mean she was eternally lost.

Of course, as she researched the book, the internet had tons of stories about the magick contained therein as well as the author. Many people claimed it was a hoax—that Blake Longstreet was a sham artist who wrote it as a joke to sucker people out of money, especially those with a grudge or looking for revenge. Others claimed it worked and created awful devastation in the lives of their targets. And still more claimed the truth was somewhere in between—that Longstreet wrote it as a hoax, but was unwittingly guided by an evil hand directing him what to write and draw. Kiara had no idea who was right. Nor did she care. She kept it in her library more as a remembrance of Derek than anything. Not only did it remind her of the good times they had together, but it also reminded her that good people can go bad. That light is always balanced out by dark. And evil is not just a figment of the imaginations of the holier-than-thou crowd. It is real and one has to work to avoid it.

* * *

Tanya lay in bed beside Paul. He quietly snored as she checked social media on her phone. She glanced over at him. He looked so sweet and innocent. She wasn't sure what drew her to him. He had many good qualities beyond his great build and pretty face. Still, she couldn't help but wonder what she saw in him. Earlier, he made her feel so small when he started bashing what she believed.

But maybe that was another thing she liked. He was certain of himself. His confidence was contagious sometimes. He was the kind of guy that could say, "Let's jump off a bridge" and tons of people would line up to do it, just because he suggested it. Hell, he could probably say, "Y'all go first," and they would all jump before he did. Sure, he could be a dick. But that was part of his charm.

Tanya looked at the red numbers on clock on the bedside table. 3:16. Soon enough, they would be prepping for the party.

She wondered about his reading again. The majority of his cards were Major Arcana with a relatively balanced number of upright and reversed cards. He needed to listen to her. But he wouldn't. Then again, he was partially right. Without knowing what signs to look for, how could he stay or alter his course? It would be almost impossible to drive from Keller Falls, Alabama to Spokane, Washington if none of the interstates and roads were marked. Still, she worried about the life-changing events coming his way. All sorts of bad scenarios whipped through her mind. A car accident that left him paralyzed. His parents dying in a fire. A blow to the head during a fight that gave him permanent brain damage. Yes, it was possible some-hing *good* was coming his way, but it didn't *feel* like that. For some reason her mind swelled with dark projections. She was usually pretty optimistic, and the cards weren't specific on whether this change would be for the better or worse, but her intuition or spirit guide kept nudging her toward the notion that something horribly bad was going to happen. And happen *soon*.

* * *

Kenna picked at her kung pao chicken, taking her time. She was in no hurry to finish. No, she was finished before she started. She was in no hurry to return home, even though she knew she had to at some point. She had the perfect outfit already picked out for the night and there was no way she was going without make-up.

Her gaze shifted from her plate to Chase. He was looking at her. Something was on his mind.

"What?" she asked.

"What what?"

"I thought you were going to say something."

Chase looked away, the overhead lights glinting in his green eyes. "Nope. Just enjoying my meal."

She took a sip from her can of Diet Coke. "What time you wanna go tonight?"

Chase's eyes returned to hers for a second. He looked at his plate and grabbed a piece of broccoli with his chop sticks. Just before popping it in his mouth, he said, "Nine?"

11

Dead Town

"That late?"

He swallowed. "Tristan said it started at eight. We could come early if we want to help set up." With his free hand he ran his fingers through his long shiny blond bangs, brushing them back over the top of his head. "But I don't want to do that."

"Isn't Bloody Mess playing there tonight?"

Bloody Mess was another friend's band. As far as college garage bands with a hard edge went, they were pretty popular locally. They played a lot of parties and some of the bars, even though half of them were still too young to legally drink.

"Yeah, but you know how he gets. Put this here. Put that there. Do this. Do that. Then he dicks off or spends an hour in the shower while I do most of the work. I'd rather sit at home and have a primer party."

Kenna preferred that idea. She knew exactly what Chase meant. One time she got suckered into helping Tristan. He sat and played Xbox while she set out red Solo cups, prepped the garbage can for the coming keg, swept, put ashtrays around the place, etcetera. It was no easy feat. Tristan and three of his friends rented a large Victorian house in the heart of Keller Falls. His bashes were always big and noisy. Fortunately, the house next to him had been vacant for almost a year and the neighbor on the other side was relatively young and still cool with loud music. It was a perfect place to party.

"What time is kickoff?" she asked.

"Sevenish?"

She looked at her phone screen. 3:16. She wasn't about to spend the next three or four hours at home. "*Sevenish*?" She repeated, hoping he would get the hint and invite her over.

"Why? What time you wanna start?"

She looked at her phone screen again. "Three-twenty?" She smiled.

It was Chase's turn to check his phone. "*Now*?" he asked.

"Why not?" She watched his face change from expressionless to one of almost confusion then added, "It's Friyay."

"I ain't got the booze from my cousin yet."

For someone who always did well in school and was considered smart, he sure could be an idiot sometimes.

"I got it covered." She pushed her plate away. "Let's go."

They went their separate ways in the parking lot. A few minutes later, she pulled off the road onto the dirt driveway.

Please. Please. Please, she thought. *Don't be here.* As she rounded the corner slowly, she was relieved to see the warden's car was there in the same place but the blue car was still gone. Hopefully, that was a good sign. She pulled up and parked. When she got out of her vehicle she didn't bother closing the door.

As quietly as she could, she opened the front door and crept in. The place was silent. Dead. But maybe the warden came home and passed out again.

As she crept down the hall, Pepe ran out to greet her. He jumped and pawed at her leg, grunting and snorting. She picked him up and held him tightly to her breast until she reached the warden's open door. The bed was still just as sloppy as ever, but no one was on it.

"Hi, baby," Kenna said, stroking Pepe's head.

She entered her room and set him down on the bed. Rather than change there and risk the warden coming home and finding a reason to make her stay in, Kenna grabbed her clothes and makeup bag then headed for the front door again.

Pepe followed her, looking up as if asking, "That's it?"

"I can't stay," she said. "Mama's gotta go. I'll be back later. Okay?"

She stepped out of the house, hurried to her car and got the hell out of there as fast as possible.

* * *

Chase opened the apartment door and let Kenna in. He thought she was going to change, but she still had on the same sexy skirt and boots she wore to class. In one hand she held a small bundle of clothes. In the other she had a little yellow makeup bag.

She walked in.

"I got Coke in the fridge if you want to mix—"

"Fuck! I forgot the liquor."

She looked panicked. Her eyes darted around the living room.

"No worries."

13

She followed him to the sofa and plopped down beside him, letting out a little sigh before turning to face him. Her bright eyes had a way of burrowing deep into him and making him feel as though there were feral cats clawing at his stomach from the inside.

"We can go back and get it," she said.

"Not a big deal. James will be here after he gets off work."

Kenna set her stuff down between them then leaned back and let out another sigh.

"Got any gas?" she asked.

Chase looked at the coffee table where the bong had been. "Paul," he shouted. "Hey, Paul!"

A few seconds later, Paul's bedroom door opened. He turned and saw Tanya walking toward them.

"He's sleeping," she whispered.

"Anything left in that bong?" Chase asked as she sat in the chair he used earlier.

She shook her head side to side. Her voice rose to a normal level. "But he's getting more before we go tonight."

"It's all good," Kenna said. "We'll just run to my place real quick. You drive."

Chase cocked his head and looked at her. In all the years he had known her, he had only ever been to her house a couple times. And that was back when they first met. He knew she was embarrassed by her mom and had problems with her, but usually she came up with excuses for why she didn't want people over or dropping her off.

As he stood up, Tanya said, "A friend of mine is coming over from Huntsville tonight. Y'all think it'd be okay if she hangs with us?"

Chase looked at Kenna then back at Tanya and grinned. "Is she hot?"

Kenna slapped his arm. He looked at her again. "What? You jelly?"

"You wish." She stood up, leaving her things behind.

"Doesn't matter to me," he said without looking at either girl so both could take it however they wanted to.

He grabbed his keys off the table. "Let's go."

A few minutes later, they were in his Nissan Altima, speeding toward her house and streaming music loud enough that a conversation was impossible. That was okay by him, because as much as he wanted to talk to her and ask her out on a real date, he equally feared the same. As things stood, they were best friends and he could hang with her tonight and any other time. But if he were to ask her out now and she shot him down, everything going forward would be forever changed. Just going to the party with her would be awkward. A little of something is always better than a whole lot of nothing, right?

Kenna turned the stereo down and pointed at a dirt driveway. "Turn here."

"I remember."

"Go slow," she said. "Real slow."

He turned the wheel and slowed to a crawl.

As they rounded the curve, Kenna said, "Fuck."

"What?"

She pointed to the two cars parked out front. "They're back."

"Want to turn around?"

He stopped the car and they looked at each other for a long second.

"It'll be ok. Just wait in the car. Okay?"

Chase inched forward until they were by the other vehicles. As he stopped, Kenna stepped out and closed the door, but not completely. Just enough that it wasn't wide open.

She ran on tip toes up to the door, slowly opened it and slinked in.

* * *

Kenna crept into the house as quietly as possible, leaving the front door half-open. Nineties-style hip hop music flowed down the hall to the living room from the warden's room. Grunts and groans topped the music. They were definitely hard at it.

She padded lightly to the kitchen and opened the cabinet next to the sink where the warden always had numerous bottles of assorted liquors. The warden called it her *liquor cabinet*. How clever.

Kenna snagged a couple bottles of clear liquor and turned around. As she did, one of the bottles brushed a glass filled with Coke and knocked it to the floor where it shattered.

"Fuck," she whisper-shouted.

Dead Town

She stood motionless for a second. The music still thumped from the warden's room, but the moaning stopped.

Kenna turned quickly and grabbed a couple plastic grocery bags from under the sink. She shoved the bottles in and set them down by the doorway, trying to hide what they were.

As she bent over to pick up the pieces of busted glass, the warden and Matthew stormed into the kitchen.

"Jesus, girl! What the fuck is wrong with you?" the warden shouted.

They were both standing above her, buck naked. The first thing Kenna noticed was Matthew's short, fat hard-on that was starting to drop. The next thing she saw was the pistol in his hand. Her eyes flashed to his then the warden's. Both looked strung out as fuck. Their eyes were wild, their hair wet and matted, their skin pasty white and dripping with perspiration.

"Yeah. What the fuck is wrong with you girl?" Matthew asked.

Kenna carefully picked up the big chunks of glass and transferred them from her right to left hand. "I'm cleaning it."

Matthew set the gun on the counter. "I'll tell you what you *ought* to be cleaning. *This.*" He grabbed his nuts and mostly soft dick with his left hand and shook it. "You ought to be cleaning your mama's juices off with your mouth. Whaddaya say?" He grinned and showed a mouth full of black and white teeth.

Kenna rolled her eyes.

"Huh?" he asked, then looked at the warden. "What you think, darlin'? A little mother-daughter action for your old man?"

"Get her some molly."

* * *

Chase sat in the car, drumming his thumbs on the steering wheel and staring at the semi-open front door. He wondered if Kenna's mother caught her or had her doing something. After a couple minutes, he heard muffled voices coming from the house. They got louder, but he still couldn't figure out what they were saying. Then he heard a guy shout something.

"Nooo!" Kenna screamed.

Chase bailed out of the car and dashed into the house.

He couldn't believe it. Kenna's mom and a guy stood there completely naked in the living room. They had Kenna backed into a corner.

"Bitch, get over here and suck my dick," the man said.

Chase stood paralyzed for a second, but came to his senses when Kenna looked over the naked man's shoulder at him.

"What the fuck?" Chase said.

The naked couple spun to face him.

"Just get the fuck out of here, boy," the man said as he clenched his fists. "I mean it. Go on. This ain't none of your business."

Chase looked at Kenna's mother. She was maybe in her early forties, but had about sixty years on her face and body. She had been rode hard by life.

The warden turned back to her. "Kenna, baby. Come on. For mama."

"No!"

"Kenna-Grace, I ain't gonna ask you again. Now if you don't—"

"Fuck you!"

At that, the wiry little man whipped around and said, "Don't you dare talk to your mama like that."

He drew his arm back. Chase dove forward and tackled him before he had a chance to hit her.

For a couple seconds he and the naked man rolled on the floor. Chase was aware of both girls screaming, but couldn't make out what they were saying.

"Ima fuckin' kill you, boy," the man said. "Then Ima fuck that girl *and* her mama."

Chase managed to get some leverage and rolled the man one last time. He quickly mounted his waist and started raining bombs down on his face and head.

"You're gonna do *what, boy*?" he said, punctuating the boy. "You want to hit someone? Hit *me*."

The man covered his face with both fists, but Chase kept pounding on him. Blood ran from his nose and lips. Then for good measure, Chase dropped a couple elbows to his head. One landed, leaving a long cut above his left eyebrow. It gushed blood.

Dead Town

When the man stopped moving or even trying to defend himself, Chase punched him a few more times.

He looked up at Kenna's mother. "What the fuck is wrong with you?"

He stood up and grabbed Kenna's hand. "Come on. Let's go."

She jerked away from him. "Wait."

He couldn't believe she wanted to stay there after all that. He watched as she darted out of the room. A second later she returned with a large white grocery bag.

She took his hand and tugged. "Now."

They jumped in the car. Chase backed up a little then pulled a U-turn and started heading down the dirt drive.

"Kenna," he said.

"Don't"

"What the fuck?"

She looked down. "Will you just shut the fuck up and drive?"

* * *

Tanya felt uneasy as she looked at the cards she had laid out on the coffee table. Something big was going to happen. Like Paul, she was in for a life-altering event. Good or bad, she wasn't quite sure, but she leaned more toward the bad—just as she had with Paul's reading. Something inside her told her these changes were *not* going to be pleasant.

She wondered if their fates were linked together. It was possible. Perhaps soon they would break up or get much more serious. Either would be life-changing.

"What're you doing?" Paul asked, stumbling sleepy-eyed into the room.

Tanya put both hands over the cards and started drawing them together, trying to clear them away before Paul said anything.

"Good nap?"

He sat beside her and lit a cigarette.

"Guess so. Weird as fuck dreams. More like acid dreams than pot." He took a drag off his cigarette. Laughed a little. "I think a fucking dinosaur or some shit was chasing me."

Tanya's face tightened.

"What?" she asked, even though she heard him clearly.

"A dinosaur or something. Chasing me the whole time."

Tanya tried to put her cards in their bag without drawing attention to them so he wouldn't belittle her again.

"You think it was a *sign*?" he asked, his eyes growing big.

Her stomach dropped a couple inches. She set the bag of cards on the other side of her.

"Could be," she said. "Maybe the universe is trying to tell you something bad is coming for you."

"Yeah," Paul said. He took a puff off his American Spirit. "Like if I don't change my wicked ways, I'm going to find and get trapped in a real Jurassic Park. Or maybe—"

"I'm serious."

"So am I. Maybe I will find a dinosaur egg and hatch it and—"

"Okay. Stop. I get it."

Paul let out a charming giggle.

"You can be such a dick sometimes," Tanya said. "Why do I stay with you?"

"Because I look good. I smell good. And I'm confident."

A key turning in the lock drew her attention from the conversation. It was just as well. She wasn't quite sure how to respond to that anyway. He was right.

The door swung open and Kenna entered, followed by Chase. His face was a blotchy red and under his left eye, blood was beginning to pool.

"What the fuck happened to you, man?" Paul asked.

Before Chase could answer, Kenna cut her eyes at Chase and said, "Nothing."

Chase looked at Kenna then Paul and shrugged his shoulder. "Nothing."

"You got a fucking black eye, bro. *Something* happened."

Chase glanced at Kenna then turned his attention to Tanya and Paul. "I guess no really means no when *she* says it." He poked his thumb out in Kenna's direction.

They all laughed a little and somehow that ended the conversation, even though Tanya knew there was way more to it.

CHAPTER 3

Hayden Smalls opened the drawer of the cash register and passed the appropriate change to the woman in front of him. At thirty-something, she was too old for him, but she still looked good. Something about her made him want to look at her. She had long auburn hair and olive skin with large, dark eyes.

"You need your receipt?" he asked.

"That's some interesting ink you got there." She declined her head toward the numerous tats on his arms and hands.

He held the receipt out for her.

"I don't need it," she said. "That's cool." She pointed to a color image of Baphomet on his left forearm.

Hayden thought, *Oh great. I'm about to get invited to yet another church.* It was only his third day working at the Gas-n-Save and already he had over two dozen invites to various churches because of his tattoos.

"You get those done around here?" she asked.

"My artist is in Nashville."

The lady picked up her drink and candy bar. "One last question."

Here it comes, he thought.

"No, I'm not going to invite you to church. I was just curious if you've ever been to Dead Town."

"That a club or something?"

She smiled and lowered her eyes. "Or something."

The woman turned and walked out.

Hayden tried to see what type of car she got into. He bet it had to be a Mercedes or something expensive, but he lost sight of her somehow.

* * *

From Chase's perspective, other than having a black eye, the night was shaping up perfectly. The four of them had just spent the last few hours playing Cards Against Humanity as a drinking game. They just about polished off the two bottles of liquor Kenna-Grace swiped from her mother. Paul's hookup came and dropped off a couple of exceptionally large buds of grass. And Chase's cousin brought him the booze he was waiting on.

Soon it would be time to head to Tristan's for the real party.

Chase grabbed his phone and texted his friend Dave.

--WYA

--Ain't gonna make it

"Fuck!" Chase said after a few more texts. Everyone stopped talking and looked at him. "No DD tonight. Dave just bailed."

"No way I'm driving," Kenna said. "I'm already lit."

Paul said, "Don't look at me. I'm still in classes for the last DUI to keep it off my record."

"I'll see if Kiara can drive," Tanya said.

"*Who?*" Paul asked.

Tanya looked at Chase and Kenna. "The friend I asked y'all about." She turned to Paul. "You were sleeping."

Tanya plucked her phone from the table and stepped away.

The puzzled look on Paul's face told Chase he needed to explain. "Friend from Huntsville. Wanted to come out with us."

Paul lit a cigarette. As he exhaled he said, "Cool. Three-way!"

Kenna rolled her eyes.

Tanya returned and sat. "I hope it's okay. She asked if her friend Hayden could come too. She said Hayden has a Four Runner, so we can all fit in."

"More the merrier, right?" Kenna asked.

"Just as long as I ain't getting another DUI, I don't give a fuck," Paul said.

Tanya picked up her phone and started texting.

"I sent her the address here."

Everything was shaping up just fine. This was going to be a great weekend. If Chase played his cards right and grew a set, or got drunk enough, he'd finally try to take that next step with Kenna.

He glanced at Kenna, sitting beside him. She was looking at him, smiling. Her eyes, slightly bloodshot, looked brighter and sharper than ever.

Come hell or high water, this was his weekend to seal the deal with her.

* * *

Kiara waited on the sofa, thumbing through one of the magick books Hayden had on his table. She could smell the age and dust as she flipped the pages.

"Where did you get this?" she said loud enough for him to hear in the bedroom where he was changing.

Hayden poked his head and shirtless torso out the door and looked at her. "You know I can't see through walls, right?"

Kiara glanced at him for a second. She never really thought about him in a romantic way, though he had often been blatant about wanting her. Still, with his black hair and dark eyes, there was something attractive about him. She looked at his bare chest. Relatively small, but muscular enough. At least he didn't have the dad bod so many girls were suddenly craving.

Kiara held up the book and shook it a little, showing it to him.

"Oh that," he ducked back into the room. "Estate sale a few years back."

"Looks dark as fuck."

Hayden returned wearing a tight black V-neck T-shirt.

"Some of it," he said. "Mixed really." He took the book from her and opened it. "Actually, the spell that's going to have you dragging me to bed to lay you down and sex you up is in here. But so is the counter-spell. Can't have you seeing that yet."

"So, I was right," Kiara said with a smirk, "Really bad juju in there."

Hayden set the book on the table and extended his hand to help her up. "Know where we're going?"

She looked at his hand, but didn't take it. She pushed herself off the sofa. "Yep."

A few minutes later they were in his SUV heading for Tanya's boyfriend's place.

"You okay being designated driver?" Kiara asked.

"As long as my passengers are okay with having a drunk driver."

"Seriously."

"I *was* being serious." He grabbed his Kools from the console and lit one. In the dim light of traffic and streetlights, she glared at him.

"I will stay *mostly* sober. *Okay?*" He took a drag and exhaled, then cracked the window a bit to let the smoke escape. "I won't get completely shitfaced. Just a little. But I'll be fine to drive."

She had been out with him enough to know he was a decent driver if he hadn't had too much. It was just keeping him from the *too much* that was difficult. Somehow, he often went from just two or three to eighteen or twenty. But she'd make this work.

After guiding him the rest of the way, they finally pulled up outside the apartments and found 112. They parked and headed for the door.

"Oh," she said suddenly remembering. "Tanya's okay, but I don't know how cool the others are with the whole witchcraft Wicca thing. So, we might want to keep it quiet."

"Right. No drinking and definitely no black mass tonight. Don't want to scare the good Christians who are trying to get drunk before having to repent on Sunday."

"That ain't what I said."

"I'm fucking with you, Kee-kee. Why you so worried anyway?"

She paused a second. That was a good question. Why was she worried about what the others thought? Shit, she didn't even know them. The only people she knew were Hayden and Tanya, but she hadn't seen Tanya in months.

* * *

Kenna picked up the clothes she had brought and stumbled off to Chase's bedroom. *Someone* was going to notice her tonight.

She took off her shirt and slipped out of her skirt. She stood before the dresser mirror looking at herself. She guessed she had an okay body. Her B-cup breasts were smaller than she wanted and her abs, although kind of present, were not as pronounced as she would have liked.

Dead Town

Kenna slipped the little black dress over her head and tugged it down. It was shorter than the skirt she just took off and definitely tighter than the shirt. She picked up her discarded clothes and tossed them on Chase's bed. Then she walked out of the room.

"Can you help me with this?" she asked Chase.

She turned around and lifted her hair, exposing her back and neck to him. After a few seconds, he got the hint. He grabbed the zipper at the small of her back, just above her panty line and zipped slowly upward.

"Dayum," Chase said.

"What?"

Before he could answer, a knock on the door interrupted them. They turned their attention in that direction as Paul opened the door.

* * *

Paul quickly studied the pair standing outside his open door and decided they weren't his usual type of friends. That was neither good nor bad. Just an assessment. The guy, Hayden he assumed, was about five-ten with jet black hair and dark eyes. Either he had some of the thickest lashes ever or he was wearing guyliner. He was gauging his ears and could already pass dimes through the lobes. Around his neck he had a black leather strand with a pewter or silver pentagram hanging from it. Definitely more Tanya's type.

The girl, on the other hand was different but attractive. She was maybe five-six and probably weighed about a buck-thirty with the currency in all the right places. Her long brown hair flowed smoothly to the middle of her back. Just above her bright green eyes and thick eyebrows she wore a thin white lace headband that looked like flowers strung together. The neckline of her lightweight black top with a pink and white flower print was cut low enough to expose a little cleavage and the tail end of a tattoo above her right breast.

Paul eyed her up and down. The shirt hung loose and barely came to her waist, exposing just a bit of her abs. Below that, tight blue jeans hugged her legs all the way down to her ankles and well-worn cowboy boots.

"I'm Kiara," she said. "Is Tanya here?"

"This is the place," Paul said. He stepped aside. "Come on in."

"This is Hayden," she said.

Hayden stretched out his hand as he entered.

"Paul." He closed the door. "That fool there is Chase. That crazy girl in the dress two sizes too small is Kenna-Grace and y'all know Tanya."

The new couple waved and smiled. As they walked into the room toward the others, Paul couldn't help but sneak a glance at Kiara's ass. Her jeans may have been faded blue, but it reminded him of a red delicious apple. *I'd take a bite out of that*, he thought.

* * *

Kiara looked around the room at the unfamiliar faces. They were friendly enough, but she had mixed emotions. The first person she noticed was Paul. He had that muscular build like a pit bull that attracted her to the breed, and she supposed he was cute, but still she hadn't quite sized him up or decided what she thought about him. The next person was Kenna. She was an attractive girl with striking eyes. Kiara felt an immediate connection to her when their eyes met. She wondered if she was into girls or strictly dickly. Tanya, she knew. Although she hadn't seen her in a while, she was as pretty as ever. The other guy, Chance, Chase, whatever his name was didn't do much for her.

He seemed nice enough when he said, "Come on over and have one or six before we go." But other than that, there was no chemical romance. Not that she was looking for one. Tonight, she wasn't looking for love or a good lay. She was just looking for some fun.

Kiara walked over to where Chase stood holding a two-liter bottle of Coke and a liter of Jack Daniels.

"My kind of man," she said.

She took the Jack and poured a few fingers into a red Solo cup then downed it.

Chase smiled, "My kind of woman."

Chase looked at Hayden and waved him over. "Don't be scared, bro. We don't bite until after the second drink. So, come get one."

That's when Kiara decided she rather liked Chase. She could tell he had never met a stranger in his life.

Dead Town

Paul sat at the table with Tanya on his lap. Kenna took the chair beside them to Paul's right.

"You two sit," Chase said, offering them the only other two seats.

Hayden plopped down in the chair across from Paul and looked at Kiara, patting his knee. "You can sit here."

"Or I can stand." She gave a warm smile to show she wasn't trying to come off as bitchy as it sounded.

Chase pulled the remaining seat out. "Sit," he said. "I'm good."

She sat and Chase dipped out of the room, down a hallway. A moment later he returned carrying a crimson and white folding nylon chair with a giant University of Alabama logo on it.

"Roll mother fuckin' tide," he said loudly as he plopped it down between Kenna and Kiara. He sat in it and looked at both girls. "Y'all try to keep your hands to yourselves. I know you want *this*," he took both hands and slowly stroked from the top of his chest to his waist, "but you gotta wait and wrassle later to see who gets it."

Kenna leaned forward to look past him at Kiara. "He's a little drunk and a lot stupid, but he's ours and he's harmless."

Chase looked at Kiara. "She's right. You see this?" he pointed at his black eye. "She did this. Know why?"

Kiara shook her head, glanced at Kenna then back at Chase.

"Because I asked her to stop touching my ass when I was washing her dishes. It's bad enough she made me wear a man-hammock when I did her laundry, but this . . ." He shook his head and lowered it.

Paul poured some whiskey into his cup. "If you haven't figured it out, Kenna forgot to mention he's also full of shit."

"That's fine," Kiara said. "I got a shovel outside and shitkickers on." She lifted the square toe of her boot to show it off.

Chase looked at Kenna. "Ooh . . . I *like* her."

Then he looked at the others and said, "Enough of all this talking bullshit. Let's drink. Paulie, get a deck of cards. We'll play War."

"*You* get 'em. I'm getting a lap dance right now." He wiggled Tanya a little and she purred.

Kiara looked at Paul. She knew what it was like to have Tanya on her lap. There were a couple drunken nights when they hooked up. What she couldn't figure out, though, was why she suddenly wondered what it would feel like to sit on Paul's lap. Paul looked at her and, though it was only a second before she looked away, his bright green eyes grazed her soul like a cat peering deep into her.

"Ready for another?" Paul asked, passing her the bottle of Jack.

She took it, looking at him again. This time his gaze didn't penetrate her.

Damn, she thought. *That was weird.*

That first glance was like having sex and the second was the post-orgasm cigarette.

"Thanks."

Chase left the dining room and hurried to the kitchen. Drawers opened and closed.

"Found them!"

He sat back down with the cards and started dealing them out.

"Booze War," Chase said. "Just like War when we were kids, but losers all drink."

"Unless there's a war," Paul said. "In that case, those two battle it out and the loser drinks the total card value of the winner's hand."

"Damn," Hayden said.

"That's right, cupcake," Chase said, looking at him and grinning. "This ain't for kiddies. Serious drinkers only."

Kiara looked at Hayden to see how he responded to being called cupcake. She didn't think Chase meant anything by it, but Hayden could have a bit of a temper when he felt his masculinity was in question. He seemed to take it in stride.

"I'm DD," Hayden said, "but if you're okay with DD standing for drunk driver, I'm down."

Chase tapped Kenna's leg. "I like him, too."

"It's your license, not mine," Paul said.

After just one once-around the table, Kiara was already feeling the effects of the whiskey circulating through her veins. Chase wasn't joking. This was definitely a game for professional alcoholics. She only had to lose one war to realize how ugly things could get. She ended up downing thirteen points of whiskey. She took small gulps, but that was still about half a cup.

Her stomach burned already. When Paul produced a small red bong from under the table, shit started to get more out of hand.

Kiara took a couple hits then said, "Okay. I gotta slow down. If I don't, I won't make it to this party."

"Oh fuck, *the party*!" Paul said. He looked at his phone. "Totally forgot about that shit. Let's go."

"We can just stay here," Tanya said. "We're fucked up enough already."

"But Bloody Mess is playing," Kenna said. "I told Jarrett we'd be there."

"I love them," Kiara said. "You *know* them?"

"Know them?" Chase asked. "She *slept* with all of them. No wait. Never mind. That was me."

Kenna slapped Chase's arm.

"See how violent she gets?"

"Hayden, you good to drive?" Kenna asked.

* * *

Because of his height, Kenna suggested Chase sit up front with Hayden. She and Kiara would sit in the third-row seats since they were the smallest, and leave the middle row for Tanya and Paul. Now that they were back there, she had her doubts about the arrangement. The space was cramped. And, while Hayden was doing a decent job driving, Kenna was getting sloshed around a bit too much for her inebriated state. She needed some air. Fortunately, it was a short stint to Tristan's place.

They parked four or five houses down and poured out of the vehicle. Even from where they were, Kenna could see the people milling about outside and hear the din of the crowd.

She looked at her phone. 10:12.

"Think they played already?" she asked Chase.

"Is it past midnight?"

They naturally paired off. Paul and Tanya led the way. Kiara and Hayden followed. Then Kenna took up the rear with Chase.

"You okay?" Kenna said quietly, so the others wouldn't hear.

"What you mean?"

"Sorry about earlier."

"I don't know what you're talking about."

"You *do*. Stop." Chase stopped walking. She grabbed his wrist and tugged. "I didn't mean stop walking, dumbass."

"Look, Kenna," Chase said, his voice grave. "You got nothing to apologize for. I'd do it all over again and more if I was back in that situation again."

Kenna held his hand playfully. It was warm around hers. She liked the way it felt, but she doubted he knew that. She tried numerous times to drop subtle hints, but either he was too daft to see or was kind enough to pretend he didn't see to spare her feelings. Still, she wished she knew what he thought about her. Wished he was as curious as she was about trying to date.

CHAPTER 4

Kenna took his hand and tugged. "I didn't mean stop walking, dumbass," she said.

Chase wondered how long the moment would last. As friends, they sometimes touched and held hands for instances like these, but they were always brief, too brief. He always wanted them to linger and, at the same time, he always worried he lingered too long. One day she would call him out on it and that would be the end of their friendship. She would be like that woman in that Prufrock poem and say, "No, that ain't what I meant at all" or whatever it was she said. Then the distance between them would grow greater every day because they would both feel so damn awkward about it. After a while, the separation would be a habit. And then they would slip further apart, like the continental drift, until they were two islands complete to themselves, their lives inhabited by other people.

After reassuring her she had nothing to be sorry for, Chase held her hand a tad longer. It was soft and delicate, like she always was, even in her most brash moments.

Get a fucking grip, he told himself. *She's just another fucking girl.*

But she wasn't *just* another girl.

Chase let her hand fall from his as they approached the house. He would linger another time. But not now. Right now he needed some liquid courage.

They filtered their way through the crowd congregating on the front lawn. Guys and girls mingled in clumps of fours and fives talking loudly. Laughing. Arguing. Debating nonsense. As they made their way through the open door into the large house, Chase noticed the band gearing up in the living room. He closed the door behind him.

Paul led the group to right near the band. He said hello and fist-bumped several of the members. The band nodded and waved at Kenna and Chase.

A moment later, Bloody Mess ripped through the noise of the crowd with some bold drums and loud, raw electric chords on Jamie T's guitar.

A horde of people filled the room, pushing Chase and the others forward. It was a great place to be with one exception. They didn't have their drinks yet.

Tristan made his way to the front with them. In his right hand he held a lit cigarette—in his left a bottle of Tequila.

"Glad you finally made it!" he shouted in Chase's ear.

Chase snagged the bottle, uncapped it and turned it up. After gulping down a few large swallows, he handed it back to Tristan.

Chase smiled.

Tristan bumped Kenna's shoulder with the bottle. When she turned and saw him, she scooted past Chase to give him a hug. Tristan kissed her on the cheek, pushed her back a bit and pressed the bottle into her hand.

"Oh, hell yeah!" she said.

Kenna chugged some tequila and passed the bottle back.

As soon as the song ended, Kenna grabbed chase's arm and screamed in his ear almost loud enough for him to clearly hear. "Let's get some beer."

They shouldered their way through the throng like a couple of salmon going upstream until they made it to the hall, then headed down to the kitchen at the back of the house where the keg was always stationed.

As they stood in line, in the relative quiet of the kitchen, each holding two plastic cups, Kenna-Grace asked, "So, what you think about her?"

"Who?"

"The hot chick that came with us. Don't play dumb."

"A hot chick came tonight?" Chase asked, grinning, hoping he would catch a glimpse of jealousy or some hint she might be interested in him.

Kenna looked down at her dress then back at him, raising her eyebrows. "You saying I ain't hot?"

Chase looked down then back up again. "Well," he started.

"You don't think she's hot?"

Dead Town

Chase lied. "Didn't notice. I was too busy drinking."

There was definitely something to Kiara that Chase found attractive. She had a beautiful smile and that whole *earthy* hippy thing going on with that band around her head. Ordinarily, he would have been all over her from the get go, but he was more interested in Kenna-Grace. Over the years they'd known each other, both had dated other people, but this was Chase's weekend to put an end to that. This was his weekend to show her it was always her he was interested in most.

"Sure you were," Kenna said, eyeing him suspiciously.

Finally, they made it to the keg and Kenna bent over to fill her first cup of beer. Chase couldn't help but stare. The tight skirt clung to her compact body like Saran-wrap.

Do or die, he thought.

"Hey, got a question for you," he started.

Kenna looked up at him as he bent over slightly to talk to her.

"I was thinking . . ."

Bam!

Before he knew what happened, Chase was on top of Kenna on the floor. He looked up. Two guys, Allen Smithson and Cooper something, were fighting and had each other in headlocks. They crashed across the room again as people tried frantically to get out of their way. When they hit the cabinet by the sink, they sputtered to a stop.

Chase leapt to his feet and pulled Kenna up. About that time, Paul charged into the room and grabbed Allen from behind. He whipped him down to the ground and reached for Cooper. Cooper was a bit taller than Paul, but not quite as wide. He launched a quick haymaker that caught Paul upside the head. Paul swayed a tad from left to right then unleashed a flurry of fists, bending Cooper backwards over the sink. When he twisted and gave up his back, Paul took the opportunity to put him in a choke hold.

"Calm the fuck down!" Paul said.

Blood poured down from Cooper's nose over his white Bama T-shirt and onto the linoleum floor.

Allen jumped up and looked like he was about to attack Cooper again, but Tristan and a couple others ran into the room, grabbed him and rushed him out as Paul followed with Cooper.

Chase and Kenna brushed off the beer she had spilled on both of them. Someone handed them fresh cups and they filled up.

"Damn, that was crazy," Kenna said. "Wonder what that was about."

Chase just shrugged. It took him years to muster the courage to ask her out and only two drunk assholes and one second to snatch it away from him. He led her back to the living room where the band continued to play. As Chase and Kenna entered, Bloody Mess faded out of one song and into Chase's favorite—*Hellbound*.

* * *

When he first arrived, Hayden felt more uncomfortable than an anorexic in a bikini contest. He wasn't usually self-conscious, but here, now, he felt like people were staring at him, wondering why he was there. He kind of wondered the same thing. But then he knew why he was there. Kiara invited him. Well, he invited himself when she said she was coming to Keller Falls. He had only lived in town a month and figured it would not only be a great way to meet some people, but also an excuse to spend more time with her. Eventually, she would come around and take him up on one of his offers.

By the time the band finished their second set, it was after one in the morning and Hayden felt a whole lot better about almost everything. The people there, ranging in age from eighteen to mid-forties were settling down and chilling. The crowd had dwindled from about two hundred down to around fifty. Hayden wasn't drunk, but he wasn't sober either. He had a good buzz going on from the beer and a couple blunts he hit throughout the night.

And at some point during the band's second set, a brunette came over and started chatting with him. She was tall and well-proportioned with doe eyes and one of the best sets of lips he had seen on a girl in a while.

"I like your tats," the girl said.

She didn't look like the normal type girl that commented on his artwork. Then again, as he looked at her closer, he thought he might be wrong. The little black dress she wore had thin shoulder straps and was low-cut enough to show a good portion of her pale round breasts. The dress cinched around her narrow waist and flared at her hips, not even making it a third of the way down her shapely thighs. From beneath the dress extended some black and red garter belts holding up her black spider web nylons that flowed down into a pair of black Dr. Marten boots.

"Thanks." He stuck out his hand. "Hayden."

"Olivia. But my friends call me Liv."

"What should I call you?"

She pulled her cup up to her face and peered over it. "Whatever you want to. As long as you call me." Then she smiled and took a swig.

It was about that point Kiara took her leave. Since then, Hayden and Liv had swapped snap codes, made out, and parted ways when her friends came over and said it was time to go.

A few minutes after they were gone, Liv sent him a snap of herself cuddled up in bed. On it she wrote, "Safe."

As he closed the snap, a man about thirtyish approached Hayden. He was short, maybe five-eight with bright blond hair in a bowl cut and little round glasses. He had a space between his two front teeth.

"Baphomet, huh?" the man asked, pointing at Hayden's forearm. He pointed at another tattoo. "And Vegvísir, huh?"

"You *know* what it is?"

"I did my doctoral thesis on Norse religions." He stuck out his small hand. "Richard. Richard Garrett."

"Hayden."

"You know that symbol may not be what it's supposed to be, right?" Richard pulled an off-brand pack of cigarettes out of his shirt pocket and lit one. "It really only showed up in one manuscript and that was tainted by Christian mythology and other stuff over the years."

"Never heard that."

"Look up The Huld manuscript. Read about it. You'll see." Richard took a deep draw from his smoke and exhaled, studying Hayden's arms the whole time. "But that doesn't mean it isn't true. There's a lot of power in the Runes and other magical symbols."

Richard lifted the hem of his shirt and exposed his semi-hairy belly. Beneath the blond hair was a large tattoo covering his abdomen and disappearing up under his shirt on his chest. It was a mish-mosh of runic and other pagan symbols all strung together. Some Hayden recognized as being for protection and strength. Others he had never seen.

The two men walked to the keg and each poured a cup. They stood in the kitchen talking about magick and mythology. They had a second cup. And a third as the conversation continued on. Then Richard surprised Hayden.

"Have you ever been to Dead Town?" he asked.

"You're the second person today to ask me that. What is it? A store?"

Richard let out a raspy laugh. "No. It's a place. A *dead* town."

"Never heard of it."

"You want some power? Go there."

"Where is it?"

"A few miles from here."

"*What?*"

"You want to go?"

"Do bears fuck in the woods?"

"Finish that. Let's go."

Hayden looked around. "Can't. I'm driver tonight."

Richard chugged his drink and said, "Tell you what. Get your friends together and wait here. I'll make a run to the package store and get a bottle of something before it closes." He looked at the black plastic Timex on his wrist. "It's almost two. I'll be back in ten minutes. What do you and your friends drink?"

"Whiskey?"

"Deal."

Hayden walked through the house with Richard and out the front door. Richard stepped to the side of the house, grabbed a cruiser-style ten speed bike and hopped on. As he rode away, Hayden shook his head, figuring he wouldn't see the man again.

Among the people milling about the front lawn, Hayden spotted Kiara, Paul and Tanya sitting beneath a large magnolia. He headed over.

The three were lit.

"You seen the others?" Hayden asked.

"Not out here," Paul said. "You look inside?"

Kiara laughed.

Hayden glanced at her wondering if he was the object of her laughter or something else.

"Wait here."

Hayden walked into the house. Eventually, he found Kenna and Chase sitting in the formal dining room at a table playing quarters with several people.

"You two about ready?" he asked.

"Bout ready to make her drink!" Chase bounced the quarter into the shot glass and pointed at Kenna. "Do it!"

Kenna chugged some beer.

Hayden shook his head. "Everyone else is outside."

"You're seriously ready to go home, bro?" Chase asked. "It's not even two yet."

Hayden wondered about it. No, he wasn't ready to call it a night. He was just ready for something different. Liv and Richard convinced him of that.

"Home?" Kenna said. "I want some Waffle House."

"And more whiskey. Keg's dry anyway." Chase said.

Hayden lit a cigarette. "Then come on. Everyone is outside waiting."

"Waffle House!" Kenna said again.

* * *

Kiara sat under a magnolia with Paul and Tanya. Something inside her stirred, but she wasn't sure what. Sure, she had hooked up with Tanya a couple times. And yes, she was feeling a bit anxious to get a piece of something. But she wasn't sure whose piece she wanted. She had so many options at the moment. Tanya swore it would never happen again, but she said that before the last two times, too. Paul was something. The more Kiara talked with him, the more she felt a connection. And Kenna. Kenna was electric. If she had to, she knew she could always get a piece of Hayden or even Chase, but she wasn't that desperate yet.

Hayden emerged from the house with Chase and Kenna a few steps behind. Kiara watched the two of them laughing as they stumbled through the doorway. She wondered if they saw the same fireworks between them that she could see from twenty feet away.

"Who wants Waffle House?" Kenna asked, practically shouting.

"I'm down," Tanya said.

Kiara smiled. "I can definitely do an All-Star or whatever the hell it's called."

Kiara took a sip from her beer, wishing it was whiskey. As she sipped, she looked over the rim at Paul. Damn, he was cute.

Don't do it, she told herself. *Tanya's your friend*. But still, there was something there. Maybe she was mistaken, but she thought she caught him looking at her, too.

"We need some Jack Daniels," Kiara said. "Let's get more before the stores close."

"Already done," a weird-looking man said as he rode up on a bike.

Kiara turned to face him. He looked like that singer her grandma liked, Bob Denver or something like that. The guy that sang "Rocky Mountain High."

"Sorry?" Kiara said.

The stranger dismounted his bike. From a basket on the back he produced two brown paper sacks. He held them in one hand from beneath and pulled out the top half of a bottle of Jack Daniels. He lowered it back into the sack and pulled the top of the other bottle, Gentleman Jack.

"My new best friend," Kiara said with a large smile.

"Hi," he said, walking toward her.

"Oh. This is Richard," Hayden said. "He was gonna take us somewhere to drink." Hayden held out his left hand and pointed at each person as he said their name. Once finished with that, Hayden said, "We're hitting Waffle House first. You down?"

"Do I look like I turn down food?" Richard said, rubbing his stomach and grinning.

Kiara looked at him. The man wasn't fat, but he wasn't skinny. The honest answer was *maybe*. She didn't want to get into that with him.

"What kind of place?" Kiara asked.

"What?" Richard leaned toward her a bit.

"What kind of place are you taking us to?"

Dead Town

"Magical," Richard said. "Dead Town."

"What the fuck is Dead Town?" Chase asked.

"Just an old part of Keller Falls."

"I grew up here," Chase said. "I never heard of Dead Town."

"Most people haven't. It's kind of like peeing in the shower or masturbating. People do it. They just don't talk about it. Those that know about Dead Town pretend they don't. They hope it will just fade away. And it has for the most part."

"What the fuck are you talking about, man?" Paul asked. "You drop some Vitamin A or something?"

"Vitamin A?"

"Acid? Shrooms? You sound like a nut." Paul shook his head and Tanya laughed.

For the most part, Kiara agreed with Paul. The man sounded like he had one trip too many and the last one was one-way. Still, there were five things that interested her in the place. Jack Daniels, Gentleman Jack, the fact Richard called it magical, Kenna, and Paul—not necessarily in that order. If Paul and Kenna were going, Kiara definitely wanted to be there, because she wanted to figure out which one had her stomach twisted all night.

"Could be fun," Kiara said. "But food first."

Everyone looked at Richard. He didn't react, just stood there with the two sacks.

"Waffle House," Chase said.

"Mmm waaaaaffles," Kenna said, giggling.

Richard looked at the bags and then his bicycle. "You have room for me in your car?"

"Ditch the bike," Hayden said.

As Richard walked his ten-speed to the side of the house and leaned it against the wall, Paul stood up. He extended his hand to Tanya and helped her up off the ground. Once she was up, he thrust his hand and muscular arm toward Kiara. She gladly accepted.

His hand was strong, but gentle. Warm and soft. It completely and perfectly swallowed her hand.

"Thank you," she said when she was on her feet, flashing him a smile.

He smiled back. His teeth were perfect. In the glow of the house-lights and moonlight, his eyes sparkled.

Kiara suddenly realized she was still holding his hand. She dropped it, feeling awkward not only because it seemed like she was fawning over him, but because Tanya was right there.

As everyone started walking toward Hayden's vehicle, Tanya and Kiara took up the rear. Tanya seemed to linger to make sure they were straggling behind. Once they were a good eight or ten feet from the others, Tanya extended her arm and touched Kiara's, stopping her.

Kiara looked at her, thinking, *Oh shit, here it comes.*

"What's up?" Kiara asked, trying to sound nonchalant.

Tanya's gaze dropped to the ground, then back to Kiara. "I don't know," she said. "Something's not right."

Kiara glanced at the others getting away from them. She tried to play innocent. "What do you mean?"

"This. Tonight," Tanya said. "I got a bad feeling."

"Bad feeling like what? *Sick*? Drink too much?"

Tanya shook her head side to side. "Bad feeling like something awful is about to happen."

"We *are* going to the Awful House," Kiara said, giggling a little. She grabbed Tanya's arm and tugged gently.

Tanya started walking with her. "I'm serious. Something really bad is about to happen." She paused a second. "And whatever it is, we're kicking the wheels into motion."

Kiara knew exactly what she meant. Or at least how she *felt*. She, too, felt the strange tug all night, but she supposed for different reasons. *One man's rebel is another man's freedom fighter*, she thought. Perhaps they were both feeling the same upcoming change, but from opposing sides, so it didn't seem like such a crisis to her.

"It'll be okay," Kiara said. "You'll see. Everything is gonna be fine."

* * *

The ride to Waffle House was aligned almost identical to the earlier ride, but with Richard on the middle row seating with Paul and Tanya. Richard and Hayden talked back and forth about some shit Paul had no interest in. Something about ley lines and spells and summoning. It all sounded like a load of bullshit. But the man had a couple bottles of whiskey and the night was still young.

They couldn't fit seven into a single booth, so Paul and Tanya sat in one with Kenna and Kiara sitting opposite them while the three remaining guys took the booth behind them.

Once everyone was seated, Chase turned around and looked at Kenna who was directly behind him and across from Tanya.

"Wait a minute," Chase said. "You need to come over here." Then he looked at Paul. "Why do you have all the girls at your table while we look like we're having a sausage fest over here?"

Paul shrugged his shoulders and laughed. "It is what it is, man. Don't hate."

For the most part, Paul sat quietly drinking his Coke and drifting off into thought as the three girls talked about various things that failed to hold his interest. A couple times, his ears perked up and he listened. Usually, when Kiara was speaking. Something about the sound of her voice and the way her red lips moved, exposing her teeth while she talked, captivated him.

As Kiara finished speaking, a heavyset waitress with a front tooth missing and a name tattooed on her neck walked up with several plates stretched across her arm.

She began passing out the food and everyone fell silent, with exception to quiet *thank yous* spoken as a plate was set before them.

"What's this place we're going to?" Paul asked after swallowing a bit of egg.

The girls swapped quizzical glances.

Kiara said, "Just somewhere to drink, I think."

Paul watched her. After carving all the white off around her over-medium eggs, and eating that, she slid the fork under the yolk, scooped it up in a single piece and slid the whole unbroken yellow in her mouth. She did the same with the other.

"I can certainly drink some more," Paul said. "Especially after eating."

Tanya reached over and rubbed his leg gently. Paul smiled at her then returned his attention to Kiara. There was something magnetic about her. Not only her looks, but her personality and mannerisms. He watched as she started to eat her waffle. Unlike most people, she didn't start by cutting one of the intersecting two lines and forming a triangular wedge. Instead, she cut the crosshairs in the middle, then cut a small hole in the center.

"I have a peculiar way of eating, I know," she said when she noticed Paul staring.

"It's all good," Paul said.

Kiara just kept going, working her way around that center hole, making it larger and larger until she left a giant O on her plate. Then she was done.

After devouring their food, they paid and walked out to the parking lot. Tanya stopped Paul and kissed him lightly on the lips.

"You sure this is a good idea?" she asked.

"Drinking?"

"We don't know him," Tanya said. "And I have a bad feeling. The cards—"

He cut her off. "The cards don't rule me. And besides, how bad can this guy be? I'm sure if he gets stupid, Chase, Hayden, and me can take him out."

"But—"

"It'll be fun. You'll see."

CHAPTER 5

Kenna and Kiara crawled to the back like before and Chase offered to let Richard sit up front so he could direct Hayden to where they were going. For a few seconds Kenna watched the back of Chase's head bob to the music flooding the tight SUV. She looked at Kiara sitting next to her, the overhead streetlamps lighting her periodically. Then she looked out the window at the black skin of the river as they crossed over it. In the distance a boat floated.

Kenna looked at Chase again. In front of him, Hayden and Richard talked, but she couldn't make out what they were saying above the music. She turned her attention to Kiara once more.

Kiara was looking at her. Whether it was the lights playing with the shadows or not, Kenna couldn't tell, but Kiara's lips looked almost turned up in a smile, though she wasn't smiling. It was an impish sort of grin.

Kenna leaned in the opposite direction, her forehead on the glass, her eyes fixed on the fields whipping by.

The music went silent.

"Here," Richard said.

The car slowed and made a U-turn on the highway. A few seconds later, they pulled onto the shoulder and parked.

"What the fuck are we doing here?" Paul asked, voicing Kenna's thoughts.

Richard turned around in his seat. She couldn't see his face, just his silhouette.

"That's the entrance to Dead Town," he said, pointing out the windshield.

"Just looks like some fucking woods," Chase said.

"Camouflage," Richard said.

Kenna looked out the side window and saw nothing but trees set back about twenty feet off the road.

"You'll see when we get in there." Richard opened his door and the cabin lights came on. "It's perfectly safe."

"Why's it called Dead Town?" Kenna asked, but by then, Richard was out of the vehicle.

Chase opened his door and stepped out. Tanya and Paul followed.

"As long as there's somewhere to piss, I'm down," Paul said.

Kenna climbed out into the night with Kiara right behind her. She wrapped her arms around herself, feeling a chill in the air for the first time that evening. They were supposed to be in a house where it would be warm. Maybe she was just sobering up a bit after eating. No one else looked cold, but no one else was wearing a little black dress, either.

Kenna looked up at the moon and then at the others standing on the side of the highway with her. *This is fucking crazy*, she thought. But when everyone else started following Richard, she did too. There was no way she was going to be left alone in the middle of nowhere.

Richard led the pack down the gravel shoulder for a short distance. Suddenly, the loose stones turned to broken asphalt like an old drive-way or road covered in dead leaves, grass and twigs. They made a right and followed the path to a tiny clearing in the trees. It was almost impossible to find without knowing what you were looking for. No one would ever notice it while driving down the highway.

At the edge of the woods, just inside the tree line, were concrete pillars about waist-high, one on either side of the path. A thick, rusted metal cable hung between the two to prevent cars from entering.

On one of the trees was an old faded white sign with red lettering: POSTED NO HUNTING OR TRESSPASSING.

"Is it okay to be back here?" Tanya asked.

"No one's going to know," Richard said. "No one ever comes back here."

"But the car," Hayden said.

"Looks like a stranded motorist." Richard stepped over the cable and almost disappeared into the swelling darkness. His pale hand and arm extended from the black into a bit of moonlight and glowed as he helped Tanya over.

Paul followed, then Chase. Paul helped Kiara when she got there and Chase helped Kenna.

Dead Town

When they were all inside the perimeter, covered in heavy shadows and dappled by small rays of moonlight, Richard said, "Welcome to Dead Town."

* * *

Chase pulled out his phone and turned on the flashlight. He was amazed to see a wide swath of cleared area before him. He looked down. It was definitely a road, covered in dead leaves and natural debris. Ahead, small saplings extended randomly from fissures in the pavement.

Richard began walking. After only ten yards or so, the canopy of leaves overhead parted, allowing the moonlight to flow into the area. Chase turned off his phone's light.

"This way," Richard said. "It's the perfect place." He spun around, his glasses briefly reflecting the moon.

He continued walking with loose pairs behind him. First Hayden and Kiara, then Paul and Tanya, and finally Chase and Kenna. Their walking was an almost constant shushing and crunching of leaves and twigs.

Chase looked side to side, half-expecting to see a pack of hungry coyotes and half-expecting an evil clown or hatchet-wielding madman to jump out. He never saw any of that, but he did notice they passed what looked like several roads branching off to the right.

The path curved to the right and just at the end of the curve a good-sized oak had fallen across the road, with the top on the left side of the path and the thick trunk suspended a few inches off the pavement.

"Who's ready for a fire and some whiskey?" Richard asked.

"Fire for sure," Kenna said.

Paul kicked and scooped some dry leaves together a few feet in front of the tree. Then all the guys walked around gathering twigs and branches and set them on the leaves. When they had a small stack, Paul got down on his knees and lit the leaves. Within a minute, the pile was burning and crackling, giving off a good amount of heat. Everyone gathered in a circle around it as Richard handed one sack to Paul, who was next to him, and pulled the bottle of Gentleman Jack out of his sack. He tossed the paper on the fire and passed the bottle to his left, to

Kiara. She quickly uncapped it and chugged down a few swigs. After replacing the cap, she handed the bottle to Hayden.

"You first," Paul said, holding the Jack Daniels out in front of Richard. "You bought it."

Richard and Hayden swigged simultaneously. Then they passed the bottles in opposite directions.

Kenna turned the bottle up. After a few swallows, she pitched forward and exhaled, shivering.

"Yech!" she said. "Need some Coke or something with that."

Chase and Tanya drank simultaneously then swapped bottles.

As they passed the bottles back and forth like that, the conversation began.

"What exactly *is* this place?" Paul asked.

"Exactly what I told you. A dead town," Richard said.

"Like a *ghost* town?" Kenna asked with a somewhat nervous voice.

Chase looked around. "I don't see any houses."

"Supposedly, there is one left," Richard said. "But I haven't found it. Then again, I haven't looked everywhere." He fished a cigarette from his shirt pocket and lit it. "I *have* found a couple buildings. I think they were probably for a community pool or park or something."

"So, where's the *town*?" Tanya asked.

Paul exhaled a long blue cloud of smoke. "Dead."

* * *

Tanya felt something, but she couldn't explain what. It was more than the cold on her back and the heat from the fire warming her front. It was a *buzz*. Not an alcohol and weed induced buzz, though she felt that, too. She felt like a firefly, plugged into a wall socket. Like she was glowing with a current flowing through her. It was a completely foreign feeling, but whatever it was, it was remarkable.

"I don't get it," Tanya said. "This is still part of Keller Falls, right?"

Richard swigged some whiskey then nodded as he passed the bottle. "Technically." He took a drag off his cigarette and exhaled in her direction. "And technically not, I think. I don't know. I'm not a lawyer or expert on government things. This *used* to be the far edges of Keller Falls back in the Fifties."

"Used to be?" Paul said.

"After everything happened, I think the city council decided to un-incorporate this part of town."

Heavy shadows cast by the fire's light and the moon marred the already dark trees.

"What happened?" Kiara asked.

Richard picked up a large stick and tossed it on the fire, sending red embers into the air like squiggling snakes. He took a swig of whiskey, passed the bottle and started his story.

"Somewhere around nineteen fifty-six or seven a man, James Thornton, moved down from New York. He was an architect and city planner by trade, but also an Irish Catholic, disillusioned by his time in Europe during the war."

"Disillusioned?" Paul asked. "What the fuck does that mean?"

"He lost his faith," Richard said. "He stopped believing in a benevolent God. At the same time, he started picking up pieces of occultism and ancient religions."

Tanya watched as the firelight played with Richard's lips, nose and brow line to cast disfiguring shadows across his otherwise glowing face. He looked almost monster-like as he continued.

"Rumor has it he figured since this was the buckle of the Bible Belt, it was the best place to start unbuckling the belt and setting people free from the antiquated notions of Christianity—things like good versus evil and body versus soul." He took a drag from his cigarette and continued. "He bought a few hundred acres with a large old farmhouse on it on the edge of Keller Falls. This property here."

Richard waved his hand like a model on a game show presenting the woods before them.

"It was meant to be a hellish paradise on earth. And so it was."

* * *

Chase listened as Richard spoke. Ever since he was a Cub Scout, he always loved good old ghost stories by the campfire, but this one was too weird. Yes, the area looked like an old neighborhood, but a ghost town in Keller Falls? He wanted to call bullshit, but he didn't. He just listened and watched the light of the fire dancing on Kenna's face. God, she was beautiful. But also shivering.

"You cold?" he whispered.

She nodded.

He wished he had a jacket to give her. He thought about wrapping his arms around her. Keeping her warm would be a good excuse to hold her, but he didn't know how she would react. A rejection in front of all these people would be embarrassing. Chase did the best thing he could think of.

He said, "Me too."

Hayden said, "Wait, go back a second. Did you say a hellish paradise? That's a complete oxymoron."

Richard tossed his cigarette into the fire. "Not necessarily. You only see it that way because of how *you* perceive hell. My guess is your parents and grandparents talked about a place of fire and brimstone and eternal torment. But those are the Christian versions meant to scare people into warring with themselves over how they feel and act. If Hell is a place of complete liberation and freedom from the antiquated mores of our forebears, then it *could* be a paradise."

Paul passed the dwindling bottle to Richard.

"For Thornton, complete freedom, Hell, and Paradise were synonymous." Richard said before taking a couple gulps of whiskey and passing it on.

"You people are making my fucking head hurt," Kiara said. "Can't we talk about something other than religion?"

"How do you know all this?" Paul asked. "I mean, if no one talks about it . . ."

"My grandfather had some involvement," Richard said, straightening up a tad as if he were trying to dignify his response.

"Your grandfather was one of his followers?" Tanya asked, sounding astonished.

Hayden finished the bottle of Jack Daniels and tossed it into the fire, causing a flurry of red embers to shoot up.

"No," Richard said, looking at Tanya. "He was involved *after* the fact."

Dead Town

"After *what* fact?" Paul asked. "You still ain't told us what the fuck happened and why this place is a ghost town."

"I'm trying to," Richard said. "You want the whole story or the short version?"

"Short version," Kenna said. "I'm fucking freezing."

"Ok. Short version. They all died. Including Thornton."

"I gotta piss," Paul said, turning around. He looked over his shoulder at Richard, "but I gotta tell you, that ain't much of a story." Paul took a couple steps to the edge of the woods and relieved himself.

Chase pulled out his cell phone and looked at the screen. It was almost 4:30 already.

"We should probably go," Chase said, not only feeling the cold biting at his extremities, but all the alcohol rushing through his veins. In his mind, he felt sober enough, but he could feel himself swaying as he stood in place. He knew as soon as he started to actually move the shit would hit him hard.

A couple others agreed.

Kiara polished off the last of the Gentleman Jack and set the bottle down.

Tanya and Kenna stood to the side, as the guys and Kiara kicked and stomped at the fire until it was just about out. Then Hayden and Chase unzipped and pissed on the embers, causing them to sizzle loudly. The girls, backs turned to the scene, laughed.

"Guys will use any excuse to piss outdoors," Kiara said, picking up the empty bottle beside her boot.

They kicked out the remaining embers and headed back to Hayden's car.

Paul paused and lit a cigarette. "You going to give us the long version on the way home?"

Richard smiled in the darkness, his teeth an eerie blue. "Of course."

* * *

Once the fire was out, Hayden immediately felt the chill in the air. It was like a cold fist encircling him, squeezing him.

48

As they stumbled through the darkness back to the car, two things kept running through Hayden's mind. He drank way more than he should have. And there was something amazing about this place. He wondered if Kiara felt it, too. Then again, maybe it was just the power of suggestion. First the woman and then Richard mentioning it. Then Richard's story. He still didn't know everything, but it was possible it was like a placebo effect. Either way, real or not, he liked the place and wanted to come back to look around. Besides that, it was just a cool place to drink around a fire.

"Turn on the heat," Kenna said from the very rear of the vehicle as soon as everyone was in.

Hayden kicked over the engine and turned the air up as hot as it would go.

As Hayden put the SUV in drive and pulled onto the highway, Paul asked, "You going to tell us the rest now?"

Richard turned in his seat to look at everyone else. "Where were we?"

"Paradise," Chase said.

"Yeah. So, Thornton had a few people move down and they started developing his land, building a subdivision. I don't know if it was because it was too far from town or they kept it private, but it was only his acolytes that lived there."

"Only his *what*?" Paul asked.

"His followers." Richard turned to face the front, lit a cigarette, then twisted back and continued. "In all, I think they had at least a dozen houses here. Then rumors started circulating about them. They were Satanists. They used drugs. They had bisexual orgies. Some even said there were a couple of black women who lived in Thornton's house who were his willing sex slaves. They tried to quash the rumors by building a small, unused church on the grounds, but in the end, it didn't work."

Hayden looked at the shimmering black river as they crossed it back into town.

"So, what the fuck happened?" Paul asked, sounding frustrated.

"In all, eighteen people died horrific deaths. Supposedly some were disemboweled, some hanged, some bludgeoned to death."

"In *one* night?" Tanya asked.

Dead Town

Richard took a drag off his cigarette and exhaled. "In one *house*."

"I never heard about this," Chase said.

"One of Keller Falls and Alabama's best-kept secrets," Richard said. "That rug's got a lot of things swept under it."

"Well, who did it?" Hayden asked as he turned down the road to Tristan's place.

"No one knows. Some people said a mob of townspeople got together and killed them for being homosexual Satanists. Others blamed the Klan, because of the interracial stuff. And some said it was ritual murders. In the end, the *official* story," Richard held up his first two fingers on each hand and made air-quotes for the word official, "was it was several murder-suicides."

"So, where does your grandfather fit in to all of this?" Chase asked.

"He was a cop at the time. He said a call had come into the station that night. A woman was frantic, saying something about 'they're killing us.' He was one of the first ones on the scene."

Hayden pulled over in front of Tristan's house. The street was dead. Everyone in the car was quiet as could be except Richard.

"Anyway, he said it was the most gruesome thing he ever saw, and he was at Guadalcanal during the war. Bodies everywhere. Most of them naked. Blood. Guts. I never asked if he was in the Klan and he never told me, but he did say he had it on 'good authority'" air-quotes again "the Klan had nothing to do with it. He didn't think a mob did it, either. He said he didn't see how any person could do some of those things to other people."

Richard rolled his window down a bit and flicked his cigarette butt out. "And, if a mob did it, that was the most tight-lipped mob ever, because no one ever said a word about it. Anyway, at some point, the State Troopers came and took over the case, saying Governor Folsom wanted to get to the bottom of it. With all the Civil Rights stuff going on, it was easy to bury the story. All people knew was there were some murders there. That was enough to keep people from moving into the subdivision. Since no one would pay for the existing houses or build new ones, nature reclaimed the property. The city unincorporated it and the state eventually took it. Somewhere in the Seventies, there was a big fire and most of the buildings burned down. And now we're left with Dead Town."

"That's a helluva story," Paul said as Richard opened his door and the cabin lights came on.

"Truth is often stranger than fiction," Richard said. He dipped his head as if tipping a hat and closed the door.

As the lights went off, Hayden watched Richard hurry awkwardly to his bicycle on the side of the house. Once he had mounted it and rode in front of the SUV, Hayden drove away, heading for Paul and Chase's place.

* * *

Kenna-Grace sat in the back with Kiara, half-listening to Richard, though it was a struggle to hear much of what he said, and drifting off in her own thoughts.

As for all that shit Richard was slinging, she was even less certain about it. Satanists. Mass murders. Ghost towns. It all sounded like a lot of bullshit folklore someone made up to justify a subdivision going belly up years ago. There was probably a much more normal reason than any of that.

When they got back to Chase's place, everyone except Hayden poured out of the car.

"Text me when you get home," Tanya told Kiara. Then Kiara climbed into the front passenger seat and closed the door.

Kenna walked slowly toward her car with Chase. She was *not* looking forward to going home. She didn't know if the warden would be there or not, but she dreaded the thought of facing her and that guy again.

"I am so fucking tired," Kenna said.

He got the hint. "You want to crash here?"

"You mind?"

"Beats the alternatives of getting a DUI or going back to that fucked up situation, right?" He smiled gently and she returned the gesture. "You can sleep in my room. I'll take the sofa."

As they followed a few feet behind Paul and Tanya, Kenna said, "I don't want to take your bed from you."

"You want the sofa?"

He could be so daft at times.

"I trust you," she said, smiling.

They walked into the apartment and Tanya and Paul immediately headed for his room. Kenna and Chase stood in the living room looking at each other.

"You want some water or something before we . . .?" his voice trailed off.

Kenna turned around and lifted her hair slightly to expose her neck. "You mind?" When Chase didn't do anything, she said, "the zipper."

"Oh."

His warm hands brushed the back of her neck as he fumbled for a grip on the dress. Slowly, he started to undo it.

"Wait," she said, almost whispering. She led him back to his bedroom, turned on the light and closed the door. Then she turned around again. "Okay. Now."

The truth was, from as far as he had already unzipped her dress, she could have finished, but she wanted to feel his hands on her. She wanted to entice him to act.

Chase grabbed the zipper more gently this time and, pinching a bit of her dress in one hand, continued to unzip all the way down to the top of her teal thong.

"Thanks." She turned around to face him, their lips just inches away from each other's. "You've had some experience doing that, huh?" She raised her eyebrows.

Then Chase did something completely unexpected.

He stepped aside and opened the middle drawer on his fake walnut dresser and pulled out a pair of grey sweatpants and a white V-neck T-shirt.

"You want to sleep in *these*? Or . . .?"

Kenna looked at them then back at him. She wouldn't be getting laid tonight. Not the way things were going.

"You got a pair of boxers I can wear?" she asked as she plucked the T-shirt from his hand.

Chase opened another drawer and dug around until he produced a pair of red plaid boxers and handed them to her.

"I don't think you'll be able to keep them on," he said.

Kenna grinned. "You *that* confident?"

Chase's cheeks reddened a bit. "I meant—"

"I know what you meant." She giggled. She also knew what she hoped.

She stepped into the boxers and pulled them up under her dress, twisting one side of the waistband tightly and tucking it in like a make-shift knot to keep them up.

"Want to see my wiener?" Chase asked, sounding a bit like a little boy trying to show off a new toy.

Before she could react, he unbuttoned his jeans and pushed them down to his knees then stood back up. He was wearing a pair of navy blue boxers with a light brown dachshund taking up most of the space. Its butt was near the left-hand side of the boxers' fly. The body circled all the way around the back until its nose was almost touching its rear.

"Oh my God. You're such an idiot," Kenna said, laughing.

Chase pulled on the sweatpants and turned his back to her. "This okay? Or you want me to leave so you can finish changing?"

"Done." She tossed her dress over his shoulder.

If she were at home she probably would have just left the dress on the floor by her bed, but Chase folded it and set it on top of the dresser. His movements struck her as incredibly careful and delicate, as if the dress were studded with diamonds and jewels instead of something she picked up on sale at Forever 21. She liked that. Especially when she watched him pick up his jeans and just kind of roll them up into a bundle and pitch them next to her clothes.

Kenna grabbed the thin lacy bra strap through the right sleeve opening and contorted herself until she worked it down her arm. She did the same with the left then reached up under the oversized shirt and spun the bra around her torso. As she unhooked Victoria's Secret, the knot she worked in the boxers came unbound and they fell to her ankles.

"Oops!" She giggled, letting the shirt hem fall as she pulled the bra from beneath. She'd swear she saw a flicker or twinkle in Chase's eyes at that moment—just before he looked away.

She tossed the bra over Chase's shoulder just to see what he would do. He folded it and set it on her dress.

Kenna looked down at the shirt that came to mid-thigh. "Meh. I guess it's long enough. Don't need *these* either." She stepped out of the boxers, grabbed them with the toes of her right foot and kicked them at Chase.

They fell to the floor. He bent over and picked them up, wadding them into a ball and tossing them on his jeans.

"I think you're a little drunk," he said.

"You think?" She laughed playfully. "Now take me to bed."

* * *

Chase couldn't believe he was standing there in his room getting undressed with Kenna. Countless times he had thought about it. Hoped for it. And now it was happening.

When her boxers fell, he saw the small, blue-green triangle of her panties. All he could think, though, was *Don't stare like a perv.*

Then she threw her bra at him. It was soft and still warm as her breasts.

He didn't know what to think when she said, "Now take me to bed." It was like the universe was fucking with him. He knew she didn't mean it the way he hoped, but there she was—barely clothed—in his room, her erect nipples poking at the thin fabric of his shirt she wore. Could it get any worse?

"Here," he said, pulling back the covers of his double bed. "Crawl in."

As she did, the shirt stretched tightly against her small round ass, conforming to both cheeks and dimpling slightly in the middle.

He pulled the covers up to her shoulders as she nestled her head against the pillow.

Chase walked to the door and flipped the lights off, then navigated back to the bed, making his way around the far side.

As soon as he climbed in, Kenna rolled away from him.

"Night," he said.

She reached back, grabbed his hand and pulled it over her, hugging it to her sternum. "Sweet dreams," she whispered.

Chase lay there feeling her ribs expanding and contracting with each breath. Over the years, he had wondered so many times what this and more would be like with her. And now here he was, holding her. It wouldn't go down like this. Not with them both lit like Christmas trees. Besides, rather than thinking about sex, all that kept running through his mind was the fucked-up situation at her house earlier. He still couldn't believe her mother tried to get her to hook up with that creepy fucker. Chase smiled a little when he thought about pounding the shit out of him. He just wished he'd hit him a few more times, maybe knocked a few of his teeth out or broke some bones.

Chase inched closer to Kenna-Grace and held her tighter as they spooned. Her breathing slowed enough to indicate she had fallen asleep. That was fine by him, because he was dog-ass tired. Besides holding her, all he wanted was for her to have some peace and, hopefully, some good dreams where she was far away from the warden.

* * *

Paul lay in bed naked with Tanya. As soon as he closed his eyes, the bed and room began spinning. He opened them again and stared at the dark ceiling. Everything still whirled around him, but at a much slower pace.

Tanya rolled toward him and began rubbing his chest. He lay motionless, hoping she would think he was asleep, but her hand drifted south, down to his abs.

"You awake?" she asked. Her hand went down a few more inches and her fingers stroked the skin just above his pubic hair line.

As her hand moved down even further, he closed his eyes and the bed whirled. He liked Tanya. She was a cool chick and fun to hang out with. She was definitely good between the sheets, but as she touched him and got him hard, he found his thoughts drifting. He imagined it wasn't her hand stroking him, but Kiara's. Something about that girl— the way her lips moved when she talked. The way her eyes flashed like two small green flames when she smiled.

Paul's hand slid between Tanya's legs. He wondered if Kiara was completely shaved, too, or if she had a patch of hair still. As his fingers worked around and into her warm moistness, he opened his eyes and looked at Tanya. In the darkness, he could barely see her. The dim streetlight pushing through the edges of the vertical blinds made her hair look darker. That made it easier to imagine he was kissing Kiara's soft lips.

Soon, Tanya rolled over and straddled him. His hands grabbed her narrow waist and guided her gently down. As she rocked and bobbed slowly, letting him enter her an inch at a time, he closed his eyes again. Let the bed and room and world spin madly, but let him picture Kiara's body in his hands.

Her waist was probably a little thicker than Tanya's. And she was a couple inches shorter, but they weighed about the same. His hands slid down her backside, over her ass. Tanya didn't have much back there. Enough to be enjoyable, but Kiara definitely had more. He squeezed her cheeks with both hands. Kiara's would fill his hands better, would be more to play with, more to enjoy.

Tanya leaned down to kiss him, grinding her hips against his. Her mouth tasted like whiskey. It was on her breath when she said, "You feel so good."

"Shh," he said. "They'll hear you." But that was *never* a concern for him. Chase often heard him having sex and they joked about it. The truth was, her voice pulled him from his fantasy and made him remember it was she he was buried deep within, not Kiara.

CHAPTER 6

The angry buzz of the alarm clock scared the hell out of Hayden when it went off at seven. He forgot he had picked up the eight-to-twelve shift Saturday morning. That was part of the reason he was going to be designated driver. He figured he might drink and smoke a little, but nothing ridiculous. He hadn't counted on how wild the night—and he—would actually get.

He was still drunk as he stumbled down the hallway toward the bathroom for a hot shower. As he stood under the powerful stream trying to sober and wake up a bit, his mind drifted back to Dead Town. There was something alluring about the place. Maybe it was the power of suggestion and the crazy tale Richard told. He couldn't put his finger on it, though. It didn't look any different from any other woods he had ever camped or partied in. Still, it was like a powerful magnet strong enough to tug all the iron in his body and, consequently, him toward itself. He thought he felt something . . . *magickal* there. He wondered, though, if Richard had not said anything, would he have still felt it?

No, it wasn't Richard. The moment they crossed over the cable and began walking down the path, Hayden sensed something mystical. The sensation grew the deeper they travelled into the dark. At one point, he actually thought his feet weren't even touching the ground. He was certain if he tried, he could have willed himself to levitate above all the others. But at the time, he attributed that floating sensation to the booze and weed. Now, he wondered. He didn't wonder if he was actually hovering in the air, but if he *could* have. If that floating feeling was his spirit revealing to his mind and body the immense power circulating in the air, waiting to be harnessed by a user. Whatever it was, there was *something* there and he wanted to learn what it was and how to use it.

After drying off, Hayden returned to his room with a towel around his waist and dressed for work, throwing on a pair of jeans and a fresh Gas-n-Save polo. He tugged on some socks and walked quietly down the hall, through the living room, past Kiara sleeping on the sofa, and into the kitchen for a cup of coffee.

As the maker brewed a single cup of extra strong dark roast, he stared over the breakfast bar. Kiara was wrapped tightly in the light blue blanket he had provided. He offered her the bed, but she insisted on sleeping out there. He had hoped she would find the sofa too uncomfortable and crawl into bed with him in the middle of the night, but that didn't happen. He didn't think it would, since she always turned down or ignored his advances, but still, a guy could hope. Hollywood taught him that. Shit, every teen movie is about an overlooked, outcast guy or girl like him trying to garner the affection of some incredible person like Kiara. At first that object of desire always has misplaced interests, only to learn at the end he or she *belongs* with the outcast.

But this was no movie. When he first met Kiara, he thought about casting a spell to make himself more desirable to her, but then he thought not only about other movies and how shit like that *always* backfired, but also about her free will. If he did something like that, he would never know if she *wanted* to love him or was *bound* to love him like a slave. Besides, he also knew magick should never be used for personal gain or evil. Stealing someone's freedom to love whom they wanted was definitely evil. Nothing good could ever come of it. So, he decided he would do it the good old-fashioned way. He would hit on her until she accepted or until he found someone else. Either way, he trusted it would happen. Everything always turns out the way it's supposed to in the end.

As he stirred some sugar and cream into his coffee, Kiara mumbled.

"What time is it?"

"Early." He walked out into the living room and sat on the sofa near her knees. "I forgot I got to work. Why don't you crawl into bed and get comfy?"

"I'm good," she said without opening her eyes.

"You sure?" He rubbed her thigh lightly, in a more fraternal than sexual way.

She tugged the blanket up tighter to her chin and nodded. "Couldn't move if I wanted to."

"Okay. You know where everything is. I'll be back around noon. You going to be here?"

"Probably still sleeping," she said.

Good. He hoped she would stay. Even if there was no chance of romance, he still loved hanging out with her. And he wanted to try to get her to go back to Dead Town with him later.

* * *

Once Paul and Tanya finished and cleaned up, they fell asleep with him spooning her. Within seconds of closing his eyes he was in another place with another person—Kiara. It was one of the most vivid, sexual dreams he had since the occasional wet dreams he experienced during puberty.

"You okay?" Tanya asked, waking him. She was leaning on her elbow and holding him with one hand. "You were groaning."

Paul closed his eyes and lied. "Fucked up dream."

Tanya kissed him on the forehead then lay back down.

Paul grabbed his cell phone from the bedside table and looked at the screen. It was almost eleven o'clock. He didn't think he had slept that long.

Part of him felt bad for lying there with Tanya, thinking about her friend. The other part of him knew whatever he had with Tanya was bound to fizzle out at some point anyway, so what did it matter? He flipped from girl to girl often. Most of his girlfriends knew that. What he didn't do, though, was obsess over some girl he just met. There were too many bass in the river to worry about just one. He'd catch and release. Catch and release. Until the day he found that one great fish he could not let loose. He was far too young to be thinking he had already caught the best fish ever.

* * *

Chase woke with the sunlight pushing through his blinds and his arm around Kenna's waist. She was snuggled against him, her warm body pressed tightly against his. When he realized his morning wood was riding straight up and down her butt crack like a bratwurst on a bun, he created a little space between them. He loved the feeling, but didn't want her to wake feeling his dick all over her. It might freak her out. One day. Just not today.

Kenna rolled over and looked at him. "You finally awake?" she asked.

The faint trace of whiskey was still on her breath. He didn't answer. He just looked at her and marveled how she could look so good first thing in the morning.

Her eyes, though heavy with sleep, were brighter than the room. She smiled.

Then it struck him and his ears burned a little. She was awake before him. She had to have felt him pressed firmly between her butt cheeks. Thank God she didn't say anything about it, because he probably would have shriveled up and died right there beside her.

"What you wanna do today?" she asked.

He hadn't even thought about the day. Shit, he was too comfortable laying right there with his arm still draped across her.

"Breakfast?" he asked.

She smiled warmly. "It's almost lunchtime."

"What?"

"MmHmm." She nodded, then pulled her phone out from under her pillow and showed him the display. 11:42.

"No wonder I'm fucking hungry."

"Same."

"Well?" Chase smiled inside, when he realized she didn't squirm from beneath his arm. That *had* to be a good sign.

She pulled the covers back and looked down at his sweatpants then back into his eyes. Fortunately, his pants were no longer poking out as much. "Rise and shine?" she asked, cocking an eyebrow. Then she rolled away from him, out of his embrace and stood.

Chase studied her lithe body for a moment before moving. His shirt draped over her, catching on her nipples and sticking out just a little more at those two points. He had always wanted her, but never more than at that second. It wasn't because she was half-undressed before him. It was because of the way the sunlight caught her body and echoed off it, shimmering through her delicate movements. It was almost like a thin halo or aura around her entire being. *Angelic*. She looked angelic. That was the word he was searching for.

When they walked out to the living room, Paul and Tanya were already there sipping coffee and watching one of the Fast and Furious movies with the sound turned almost all the way down.

"Wakey wakey," Paul said, "Time to get bakey bakied." He picked his bong up and held it out toward Chase and Kenna-Grace.

"Time to get some damn food," Chase said.

Chase walked to the kitchen and began pouring a couple cups of coffee for Kenna and himself.

"Y'all want to get something to eat?" Kenna asked.

"Yes," Tanya said, sounding almost as if she slobbered on herself while answering.

They hashed out the where and when. Waffle House after they finished their coffees and got dressed.

Kenna sat in the chair by the sofa, tugging her shirt down to cover herself. Chase sat near her feet.

"That's quite an outfit you got there, girl," Paul said, raising his eyebrows and grinning like a letch. "Something you kids want to tell us?"

"Nothing happened," Chase quickly said.

"Sure. We believe you." Paul looked at Tanya. "Don't we?"

"Seriously," Chase said.

Tanya's eyes bounced back and forth between Chase and Kenna. "I don't know," she said, but the way she dragged out the words, he knew she was toying with him.

"I believe you," Paul said, winking.

"I'm—"

Kenna cut him off. "He fucked me just right," she said. "I'll be sore for days."

"That's my boy!"

Chase shook his head and rolled his eyes. He looked at Kenna.

She said, "We might as well tell the truth, darling. They'll know when the baby comes and has your eyes."

"Get the fuck out of here," Paul said. Then he looked at Chase. "You let me down, bro."

Dead Town

As they sipped their coffees, Tanya pulled out her tarot cards. She shuffled them quickly and dealt three out. Past, present, and future. She flipped them slowly, studying each. The Eight of Cups reversed. Seemed accurate for her *past* card. Before Paul, she had quite a few short-lived relationships that always left her wanting more—even at their best. Her present? The Tower. A quick change, upheaval. That was fair enough. Everything changed when she and Paul started dating. She rarely spent a night at home. She enjoyed life more. She actually had a boyfriend who did not leave her dreaming and aching for something better to come along. Finally, those things to come—the Three of Swords. Grief, heartache, loss.

She didn't want to think about it.

Tanya pulled the cards together and began shuffling again, trying to listen to the conversation between Paul and Chase, but try as she did, she couldn't stop her mind from wandering back to the readings she did yesterday and how they related with this one. Bad shit was heading their way.

Tanya contemplated a few quick scenarios in which she and Paul broke up. She hadn't used the L-word yet, but several times she had come dangerously close. Did she love him? Probably. If ever she loved anyone in a romantic way, it was most definitely Paul. She had used the word a thousand times before—from her middle school boyfriends on up—and each time she did, she believed it. But after her last long-term relationship, a fourteen-month ordeal with Jeremy that ended over a year ago, she realized she never truly loved any of them. She just loved the *idea* of love. After Jeremy, she promised herself she wouldn't use the word again until she meant it—until she burned for the guy every second he was near and yearned for him every second he was absent. Paul had the material to *become* that guy, but he wasn't quite there yet. He was fun and she loved hanging with him and getting stoned with him, but when they weren't together for whatever reason, she didn't spend all her time wondering what he was doing or if he missed her. Maybe she was growing up a little. Maybe she was enjoying the taste of freedom and the thrill of individualism—of becoming her own self instead of who someone wanted her to be. Or maybe she was secure in a relationship for the first time. Whatever the maybes were didn't matter, because if something didn't change—if she didn't read the signs correctly—they were bound for a split. The cards said it and she believed it.

But maybe the cards didn't say that. Maybe the cards were predicting some other heartache. Her parents were getting old. They were both over fifty. There was no telling how much time she had left with either of them.

Stop thinking about this shit, she told herself.

"It's all bullshit," Paul said.

Kenna sipped her coffee. "Something was there."

"That doesn't mean shit," Paul said, laughing a little to emphasize how preposterous he found her assertion. "What do you think?" he asked Tanya.

"About?"

"That guy's stories last night."

She lit a Newport and took a deep contemplative drag, enjoying the rush of mentholated smoke. "I hadn't thought much about it."

"But did you *believe* him?"

She remembered the electrical buzz circulating through her body. "I don't know. Maybe?"

"You seriously believe a bunch of Satanists moved here and committed mass suicide or were murdered and left a ghost town?"

"Well, if it's true," Chase started "I sure as fuck wouldn't move there."

"Why not? Could probably get the land cheap as fuck."

"Still," Chase said. "Just too—"

"What? Scared of ghosts?"

"Fuck ghosts. I don't believe in them. But that would be creepy as hell knowing you lived where someone was slaughtered."

"There could be ghosts," Tanya said. "I mean if they were murdered or something. There are tons of stories about people with unfinished business or victims lurking where they died."

"Bullshit!" Paul said.

"There *are*."

"I know there are tons of bullshit stories like that. But they are all *bullshit*."

"There were definitely roads and stuff," Kenna said.

"That just means there were roads. It doesn't mean houses were there or Satanists were murdered or offed themselves."

"I know I never heard any of those stories," Chase said. "Hell, I've driven past those woods a million times and never even knew that shit was back there."

"We should go back," Paul said, grabbing his bong. "See if we find any houses or those buildings he mentioned."

Tanya shook her head as Paul lit the bong and took a big hit. She liked the feeling she had while there—the energy and all—but if the stories were true or the place was haunted, she didn't want to mess with it.

"I don't know," Tanya said.

"We'll go after we eat," Paul said after exhaling. "It'll be day. Everyone knows ghosts don't come out 'til night." He grinned impishly, clearly amusing himself.

"I'm down," Chase said. "Would be cool to see what else is back there." He looked at Kenna. "You in?"

Tanya hoped she would say no, but after a few seconds of just staring at Chase, Kenna said, "Sure. As long as we are gone before dark."

Paul started to take another hit off the bong, but stopped. "Don't tell me you're scared, too." He looked at Chase and rolled his eyes. "Fucking women, scared of everything."

"The only thing I'm scared of is being lost out there in the dark and cold," Kenna said.

Paul looked at Tanya, waiting for a response. She took the bong from him and lit it.

After filling her lungs with smoke and exhaling, she said, "Whatever." But something inside her told her she would regret it.

* * *

Kiara rolled off the sofa and headed for the bathroom. She hadn't brought a change of clothes, but she needed a hot shower.

As she stood under the steady stream of water, she contemplated the previous night's events.

Something about Paul's cocky, self-assuredness was attractive. He was funny, too. And it didn't hurt that he was cute. He had a gorgeous smile. He was more muscular than she usually preferred. Or was he just more muscular than the kinds of guys she usually dated? No. He looked good with those bulging muscles. He wasn't one of those disgusting freakish looking guys on the covers of magazines with legs bigger than bulldozers. *Bulging*, the word struck her and she smiled to herself. *Wonder what his* other *bulge is like*.

Kiara shook her head, feeling a little guilty. She had never cheated on a boyfriend. And never dated a guy that had a girlfriend or wife. And now, here she was thinking about her friend's boyfriend. Somehow that seemed like the worst of all three possibilities.

Yes, she wanted him. But she wouldn't do anything with him. Not while he was dating Tanya.

But if they broke up? Maybe not even then. She didn't know. Why worry about it, though? It wasn't as if Paul had hit on her or asked her out.

Kiara finished her shower and threw her same clothes on. They reeked of campfire smoke.

She looked at her cell phone. It was after noon. She texted Tanya.

--WYD
--Abt to eat. WYD
--Still at Hayden's
--Oh???
--Not like that
--Wanna come?
--IDK. Maybe. Where?
--Awful house

Kiara was about to pass, but figured Paul would be there. She wanted to see him during the day when she was sober to see if she still felt the same way about him.

--K

Ten minutes later she walked into the Waffle House and, after spotting the others in a booth, made her way to them. To her left sat Tanya and Paul, with Tanya on the inside. To her right were Kenna and Chase. Both boys scooted in and she had her choice which she would sit next to.

Dead Town

Her first instinct was to draw up to Paul and feel him close beside her, but she chose to sit beside Chase instead. That way she could look at Paul and he at her.

She smiled at Paul and Tanya.

"So, you survived, huh?" Paul asked.

"I wouldn't bet on it," she said, shaking her head and grinning a little.

The waitress, a pale, skinny woman with mostly black teeth and a neck tattoo that said *Sweetie* walked up and set down drinks before the others.

"Can I get a coffee?" Kiara asked.

"In a second, baby." The woman couldn't have been over twenty-seven, though she looked like she got rode hard and hung up wet more than a few times. "Y'all ready to order?"

Everyone, including Kiara, nodded or said, "Yes."

Kiara looked at the nametag on the woman's breast. Donna. She didn't look like a Donna.

A couple minutes later, when everyone's meal was ordered, Donna walked off and returned with a cup of coffee for Kiara. After setting it in front of her, she called out the order to the cook.

Kiara watched Paul as he drank his Coke through a straw. She glanced at Tanya, then back to Paul. He had some beautiful eyes. They reminded her of pale, unpolished emeralds.

"What you doing after this?" Tanya asked.

Kiara shrugged her right shoulder and raised her eyebrows. "Why?"

"We're going exploring," Paul said.

"Going *what*?"

Tanya shook her head. "He wants to go back where we were last night and look around."

"Why?"

"Shits and giggles," Paul said.

Chase turned to Kiara. "He thinks that guy was full of shit. He—"

"*Full* of shit," Paul reiterated.

"He wants to prove it to Tanya."

Kiara looked at Paul. "How?"

"By *looking*," Paul said.

She stared into his eyes. "How is looking going to prove anything? I mean, what are you looking for? A sign that says, 'Satanists died here in nineteen fifty- or sixty-something'?"

She watched his mouth as he spoke. "I don't know. If there *is* a house hidden back there, that would be cool as fuck to find. And even if there isn't, Halloween is coming up in a couple weeks. It would be a cool ass place for a party. We can even invite that Richard dude. Someone has to know how to get ahold of him. He'd scare the hell out of everyone."

Paul and Chase both laughed.

Kiara realized she was staring at Paul. She looked at Tanya for a second, but she was looking at Kenna. Kiara's eyes naturally glided back to Paul.

"So, you find a house. Then what?"

"We go in and look around."

"For . . .?"

"*Clues.*"

Kiara looked at Tanya. "What are you two like Fred and Daphne from that old Scooby-Doo movie now?"

"Not me," Tanya said. "Him."

"Okay, Fred," Kiara said, smirking. "Even if there was a house, it's probably rotted to the ground by now."

Paul looked at Chase. "What'd I tell ya? Girls—too scared of—"

"Here ya go," Donna said as she leaned over the table and began passing out food.

Paul pointed at Kiara's All-Star breakfast. "Didn't you eat that last night?"

"I ain't scared of shit," Kiara said. She cut some white off her egg with the edge of her fork and scooped it up, pausing just in front of her face. "It's the only thing I eat here."

"*Shit?*" Paul asked.

Everyone laughed, including Kiara. "Dumbass."

"Then you're coming, too?" He sounded excited at the prospect.

She moved her gaze to Tanya. Kiara couldn't tell if that was suspicion in her bright blue eyes or something else she was trying to convey without words.

"That okay?" Kiara asked Tanya.

"Why *wouldn't* it be?" Tanya said before taking a bite of her cheeseburger.

"Can I run an errand before we go?"

"Depends on how *long* an errand," Paul said. "They're all scared of the dark." He pointed at everyone else.

"Not me," Chase said. "I'm up for another fire. Let's get some marshmallows and whiskey."

"There's a good combo," Kenna said. "Guaranteed to make you vomit."

"Hotdogs?"

"Won't take long," Kiara said. "Like twenty or thirty minutes."

Kiara smothered her waffle in syrup. "Want to go with me?" she asked Tanya.

"Where?"

"Just need to run to the store."

"Fine by me," Kenna said. "I could use a shower and change of clothes anyway."

They quickly finished their meals and paid. As Tanya climbed in the passenger seat of Kiara's car, she said, "Where we going?"

"I need some damn underwear. I'm going commando right now and it ain't fun."

"What? *Why*?"

Kiara explained she wanted to hit Victoria's Secret at the mall because she wasn't about to put dirty underwear back on after showering.

As they pulled out onto Sixth Avenue, Tanya asked, "What do you think of Paul?"

* * *

Hayden was ready for his shift to end. He was tired as hell already and to make matters worse, there was a never-ending line of people coming in. Every now and then he thought he was about to get a break to plop down on his stool behind the counter and relax for a few minutes, but just about every time he sat, someone else came in needing cigarettes or drinks. It was probably just as well, since he was likely to fall asleep if he sat too long.

Already, it was well past twelve and Deante, his replacement, hadn't shown. He had called an hour earlier and said he was having some car trouble and would be there as soon as possible. Hayden agreed he'd stay and cover for him. By a quarter after one, he regretted that decision. He didn't mind helping someone out. He wouldn't mind the extra few bucks on his paycheck. But he was ready for a nap.

Finally, though, there was a lull in foot traffic and Hayden could relax.

He sat on the stool and checked his phone, running through his various social media pages and Snapchat messages.

The door chimed as it opened and Hayden stood. One of the house rules—no sitting while people were in the store. He looked over the counter at the attractive woman walking in and toward the drink fountain. He recognized her immediately.

After filling a large Styrofoam cup, she approached the counter.

He was anxious to talk to her.

"How you doing today?" he asked, trying to sound more excited than he had the day before.

"Well. You?"

"Ready for bed." He smiled. As soon as he did, he worried she might take it the wrong way.

"Long night, huh?"

He rang her up.

"One forty-one. Can I ask you something?"

She reached into her small purse and started retrieving exact change. "Sure."

"What do *you* know about Dead Town?"

Her fingers immediately stopped fiddling in her purse and she looked up with a semi-shocked expression as if he had just farted loudly.

"I know you shouldn't go there."

"Why not? I mean . . . the stories . . ."

"Why are you asking?" She sounded almost perturbed. "Yesterday you didn't even know what it was."

The lady bowed her head back down and found the rest of her money. She plopped it on the counter.

"Last night someone else mentioned it. Then took us there."

69

Dead Town

Again, she looked at him, this time more worry than shock etched on her face.

"Whatever you heard about Dead Town, if it was horrific, it was probably true," she said. "There are a lot of bad things in Keller Falls and a lot of good. But at Dead Town? There is *nothing* good up there."

"Have you been?"

She looked at his name tag. "Trust me, Hayden. Please."

"It felt like a lot of power or energy up there."

"Probably way more than you realize."

"So, you've been?"

She picked up her drink. "You want to know what I know about Dead Town? I know you shouldn't mess with things you don't understand."

He'd be lying if he said he didn't take offense to that last comment. He'd studied this kind of shit since he was thirteen or fourteen.

His contempt must have been scrawled on his face, because she softened a bit in tone and became almost mother-like. "I'm serious about nothing good being there. And nothing good can come from going there. I probably should never have said anything to you in the first place, but I did. That was *my* mistake. I guess I was trying to see how serious you were with all your tats."

She took a sip of her drink. At the same time, the door chimed and a chubby black man in his fifties walked in.

"I don't really have time to talk right now," she said as she picked a pen up from the counter. She flipped her receipt and wrote on it. She wrote her name—Amber—and her number on it. "Call or text me and we'll talk. Ok?"

Hayden nodded. "Sure."

"Just promise me you're not planning on going up there again."

"I'm not," he said.

"Good."

With that, she turned and walked away.

A couple customers later, Deante entered. Hayden looked at his phone. It was 2:13.

"Sorry, bro," Deante said, smiling. "Still didn't get my car running. Had to catch a ride." He went on with his story about what happened and what he tried doing to fix it, but Hayden didn't give a fuck. He was ready to get out of there and back home.

As soon as Deante clocked in, Hayden clocked out.

Hayden had just gotten home, stripped down to his boxers, and crawled into bed when his phone alerted him he had a text message. He thought about ignoring it and closing his eyes, but curiosity got the best of him. He pulled the phone out from under his pillow and looked at the message from Kiara.

--Going back to Dead Town in a few. Wanna come?

Hayden thought about Amber's admonition. He just told her less than thirty minutes ago he wasn't going back and now here was the temptation pulling at him like a winch attached to his waistband. Actually, what he told her was he didn't *plan* on going back. It wasn't as if he lied. Hell, it wasn't as if it was any of her business anyway. Besides, this would give him more time with Kiara.

--Sure. When? WYA?

* * *

Kenna was relieved when Chase asked, "Want me to drive you home so you can get some clothes?"

"You mind?"

She knew she had to go back eventually and she had been dreading it all morning. Half her meal was spent worrying and conjuring up images of what was going to happen when she walked in. The hope that the warden and Matthew were not there quickly gave way to more dark visions of the two of them cornering her again. Would the warden help him rape her? Or would she just stand by all bleary-eyed and stoned, watching? Maybe she would escape the rape and get off with just an ass-whooping from him.

A short while later, they turned up the dirt drive to her house. She held her breath as they rounded the curve. Both cars were parked out front.

Chase reached over and placed his hand on her thigh.

"It's gonna be alright," he said, slowing the car to a quick, quiet stop. He looked at her. "I'm here for you. I'm *always* here for you."

71

She tried to force a smile and hide her fear, but she suspected she was failing miserably. "I know."

Chase gave her leg a couple gentle pumps and took his foot off the brake, allowing the car to inch forward toward the house. "I'm going in with you."

"No. That's al—"

He repeated it slower, bobbing his head with each word for emphasis. "I'm. Going. In. *With* you."

Somehow, the assuredness and confidence he exuded made everything better that moment.

"Okay."

They pulled up alongside the other vehicles and got out. Then Chase surprised her. He walked over to her and took her hand, squeezing it gently. He didn't interlace their fingers like lovers on parade, but cupped her palm in his. It reminded her of how her father used to hold her hand when she was little and walking across a street or through a store with him. It was sweet. It was nice. It was *good*.

Kenna opened the front door and stepped in with Chase on her heels, still holding her hand. She gripped his hand tighter as she held her breath. The living room was empty. Maybe they were passed out or busy fucking in the bedroom.

No such luck.

The warden stepped out of the kitchen wearing just a pair of panties, her small aging breasts sagging and clinging to her ribs like a couple of drooping pancakes.

"Oh, it's you," the warden said, sounding as if she expected someone else.

"Why don't you cover up?" Kenna asked, feeling the embarrassment for her mother burning her cheeks and ears.

"Why? Ain't he ever seen tits before?" She looked at Chase. "You ever seen tits before, boy?"

"Not like those, I haven't," he said.

Kenna picked up the sarcasm in his voice, but clearly the warden didn't, because she cupped her breasts and lifted them up, pushing them together a bit. "I know. *Nice*, huh?"

Kenna tugged at Chase's hand to pull him back toward her bedroom. As they started to move, Matthew came out of the kitchen buck naked.

"What the fuck is that faggot doing here?" he asked.

Chase let go of her hand.

She looked over at him. He clenched his jaw tightly and glared at Matthew.

Kenna took his hand again. It was limp. He barely held hers if he held it at all.

"Come on," she whispered. She tugged gently, but Chase didn't move.

"Don't you eyeball me, boy," Matthew said. "I fucked boys like you in Kilby all the time."

Kenna waited for Chase to explode. She could feel his hand trembling in hers. It didn't feel like *fear* that had him twitching, but anger and anticipation. It was like holding the lit wick of a stick of dynamite, feeling it buzz as it burned, waiting for it to go off.

Then it stopped.

"I bet you did," Chase said. "Bet you loved every minute you were bent over, too."

"You wanna *try* me, boy?"

Kenna pulled at Chase again. This time he moved as he said, "Already did. Already whooped your ass, too, *boy*."

Kenna led Chase down the hall to her room, closing and locking the door behind them. She could hear the Warden and Matthew arguing outside.

She grabbed a pair of panties, a bra, some jeans and a T-shirt as Chase stood by the door like a Rottweiler guarding it.

He looked at her and gave an awkward smile.

"Why don't you pack a few changes of clothes?" he said. "You can crash at my place for a while until this loser is gone or cools off."

His words were like a crane pulling a two-ton boulder off her chest. She almost asked, "Are you sure?" but she didn't.

She pulled a small nylon bag from her closet and began jamming clothes into it. She only halfway paid attention to what she collected. She didn't bother counting changes of undies or even hiding them from

Chase's view. Ordinarily, she would have been a little more modest with those intimate items.

Once the bag was full to the point it could only zipper about three-quarters of the way, she said, "Let's go."

She opened the door and yipped like a surprised dog.

Matthew stood there, still naked, holding his shiny silver pistol and pointing it at her.

Kenna jumped back into the room, dropping her bag and falling to the ground. Chase gave her a quizzical look as she scampered back.

"Where's that faggot?" Matthew said, stepping into the room.

Matthew blocked the door directly in front of her. Chase was to her right, only a couple feet away from Matthew as the latter spun and swung the pistol toward him.

"Come on, boy. You wanna try me *now*?"

Chase raised his hands about shoulder high and shook his head.

"You got a smart mouth on you, boy. Bet it's a good dick sucker."

Chase slowly backed up a couple steps until he bumped into a dresser. "Put that shit away, bro."

Matthew inched toward him. "Come on, boy. Say something. Eyeball me again!"

The warden stepped into view in the hallway. She looked down at Kenna-Grace then over to Matthew. Kenna hoped she would say something, but the bitch kept her mouth shut.

"Get the fuck out of here!" Kenna screamed. "Go!"

Matthew turned toward her, waving the gun in little circles. "Oh, don't you worry, missy. You gonna get your chance with this, too." He thrust out his pelvis, causing his short fat dick to bounce.

The nasty grin on his face revulsed her.

"Get out!"

The warden smiled at her. It wasn't a happy smile. It was one of those shit-eating smiles that seemed to say, "Now you're going to get yours."

CHAPTER 7

Chase stood in Kenna's room, waiting for her to get her bag packed. When she was ready, he tried to help her zip it. She had the thing so chock full of shit, they couldn't get it closed all the way. That was fine by him. She'd be able to stay gone longer. Yes, he wanted her crashing at his place so he could find the opportunity to make a move. But more than that, more than anything at the moment, he wanted her out of this fucked up place for a while. He didn't give a good fuck if that meant at his place or at some Eskimo's igloo in Alaska.

She grabbed the small pink bag and scooted past him.

As she opened the door, she yelped and stumbled back, falling.

He looked at her trying to figure out what just happened and why she was crawling backwards, but he knew as soon as he heard that asshole.

He came into the room waving a nickel-plated revolver. A .38 or .357.

Chase threw his hands into the air and backpedaled until he bumped into something. He reached behind him and touched the dresser with his right hand, knocking over a small framed photo of her father as he said, "Put that shit away, bro."

Chase wasn't afraid of guns. This was Alabama. He grew up around guns. But he was smart enough to be afraid of a fucked-up meth-head with a grudge and a gun. There was no telling what a loser like this would do.

Kenna screamed at the man to leave. Then he twisted his body and waved the gun at her, threatening to rape her.

Chase glanced over his right shoulder. By his hand was a large ceramic lamp. He grabbed it with both hands and spun. The power cord broke with a snap and a loud fizzle as he lunged at the man's head. The base shattered against his skull. The white plastic lampshade fell to the floor.

Dead Town

BANG! The gun went off.

The creep stumbled backwards and hit the open door, breaking it.

For a split-second Chase stood there, empty-handed, wondering what to do. But when the man began to raise the pistol, Chase stopped thinking.

He charged him like a safety hitting a wide-receiver about to make a game-winning catch. The gun went off again before the man fumbled it.

They tumbled to the floor at Kenna's feet. She scrambled to get out of the way.

The way and place they landed put Chase at a disadvantage. They rolled and the man ended up on top of him in a full mount, his legs straddling Chase's waist.

Blood poured from the man's forehead, running down his cheeks and dripping, streaming, onto Chase's face and chest.

Trapped on a narrow swatch of carpet between the foot of the bed and closet, Chase couldn't get the leverage or find the space he needed on either side to roll the man.

Several blows rained down on him. The first made his teeth clack shut. The next couple hit his cheek and temple as he tried to cover up. The man kept dropping bombs.

"Say something smart now, boy," he shouted.

Bam! Bam! Bam!

Chase tried to thrust his hips up and buck the man, but failed. It did, however, give him a second to reach up and grab the guy by the throat with one hand. He jerked free from Chase's grip.

"Come on, boy. Open that pretty little dick sucker and say something now."

Bam!

Chase did what he could to defend himself. He worked his arms feverishly, trying to block the flurry of blows.

Then . . .

BANG!

The gun went off again.

They both froze.

The man twisted toward the door. Chase looked past him, over his bloody shoulder, at Kenna standing near the wall. She had the pistol pointed at the creep's head.

"Get off him now or I will blow your fucking head off," she said through gritted teeth.

The man turned back toward Chase and raised a fist.

Click. The hammer cocked back.

His body went limp and he rolled off Chase.

As Chase stood, he looked at him. It was over.

"Good thing you had that bitch here to save you," the guy said.

It *wasn't* over. Chase kneed him as hard as he could in the face. He slammed into the closet door behind him with a loud thud. Then sat there, his face and shoulders drenched in bright red blood.

Chase picked up the pink bag and handed it to Kenna. He took the gun from her and pointed it at the warden's boyfriend.

The bastard grinned. "What're you gonna do, *boy*?"

Chase stared at him. No, it wasn't over. Just as he was always taught. He took a deep breath. Exhaled half of it. Held it. And slowly squeezed, not jerked, the trigger.

He grabbed Kenna's wrist and yanked her out of the room, knocking her mother over in the process. They ran down the hall, out the door and jumped in his car.

* * *

Paul sat on the sofa with Tanya, smoking a mango passion fruit blunt he rolled. After she hit it, she passed it to Kiara, who was on the chair. Paul watched her full lips wrap around the end and her cheeks pucker in as she inhaled. She looked at him as she did.

Damn, she looked good, sitting there in her tight blue jeans and new shirt she bought at Victoria's Secret. It was a thin heather gray shirt with *Angel* scrawled across the front in black. She might have had an angelic face, but there was something devilish about her, too. And *that* was the side Paul wanted to see.

Kiara rose and passed the blunt to him. He took a couple sweet, potent puffs then handed it to Tanya. Too bad they were friends. If they weren't, he would probably flirt a little with Kiara. Side ass wasn't his style. He'd been cheated on by a girl in high school and didn't like the feeling when he found out. But he also believed women were like jobs. You never quit one until you have another one lined up. But lining up your girlfriend's friend? Too complicated. Especially when he didn't know how Kiara would react. Sure, she might flirt back and line up. But she might also go straight to Tanya and say, "Your boyfriend just tried to hook up with me."

The blunt made another full circle back to Tanya. As she hit it, Paul's phone dinged with a message.

--WYA WYD

It was Ladarius.

--Home. Smoking. WYD

--BRT LOL

--Come on

--Srsly???

--Yea. I'll roll another. But hurry.

--K

Less than ten minutes later, there was a knock at the door. Paul stood and the power of the smoke hit him, making his legs wobble a bit. It was a new batch from his friend and stronger than the last. Definitely not reggie or even mid.

Paul opened the door and Ladarius stepped in.

He was a couple inches shorter than Paul and scrawny. He looked like a gentle breeze could snap him in two, but he was one of the best scrappers Paul ever saw. He was a pit bull in a Chihuahua's body. But he was also chill as fuck as long as you didn't mess with him or his friends.

Ladarius looked around and smiled a big smile. "Y'all got the good shit cooking in here, huh?"

"This is some top shelf shit," Paul said, walking back to the sofa and picking up the small baggie of weed on the table to show it off. He sat beside Tanya.

She scooted over to make room for Ladarius on the other side of her.

Ladarius walked over to Kiara. "Ladarius," he said, offering his hand and a bigger, warmer smile. "My friends call me Dari, but you can just call me Bae."

In the four years Paul had known Ladarius, he had never seen him date or even hit on a black chick. Although he was black, he always had a thing for white girls and Latinas.

Once, Paul joked with him and pointed it out, asking, "What are you, some kind of racist, man? You don't like black girls?"

Ladarius laughed. "You sound like my mama. Always telling me to stick with my own kind. I'm gonna tell you what I tell her. I'm doing my part to create racial harmony . . . one girl at a time." He laughed again, then added, "Unless they're down for threesomes. Of course, I *don't* tell her *that*."

And that's how he was. Cool with everything and everyone. He never defined himself by his skin color and hated when others tried defining him or themselves like that, regardless of what color they were.

"Kiara." She shook his hand. "My friends call me Kiara, but you can call me unimpressed by that cheesy pickup line."

She grinned mischievously.

"Fair enough." Dari smiled again.

"Sit your ass down," Tanya said, patting the seat beside her. "Quit harassing the guests."

As he turned to face Tanya, Dari wrapped his arms around himself and feigned a shiver. "Damn. It's cold in here."

Paul rolled another blunt and the four of them smoked it as they waited for Chase and Kenna to return. At the same time, Paul texted Tristan, asking if he knew how to get in touch with Richard. He did. He gave him his number and told him where he lived.

Paul texted Richard. They were going back to Dead Town. Did he want to join? Absolutely. Paul texted his location and told him if he'd pick up some whiskey on his way they'd pay him when he got there.

Halfway through the blunt, Paul asked Dari, "You coming with us?" He puffed and passed to Tanya.

"Where?"

"Dead Town."

Puff. "What the fuck is Dead Town?" Pass to Kiara.

"A hidden ghost town just across the river."

"*Ghost town?*" His eyes grew wide. "Come on man, you know us brothers don't do ghosts."

"Ain't no ghosts there." Puff. Puff. Pass. "It's just some woods."

"Some *woods*?" He took the blunt from Tanya. "Make up your mind. Woods or ghosts?" Puff. "Which is it?" He leaned forward and almost fell over as he passed the dwindling blunt to Kiara.

"This weird guy, Richard, said there used to be some houses and shit there," Tanya said. "Paul wants to look for them."

"In the woods . . ." Ladarius said, half-question and half-statement.

Paul nodded as Kiara handed him the blunt. He looked at it and passed it to Dari without hitting it. "Let him kill it," he told Tanya. Then he looked at Dari. "We smoked one before you got here. You need to catch up."

Ladarius nodded. "Cool." He toked a few times in rapid succession. When it was spent, he crushed it out in a large black plastic ashtray on the coffee table.

"It'll be fun," Paul said.

"What?"

"Exploring. Come on."

After a little chiding and prompting from the girls, Dari finally agreed to go.

The front door opened and Kenna walked in followed by Chase who was carrying a pink nylon gym bag. His face was red and splotchy. His left eye was swollen. And he had crusted blood under his nose.

"Dude! What the fuck happened to you?" Paul asked.

Chase shook his head. "Long story."

"I got time."

"You alright, bro?" Dari asked.

"I'm fine."

"We need to handle some business?" Dari looked like he was about to jump off the sofa.

Chase handed the bag to Kenna, then with a grand sweep of his arm motioned for Kenna to head down the hallway toward the bedroom.

"It's handled," Chase said.

Everyone looked at Kenna for answers. She seemed to shrink into her shirt like a turtle.

"The warden's new beau," she said.

Everyone but Kiara nodded. No more needed to be said. They may not know the guy, but they all knew about her mother.

Kiara gave Paul and Tanya a questioning look, then looked away as if she suddenly realized it was probably none of her business.

Kenna disappeared down the hall. When the door clicked shut, Paul whispered, "Seriously, dude. What the fuck is going on?"

"Don't worry about it."

Ladarius leaned in closer. "Chase . . . you *know* if you need help I'm here. I always got your six."

Chase nodded. "Yeah."

"Or my cousin—"

"No. It's all good."

"You sure?" Tanya asked.

"Just let me wash up some."

Chase walked down the hall to the bathroom.

As the water ran, Ladarius asked, "So, when we going?"

Paul said, "We're just waiting on that dude Richard. He's picking us up some whiskey, too."

"And Hayden," Kiara said.

Everyone looked at her as if they had all forgotten she was in the room.

"I hope you don't mind," she said. "I just texted and invited him a few minutes ago." She lit a cigarette, exhaled a small cloud of blue smoke and shrugged her shoulder. "I mean . . . I'm staying at his house. But if you don't want him there we can—"

"No. That's fine," Paul said. He started taking a mental count. "We just need to get eight of us over there now."

"Doesn't sound like a problem," Kiara said. "Sounds like a party."

Everyone laughed.

The bathroom sink stopped running and a few seconds later Chase returned to the room. Despite the absence of dried blood from his face and neck, he still looked a mess. His black eye from the day before was darker and fuller. In fact, his whole face appeared a little puffy and the blood stains on his shirt made him look like a serial killer that just got done butchering a victim.

"You want to sit?" Kiara asked, beginning to rise from her seat.

Chase waved his hands. "I'm good. Thanks."

Dead Town

Kiara relaxed back in her seat as Chase headed for the kitchen.

After a couple minutes, Kenna emerged from the bedroom wearing a pair of jeans and a bright red Fireball Whiskey T-shirt.

"You okay?" Dari asked her.

"Ain't I always?" She walked over and sat on his lap.

"Be a good girl and wiggle a little for Santa," Dari said, grabbing her by the waist and shaking her.

She slapped his arm. "Quit." She smiled. "If you're *really* Santa, you *know* I've been deliciously naughty all year."

"Just the way I like 'em," he said, laughing.

Chase walked back through the living room and headed to his bedroom. About the same time, Richard arrived. Paul paid him for the whiskey. Everyone took a swig from the bottle and waited.

CHAPTER 8

Chase and Kenna agreed they would drive over in his car, following the others as they rode with Hayden. Once they were near Dead Town, they would park on the shoulder across the highway and walk over so there weren't two cars parked next to each other. To passersby, it would appear as if motorists were stranded on different paths.

Chase looked at the clock on the dash radio. It was already almost three. He wasn't sure how much *exploring* they would get to do before darkness set in, but he was interested to see what they found, especially since Richard retold the story to Dari while they waited on Hayden to show up. The tale was less spooky and more alluring in the daylight and comfort of his living room. Instead of a ghost story, it now sounded more like a mystery.

Chase lit a cigarette and cracked his window as they crossed the river. He looked down at the whitecaps on the murky gray water then over to Kenna.

"Sorry about shooting your closet door," he said.

"Are you kidding?" She fumbled with her pack of Marlboro lights. "I thought you were going to blow his head off."

She sounded relieved he hadn't.

"I hope I didn't wreck any of your clothes or stuff."

She popped the filter in her mouth and spoke, the cigarette bobbing from her lips. "Wouldn't matter. I just hope that fucking asshole learned a lesson." She lit the cigarette.

"Same."

The guy was an unpredictable attempted-rapist and drug addict. There was no telling what would happen when they ran into each other. Maybe they would all get lucky and Kenna's mama would dump his ass before that happened. Somehow, though, that seemed unlikely. The crazy bitch just stood there both times. Fuck, she even encouraged

Dead Town

Kenna to have sex with the creep. What kind of mother does shit like that? *Her* mother. A fucking *mom*ster.

As they stepped out of Chase's car, a murder of crows—six of them—hopped a few feet from them, focusing on something in the grass.

Chase looked to his left. No cars coming.

"Let's go," he said, stepping onto the pavement.

Kenna followed.

They jogged across the grassy median and to the opening of Dead Town without seeing a single vehicle. After crossing over the cable, they waited and watched as Hayden pulled his SUV off the road.

In the daylight, everything looked different. It was a tangled mess of trees and plants and leaves and vines and dying flowers. There was depth and space and color that didn't exist in the darkness of night—varying shades of greens and browns, leaves changing colors—burning red, yellow, and orange—pink blooms wilting and browning.

Small saplings and long grass rose through cracks in the road. Chase looked up at the canopy of thinning branches arching over the roadway. It had been a warm fall, so most were still covered in leaves, though some were changing colors.

The place seemed like any normal patch of woods, except for one thing. Chase realized other than the sounds they made, the place was deathly quiet. When everyone stopped talking there was no sound at all other than the occasional car or truck whipping past on the road.

Chase scanned the ground and trees. He couldn't spot a single bird or squirrel. Maybe they all scurried for safety at the sight of humans. There was no telling the last time they actually saw a person.

The dried leaves crunched like small bones beneath their feet as they walked.

When they came to the first road that branched off to the right, Richard said, "I've been down that way a little. That's where I found the building I told you about."

Chase peered down the path. About twenty feet in, a fallen tree—swallowed by tall weeds and briars—blocked the way. He couldn't tell what lay beyond it other than a mish-mosh of limbs and brush.

Richard said, "It gets messy back there."

"I see that."

"Yeah, other than this road," Richard waved his hand at his feet then down in the direction they had gone the night before, "this whole place is overgrown."

Kiara pulled out a cigarette and lit it. After exhaling a large blue cloud, she said to Paul, "Pass that whiskey over here."

Richard began walking again. Paul handed the bottle to Kiara, then he and Tanya followed Richard. After Kiara knocked back a couple big gulps, everyone else moved.

They were heading right back to where they had already been. This wasn't exploring. This was a fucking field trip. A teacher and a whole bunch of kids lined up like ducklings.

"How much time have you spent out here, Richard?" Chase asked.

Richard stopped and pulled a soft pack of cigarettes from his shirt pocket.

"Not much," he said.

He bumped the package against his left forefinger, causing a couple butts to jut out. He raised the pack and, with his mouth, withdrew the one sticking out furthest. After tucking the pack back in his shirt, Richard dug into the front pocket of his blue jeans and fished out his lighter. He lit the cigarette.

"I didn't even know where the place was until a couple weeks ago. So, including last night, this is only my third time here."

"So, you don't really know where we are . . ." Paul said, his voice trailing off.

"I know we're in Dead Town," Richard said. He took a drag off his smoke. "And I know where that building is. But other than that, and the place we had the fire last night, I haven't gone anywhere else back here."

Kiara passed the bottle of Jack Daniels to Tanya. After uncapping it, she took a big swig. "Yech!" she said, making a face. She wiped her lips with the back of her hand. "*Smooth.*"

"What are we looking for?" Ladarius asked. "Anything in particular?"

"Supposedly, there's a house up here," Hayden said.

Paul took the whiskey from Tanya and drank a little then passed it on to Dari.

Dead Town

"Are we trying to find it?" Kenna asked. "I mean, *seriously* trying to find it? Or are we just walking around?"

"I'd *love* to find it," Richard said.

"Fuck yeah!" Paul said.

"Then why are we sticking together?" Kenna asked, taking the bottle from Ladarius.

Richard looked confused. Chase knew where she was going.

"We should split up and look in different places. If you find something, call the others."

Ladarius was quick. He looked at Kiara. "What's your number? I'll put it in my phone in case I need to call you."

She rolled her eyes and huffed a playful sigh. "I'm sure you'd find the need."

Dari looked at Paul and grinned. "I *like* her. Where'd y'all find her?"

Tanya grabbed her arm. "She's mine."

"In all seriousness," Dari asked. "How y'all want to break up? Twos? Fours?"

Hayden said, "Why don't Kiara and I go with Paul and Tanya? The rest of you go together. Start as foursomes and break down if we need to."

Everyone agreed that made sense. It also made sense that Richard's group would take the first cutoff where Richard had already been. He'd be able to lead Kenna and Chase to the other building easily and then they could go on after that.

Chase was fine with the plan, but he was actually hoping they'd break down into pairs so he could have some time alone with Kenna. Suggesting it, though, might make him appear overanxious. They might have known each other a long time, but that didn't mean he didn't still need to play it cool. Hell, their friendship probably demanded he play it cooler than ever, because if he fucked this up he might not only lose his opportunity with her. He might lose their friendship by letting her know how he felt.

The two groups parted ways and Chase began thinking of scenarios in which he and Kenna might *need* to branch off from the group. He'd find the perfect opportunity. He just hoped it came soon.

They started down the first road.

"Shit!" Kenna said.

Everyone stopped and looked at her. Chase thought maybe she got hooked on a thorn bush.

"They got the Jack."

Dari shook his head. "Damn, girl. I thought you hurt yourself."

They inched through briars, carefully moving them aside or holding them up, crawled over downed trees, ducked beneath low branches and walked until they saw a large lump of vines, briars and twisted branches towering at least twelve feet high. As he looked closer, Chase noticed some paint through some of the openings. There was a building under that living mess.

Just as Richard had described, it looked like it was once a park bathroom or such. The first doorway they came to lacked a door, but inside there was a white porcelain sink, a rusted stall wall, and a toilet behind it. It was fairly well preserved. They exited and made their way down a few feet to an open door. The paint and symbol had long since faded. Inside was another sink and toilet. Dried and decayed leaves, small limbs, and construction debris littered the floor. Chase looked up and realized a huge chunk of ceiling had caved in.

They worked their way beyond the building to another large, fallen tree.

"This is as far as I've been," Richard said.

Chase could see why. Small saplings rose through the gnarled branches or grew from the dead tree. To their right was the larger, more tangled mess of the tree's top. To their left was the base, covered in briars and surrounded by a wall of roots, trees, fallen limbs and other stuff. Their best option, which looked dicey, was going over and through the section before them.

"Looks snaky," Kenna said.

"*Snakes?*" Dari repeated. "I fucking *hate* snakes."

"You know, they're more scared of you than—" Richard started.

"Yeah. Yeah. I heard all that bullshit before," Dari said. "I still don't like 'em."

* * *

Dead Town

Hayden was happy to let Paul lead the way. If they ended up lost he didn't want to be the one who got blamed. Besides, since they were walking in pairs, it meant he could focus on a conversation with Kiara instead of where they might be heading.

Hayden sipped some whiskey then puffed on the cigarette he had in his other hand. He passed the bottle to Kiara.

"What you think of this place?" he asked, hoping she would answer a particular way, but not wanting to influence her.

"Not as weird in the daylight."

He had to agree. Somehow, all the magick he felt the night before had drained, leaving the place looking and feeling like any other clump of woods in Alabama. Only the knowledge of the property's past gave it any additional character.

They reached the ashes of their fire. Hayden looked around. It was such a perfect place for drinking and hooking up by campfire, he expected to see evidence other people had partied there, but nothing even hinted at that. There were no empty cans or bottles, no ripped condom wrappers, no burnt logs, none of the stuff he saw around Swan Creek and other places where friends hung out and got wild in the wee hours of night. That was probably the weirdest part about the place in the daytime. One thing was sure—that feeling like he could command his body to ascend into the sky and it would obey, was gone.

He supposed it was a little like when he was a kid and thought someone was in his room at night. Every shadow seemed to grow and move, like it had a life of its own. Then, once he turned a light on, everything was where it should be. Hayden wasn't afraid of the dark and the shadow beasts anymore. He supposed it was just the circumstances that had given him the creeps last night.

"It seemed so *different* last night," Kiara said, as if reading his mind. "It felt like the air was saturated with electricity."

"You felt it, too?" Tanya said, turning on her heels.

"Like that sensation of great force and foreboding just before a big storm," Hayden said.

"Yeah." Tanya took the bottle from Hayden. "I thought it was just me."

"It wasn't," Kiara said.

Tanya passed the bottle to Paul. "Well, I don't feel *shit*," he said, then took a swig.

"I don't either," Hayden said.

"Not *now*," Tanya added.

Paul replaced the cap. "Y'all are fucking crazy." He looked at Hayden and Kiara. "Y'all think you're witches, *too*?"

"For lack of a better term, yeah," Hayden said.

"Please tell me you don't buy into all that tarot Ouija crystal hoodoo spell shit."

Until that point, Hayden liked Paul, but he didn't like this new offensive, obnoxious side he was seeing. Crass jokes and shit were one thing, but this close-mindedness was different.

"That tarot crystal hoodoo spell shit, or whatever you called it, works." Hayden said. He felt almost certain Paul was about to invite him to church and prove he was a hypocrite like so many others.

"You know what you need, bro?" Paul asked.

Here it comes. You need some Jesus in your life.

"You need a fucking woman so you can stop pretending you're Harry Potter and you can slip her the hairy putter."

"Oh God!" Tanya slapped his arm while laughing.

"Funny," Hayden said.

"I'm just fucking with you, bro," Paul said. "Good for you if you got something you can believe in. Some *higher* power. I just don't."

"You don't believe in *any*thing?" Kiara asked.

"Me." He shrugged his shoulders. "What's left of my family. And my friends. But otherwise, no."

"That's sad," she said.

"What? That I believe in what I can see and hear and taste and smell?"

"That you have no *hope*."

Paul pulled out a cigarette and lit it. "What the fuck you talking about I have no hope?"

His words were harsh, but Hayden didn't see the same hostility on his face. He was smiling in disbelief as he said it.

"Because if you don't believe there is something bigger than you out there, some*one* or some*thing* you can rely on for external strength, power and direction—especially when you're at your weakest—you are fundamentally alone and without direction," Kiara said.

"I get strength and direction from my friends and family, especially my dad."

"What about when they're all gone? One day your dad will die. Then what well will you draw from?"

A pensive expression fell across his face.

"Another thing," Hayden started. "One thing you didn't mention was what you can *experience*."

"Like?"

"You can't see, touch, smell or taste love, but . . ."

Paul shook his head. "You got me there. But casting spells and fortune telling and ghosts?" He shook his head again. "I'd have to see it—or *experience* it—to believe it. Know what I mean?"

Hayden nodded. Okay. Paul wasn't the complete ass he seemed just a minute ago. At least he was reasonable and willing to admit he was wrong—even if only on one minor point.

"We can test it out tonight if you want," Hayden said.

"What're you talking about?"

Hayden pulled his phone from his back pocket and held it up. "I took some pictures of a few incantations and shit we can try later."

"Un uhn," Tanya shook her head. "I don't want to do that."

"From where?" Kiara asked.

"That book," Hayden said, tucking the phone back in his pocket. "The one you asked about."

"The dark—"

"Yep."

"Cool." She pulled the bottle from Paul's hand and took a sip. "Count me in."

"We'll see," Paul said.

"Scared?" Hayden asked, even though he knew the answer.

Paul laughed. "*She* is." He poked his thumb out toward Tanya.

"You damn skippy," Tanya said. "I don't want any bad shit happening."

"Nothing bad is going to happen," Hayden said. "I've been practicing this shit for a while now. I got the words and everything straight. As long as I can read it."

"Come on, Tanya. It could be fun," Kiara said.

"What's the worst that can happen?" Paul asked.

Suddenly, Hayden wasn't sure anymore. It seemed like every damn horror movie he ever saw, someone always asked, "What's the worst that can happen?" And then shit went haywire and got even worse than they could ever imagine. Okay, this wasn't a movie. It was real life, but still . . .

* * *

Ladarius hated snakes. Even the thought of them. They were sneaky little fuckers. Passing in and out of holes, hanging from trees, slithering over the ground and water, camouflaged better than the world's biggest redneck on opening day of deer season. One time, when he was about eight at his Meemaw's house, he was playing with some toy trucks and cars in a patch of red dirt she just tilled for a garden.

She walked out to check on him and gasped. Her eyes were big as cue balls.

"Don't move, Boo," she said. The tone of her voice scared him.

Ladarius started to look around.

"I said *don't move*!" She turned back toward the house and hollered. "Frank! Frank, git out here!"

Pawpaw, came out wearing his blue jean overalls and a white T-shirt. When he got to her, she pointed toward Ladarius.

By this time, Ladarius was almost ready to cry. He thought he was in trouble for something. Every time he started to twist, she shouted at him.

"Just stay right there, boy," Pawpaw said.

He walked off to the shed and came back with a shovel.

Pawpaw was much smaller than Meemaw. He was about the same height, but he was a rail of a man from years of hard work and she was at least twice his weight—probably thick from trying out all that good food she used to cook.

He was smaller, but he wasn't scared. He talked in a low, quiet voice to Ladarius. "Just stay put, boy. *Stay put*." He crept out into the clumps of turned dirt and clay. When he was right next to Ladarius, Pawpaw raised the shovel and jammed it down behind him.

Dead Town

Ladarius jumped up and turned around. There, behind him, was the squiggling body of a copperhead. It had snuck up and was only a foot or two away. If the thing wasn't moving after Pawpaw chopped off its head, he probably never would have noticed it. It blended in that well with the ground.

As soon as Kenna mentioned snakes, Ladarius felt uneasy. In all this brush there were probably hundreds of rattlesnakes, copperheads and only God knew what other kinds of snakes. He was ready to get back to civilization—where at least the snakes had two arms and two legs and he could punch them if they struck at him.

"You got any gas on you, Chase?"

"Paul does."

"Paul ain't here," Dari said, laughing nervously.

At least after they stopped by the bathroom building and climbed over another fallen tree and clump of brush, the path widened and the road became somewhat visible. That didn't mean there weren't any snakes coiled up and waiting for him to draw closer. But he had a better shot of seeing them before he stepped on them.

A few hundred yards down, the road forked with a large thick tree standing in the middle. Dari looked left and right.

To the left, the path was relatively flat and clear like the terrain they were currently on. Shoots of grass and saplings grew from fissures in the concrete, but it was still a clearly defined road. About forty feet from them to the right, a large tree next to the road had caused the pavement to buckle. Yellow and green grass created about a three-foot-high wall across the road. Beyond that, the woods grew more dense and the overarching limbs and branches of trees closed in and strangled the road.

That looks snaky as fuck, Dari thought.

"Guess I'll go this way," Richard said, pointing left.

Not really knowing him, Dari would rather have gone with Kenna or Chase, but he didn't want Kenna with a guy they barely knew in the middle of nowhere. And he sure as shit didn't want to walk through that snake-infested patch to the right. Plus, he knew Chase had a thing for Kenna.

"I'll go with him," Dari said, pointing at Richard. "Call me if y'all find anything."

"You sure you want to split up?" Kenna asked.

"Sure. Why *not*?" Chase said.

Dari grinned at him. He *knew* why Chase sounded so eager.

"That was the plan," Richard said. "We'll cover more ground this way. And like he said . . . if you find anything interesting, call. We'll backtrack."

It was settled.

Chase and Kenna walked off to the right. Ladarius lit a Kool. When they got to the buckled pavement and wall of grass and weeds, he shouted, "Watch out for snakes over there."

* * *

The longer they were out there, the more anxious Tanya found herself. She would rather be at Wal-Mart on Christmas Eve, a hundred people back from the register, with an armload of heavy stuff, than in the woods right now. Already, the sun sank onto the tops of the trees. She could only catch a glint of it through the thick foliage to her left.

Tanya pulled out her phone and looked at the display.

"What time does the sun set?" she asked.

"Do I look like a weatherman?" Paul said.

"I told you I don't want to be out here in the dark."

"Why not?" Kiara asked. "It isn't like anything bad happened last night."

"That was different."

"How?" Paul asked.

"For starters, Richard was with us and he knew where he was going. And we didn't go all that far. But now we're just four idiots out in the woods with no idea where we are and no clue where we're going."

"We know where we are," Paul said. "Dead Town. And we know where we're going. Sort of. As long as we stay on the road, we can't get lost. We just turn around and walk the opposite direction. *Easy*."

The road curved to the left and appeared to go on for a good distance. Though it was covered in leaves and had small trees popping up everywhere, it was still barren enough compared to the wilderness swallowing the edges to make it obvious where the road lay.

Dead Town

Everyone paused to light a smoke and have a sip of the dwindling whiskey. Tanya already felt its effects tingling in her brain, but wanted more for courage. About two hundred feet into the curve, there was a clearing to the right. Paul stopped and peered into it. He took a few steps and swiped at the leaves on the ground with his foot, sweeping them away.

"It's another road," he said. "This place must have been pretty big."

"He said the guy bought over three hundred acres," Hayden said.

"What's *that* mean?" Kiara asked. "I mean, who the hell knows how big an acre is?"

"About three-quarters of a football field," Paul said.

Everyone looked at him in disbelief.

"Seriously. It's like from the back of one end zone to the other team's twenty yard line."

"How do you know that?" Kiara asked.

Tanya cocked an eyebrow. "*Why* do you know that?"

"Eighth-grade science class."

The clearing went back about fifty or sixty feet then must have turned because it appeared to end abruptly.

Paul looked at Hayden. "You and Kiara want to go down that way? Or take the road we're on?"

"*What?*" Tanya didn't bother to hide her feelings about the suggestion.

"That's what we said we were going to do," Paul said. "If you find something cool, call us."

"We *also* said we weren't going to be out here after dark."

"Quit worrying so much, baby." Paul took a drag off his cigarette and exhaled. "What time is it?"

Tanya looked at her phone again. "Time to leave."

He glared at her. "Seriously."

"Four-fifteen."

"Okay. How's this? We'll go this way. Y'all go that way. If we don't find anything in twenty minutes, we turn around and meet back here."

He lowered his head and looked at Tanya again. She had been with him long enough to recognize his *you-happy-now?* look. She wasn't.

But she knew it was the best concession she was going to get from him. That tacked on at least forty more minutes to their stay there. The difficult part would be trying to keep him on schedule. She knew him well enough to know he would push that full twenty minutes and try to eke out a few more minutes if he could find an excuse.

Tanya tapped the Google bar on her phone and searched for sunset times. She watched as the wheel spun round and round. She looked at the upper right-hand corner of her screen. *1X*. Not even 3G out here. Finally, the page loaded. Sunset was at 6:17. She felt a little better armed with that knowledge. That should give them a couple hours before nightfall and plenty of time to get the hell out of this place.

Paul dropped his cigarette to the ground and crushed it out beneath the ball of his foot. "Ready?" he asked.

Paul looked at the others. "Be safe. See y'all back here in a few." With that, he turned and started to walk without waiting for her.

When they were alone, he asked, "What are you so scared of?"

It was a good question. A question for which she lacked an answer. Tanya thought about it. She actually had a good time out here last night. Truth be told, she loved that electrical buzz she felt. But at the same time, she had this incredible sense of dread. It was like half of her being was drawn to Dead Town and the other half was repelled. Two voices in her head. One saying, "Come. Come sit for a while." The other shouting, "Run. Run like hell!"

"I don't know," she finally said. "I can't really explain it."

Paul glanced over and gave her a warm smile. "How can you be scared of something, but not know *what*?"

"It's just a *feeling*. Like something really bad happened here. Or is *going* to happen."

"I can tell you why you feel like that."

She bent over and stepped on the ember of her cigarette, pulling the filter until it popped off. Not wanting to litter, she tucked it in her pocket.

He slowed his gait as she hurried to catch up. "Because something bad *did* happen here. Or at least that's what we were told last night." Paul began walking faster again and continued, "Seems logical. Hell, I bet if Richard never told that bullshit story, you'd be loving this place."

Dead Town

His explanation sounded logical. Despite that, it also sounded wrong. Maybe it was the story combined with her recent tarot readings that set her nerves on edge whenever she thought about being there after dark. It was illogical, she knew. What was the difference between day and night? It wasn't as if shit storms had to wait for the sun to go down before their winds could blow. Bad things can happen in the daylight just as easily.

The road made a sharp turn to the right then narrowed. Trees and brush grew in from both sides. From under a thick covering of dried and rotting leaves, sparse grass grew at least knee-high and thin trees sprouted, some only a foot high, others ten or twelve feet. Had she not known a road existed there, she might have mistaken it for just a natural path through the woods.

She was glad he was confident enough for the both of them. At the same time, she wasn't. Not only did she hate feeling nervous over some unknown, unforeseeable event that may or may not ever come to fruition, but she knew the universe had a way of knocking over people who got too cocky.

They meandered down what they thought was the road as the sinking sun dipped below the tree line, leaving them in shade. Every now and again as they wandered, she saw a glint of sunlight through a gap in the trees, but for the most part, there was none. It was as if the sun was setting at least an hour earlier than it should in the woods. Along with its setting, it took its heat. Already, the temperature dropped at least five or ten degrees since when they arrived.

"You really think we're going to find anything?" she asked.

"Does it matter?"

"I wouldn't ask if I didn't care what you thought."

"I meant does it matter if we find anything? A, this is a cool place. B, if we can get a good lay of the land, we can have a helluva party out here on Halloween and scare the shit out of people. And C, if we *don't* find anything you can pretty much rest assured Richard is full of shit. Or at least his story is."

Tanya wanted to point out the flaw in his logic and tell him just because they didn't find anything wouldn't mean something horrific didn't happen here sixty years ago. It only meant they didn't find something. But instead of saying anything, she simply nodded as if she understood or agreed.

Paul held up a low limb and ducked beneath it. From the other side, he continued to hold it until she cleared it. Then he let it drop. The road narrowed more. The overarching limbs closing in on it made it appear like a dark throat with an unseen end.

As they stepped into the thicker foliage, Tanya shivered. She was ready to go home. It wasn't just the chill that was settling into the air. It was something much worse discomforting her soul. It was the electricity in the atmosphere. She thought she had felt it a few minutes ago, but it passed. Now she was certain. It was like she was a light bulb on a dimmer switch. Only the darker it grew around them, the more juice she felt flowing into her.

She looked at her phone.

"It's four-thirty-five. We should probably start heading back."

"We said twenty minutes. It ain't been twenty minutes yet."

"I'm getting cold," she said. "And does it matter if we get back one minute before them?"

"No more than it matters if we show up one minute *after* them."

Paul pulled out his pack of American Spirits and paused to light one. He nodded down the dark path.

"See that tree sticking out into the road down there?"

She nodded. About a hundred yards away from them, a large tree with low branches jutted out into the road, covering half of it.

"Let's just go to the tree and see what's beyond it. Then we'll turn around and head back. Okay?"

Finally, the end of this stupid trip was in sight.

Tanya lit a cigarette. "Okay."

As they drew closer to the tree, Paul stopped. "Shh."

He pressed one finger against his lips.

Tanya looked around. Her heart raced.

She heard it. Beyond the tree, something rustled. A twig snapped. More rustling in the leaves.

Paul crept slowly and cautiously down the road. She did her best to follow without making any noise as she stepped on the dead leaves.

As the sound grew nearer, her heart pounded harder. Not only was that dimmer switch getting dialed up more, but she suddenly realized this was the first time she had heard anything out there. She couldn't remember seeing or even hearing a single bird this whole time. It was as if the place lived up to its name—*Dead* Town. It was deathly quiet all the way up to this point and now something big was moving toward them.

"What if it's a wolf?" she whispered.

Paul stopped. "Shh. Wolves don't live in Alabama."

"A coyote? Or bear?"

Visions of being mauled to death by wild animals flashed through her mind faster than she could keep up with them.

* * *

Kenna walked beside Chase, loving the peace and solitude surrounding them. It was like they were the only two people in the world and everything and everyone else had faded away into nothingness. Occasionally, her worldly demons—like the warden, Matthew, and the dozens of losers before him—invaded her mind, but they quickly vanished. It was more like the visions came just to remind her they were once there but were gone now. Then she retreated back into the safety of this island of land where only she and Chase existed.

They were supposed to be looking for a house, but she was too deep in her own thoughts to concentrate on her surroundings.

Kenna glanced over at Chase. He was so cute with that pensive look on his face.

"What you thinking?" she asked.

Chase seemed startled by her voice.

"Nothing," he said.

"You're a horrible liar. You know that?"

She hoped he was thinking about her or would at least *tell* her that. Instead he said, "All the animals around here."

She looked around. "*What* animals?"

"That's my point. Have you seen any?"

"I wasn't looking."

"Well, *look*. Do you see any?"

She peered into the trees to her right then her left. She looked up.

"You don't, *do you*?" he asked.

"I guess not. What's your point?"

Chase stopped walking. When she stopped, he turned to face her.

"I've been looking for a long time now. I haven't seen a squirrel, a bird, *nothing*. I haven't even fucking *heard* one."

Kenna listened. *Nothing*. With no breeze, not even the leaves skittered against one another. She hadn't thought about it, but now that he mentioned it, she realized the place was quieter than an empty mausoleum. It was perfect and creepy at the same time. They weren't just the only two people left in the world. They were the only two *heartbeats*.

"Weird. They're here *somewhere*," she said.

"Weird is right." He pulled out his cigarettes and lit one. "I've never gone to the woods and *not* seen *something*."

She lit a cigarette for herself. As she exhaled, she looked around, feeling somewhat nervous, anxious for the first time since arriving.

CHAPTER 9

Richard scoured the landscape with his eyes looking for some sort of anomaly, but all he saw were trees and limbs and weedy vegetation.

When his grandfather first mentioned Dead Town a couple weeks ago, he didn't think much about it. He was visiting Grampa Meyers in the nursing home where he subsisted for the past two years since Gramma Meyers died. His dementia set in several years before her death and now he was in no condition to care for himself. There was no way Richard's mother could take care of him, either. She was busy trying to keep her own boat afloat, so to speak. Between her two jobs, she worked at least sixty hours a week trying to pay off the bills left behind when Richard's dad died.

Part of Richard's salary from his job as a religious studies professor at the community college went to her each month, but that wasn't nearly enough to stave off all the wolves trying to get a piece of the carcass left behind by a man who was dropped from his health insurance due to a *loophole* after it was discovered cancer riddled his body.

At the time, Richard was sitting by his grandfather's bedside when the man just started blathering about when he was a cop in the Keller Falls Police Department. Richard sat, only half-listening at first, because he had heard the stories repeated so many times over the past few years. Sometimes, he heard the same story back-to-back. But then a few words caught his attention and he realized he hadn't heard this tale. His ears honed in on his grandfather's words as he talked about the mysterious *Dead Town*.

"Bodies *every*where," Grampa said. "So much blood." His eyes swelled with tears. "The floors, the walls, even the ceilings were covered."

"Where?" Richard asked. He had never heard of Dead Town.

His grandfather's thoughts seemed to shift. "I thought for sure Plug and me was gonna die at Tawara when we got hung up on that damn reef, but the good Lord saw fit to help us make it through the surf to Red 2 Beach. God that was a mess."

Richard figured he must have missed something. Still, stories about his grandfather's time in World War Two were rare. As a kid, he remembered hearing short snippets about the Marines and *good* memories, but never about battles and friends who died.

"Pinned down all day and all night by artillery and pillboxes everywhere. We just knew those filthy Japs was gonna get in behind us on that wrecked Jap steamship and tear the hell out of us, but it didn't happen."

Grampa Meyer's eyes scanned the room with a distant vacant look as if they weren't seeing the walls, but a horizon far and long ago.

"When we got the order to push, we pushed. Plug and me made our way to one of them Jap pillboxes. His crazy ass got right up alongside it. He was touching the wall next to the machine gun slit. Pulled the pins on two grenades and dropped them in there. *That* silenced 'em."

The story continued. Grampa Meyers rushed the rest of the way up. He and Plug made their way around back and bust in.

"There was four of them in there. All mangled and bloody. One was still alive until Plug put that muzzle in his face and sent him to meet his maker. You never can forget the sound a man's head makes when a bullet tears through it."

Damn, Richard thought. *No wonder he never talked about this.*

"Plug got cut down later, though. Machine guns dropped him. Before I could get over to check on him, an artillery shell dropped by him. His body flew twenty feet into the air. In two different directions."

Richard watched a tear run down his grandfather's cheek as he drifted through history.

"Bodies everywhere. The beach. The bunkers. Pillboxes. Japs, Koreans, our boys. You could smell the iron and taste the copper from the blood in some of those cramped spaces. I *still* taste it."

Richard didn't know what to say, so he sat silently listening. He never knew the hell Grampa Meyers experienced in his life. He always seemed so happy and peaceful.

"Dead Town was like that," he said. "As soon as I walked into that house, I tasted hell all over again." Again, his eyes focused beyond the walls and present. "Blood, bodies, body parts *everywhere*." He sobbed loudly. "For the love of Christ let me die and make it end."

"Where *is* Dead Town?"

His grandfather looked at him with a puzzled expression. "Plug, what the hell you doing here, you crazy bastard?"

"It's Richard, Grampa."

"Aw, quit clowning, Plug."

Richard was at a loss for words again. So, he just let the man believe what he thought he saw. He rolled with it and asked again how to find Dead town.

His grandfather told him roughly where it was, then quickly added, "But don't you go there, you crazy sumbitch."

"I won't."

Richard stayed with him a while longer, hoping for more information. He got a little, but then the conversation weaved in and out of various stories about growing up, pets he had as a kid, etcetera. When Grampa Meyers fell asleep, Richard slipped out.

"I tried checking this place out with Google Maps," Richard said, trying to break the monotony and silence, "but couldn't really see anything because of all the trees."

"You know there probably ain't a house out here, right?" Dari asked.

"I hope there is."

"Why? What does it matter?"

"I think it would be cool to find an old abandoned house. If no one ransacked it, there's no telling what we might find."

"What? Like money?"

Richard scratched his eyebrow. "Hadn't even *thought* of that. I was thinking more along the lines of who they were, what they were really into and stuff."

Dari nodded. "I'd rather find a bunch of gold jewelry."

They both laughed.

"That'd be good, too."

The road grew darker every minute as the sun slid down below the treetops. There was no longer any direct light as they followed the road through a curve to the right then a wide one to the left.

"How long you think we gonna be out here?" Dari asked.

Richard hadn't thought about that. When they splintered into their various groups, no one had the forethought to coordinate a return time.

Richard pulled out his phone and looked at the clock. It was pushing five already.

"We'll give it a few more minutes, then you can call the others and see about heading back. The sun doesn't normally set until a little after six, but it'll probably get dark in here long before that."

"K."

About two-tenths of a mile further down the road, the path made a sharp left and ended on another road.

Richard couldn't believe it.

"Call the others," he said.

* * *

Kiara held the bottle of Jack, resisting the temptation to sip from it every couple minutes as she walked alongside Hayden. She couldn't get her mind off Paul. She knew if she were Tanya, she'd be fucking his brains out right now. Screw looking for a house, let's have some *fun*.

Not that this wasn't fun. It was. It was like playing the Powerball or scratch-offs. You knew you weren't going to win, but you still got antsy while you waited for proof you lost.

As the woods darkened, Kiara felt something. It was a small buzz in her bones, like when she was a child and would touch a near-dead nine-volt battery to her tongue to see if it had any juice left. At first, the battery was lifeless. Then it held a slight charge. As the details of trees faded into the shade of a sunless sky, the battery recharged, growing stronger and stronger.

Hayden talked about something, but she wasn't really listening. She answered him, too. But without paying much attention to what she said. It was like she was on auto-pilot.

It wasn't until he said, "It's okay. I know I'm your nothing-better-to-do friend," that she rewound the conversation in her head and started contemplating it. He asked her about dating, not in general, but particular. Likes. Dislikes. Past. Future. Then moved on to even more specific questions. Why hadn't they dated? Why did she always turn him down? Then *that*.

"My *what*?"

"I'm your nothing-better-to-do."

"What the fuck does that mean?"

"It's okay. It's all good."

He picked up a stick and tossed it into the woods.

"That's not true."

"How about your *sure-why-not*?"

Kiara's ears burned even though it was getting cooler out. Now, more than ever, she wanted to turn the bottle up. She wanted to turn it up and chug until there was nothing left. Then hit him over the head with it.

"Why you being so hateful all of a sudden?"

"Telling the truth isn't *hateful*. It's okay. I just understand I'm the friend you hang out with when no one else is around to hang with."

She grabbed her cigarettes and fished one out of the pack. "That is *so not* true."

Between the electricity circulating through her body and this conversation, Kiara felt ready to explode. It wasn't his words, though. She liked Hayden. Just not like *that*. What pissed her off was that he *felt* like she considered him a last resort friend. He wasn't. Sure, she had been busy and hadn't seen him in a while before this weekend, but she didn't have *anyone* that low on the list. Either she wanted to be your friend fulltime or she didn't. She didn't have time to dick around with fake friendships. She was an all-or-nothing kind of girl. She expected it of herself and those around her. Friendship goes both ways. If one person isn't willing to give a hundred percent to the cause, they aren't worth one percent.

"Sure about that?" he asked as he picked up another stick and smacked it against a limb, breaking it off in his hand.

"Who invited whom out this weekend?" She took a drag off her cigarette. "Who already had plans and called you up and invited you to come out and hang? If you were a *sure-why-not*, why the fuck would I have hit you up?"

"Shh!" Hayden said, stopping abruptly. "You hear that?"

Kiara looked around, listening. "I don't hear anything."

She took another drag.

She held her breath when something rustled not far from them, ahead and to the left. Whatever it was, it must have heard them, too, because it suddenly stopped. Then, after a few seconds, it started moving again. It was much quieter now, like it was stalking them.

She looked behind them at the road they had travelled and wondered if they should turn around and run. Whatever it was in the near distance, it headed almost straight for them.

A deer, she thought. It was definitely something large. It wasn't like a squirrel scampering in the leaves. She crept forward, trying to be as quiet as possible. If it was a deer, she wanted to get as close as possible before it bounded away.

The road made a sharp turn to the left. She peeked around the corner and screamed.

"Holy shit!"

* * *

Paul inched toward the noise. It was just on the other side of a thick, leafy limb. Whatever it was, it was close. He tried to be quiet as possible, but couldn't keep the leaves from crunching beneath his feet.

"Oh my God!" Tanya screamed as she jumped back and clutched at her chest.

Paul jumped, too.

"Holy shit!" Kiara said as she poked her head around the limb.

It took a second, but Paul regained his composure, despite his rapidly beating heart.

"I thought you might be a deer," Kiara said, laughing.

Paul grinned. "I might be a dear."

Kiara cocked her head and looked at him, clearly not catching his pun. Then it must have hit her because she smiled and nodded. "Cute."

"I am. Can't help it."

Paul realized he was flirting and turned around to look at Tanya to see if she noticed. She didn't appear to.

"What the hell are y'all doing here?" Paul asked.

"Road led here."

"Ask a stupid question . . ." Paul said then smiled.

He looked down at Kiara's hand and saw she still had the bottle. "Can I get some of that?"

She handed it to him and he opened it. He passed it to Tanya after taking a sip.

"You see anything?" Hayden asked.

"Not a damn thing," Paul answered. "You?"

Hayden shook his head.

"Can we go now?" Tanya asked.

Hayden took the bottle from her. "Go where?"

"Home. This place is giving me the creeps."

"*Really*?" Kiara scrunched up her face. "Why?"

"I'm getting that feeling again."

Kiara shook her head in agreement. "Me, *too*. It's amazing, isn't it?"

"Better than shrooms for sure," Hayden said.

Tanya pouted. "No. It's fucking *annoying*." She took out her Newports and lit one. "It's like I'm high as fuck and can't come down no matter how bad I want to."

Kiara walked over to Tanya and placed her arm around her. She had an almost motherly quality to her voice as she asked, "Why would you want to? There's power here."

"Y'all gonna start that shit again?" Paul asked. "Talk about annoying."

"What if it's *evil* power?" Tanya asked.

Hayden stepped closer. "There is *no* evil power."

"Thank you," Paul said.

"There's no *good* power, either. Only *power*. What we do with it determines the goodness and wickedness. But the power itself is merely an extension of what we are."

"What the fuck does that mean?" Paul asked. "That makes no sense."

Hayden looked up out of the corners of his eyes as if thinking. Finally, he said, "You have a gun?"

"Why?"

"Do you have a gun?"

"Not on me."

"But you *own* one."

"Sure."

"Is it good or evil?"

"That's a stupid question."

Paul was trying to figure out where Hayden was going with this. "Well?"

"It's *nothing*. It's a fucking gun."

"Right. But you can use it to rob and kill someone . . . *evil*. Or you can use it to stop someone from raping a woman . . . *good*. The object itself is neither good nor bad. It is what we make it by our actions *with* it."

Paul didn't know what the hell they were talking about with all this *power* they were feeling. He didn't feel shit, other than the temperature dropping. "Finally, you're making some sense," he said.

Paul looked at Tanya then Kiara, still holding her, then back at Tanya. "See? No evil power here. Feel better?"

"I still don't like it here."

"What do you think is gonna happen? Some ghost gonna step through a tree and snatch you?"

Her eyes fell to the ground and he knew he wounded her. He didn't mean to. He just didn't understand this irrational fear of hers. In all the months they dated, she seemed like a sensible girl—other than the whole tarot, white magic thing. But hell, everyone has their quirks.

He stepped over to Tanya and put his arm around her. His hand accidentally brushed Kiara's and she looked at him. Their eyes met and he felt *power*. Not the power they talked about, but something bordering on magical. The mystical power she had over him. In only a fraction of a second, her gaze burrowed into him and clawed at his stomach in a delightfully painful way.

Kiara withdrew her arm.

"Everything's going to be okay," she told Tanya.

Tanya nodded.

"Look," Paul started. "The road we were on looped around and circled back to intersect with their road. That—" he pointed down in the direction they were travelling "is east. The way we came in. I'll bet if we stay on this road it'll loop around and we'll run right into the others."

Dead Town

When Tanya gave him a quizzical look, he said, "We can go back the way we came, which will take some time. Or we can press on. If I'm right and this road *does* make a big circle, *that* way will probably be the quickest way out of here. What you want to do?"

He waited for her answer. He'd do whatever she decided, but he hoped she'd trust his instincts, not because he was ready to leave, but because he was sure he was right *and* he wanted to see what else was up ahead. It was a win-win.

"That's fine," Tanya said.

Paul got the buy-in he was looking for from the others and led the way down the road.

* * *

The further they walked, the more uncomfortable Chase was. In body and spirit he felt just fine, but his mind wandered, drifting from various ways to broach the subject of a real date with Kenna to the mystery of the missing birds. He wondered if the land was filled with poison or radiation, but decided even *that* didn't make sense. If it were so toxic as to kill every living critter, surely there would be carcasses everywhere. But there was nothing—no evidence or trace of anything living there other than the plant life.

Chase glanced over at Kenna. Her eyes darted all around. He assumed like him, she was busy searching the trees and ground for some sign of animals. She had been quiet since he first mentioned it, and now she had the same nervous expression on her face she had when the warden and her boyfriend had her cornered. Guilt punched Chase right in the nose. With just a few words, he managed to suck the life out of Kenna-Grace.

Chase reached over and took Kenna's hand. He wasn't sure how she would react. He hoped, like before, she would continue to hold him back. When he first did it, it was more innocent than romantic, but now he found himself thinking about and loving the way her small hand felt, as if it were designed specifically for his, two odd-shaped gears perfectly engineered and meshing together. She looked up at him and smiled.

That's good, he thought as he looked into her bright eyes. But then he wondered what it meant. Was she enjoying the sensation as much as he was? Or was it a meaningless, friendly smile?

"You okay?" he asked.

"Sure. Why?" Her voice betrayed her.

"You look nervous."

Kenna forced another smile. "Just a little freaked out by this."

"What? Holding my hand?"

She raised their hands, looked at them, then back at him. "No. The whole no animals thing."

He gazed into her eyes. He had seen that look before. Not on her, but on other girls just before he kissed them for the first time.

Just do it, he told himself. He slowly leaned toward her.

Her eyes bounced back and forth, searching his face, looking into one eye, then the other, then back again.

His pocket buzzed just before his phone erupted with a snippet from a Post Malone tune.

He and Kenna both jumped and let out a nervous laugh.

Chase pulled the phone from his pocket and answered. It was Dari.

"Sup?" he asked.

"Hey . . . you won't . . . the . . ."

"What?" Chase spoke louder. "I can't hear you. You're breaking up."

Chase glanced at the large screen on his phone. He had one bar at 1X.

He hit speaker phone so Kenna could hear, too.

He could tell Ladarius was practically shouting into the phone. "I said we . . . here . . . and . . ."

Chase looked around then looked at Kenna. "You hear that?" he whispered.

"I have no clue what he said."

"No. Listen," he said to her.

He put his face near the mic on the phone. "If you can hear me, talk louder."

Chase held up a finger, indicating she should wait for it.

"I said we . . . and . . ."

"I hear it!" Kenna said excitedly.

Dead Town

Somewhere in the distance, down the road and to the left a little, Dari shouted into his phone.

Chase let go of Kenna's hand, stuffed his forefinger and pinky in his mouth and whistled as loud as he could.

He raised the phone to his face. "Did you hear that?"

"Yeah."

Then came a loud whistle in return. They were close.

"Just keep whistling every few seconds," Chase said.

He hung up, tucked the phone back in his pocket and grabbed Kenna's hand once more, tugging. "Come on."

They jogged down the road, the whistles growing louder as they got closer. The road made a wide sweep to the left. At the end of the curve was a sharp right then their road ended on another.

They ran out into the intersection and turned left. Not fifty feet from them stood Richard and Ladarius, grinning like two kids on Christmas morning.

As Chase and Kenna slowed to a walk, Dari and Richard shouted in unison, "Look!"

They pointed across the road.

Chase had been so engrossed in listening for the whistles and then excited at seeing them, he didn't even notice what lay about fifty yards in front of them. In a relatively clear area, untamed grass grew knee-high and a few thin saplings dotted the landscape.

Beyond that was a large cluster of trees. A couple sat at odd angles, most likely blown over or broken—perhaps during the April 27th tornadoes when Chase was in middle school.

Hidden deep within the shadows of their large, mangled branches was the unmistakable white façade of a monstrous two-story house.

* * *

Ladarius was relieved as hell when Chase and Kenna came running out into the road. It was like that good feeling right after a much-anticipated sneeze. Not that he didn't like Richard. The guy was okay, but Ladarius was ready to be among friends. *Older* friends. Not *older* people. More than that, he wanted to see the expressions on their faces

110

when they saw he and Richard found the house. Sure, they got there, too, but he and Richard were still *first*.

He was anxious to look inside the house, but he sure as fuck didn't want to cross that field. Shit looked snaky.

Why'd she have to bring that up? he thought.

"You call the others yet?" Chase asked.

Ladarius shook his head. "Just you."

Chase pulled out his phone and dialed Paul's phone.

After several rings, Paul picked up. "What's up, bitch?"

"We found it," Chase said.

"What?"

"I said we found the—"

"I can't understand a thing you're saying."

"I SAID—"

"Holy—"

Nothing. The call dropped.

Chase looked at his phone screen and hit redial.

* * *

Tanya didn't really give a fuck about what Paul thought. She wanted out. She had a bad feeling about this place. It wasn't just the horrible murders that took place here or her cards over the past few days or the energy that grew exponentially as the space around them dimmed to an obscuring gray. She didn't care what Hayden had to say about the neutrality of power. She had a *feeling*! Something bad was here. Something bad happened here. Worse than that, something bad was happening *now*.

Hayden and Kiara were all grins and giggles. Tanya tried to ignore them as they rambled on about the "cool energy" they felt growing inside them.

"Sun hasn't even set yet," Hayden said. "Just wait 'til it gets dark."

Tanya shuddered.

She understood the draw. It was like the first time she ever took a Roxy. A warm wave rushed over her body from her head to her feet. She tingled with a pleasing numbness. She felt everything and nothing at the same time. This power was like that. It was like an addiction calling her name, saying, "Don't worry, I won't hurt you." And a part of her believed it. A part of her wanted to join in the revelry of Kiara and Hayden. Wanted to suck it up like a plant sucking up sun and growing from it. That was the biggest part of her. But there was that little voice niggling at the back of her mind, like a mouse chewing her cerebellum. It said, "Run. Run while you still can!"

"I want to *move* here," Kiara said, laughing.

Paul dropped his cigarette and crushed it beneath his foot, grinding it into the leaves and pavement. He eyeballed Hayden and Kiara suspiciously. "You two are just fucking with me now, right?" he said. "Trying to get me to believe there's some mysterious something here?"

"What do you mean?" Kiara asked.

"Either you're fucking with me or you're imagining shit, cuz I don't feel *any*thing."

Tanya wondered how he *couldn't* feel it. It wasn't even dark and, already, it felt like her entire body was licking a fresh nine-volt battery straight out of the pack.

"Not fucking with you, bro," Hayden said. "Shit's real. And it's *lit*."

Paul shook his head. "Whatever. Enjoy your visit to La La Land. My feet are staying planted firmly here on planet Earth in the state of reality."

"Why are you so close-minded?" Kiara asked.

"What? Because I don't believe in something only the two of you are rambling on about, that makes me close-minded?"

"No. Because you aren't willing to accept the possibility that something you can't see or touch exists. *That* makes you close-minded." Kiara stopped walking, pulled out a cigarette and lit it, watching him over the flame.

"Open your inner eye," Hayden said.

"My *what*? Oh fuck! I just realized my chakra ain't in-line with my chi so my feng shui is giving my all-seeing eye of Osiris a shiner." Paul laughed. "Like I said, ain't but two of you imagining this shit. But it's all good. Enjoy the trip."

"It's real," Tanya mumbled.

He shot her a look of disbelief. "Huh?"

"I feel it, too. So, stop being so fucking condescending."

"I'm not condescending, I—"

"Little bit, bro," Hayden said.

"I don't mean to be. Seriously. I just think it's comical the way you two ramble on about this stuff, believing it the same way a little kid believes the Easter Bunny runs around laying eggs everywhere."

"That's textbook condescension," Kiara said.

"Don't hate me just because I don't share your fantasy. I don't believe the millions of people who believe Jesus saved them or Muhammad was a prophet of God, either."

"Can we *not* rehash this conversation?" Tanya asked. "We get it. You *don't* believe it. Stop being such a dick about it."

Paul's eyes dropped to the ground.

"Sorry," he said. "Really. I'm not trying to be a dick."

Tanya knew he was sincere. He was *always* a dick, but a *loveable* dick. Whenever he realized he crossed that line from loveable to detestable, he almost always quickly apologized and retreated.

About thirty feet up ahead, the road took a sharp curve to the right. A thick wall of trees obscured what lay around the bend.

"It's cool, bro," Hayden said.

Kiara shook her head. "I don't know," she said, clearly toying with him.

Dense trees encroached on the road from either side, their leafy tops coming together over the path to create a natural tunnel. What remained of the day's light barely penetrated the thick barrier. It was dark, crepuscular in there.

As they entered the deep shade, the energy blossomed within Tanya.

Kiara and Hayden must have shared her experience, because they resumed their previous conversation.

"Holy shit!" Kiara said. "That's *awesome*."

"Can you imagine this place at *midnight*?" Hayden asked.

"Okay," Paul started. "Not trying to be a dick here, but what's the significance of midnight anyway? I mean why does shit in the movies always happen at midnight?"

Hayden looked at Kiara and Tanya with an expression that seemed to ask, "You want to field this one, or should I?"

Dead Town

Kiara stepped up. "It's the time between today, tomorrow and yesterday. All three come together for just an instant. Tomorrow becomes today. Today becomes yesterday. It's also the time when the veil between the spiritual world and physical world is thinnest. It's the easiest time for spirits, demons, etcetera to cross over."

"And likewise, the easiest time to contact spirits," Hayden added. "That's why séances work best at and around midnight—while the veil is stretched super thin."

Paul's phone blared part of *Bad and Boujee*, the ringtone he had set for Chase.

"What's up, bitch?" Paul said when he answered it, putting it on speakerphone.

It sounded like Chase said, "Jaba jaba it."

"What?"

"I jaba jaba jaba the—"

"I can't understand a thing you're saying."

They continued walking. Paul looked at the others, raised his eyebrows and shrugged his shoulders. Tanya glanced around. Everyone appeared just as confused.

As they came out of the curve, the road opened onto another road that ran right and left.

Fuck! Tanya thought. She just knew Paul was going to suggest splitting up again. *No fucking way!*

"I SAID—" Chase said.

Paul and Hayden both said "Holy fucking shit!" at the same time. They looked at each other and laughed, then back across the street.

"You there?" Paul said into the phone.

No response.

Paul glanced at his screen. "Lost him."

Tanya couldn't believe it. The road before them had a wide arc and clearly curved around. Across the street looked like it was once a massive back yard. Ivy and vines covered a dilapidated wooden shed or outbuilding as it crumbled in on itself, a tree sprouting from the middle of it. Beyond that stood a gigantic clump of trees with a high canopy. A couple had fallen over and were propped up against the back of a large white two-story house.

Paul headed for the house and redialed Chase.

* * *

Kenna studied the house. From what she could see, it looked old. She couldn't tell if it was actually a Nineteenth Century relic or just built to look like it. All she could really see from here was the small, wide staircase leading up to the porch. The front door, once probably fire engine red, was now dull and dirty. On either side of the stairs were large white columns, ivy worming its way up them.

As soon as Chase's call dropped, they started walking toward the house.

Chase's phone rang again and he answered it, once more putting it on speaker so everyone could hear.

"Hey. You there?"

"Yeah," Paul said. The transmission was staticky, but comprehensible.

"We found it."

"What? *We* found it."

Chase looked puzzled. "Where the fuck are you?"

"In back of the house. Where are you?"

Chase laughed. "Dude, we're in *front*."

* * *

The closer they got to the house, the more Kiara's body tingled. She didn't know if it was the proximity or the growing darkness, but she didn't care. The shit was a rush. She could hardly wait for midnight to see what it would be like.

They cut across the lawn, weaving between the sporadic saplings as they made their way toward the front.

Despite a few trees resting on the house from different sides and angles, it looked to be in pretty good shape—even the roof looked undamaged.

Dirty white slats, several tall—fully intact—windows and black shutters adorned the outside. A large red brick chimney ran up this side of the house, promising a massive fireplace inside.

Dead Town

As they rounded the front and met up with the others, Richard called to them. "See? I *told* you there was a house here."

Kiara looked at the large front porch up about three feet from the grass. The wainscot ceiling was sky blue. There was no furniture, but she pictured people sitting out there on warm mornings, sipping coffee and smoking cigarettes.

The eight of them congregated at the bottom of the steps.

"Can we go now?" Tanya asked.

"*Go*?" Richard, Hayden and Chase said in unison.

"She's scared," Paul said.

Kiara didn't get it. Tanya was usually pretty cool. They did spells and shit together in the past. They swapped ideas, stories, even magick books. Why she seemed so freaked out all day was beyond her. As witches, they *lived* for something like this. A place full of untapped power, raw and wild, waiting to be tamed. She had to ask.

Not wanting to embarrass Tanya further—Paul did a good enough job of that by himself—she leaned over and whispered, "What's wrong with you?"

Tanya faced her and squinted a little. "I got a bad feeling about this place."

"It's just a *place*. Like Keller Falls or Huntsville or New Orleans."

"Do you buzz all over whenever you're in *those* places?"

"No, but—"

"Exactly. There is *something* here. Something different from anything we've ever seen or done or experienced."

Kiara had to agree. This was like nothing she had ever felt. The closest thing she could think of was the first time she had a real, full-body orgasm. Only this was *better*.

"Let's just check it out. If we can get in, we'll look around real quick then jet." She put her arm around Tanya's shoulder and hugged her. "We'll come back some other time when you feel better about it. Okay?"

Tanya nodded.

"Love you."

"Love you, too," she said with a quiet, unenthused voice.

Paul and Chase mounted the stairs. Everyone else followed.

"I bet you'll feel better when we get inside," Kiara told Tanya. "Being in a house, blocking out all these woods."

"Maybe."

Paul headed for the door and started to grab the brass knob.

"It's not going to be unlocked," Chase said.

Paul twisted his grip. "Sure about that?" he asked as he swung the door open.

Chase looked as surprised as Kiara felt.

Paul stood beside the open door. "Richard, it's *your* house. You want to go in first?"

CHAPTER 10

Richard couldn't believe they found the house. More difficult to believe was the untouched nature of it. The parlor, a large room with a high ceiling and white marble floor, had a large crystal chandelier hanging on brass chains. On his right, a sweeping, curved staircase worked its way up to a second-floor balcony. Directly ahead, a wide hallway extended into the bowels of the house. Although it was rather dark in there, he could see several doorways on either side.

Richard glanced at a set of mostly-open pocket doors on his left as the others filed in behind him.

"Can you believe this fucking place?" Paul asked.

"Holy shit," Kenna said.

Richard pulled out his phone and turned on the flashlight. A cone of light illuminated the room as he scanned it. Along the staircase, just below the heavy mahogany bannister, a small rectangular table with spindly legs and a malachite top stood. Upon it was a large vase. Nothing else.

Richard walked off to the left to check out the room.

A couple others pulled out their phones and turned on their flashlights as Paul said, "We should probably stick together."

Richard turned to him. "Does it really matter? It isn't like we can get lost now. We're in a house."

Chase agreed. "How hard can it be to find the front door?"

"I meant until we determine if this place was structurally sound," Paul said. "There could be water damage, termites, rotted floors, anything. I don't want to have to carry someone all the way back to the car."

Richard conceded. That made sense.

Chase started to close the front door.

"Leave it open," Paul said. "At least a little more light is coming in that way."

The room to the left was a sitting room, bedecked with furniture straight from the Forties and Fifties. A couple small sofas and chairs partially boxed in a rectangular wooden coffee table. Built-in shelves along the walls housed a number of knickknacks.

By now, everyone had their phone out and was looking at the various things on the shelves. There were small pieces of pottery, vases, miniature copies of famous statues like Winged Victory and Venus de Milo. It struck Richard these were the kinds of things you might find in any house back then or even now. Given his grandfather's story, he expected to see statues and paintings of devils everywhere. But it was nothing like that. Whoever lived here seemed like a *normal* person.

Another set of pocket doors led from the sitting room to a smaller room. On the right wall of that room was a large mahogany bar with ample space for the six barstools. Behind the bar, a mirrored wall had multiple glass shelves filled with liquor bottles.

"Jackpot," Paul said, rushing over to the bar. He stepped behind it and looked down. "Holy fuck, There's even more under here."

He reached beneath the bar and pulled out a couple double old-fashioned glasses. After setting them down, he pulled out a bottle of scotch and asked, "Who's ready for a drink?"

As Chase and Kenna sidled up to the bar, Paul said, "Don't be shy, folks. There's enough for *all* night."

Richard caught Tanya in his light as he turned. She looked scared as hell.

* * *

Chase clinked glasses with Kenna before downing the liquor. Smooth and old as it was, he figured it would be worth some money if he could find some unopened bottles. Who *wouldn't* want a bottle of seventy-something year old scotch?

In the crazy light of everyone's phones swinging this way and that, Kenna looked like a starlet.

"Fill her up, barkeep," Chase said, tapping his glass a couple times on the shiny bar top.

Paul poured him another glass and filled one for himself.

"Cheers," they said, knocking their glasses together.

119

Dead Town

The others filtered over. First Dari, then Kiara, Richard and Hayden.

"You sure that's such a good idea?" Tanya asked from somewhere behind them.

"What's wrong *now*?" Paul asked.

Chase looked at Paul who was looking back at him and rolling his eyes.

Hopping off his barstool, Chase said, "Come on, Tanya. You can have my seat."

"I don't want to."

"Don't be like that," Kiara said. "Lighten up. Have a drink and relax."

"I'm relaxed."

"Yeah," Paul said. "About as relaxed as a guy that just got strapped in an electric chair."

Finally, she came over and sat. Paul pulled out a glass, set it in front of her and filled it. "Enjoy," he said.

"Can we go soon?" she asked.

Paul leaned against the bar. "Come on, Tanya. Gimme a break. *Relax*. You wanted out of the woods. You're *out*." He reached under the bar and produced a crystal ashtray. After setting it between them, he pulled out a cigarette and lit it. He exhaled, waved his hands as if displaying the room and looked around. "You're in a house. You're safe. What're you worried about?"

Chase wondered why she was so anxious. He hoped she'd answer, but she didn't.

Her fear made no sense to him. He found the place rather inviting and soothing. If anything disturbed him, it was the fact the house remained unmolested by vandals and animals over all these years. It was as if the people who lived here left his morning and would return at any moment now.

"I'm going this way," Chase said, pointing his phone's light toward a set of pocket doors opposite the ones through which they entered. "Who's coming?"

Kenna hopped down from her stool. "Wait for me."

"Come on, man," Paul said. "Let's stick together."

"Look at this place," Chase said. "It's safe." He took a sip of scotch. "Y'all stay here. Kenna and I will check out the rest of this floor and be right back." He took another swig from his glass, walked back to the bar and said, "Top it off?"

As Paul poured, he said, "Stay on *this* floor. And *watch* where you're walking. These old floorboards might be rotted."

Chase almost said, "Quit acting like Tanya," but he stopped himself. "Bet," he said, agreeing to Paul's terms even though he disagreed with the premise. He *might* have been right, but Chase doubted it.

* * *

Richard knew more than he told.

He wanted to explore the house with Chase and Kenna, but for the moment, he was content sitting right here at the bar, satisfying the thirst he worked up walking around all day.

"What else is back there?" he asked Paul.

"Little of this. Little of that. And a whole lot of damned-if-I-know." Paul took on the pleasant tone of an employee of the bar. "What can I get for you, sir?"

Richard played along. "How about a rum and Coke?"

"Sorry, sir. We're fresh out of Coke. How about a rum and shit-outta-luck?"

Everyone, even Tanya, laughed.

"How about a bourbon and bourbon?"

Paul searched under the counter for a few seconds. He pulled up an unopened bottle of Old Forester. "This should be good."

He filled Richard's glass to the top.

It was definitely good.

The white drapes on the window across the room were fading to a dark gray. It was probably just about dark outside already. Richard could hardly wait for nightfall.

"I wonder if there's still power coming to this place," Paul said.

"I'm pretty sure the power company has a rule. After fifty years of not paying your bill, they shut you off." Kiara said, then tapped her glass on the bar. "Tequila?"

Dead Town

Paul searched beneath the bar and found a bottle. He started pouring it in her glass.

"Whoa," she said. "Shouldn't that come in a shot glass?"

"Does it matter?"

"It does if we're gonna be playing quarters."

"I'm in," Richard said. But he would be in for anything—even safety pinning his shirt to his chest—if it meant staying there longer.

A flash of light in the mirror caught Richard's attention. He turned to see Chase and Kenna returning from the other room. They each held a large candelabra with seven or eight candles on them.

"We found these in there," Chase said, nodding toward the door. "Should help light the place and save our phones' batteries." Chase set one at the end of the bar and began lighting the candles. Richard counted in his head. Nine.

The Table of the Beast, Richard thought. He remembered reading the significance long ago. 666 times one is 666. Add them up, eighteen. Add those two numbers, one plus eight, and you get nine. You could do that with any multiple of 666 at least to ten.

The long white tapered candles lit the room beautifully. Everyone shut off their flashlights. It was still just as bright as it was before the candles arrived if not a tad brighter.

"Here, take this one, too," Kenna said, passing the heavy candelabra to Richard.

"We're about to play quarters," Paul said. "You going to join us?"

Chase shook his head. "We're gonna look around a little more. Maybe we can find some more candles or cool shit. We'll be back in a few."

"Remember what I told you."

"Yes, dad," Kenna said before they exited the room again.

As Richard set the candles on the bar top and began lighting them, Tanya asked, "Are you really going to start playing fucking *quarters*?"

"Sure. Why not?" Paul asked.

"I can't fucking believe you."

Times like these made Richard glad he didn't have a girlfriend.

"It's what?" Paul said. "Like six o'clock? It's *early*. We're in a house. We were here last night and nothing happened. Right?"

"We weren't in this house."

"No, you're right. We weren't. We were out there in the middle of the woods. And it was much later."

"He's right," Kiara said. "It has to be safer in here than out there."

Tanya glared at Paul. "You just told those two we don't know if the house is safe."

"Then stay in this room or that one," he dipped his head toward the sitting room. "We *know* those are safe." Paul chugged what remained of his drink. "YOLO, baby."

Hayden, who sat on the other side of Tanya, leaned over and spoke in a soft, paternal voice. "I get that you're uneasy. The power here is immense. I can feel it. But just embrace it. Enjoy the feeling. In a little while we'll be gone and wishing we stayed longer."

"I know *I* was last night," Kiara said.

"But . . ."

Kiara got off her barstool and hugged Tanya from behind. "But nothing. You know I love you, right?"

"Yeah."

"Then don't take offense, because I say this out of love. You're being a little silly right now. It's just us here and no one's going to hurt you."

"And no one is going to *let* anyone hurt you," Ladarius said. He raised his glass to her. "Girl, you *know* I would take a bullet for you."

She nodded.

"So, just relax," Hayden said.

"Have a couple drinks," Richard said. "You'll feel better."

"If *that* doesn't work, *this* will." Paul pulled a good-sized bag of weed from his front pocket and tossed it on the bar in front of her.

"*Now*, it's a party," Richard said, causing Tanya to grin.

* * *

Kenna followed Chase back into the dining room. They scanned the room with their phones' light again. Against the back wall to the left was a large, dark antique buffet.

"We should look in there," Kenna said.

"What for?"

Dead Town

"More candles." She wanted to find more so they could stay longer, but she was also curious what was in the drawers.

There were no additional candles, only cloth napkins, serving platters, table cloths and place settings.

On the wall opposite the buffet was a doorway leading to the hall they had seen from the parlor. Opposite the door they entered, was a normal sized swinging door, through which Chase walked. Kenna followed him into a kitchen.

Tons of white cabinets lined the large open space. In the center of the black and white checkered floor was a large island with a built-in cutting board that looked big enough to slaughter a small pig on. She walked over and checked it out. The wood in the block had definitely seen use. Thin lines evidenced countless knife strokes against the grain. A long Chicago Cutlery butcher knife sat on the board where the last user left it, though it appeared clean.

Cool, she thought. It wasn't the cutting board or knife she found so interesting, but the idea they were in a house that was essentially a museum of life sixty years prior.

It's like walking through a damned time capsule, she thought.

On the wall adjacent the hall was another swinging door. On the wall directly in front of them were two doors. Paul opened the one on the right and found a butler's pantry.

"Shit," he said, stepping into it.

Kenna followed. It was a room almost as large as her kitchen at home. The shelves were filled with boxes, cans, and jars.

She picked up a box of Cream of Wheat, and was surprised to find it almost full. At her house, roaches or mice would have chewed into it and eaten it if she was gone for a weekend.

"You think this is past its expiration date?" she asked, laughing.

"Little bit."

On one of the shelves they found a couple boxes of utility candles. Beside them were about a dozen boxes of tapered candles—red, white, black, and gold.

"Shit," she began, "with all this, we can light the entire house."

"Now we just need more candle holders," Chase said.

"Fuck that. We can make redneck candle holders if we have to."

"Make *what*?"

"Redneck candle holders. Just get some plates, drip wax on them and stick the candles in the wet wax. When it cools, it'll hold them in place."

They carried the candles to the butcher block and set them down, then opened the second door. Kenna peered around Chase's arm as he shone his light down a narrow wooden staircase.

"Oh, hell no," she said.

"What?"

"That looks creepy as fuck."

"Probably a wine cellar." He started to walk down the stairs.

Kenna grabbed his shirt near the shoulder and pulled. "No you don't," she said. "You told Paul we would stay on this floor."

"Come on. Just a second."

Kenna put one hand on her hip and gave him her sternest look. "Do I need to yell for Paul?"

"What's he gonna do?"

She opened her mouth and took a deep breath as if about to scream at the top of her lungs.

"Okay. Okay," Chase said. "We'll look later."

She wasn't as freaked out by the house as Tanya was, but one thing was certain. She didn't want to go downstairs just the two of them and she didn't want to be left alone in the kitchen.

"Good boy," she said. She raised up on her toes and gave him a peck on the cheek.

"Must not have been *that* good," Chase said. Just as she was starting to feel insulted, like the kiss was a bad thing, he added, "You missed my damn mouth."

Oh, how she wanted to kiss that damn mouth,

She looked up at him and smiled, wondering, *Should I?*

* * *

Ladarius sat at the bar pounding them back. He knew he should pace himself, especially if they were going to play quarters, but he never had any liquor this old or good and didn't know when he would again.

"We can't tell anyone about this place," he said.

"What?" Hayden asked.

"Let's keep this house *our* secret. Think about it." He took a Kool from his pack on the bar. "This shit has been here *how* long?"

"About sixty years," Richard said.

Dari lit his cigarette. "Exactly, and it's all still here. Like our own private bar. But if we tell people, they'll tell people and pretty soon, some asshole is gonna loot this place."

He was glad when the others agreed with him. He just hoped they meant it. There was enough booze here to last them over a year—at least until everyone was legal. More than that, it was a cool place to hang and relax. Like owning their own party trap.

He was more glad when he looked over and saw Tanya smiling. She was finally loosening up. Poor thing was wound up tighter than Beyonce's weave.

Paul stacked a bunch of shot glasses in two columns in front of Dari then pulled out a bottle of tequila.

"We playing with tequila or what?"

"I'd rather shoot whiskey," Hayden said.

"Same," Kiara said. "You *know* I'm a whiskey girl."

Paul leaned across the bar in front of her and said, "Speaking of that, you know how a girl holds her liquor?"

"In her hand?"

"No. By the ears. Get it?"

"Oh my God." Kiara laughed and pawed at his arm.

Dari looked over at Tanya. She knew what time it was. She chugged her drink and said, "Gimme another."

Paul said, "Coming right up, my dear. Anything else?"

"Yes. Quit being such a flirt."

"I wasn't flirting. I was telling a fucking joke."

"Whatever."

Tanya gulped down her drink and slapped the glass on the bar.

Richard stood and grabbed one of the candle holders. "Let's play in there on the coffee table." With his other hand he picked up a stack of glasses and exited.

"More," Tanya said.

Paul held up the joint he had just finished rolling. "You know the rule. Smoke. Then drink. Then smoke again."

Tanya took it from him and put it between her lips. She took a deep drag as Paul lit it.

While she puffed on that one, Paul started rolling another. Just as he finished, Richard came back in.

"Are you coming or what?"

Ladarius took the joint from Tanya and hit it. With a large cloud of smoke forming his words, he said, "I'm ready to play."

Paul came around from behind the bar with three bottles—tequila, vodka, and whiskey. As Richard led the group to the front room, Hayden grabbed the other candle holder and Ladarius took the other stack of shot glasses.

Ladarius had only seen two rooms of the house, but already he was digging this place. He plopped down on one of the sofas, surprised to find it still firm and comfortable.

"Hey, Tanya," he said. "You got your cards on you?"

"In the car."

"I just wanted to see if they agreed with me, cuz I'm about to make a prediction." He took the joint Hayden passed to him and took a deep draw. "I predict I'm fixing to get fuuuuucked up."

"Same," Tanya said.

Kiara held up her glass in mock toast. "Bet."

* * *

Hayden sat on the sofa next to Kiara, his thigh touching hers. He didn't touch her on purpose, but he figured if she was okay with it, so was he. Sooner or later, she'd come around and go out with him. Persistence was the key.

After a few seconds, she looked down at their legs and withdrew hers.

"We going to do this?" she asked the group.

Paul knelt along the side of the table and Tanya got on the floor to his right. Kiara plopped down at the end of the table to his left. Hayden took the space next to her. Dari was next to him and Richard at the far end across from Kiara. They filled their glasses and smoked the rest of the joints, putting them out in a large square crystal ashtray that was already on the table.

Dead Town

The game began.

As they played, the conversation wove in many different directions. Past parties, people, the house, movies.

"Did y'all ever see that one with Liam Neeson where he was an ex-cop turned private eye?" Kiara asked. "I loved that flick."

"Taken?" Paul asked.

"No. But that was good, too." Kiara bounced the quarter into the shot glass at the center of the table. She looked around, slowly dragging her finger across everyone, until she finally landed on Tanya. "Drink."

As Tanya took her shot, Kiara said, "I ain't really into old guys, but I'd break my rule and fuck the hell out of him."

"Your *rule*?" Paul said.

She passed the quarter to Hayden and said, "Yeah. I have a rule. I have never slept with a guy I didn't know at least four months."

"What about *girls*?" Ladarius asked with a grin.

"Girls are different."

"Damn. You *got* to give me your number," Dari said.

Kiara's eyes bounced to Paul, resting on him for a second, then back to Ladarius. "We'll see," she said with a wicked smile.

Hayden knew she was a flirt and knew she wasn't his, but that never helped him with the twinges of jealousy he felt when she got like this.

"You *sure* it wasn't Taken?"

"Positive. There wasn't a sequel."

"The Commuter?" he asked.

Kiara shook her head.

"Go, bro," Dari said.

Hayden bounced the quarter. It missed the glass and landed by Paul. He flicked it with his forefinger and it slid across the table like a puck to Ladarius.

Hayden pulled out his phone to Google Liam Neeson movies. "Shit," he said. He held up his phone and showed it to the others. "No signal."

Everyone quickly checked their phones. It was the same story across the board. No one had a signal. Hayden didn't suppose it mattered anyway, though. It wasn't like they needed to call or text anyone. The only downside was no posting pics to Snapchat or social media.

* * *

Chase took the peck on the cheek as a good sign. He had hoped she would kiss him again when he said she missed his lips, but she didn't. She just said, "You're right. Not *that* good." But the playful tone of her voice told him he might have a shot at a real kiss later.

After leaving the kitchen, they crossed the hall to a large library with built-in bookshelves and cabinets from the hardwood floor to the high, vaulted ceiling. There were ladders on rollers to facilitate plucking books from the upper shelves along the wall to the left and the wall through which they entered.

There were several dark red leather wingback chairs with brass tacks pinning the leather against the frames. Their wooden legs curved down and ended as cloven hooves—like goats' feet.

Chase shone his light on the bookshelf to the left and started checking out the titles. It was *not* what he expected. There was a series of leather-bound books—maybe a dozen or so—with gold lettering stamped on them. Collected works of Aristotle, Plato, Socrates, etcetera. Beside them ran another series of books bound in green leather with gold foil announcing more modern thinkers like Hegel, Kierkegaard, Nietzsche, and so on. The hundreds of books were organized in sections—philosophy, science, law, politics. On some of the shelves, the sections were broken up by decorative bookends and space. Some had statues between them, like the white porcelain nude woman reclining between economics and personal finance titles.

Chase almost dropped his phone when his light scanned across a skull looking back at him. He jumped back, then laughed.

"What?" Kenna asked.

He shone the light on the skull.

"That's creepy," she said.

"You think whoever lived here actually read all these?" Chase asked.

"It would take Paul a year just to read the titles," Kenna said as she withdrew a book from the shelf and opened it. "No way."

"What?"

Dead Town

"Look." She held out the open book and walked toward Chase as he crossed the room.

She had in her hand a copy of Dante's Inferno. On the inside of the cover, across from the title page, the book was stamped *Ex Libris James Thornton III.*

"Fuck," Chase said.

He walked to the bookshelf and grabbed a random title, opened it, and found the same stamp.

"How cool is this?" Chase asked. No doubt, he was excited, but also felt a sudden wave of apprehension break over him. What were the odds that the only house left standing was the one where the head Satanist lived?

"We need to tell them," Kenna said, her voice full of enthusiasm.

Chase agreed, but rather than go back the way they came, they might as well walk down the hall and at least peek in the other rooms along the way.

The first door on the right led to the now empty barroom. The door on the left opened to a small powder room with just a toilet and sink.

"You think it still works?" Kenna asked. Before Chase could answer, she said, "I really have to pee."

"Go," he said. "But there won't be any water to flush."

"I don't care."

She walked in and stood by the toilet. Chase started to close the door as she began unbuckling her belt.

"No," she said. "Leave it open. Just turn around."

Chase turned his back to her.

"And don't listen," she said.

He grinned, wondering if *not* listening was even possible.

Zzzzip. Down went her zipper, then her pants. A few seconds later, a forceful stream splashed against the bottom of the porcelain bowl. She wasn't kidding. Judging by the sound, she must have been holding it for a while.

"Oh no," she said.

He spun around without thinking. She was hunkered down on the commode, her bare leg and left butt cheek visible in his light.

"What?" he asked.

Kenna laughed, but didn't seem offended he was looking at her. "No toilet paper."

Chase glanced around. He grabbed one of the hand towels hanging by the sink and asked, "Need a hand?"

She reached out and took it from him. "Go," she said, laughing and pointing at the door. "Turn around."

Once she was up and dressed, they continued down the hall. The next door was a large walk-in coat closet filled with fancy men's and women's coats from the period.

"We could make a fortune on eBay with this shit," Chase said as he examined the garments. There were leather, wool, and fur coats. The amazing thing was how well-preserved they were. No moth holes or dried, cracking leather. They all looked like they had been hung that night. They stepped back into the hall and headed for the parlor. The white wall beneath the curved staircase had large, rectangular panels bordered by trim in diminishing, but proportional measures from about eight-feet tall all the way down to a single foot near the base of the steps.

Chase paused by the malachite table and looked at the large, creamy white urn. Genuine gold highlights on the rim and the two colorful peacocks painted on it assured him the thing was expensive. Blocked from casual view by the urn was the only flaw in the woodwork Chase could see. Perhaps that was why it was there, to hide the peg-like knot about half the size of a dime jutting out a quarter-inch.

"Look," Chase said, joking with Kenna.

"What's that?" she asked.

"It leads to a secret passage." He was doing his best to keep a straight face. He wanted to see just how gullible she was.

"You're so full of shit."

"Seriously. Press it and a secret door will open."

Chase pulled out a cigarette. It wasn't so much that he wanted to smoke, but he wanted to linger there a little longer to see if temptation would get the best of her. He fumbled around, patting down his pockets as if he couldn't find his lighter. He could tell she was thinking about it.

He pulled out his lighter. As soon as she touched the knot, he would shout, grab her, and scare the hell out of her.

"You're so full of shit," she said, her finger drifting toward the protruding peg. "But . . ."

She *touched* it. Before Chase could utter a sound, he heard a click. Her hand came off the knot and it stuck out about twice as far. At the same time, there was another click to his left and one of the wall panels that stood about seven feet tall swung open a few inches.

"Holy shit!" he said.

Kenna looked as shocked as he felt.

"I was just fucking with you," he said. "I had no idea."

Chase pushed open the panel and looked. A dark wooden staircase went down to a platform then switched back and continued on. He couldn't see what was at the bottom of it and he wasn't going to find out with just the two of them. That was just a little too spooky—even for him.

* * *

Kiara knew Chase was messing with her when he told her that bullshit story about a secret passage. Still, she thought it would be cool as hell if it were true. If ever there was a house that would have some freaky shit like that, this was it. She thought long and hard about it as he worked on lighting his cigarette. She was sure he would laugh at her, but she couldn't resist.

Kenna looked past Chase at the front door. They had left it open, but now it was closed.

Maybe they got cold, she thought.

"You're so full of shit, but . . ." She couldn't pass up the opportunity.

To say she was shocked when the thing pressed in beneath her touch then popped back out with a click would be an understatement. Even more startling was the panel actually opening.

From the front room came shouts and laughter.

"Drink!" Paul told someone.

"We got to tell them," Chase said. "I can't wait to see Paul's face."

"Can we *not*?"

"What do you mean?"

Kenna was having a good time just hanging out and exploring with Chase. She wanted to check out the rest of the house. If it was in as pristine shape as what she had already seen, she might be convinced to crash there. Even if they *didn't* spend the night, though, she enjoyed the alone time with him. And she knew what would happen as soon as they told Paul. He would take over and insist everyone go down and start investigating everything.

"Let's just close the panel and find it *later*." She took the cigarette from between his fingers, took a drag from it, and added, "*Please*." She handed him back his cigarette.

CHAPTER 11

Kiara fingered the pendant hanging around her neck, waiting for her turn to come around. The increasing surge of power coursing through her body was more stimulating and numbing than the booze and weed combined. It was hard to explain, even to herself. It was like all her senses were heightened and her mind was clear, but her body was in that limbo between sleep and wakefulness.

Tanya bounced the quarter but missed. She snatched it up and passed it to Paul.

Paul leaned forward and placed the quarter on the bridge of his nose. He held it for a moment then let it roll down. It bounced on edge and hopped right into the glass.

"Drink," he said, tapping Kiara's upper arm with the back of his hand.

She poured some whiskey into her shot glass and downed it.

She took the quarter from him and tossed it against the table. It clinked into the shot glass.

Kiara looked at Paul. "Payback's a bitch. And so am I. Drink."

After Paul drank, she slid the quarter to Hayden and looked over his head at the thin white curtains beside the large fireplace. On the other side of them, the window was a large black block of night pushing its way in.

Ladarius took his turn, rung one in and called on Tanya to drink. Richard made her drink, too. Kiara suspected they were picking on her to force her to relax.

"What y'all doing?" Kenna asked from the pocket doors behind Paul.

Several of them shouted, "Quarters."

"Come on," Dari said. "We can make room." He scooted closer to Richard.

"Why ain't y'all playing on the dining room table?" Chase asked.

Kiara and Paul turned to look at them.

"There's a massive table in the room on the other side of the bar," Chase said. "Ten chairs in there."

Paul looked at Kiara. "*Now* he tells us."

She laughed as she moved closer to him. It was the perfect excuse. She patted the patch of floor between her and Hayden. "Come on, Kenna."

"I want to look around a little more," Kenna said.

Paul faced her. "Did you two find anything good?"

"A library," Chase said, leaning against the pocket door slot to his left and crossing his arms and one leg in front of the other so his toes were poking the floor. She wasn't crushing on him, but she had to admit, he looked cool at the moment—like a modern James Dean or whatever that old actor's name was.

"I said *good*." He shifted his gaze to Kiara. "I'm allergic to reading."

"And more candles," Kenna said. "Enough to last a month."

"You didn't happen to find a bathroom, did you?" Tanya asked as she bounced the quarter off the table and into the glass. "Drink, baby," she said, leaning against Paul.

"Want me to show you where it is?" Kenna asked. "No water, but it beats squatting outside."

Tanya pushed herself up off the floor and staggered a bit before gaining her balance. Kenna led her out of the room.

Kiara had to go, too, but she wanted to have a minute alone with Paul to see what would happen. She doubted he would do anything in front of all these people, but she was still curious.

Paul rolled the quarter off his nose again for another perfect shot. He grabbed Kiara's leg a couple inches above her knee and squeezed, causing her to jump. "Drink, cupcake."

"Do I look like a fat round, frosted thing to you?" she asked as she filled her shot glass.

"No. But you *do* look good enough to eat."

Everyone laughed.

"Hang on," Paul said. He filled his glass and picked it up. "Okay. Cheers."

They clinked glasses and shot their drinks.

Dead Town

Kiara took her turn, making it. "You ain't the *only* one who's played this before. Drink." She poked him in his muscular biceps. As soon as he filled his glass, she plopped hers beside it and declined her head toward it. He poured her another.

They raised their glasses in unison once more and drank.

Kiara squeezed Paul's arm while Hayden took his turn. "Damn, boy," she said. "You got some guns there don't you?"

"Drink," Hayden said, tapping her on the shoulder.

She let go of Paul's arm. She didn't want to, but she knew she'd have to sooner or later anyway.

Paul filled her glass for her.

"Here you go," Hayden said, raising his glass toward hers.

She drank with him, trying to hide the contempt she held for him at that moment. When Paul did it, it was a smooth move. This was more like a Wal-Mart knockoff version of Paul's suave nature. She knew she couldn't have Paul right now, but she didn't want him getting the wrong idea, either. She wanted him to know she was available and Hayden, as much as she liked him, had a way of clinging to her and making her appear taken—at least in "Bro-Code."

Tanya and Kenna returned. As Tanya took her position next to her boyfriend, Kiara felt a hot blast slap her cheeks and burn her ears. What was it? Jealousy? Guilt? Maybe a little of both, she decided.

Chase, still leaning against the door frame, said, "We're going to check out the upstairs."

Everyone stopped and stared at him.

Paul asked, "I thought we were going to stick together."

"We are. Kenna and I are sticking together. And *y'all* are sticking together. We'll be right back."

"Whatever."

Kiara wanted to explore the house, too. It was a cool place, but her desire to hang close to Paul overrode her curiosity. Besides, there would be plenty of time for roaming around. Tanya had seemed to come to terms with hanging there a while. With her calm now, they could probably get drunk, pass out, and go home in the morning.

Paul said, "Just remember . . . if you're gonna party, wear a party hat."

Kenna rolled her eyes.

The game resumed as soon as the two of them walked out of the room.

After a few misses in a row, it was Hayden's turn. Kiara watched as he tried to aim. The window behind him lit up slightly like a distant flashlight swept across it.

"Is it supposed to rain tonight?" she asked.

* * *

Chase offered to let Kenna ascend the stairs first, but she wasn't that bold. She would rather he lead—just in case.

The stairway terminated at a hall running to the back of the house. There were two doors on the left and three on the right. She knew it was illogical, but for some reason the fact that all the doors were closed made Kenna nervous. If they were opened or at least cracked, she'd be able to peek in and make sure no one was hiding in there with a hatchet or machete. She had seen enough horror movies—even though she hated them—to know *this* was the kind of place where escapees from prisons and psycho wards ended up. They *always* found their way to a normal looking house in the middle of nowhere.

Chase opened the first door on the right. It was a rather plain looking bedroom with a double bed—neatly made—a mirrored dresser, and a small chest-of-drawers. The walls lacked decoration. As bland as it appeared, Kenna assumed it was a guest room.

Their feet clopped as they walked across the hall to the first door on the left. It was larger than the first room with a double bed and a matching walnut armoire and dresser. In the corner of the dresser's mirror was a black and white photo of an attractive woman with her dark hair in a snood. She had a beautiful smile ringed by a heavily lipsticked mouth. On the dresser, there was another photo of her on a beach somewhere wearing a flowered one-piece bathing suit probably from the Forties or early Fifties. She looked happy.

Kenna opened the armoire to look at the clothes, all neatly folded and tucked in pigeon holes or drawers. On the other side, behind the door on the left, blouses and a couple skirts hung.

"This is kind of weird," Chase said almost in a whisper. "I feel like I've broken into someone's house and they could return any minute."

Dead Town

Kenna knew what he meant. She had that same feeling, like a voyeur or perv skulking around someone else's home. She wondered if this is what burglars felt like during their first job.

They walked out of the room and stepped across the hall toward the next door. A floorboard creaked beneath her foot. Kenna gasped and froze. When Chase looked at her, she giggled, realizing how foolish the expression on her face must have been at that moment.

That room was a small pink and white bathroom with barely enough room for the vanity, toilet and tub. She had to know. Kenna stepped up to the small mirror protruding from the wall above the sink. She tugged on one edge and it opened, revealing a cabinet with a half-used tube of toothpaste—some brand she had never heard of—a simple toothbrush, some aspirin and a couple bottles of medication with the user's name—Layla Vanderhoff.

Kenna closed the cabinet and they made their way to the second door on the left. An eruption of laughter downstairs made Kenna's heart sputter. She had almost forgotten there was anyone around besides Chase.

Chase turned the knob and pushed the door open. Their phones illuminated a large bedroom with a large bed and a masculine suit of furniture if such a thing existed. The dresser, armoire and four poster bed were dark wood with large edges and carvings in them. The feet were giant lion paws. Like the other rooms, the bed was neatly made, a simple black and white vertical striped spread covering it.

Upon the wall was a black and white portrait of a man with slicked back dark hair and brilliant eyes. They were probably blue, but the photo made them appear almost white. Despite it being only a photo, somehow the man's eyes managed to penetrate deep into her. There was a photo of him with the woman from the other room holding hands framed on the dresser. And another photo of them touching lips in a closed-mouth kiss, both with one eye looking at the camera. In all the photos, his eyes seemed to come off the paper like two tiny LED lights.

Between the bed and armoire, a doorway opened to the master bath, which was larger than the hall bath and done in black and white. The hand towel next to the sink was hung neatly, but been used a time or two. A bar of soap—yellowed and cracked—remained in the soap dish in the tub.

Kenna couldn't resist opening the drawers and cabinet to see what kind of man he was. Everything was organized. An old jar of shave cream had a small upturned brush beside it and a straight razor next to that, then a black comb with a tube of something next to it.

Kenna picked up the tube and read, "Brylcreem. For smart hair grooming." She laughed before placing it back exactly as she had found it.

The second drawer held a toothbrush, toothpaste, dental floss, and a small, evaporated bottle of *Listerine Antiseptic*.

Kenna popped open the mirror cabinet, finding aspirin, alcohol, and a bottle of Barbitol prescribed to James Thornton III.

Kenna took the bottle from the cabinet and held it out for Chase to see. "This was his room," she said, feeling an odd sort of glee. Now, she knew at least who owned the house and what he looked like. Why that mattered, she didn't know, but it made her feel more comfortable in the house.

They left Thornton's room and headed for the last door upstairs. As soon as Chase opened it and their lights penetrated the darkness, all that comfort she had just felt fled from her.

* * *

Tanya hated the feeling she loved. It was a fucking addiction waiting to happen. The electricity buzzing through her body was better than any orgasm Paul or any other person ever gave her.

She didn't want to be here, but if she *had* to be here, she might as well be drunk as fuck for it. If she could call her own name, she would. But she was pretty sure that was against the rules of quarters. So, she picked on Paul, hoping he would get tired, take her somewhere and just fuck her until they fell asleep.

That's really all she wanted. It wasn't even that late, maybe seven o'clock, and she was ready to call it a night. Not because she was tired, but because she was done with this place. It was creepy as hell and it had bad mojo everywhere. Paul may have been correct. If she had never heard the story of the murders, maybe she would feel different—but she *did* hear the stories and she was scared.

Dead Town

Not scared of the stories per se, but scared because the stories mixed with her cards spelled disaster. Her cards said an end was coming. And she wasn't ready for a breakup, whether it was amicable or not.

Now here Kiara was—cute as fuck. Tanya could see that. Worse than that was that Paul saw it, too. He was flirting with the bitch earlier. No, she wasn't a bitch. Just . . . someone there at the wrong time and place.

The window over Hayden's shoulder lit up. A storm was coming. The weatherman said a ten-percent chance of severe thunderstorms. It looked like that one-in-ten shot was on them.

Tanya tried to hint to Paul she was ready to be fucked. Either he was too drunk to notice, or he was too into Kiara. A small part of Tanya didn't blame him. She wanted to sleep with Kiara, too. But the better part—which was her worst part—took over and had her burning with jealousy. That was *her* man.

Tanya stood and walked away from the table, hoping Paul would follow her, but he didn't. She continued on into the bar and then the kitchen. She paused a couple minutes to see if he would come. When he didn't show, she figured she might as well look around the place and see what she could find.

Tanya crossed the hall to the library and began checking out the titles. When she got to the section on religion, she grabbed a book on world religions and took it back to one of the chairs. She sat back and thumbed through the index to see if it had anything on Wicca or Druidism. Unless it was under some other larger category, it didn't.

The room lit up for an instant as lightning flashed.

World religions my ass, she thought. *Doesn't even have two of the world's oldest.*

Then she remembered everything in here was printed in the more puritanical days of America's history—no later than the Fifties when women still aspired for little more than to get married and stay pregnant. When every Sunday was God and apple pie all day long. Now, Sundays were more like *Oh, God, did I really do that last night?*

She flipped to the front of the book to see when it was printed. Her guess was the Thirties or earlier. As she looked at the inside cover, her stomach churned.

Figures. Had to be his *fucking house*, she thought as she read Thornton's name.

Tanya stood to put the book back. It was time to go. She didn't care if she had to walk to the road and hitchhike home, she was getting out of here.

Lightning flashed again.

In the almost-daylight brilliance she saw it and screamed.

Then came the heavy rumble of thunder.

* * *

Paul heard the scream and pushed himself to his feet.

"Tanya?" he hollered.

He turned on his phone's flashlight and ran into the bar as fast as his unsteady legs would take him. He passed through there, through the kitchen until he saw the light of her phone in a room across the hall.

"Tanya!"

"Holy shit," she said as he ran in.

"You okay?"

"Oh my God. I just had a heart attack." She put one hand between her breasts and laughed nervously.

"What's wrong with you?"

"Look."

Lightning flared and Paul realized they were in his hell—a library.

As thunder shook the house, Tanya pointed her phone's light toward one of the walls. There, between a couple sets of books, was a human skull.

Paul laughed as he walked toward it. Just as he was about to pick it up, the others stumbled into the room with one of the candelabras and the usual questions—what's wrong? You okay? What happened?

Paul held the skull in front of his face and his phone beneath it so the light came up from under the chin.

"Well, that's unnerving," Kiara said. "Is it real?"

"Doubt it." Paul shone his light on it. He looked for a Made in China mark or something, but didn't see one. As long as it was white and not made of something like wood or cement, he would have no clue if he was holding a human skull or a mockup.

Dead Town

Paul tossed it at Kiara, who bobbled, but caught it.

The room lit up with a brilliant flash outside. Not a second later, came the thunder that rattled Paul's body. It was going to be a helluva storm.

"We need to leave," Tanya said.

"Not in *this*."

Tanya picked a book up off the floor. "Look at this," she said, flipping open the cover and holding her phone so the inside was illuminated.

"Awesome."

Hayden leaned in over Paul's shoulder.

"This is fucking Thornton's house," Tanya said.

Outside the rain started. It sounded like loud static on a turned-up car radio that had just slipped out of range of the station. *Shhhhhh!!!*

"I got a bad feeling about this," Tanya said.

"Bad feeling. You *always* have a bad feeling."

Tanya pulled out a Newport and lit it. Her face glowed like an angel's. "You don't have to leave, but *I am*. I'll fucking walk home if I have to."

"You'll fucking *die* is what you'll do if you try to leave this house," Paul said.

Kiara wrapped her arm around Tanya and pulled her close. "He's right, baby. You can't go out in this."

As if to prove her correct, lightning and thunder punctuated her point.

Wind howled, ripping through the trees. The house moaned a low, mournful note. Rain beat down on the leaves and window panes. Thunder rattled the glass and knickknacks on the shelves. An unseen tree snapped with a terrible *Craaaack!* then slammed against the ground with a thud and the lesser cracks of boughs breaking beneath the weight.

Richard, holding the candelabra, stepped closer and spoke like a father to his young daughter. "They're right. The way this storm is going right now, our safest spot is here."

She took a drag off her cigarette, spun and dumped her ashes in a large bronze ashtray standing by the chair, and turned back, focusing her attention on him.

He went on. "If a tornado hits, at least we have *some* protection here. Out there? They'd find your body parts in Tennessee or Huntsville. If you're lucky."

Paul had to hand it to Richard. He had a way of getting his point across. He was dead right, but the words he chose and the manner in which he chose to convey them seemed to have a calming effect on Tanya.

She sat down in the chair and leaned back. "Well, can we go when it stops or lightens up?"

"Bet," Dari said. "Until then, don't worry, Tanya. I ain't going to let nothing happen to you. *None* of us will. You *know* that."

She nodded and crushed out her cigarette.

"I say we smoke some green and start exploring." Paul said, heading for the door.

"Hell yeah," Kiara said.

Hayden fell in line behind Paul. "I'm down."

"I'm staying here," Tanya said.

When they got to the parlor, Paul asked, "Who closed the door?"

Everyone looked at one another with questioning looks. Finally, Hayden said, "Probably Chase or Kenna."

* * *

Chase opened the last door and marveled at what he saw.

Until this point, the house looked like any other normal house. He'd have almost sworn Richard's stories about Thornton were urban legends like Slender Man or that guy in the back seat of the car. Everything pointed to Thornton being your typical *Leave It to Beaver* kind of guy—albeit with a minor case of OCD.

But *this* . . . This was a twist.

Lightning popped like a photographer's flash, burning a negative image on Chase's retinas for a second. When his eyes readjusted to the dim light, he entered.

Against the wall beside him was a small chest of drawers. A large, high four-poster bed stood in the center of the room. Braided ropes, about eight-feet long and a couple inches thick, drooped from near the tops of each post. One snaked across the white crumpled and stained sheets of the bed. The other three fell to the hardwood floor.

On the wall to his left hung multiple whips of varying lengths and materials. There were a couple leather riding crops, a thin wooden stick with a knob a little smaller than a ping pong ball on the end, another thin rod about two feet long and an inch thick, a cat-of-nine, a long whip like cowboys used in old movies, a belt, a barber's strop. On the other side of the window in the center were more bondage toys. A leather mask with holes for the eyes and mouth. Another similar mask with no mouth hole. There was a peacock and a long white goose feather on thin shelves—the smaller above the larger. A ball gag. A coiled horsehair rope.

"Holy shit," Kenna said. "What a *freak*."

"The *original* Fifty Shades of Gray," Chase said, laughing.

Chase opened the top drawer of the dresser. There was an 8mm film camera and many stacked cans of film in there.

The second drawer was filled with photos. Chase grabbed some and pulled them out. The first picture was of Thornton holding the riding crop. A woman lay in prone position, tied spread eagle on the bed. Her legs and ass had large welts going across them.

The next picture was a thin, attractive black woman, sitting naked on the bed. She had some white guy's dick in her mouth. There was another picture of her—judging by the body—with the leather mask on. She was on all fours with a white man entering her from behind and Thornton in her mouth.

More and more pictures like this. Hundreds of them. Some depicted women being pissed on by multiple men. One had a man and woman cutting each other. The next few photos were of them covered in blood as they had oral, vaginal and anal sex. Pictures of men and women having various phallic objects stuffed in their orifices.

"Wow," Chase said, "A man before his time. This would be tame for some websites now."

Kenna scrunched up her face. "Eww! What kind of websites are you going to?"

Chase shoved the photos back in the drawer and opened the bottom one. It held about a dozen dildos, lined up side by side. He recognized one from the photos and pulled it out. Around eight inches long, it was carved wood with some sort of clear coat over it to make it slick and shiny. He held it from the bottom, between his thumb and forefinger, feeling weird holding someone else's used sex toy.

"Gross. I can't believe you picked that up."

As he turned it around, he said, "Look." It was carved to look like a bearded man.

"Is that *Jesus*?"

Chase looked closer. A thorny crown ringed the man's forehead.

"If he *wasn't* a Satanist, he probably still ended up in hell for that," Kenna said, giggling.

The other dildos were plastic penises or plain pointy rocket-ship shaped things. They ranged in size from about six to twelve-inches long and in width from two to four inches.

"Which one you want to take home?" Chase asked through a sheepish grin.

"As if."

He had seen enough.

"Ready to go down?"

Kenna's eyes got big. "Excuse me?"

"Stairs," he said. "That came out sounding bad, didn't it?"

It was her turn to don a coy grin. "Maybe."

* * *

When Chase and Kenna returned, the group—minus Tanya—had already moved the party to the dining room where they could all be comfortable. The candelabras kept the room lit enough that everyone could see well. To make things easier, they had brought a few more bottles of liquor and more candles in to have them close by.

"What'd you find up there?" Hayden asked.

Everyone kind of leaned in, waiting to hear.

Chase and Kenna both talked about the bedrooms, their organized nature. Layla Vanderhoff.

"And a torture chamber," Kenna said.

"A *what*?" several asked in unison.

"Like an S&M porn room," Chase said.

Paul laughed. "You're shitting me."

Dead Town

"No," Kenna shook her head. "All this bondage stuff and photos of orgies and shit."

"Ooh, I want to see *that*," Kiara said.

"Me, too," Hayden said.

"They're fucking with us," Paul said.

After lighting a cigarette, Kenna said, "I promise we're not."

As if he were god of the house, Paul said, "We'll go up in a little bit. Give Tanya some time to chill, then we can *all* go."

Somehow, that seemed to settle it. Even Richard, though he didn't know why, was willing to accept that as gospel.

Over an hour had passed since the storm began and it still raged ferociously. There were short periods where the rain and lightning slacked off, but just when it seemed like it was about to die out, it spun back up again.

Richard had had enough for the moment and needed a break from the booze.

"I'm going to check on Tanya," he said, even though Paul had just checked on her about fifteen minutes before.

Richard stood from the table and staggered out of the room. Before he looked in on her, he had to piss. Using his cellphone to light the way, he headed across the hall to the bathroom. As he stood urinating in the toilet, a new wave of lightning and rain came.

He shook and tucked himself back in, then stood before the mirror, staring at himself. His features were distorted by heavy shadows. His eyes looked more like empty dark sockets, his blond hair barely visible. He waited and watched. Lightning struck again and he saw himself clearly for a brief second before seeing the negative image and the colors of his aura. That was always the easiest way for him to determine his own aura. There were shades of green and brown and orange.

Richard walked out as thunder roared.

The library was dark as he approached.

"Tanya," he whispered.

"What?"

He walked in and panned the room with his light until he spotted her still sitting in the same chair, her feet drawn up under her.

"Why are you sitting here in the dark?"

"Why not?"

"I'll bring you some candles."

"Don't bother. I just want to sleep until this is over."

Richard looked around the room. When he was in earlier, he hadn't taken the time to investigate the titles. As he skimmed them, pausing only to read every so often, he found himself impressed with Thornton's collection. The man had to have been incredibly intelligent and a quick reader if he made it through even half of these.

He began opening the cabinets beneath the shelves to see what they held.

"What are you looking for?"

He had no idea. He supposed more information on who Thornton was. If he was the person his grandfather said he was.

"Just looking."

The first cabinet had Parcheesi, chess, backgammon, and a deck of playing cards stacked in a pyramid. The second and third cabinets were filled with old magazines. The fourth cabinet was more like what Richard expected. There were several decks of tarot cards on top of a Ouija board.

"That's what I'm talking about," Richard said as he slipped the large wooden board out from under the cards.

"What?" Tanya asked, sounding rather indifferent.

He held it up in his light. "A Ouija board."

"Oh, hell no."

"What?" he asked as he removed the planchette, which was leaning on edge against one of the cabinet walls.

"We are *not* using that thing in this house."

"Where's your sense of adventure?"

Tanya flicked her lighter several times. Finally, it worked and she lit the cigarette dangling from her lips.

"I left it at home this morning."

* * *

Ladarius didn't think the storm outside was ever going to end. Even when it slacked up, and the lightning shifted from near to far, the rain still came down heavily.

147

Dead Town

He stood and wobbled to the window, pulling back the sheer white curtain and peeking out. Other than trickling beads of water and his reflection on the glass, he saw nothing but blackness. Lightning streaked the distant sky as a silvery veil of rain plummeted to the green-black trees. Then everything vanished into the hungry darkness until the next flash.

"Look what I found," Richard said as he entered the room.

Ladarius turned on the balls of his feet as Richard plopped something on the table. He walked over.

"What the fuck is that?"

"A Ouija board," Richard and Hayden said at the same time as Richard set the pointer, a wooden heart-shaped object with a circle cut out near the point, beside the board.

"Fuck no," he said. "I already told you, Paul, black folks don't do ghosts and shit. And I don't know if you noticed, but I *am* black."

Paul laughed at him.

Dari was trying to keep it light and comical, but he was also serious.

"What're you scared of?" Chase asked him.

"Ain't you ever watched a movie?" Dari said. "As soon as you pull one of those things out, people start dying. And you know who *always* gets it first? The token black dude. *Always*."

This time everyone laughed—except Ladarius.

As he stood looking at the letters stretching across the board in two arched rows, he felt the buzz of alcohol and weed fading. Just the *thought* of playing with this thing had a sobering effect.

"Don't be such a pussy," Paul said. "Why's the token negro always got to be a pussy, too?"

He and Paul went way back and Paul *knew* that was one shoe that didn't fit. Other than when he was seven, he never ran from a fight. And even though that time he ran from two sixth-graders who were dropping the N-bomb and screaming, "Kill him," and, "better run, *boy*," as they chased him, he never forgot or forgave himself for it. He spent the last thirteen years proving to himself and everyone else he wasn't the chicken those kids claimed he was when they got back to school the next day. He met them on the playground and got his ass whooped by those rednecks-in-training, but he didn't run and he even got a few good licks in.

As they were in the room next to the principal's serving their In-School Suspension the next day, one of the kids he hit—Jake Brown—made the comment, "Black boys need to learn their place."

Ladarius glared at him and smiled, proud of himself for giving Jake that shiner. He boldly said, "Then you better learn your place too, *boy*, cuz you part black now." Then he pointed at his own left eye so Jake knew what he meant. That made Rick Reed, Jake's buddy, laugh out loud. And though Jake appeared a little butthurt by both of them at the moment, it gained Ladarius not only their respect, but their promise to make sure no one else ever fucked with him while they were around.

"I ain't no pussy," Dari said. "But I ain't touching that thing."

Whether she meant to or not, Kiara came to his rescue. "I'll play with it," she said. "But I'd rather go check out that torture chamber first."

Dari nodded in agreement. "Bondage and porn pics. Now *that's* an idea I can get behind." He smiled at her. "I'll go with you, girl." He cocked an eyebrow. "Ever been tied up?"

A lascivious smile made its way onto her lips. "Wouldn't *you* like to know?"

"Hell yeah," Paul said.

Richard disappeared into the kitchen and began rattling around in the cabinets. When he returned, he had a small plate in his hand.

"I forgot," he said. "I told her I would bring her some candles."

He lit a short, thick white candle, turning it sideways and allowing the wax to drip onto the plate. Then he stood the candle up in the wax and blew on it to cool it. He repeated the action two more times then slowly carried the plate out of the room. A moment later, he came back without the makeshift candleholder.

Ladarius and Hayden each grabbed a candelabra as the group headed for the stairs.

* * *

Dead Town

The content of the room amused Hayden, but the comical reactions of the others as they sifted through the photos and played with the toys entertained him even more.

Paul plucked the riding crop off the wall and told Kenna, "Get on the bed, bitch."

"No." She laughed.

Paul chased her around the bed a couple times, him saying, "I'm gonna set that ass on fire when I catch you." Her giggling.

Finally, Paul stopped near Kiara and swatted her on the ass. She jumped with a yelp, her eyes wide like a frightened horse's. Before he could hit her again, she spun around and snatched the wooden stick from its hanger. She held it up like a sword.

"Don't you dare," she said.

After a little more play and a quick tour of the other rooms led by Chase and Kenna, they went back downstairs.

"Holy shit," Chase said when they were halfway down. "I totally forgot."

"What?" a couple asked.

"I got to show you something cool."

When they got to the bottom of the steps, Chase took them to the table by the staircase.

"Check this out," he said as he reached behind the decorative vase. *Click. Click.*

One of the panels swung in a couple inches.

"You're just *now* telling us about this?" Paul asked. "What's down there?"

"Fuck if I know."

Hayden walked over and pushed the door in further. A cool air, like a ghost, billowed up out of the darkness and rolled over him.

"You didn't check it out?" Paul asked.

"Hell no," Kenna said. "That was just a little *too* weird. Like the dark hole in the kitchen."

"The *what*?" Paul, Kiara and Hayden said together.

She went on to detail the door in the kitchen leading to what they supposed was a cellar.

Hayden lingered at the top of the stairs, feeling the rising tide of power within him as he peered into the blackness. It was much stronger than when they were partying in the woods last night.

He pulled out his cellphone and turned on the flashlight, noticing the time as he did. 11:14. No wonder it was stronger. As midnight approached the veil stretched thinner. Soon, the energy would be at its apex.

"Who's going first?" Kiara asked.

"Don't look at me," Dari said.

Paul shot him a grin. "Pussy." He took the candelabra from him, said, "Excuse me" as he passed Hayden, and descended the stairs.

CHAPTER 12

Tanya listened as the others tromped around upstairs. She didn't know what the rest of them saw in this place. It was just an old house in the middle of the woods. When she thought about it that way, she wondered why she was so damned scared of it. It wasn't all that spooky of a house. In fact, besides the darkness—which was understandable—everything was completely normal—other than the fact that it had somehow managed to escape detection, vandals, fire, storms, and God knew what else for roughly sixty years, without any maintenance or upkeep.

Still, that mouse gnawed at the back of her brain, insisting something *was* wrong with this house. From the time they entered, she felt the drug of power pumping through her body. It grew more intense by the minute. And though she had never shot up any drugs, she imagined this was what heroin felt like, but in super-slow motion.

Maybe she couldn't ascribe that feeling to the house, though. She felt the same surge of energy, albeit much weaker, in the woods last night. At that point, they weren't even near the house. She would probably be inclined to chalk it up to imagination or nerves if Hayden and Kiara hadn't also felt it.

Tanya closed her eyes and tried to relax. Maybe if she could pass out for a little while, the storm would end and she would survive this place without anything bad happening.

Uncomfortable in the leather chair, Tanya grabbed the candles from the floor near her feet and walked down the hallway to the front room where she could stretch out on one of the sofas.

She set the candles on the coffee table and lay down. Despite the static strumming through her body like a plucked bass string, she closed her eyes and tried to sleep.

* * *

Paul walked slowly down the wooden steps. A couple creaked beneath his weight. He hoped they were as well-constructed as everything else in the house. He paused just past the landing and waited for the others to come clopping down. He continued.

He wasn't sure what he expected to find—probably old paint cans and tools or a furnace and boxes of stuff Thornton had stored for some other time and place. Paul was *not* prepared for what he saw. For one of the few times in his life, he was truly speechless. Not even a *damn* or *holy shit* came out.

It was a massive space running the entirety of the house or close to it—so large the candelabra didn't cast enough light to see the far end. It prompted him to think of a big black mouth, open and waiting to devour them.

There were four long, wooden church pews set in two rows near the bottom of the stairs. On either end of them were tall candle holders, each with nine half-burnt black candles in them.

Paul passed his candles to Kiara and retrieved his lighter from his pocket. As he began lighting the black candles, he told Dari, "Go light those."

The mouth at the opposite end of the room withdrew and closed a little. The new light glinted off another pair of similar gold stands about fifteen feet from them. Paul moved forward to light those. Dari hesitated at first.

Beyond those were two more sets.

The others whispered amongst themselves, barely moving from the pews. Paul turned and looked, wondering why the pews were set so far back when there was nothing in the center of the room.

As he and Dari lit the third set of candles, the darkness receded and the back wall came into view. Behind what looked like a wooden altar with a stone slab on it were two more candle holders. A red pentagram with various symbols in the different sections had been meticulously painted on the concrete wall.

"What are y'all doing back there?" Paul asked, turning toward the group. That's when he realized the center of the room was not empty at all. The same symbol painted on the wall also covered most of the open space on the floor, but in black. Massive dark patches and smudged stains from years ago colored the creamy floor, obscuring some of the design.

Richard rushed forward.

Paul and Dari lit the last set of lights. The room glowed with an eerie gold hue.

"Okay," Paul started. "Now *this* is scary."

Chase came right behind Richard. Finally, Hayden and Kiara made their way up.

"What the hell is this?" Dari asked.

Richard set his candelabra on the stone altar.

At first, Paul had thought the stone top was black or deep brown, but he quickly realized it was actually white marble at one time. Dark stains covered the center, running in misshapen rivulets to the edges where a trough about three inches deep and two inches wide formed the perimeter of the table.

"A sacrificial altar," Richard said, pointing to the trough. "As the sacrifice bled, the blood flowed through this gutter to here." He walked along the edge and stopped at the far front corner. There was a hole in the stone. "This is the lowest point. The blood would flow out and the priest, probably Thornton, would catch the blood in . . ." He looked around. "This."

Richard scampered to the back corner, bent over and picked up something. When he turned around, he was holding a large silver chalice.

He studied the base of the altar. As he did, Paul did also.

It was about seven feet long and three-and-a-half feet wide and tall. Fashioned from dark wood, maybe mahogany, it bore multiple carved reliefs. There was Adam and Eve in the Garden of Eden. A serpent curled around Eve's feet. He wasn't handing them an apple, but passing them a flame he had coiled in his tail.

There were goat heads and swords, a lion eating a lamb, a dragon with a woman crushed under one foot and a man in its mouth. From each of the corners hung a two-inch wide, thin black leather strap long enough to reach the opposite corner.

"Here we go," Richard said, grabbing a handle that fit into the art-work. He slid the center panel back, revealing a storage space. Inside were two large silver buckets. "If the sacrifice was large enough, and depending on the ceremony, they would collect the blood in these."

"What for?" Dari asked, sounding nervous. "They *drink* that shit?"

"Sometimes."

"Gross," Kiara said.

Paul had to agree with her. There was no way he was drinking something's or some*one*'s blood. He wasn't afraid of blood, but hell, he didn't even want to have sex with a chick if she was bleeding. There were some lines that just shouldn't be crossed. Blood was one of them.

Richard squatted down and began poking around under the altar again. He stood up and scanned the room with his eyes. He began in the back corners then slowly turned.

"What're you looking for?" Paul asked.

"This is too fucking weird," Dari said. "I may not go to church like I should, but I *know* I shouldn't be in some sort of demonic worship center, either."

"Something," Richard said. He headed for the pews.

When he got to the front pew, Richard knelt down and reached under it, extracting a shiny object. He walked back and resumed his position behind the altar. The candlelight blazed creepily in Richard's eyes.

He rested his left forearm, palm-up on the altar. He raised his right hand, exposing what he had retrieved from across the room—a dagger with about an eight-inch blade.

"What the fuck?" Dari asked.

Richard smiled at him and said, "Ego deditionem me ad vos aeterna potestas."

Then he gave his arm one good heavy and quick whack with the blade. The skin parted, exposing the white flesh within. Blood filled the wound and spilled over his arm onto the stone top.

"What the fuck are you doing, dude?" Paul asked, hardly able to believe what he just witnessed.

Richard smiled. "Sacrificing myself."

* * *

155

Dead Town

Tanya woke feeling fresh and comforted. Something snapped quietly behind her, but it didn't scare her. She sat up on the sofa and looked. A fire blazed in the fireplace, giving a nurturing warmth. It popped again.

Evidently, at some point while she slept, the others built the fire for heat. She glanced around the room, but they weren't present. It didn't matter. She was enjoying the quiet and solitude.

Tanya sat for a few more minutes. The rain had finally stopped. That didn't matter, either. The rest had done her good and she was no longer frightened of the house. Everything was going to be okay. She just wished she hadn't left her cards in her purse in the car. She would love to do a quick spread just to confirm the potential pitfall had passed. Maybe the real danger was the storm itself and her going out into it.

Tanya stood and walked to the parlor. The front door was still open exposing a lawn silvered by a near-full moon. Even the clouds had passed.

"Paul?" she said loudly. When there was no answer, she called him again. "Paul!"

She turned from the front door and walked down the hallway, checking into each room as she passed.

"Kiara? Where are y'all?"

By the time she got to the library, she remembered the last time she heard everyone, they were bouncing around upstairs. They probably passed out in some bedrooms up there.

Tanya walked back to the front and mounted the stairs. The power flowing through her made her feel like she didn't even need them. If she wanted, she could just say, "Rise" and she would float to the second floor.

She looked down the hallway at the several open doors. Something stirred in the last room on the right. They were there.

When she stepped through the door, her mouth fell open.

"What the fuck?" she said.

Kiara was on the bed buck naked, moaning in ecstasy as Paul lay supine beneath her, fucking the hell out of her. One of the other guys, maybe Hayden or Chase, rode her from behind, buried deep in her ass. She rocked and squirmed and squealed as the two boys ground against her, meeting her movements and grunting like animals. Their bodies glistened with sweat. The room didn't just smell like sex, it *stank* of it as if they had been going at it for hours.

They still hadn't noticed she was in the room with them.

"Hey!" she said.

Kiara turned her head and looked back at her. Her eyes were wild with passion. From beneath her sweat-matted and tangled brown hair, she smiled.

"You going to join us?" Kiara asked.

Tanya shook her head, trying to make sense of what she was seeing. Maybe someone brought some molly she didn't know about. That was still no excuse for Paul to be fucking some other chick. He could have been in the front room fucking *her*. She'd have gotten up for that.

The one on her back turned and grinned. It was neither Hayden nor Chase, but a man with slicked back hair and the most brilliant ice-blue eyes she had ever seen. They were almost a painful white.

"Yes, join us, please," he said, dismounting Kiara and rolling over so his thick hard cock bobbed and stabbed at the air.

"Dude, that's some fucked up shit!" Dari said from somewhere down the hall.

"I can't believe he *did* that!" Kenna said.

Tanya couldn't figure out why—if they were so upset about what Paul was doing—they didn't stop him while she slept.

"Holy fuck!" Paul said, his lips never moving.

Tanya gasped. Her eyes opened and she bolted upright. She was still on the sofa, the others filtering into the room. She looked around as lightning lit the windows and room. The fireplace was as empty as when she fell asleep.

* * *

"What's going on?" Tanya asked.

"Your boy is one fucked up dude, Paul," Dari said.

Kenna lowered herself onto the sofa next to Tanya. "How you feeling?"

"What happened?" Tanya asked.

Kenna shook her head side to side. "Don't ask."

Dead Town

Tanya's eyes darted to the others as they assumed positions on the sofas and chairs. "Where's Richard?"

Dari said, "Probably downstairs killing himself on the alt—"

"In the basement," Paul cut him off.

"*Killing* himself?" Her eyes grew wide.

Kenna wrapped an arm around Tanya while giving the others the stink-eye. "They're kidding. He's *not* killing himself."

After Richard sliced his arm open and said he was sacrificing himself, everyone stood dumbfounded. Kenna knew cutters in middle and high school, but she only saw the small hashmarks as scabs or scars. She had never seen *anyone* inflict a wound like that on themselves. The blood just poured down his arm, covering the pale flesh in bright red streams before dripping to the top of the thirsty altar. What the hell was he thinking?

She wondered if he could die from that.

"I just wanted to see if it would do anything," Richard had said shortly after saying he was sacrificing himself. "You should see your faces. You all look scared shitless."

She didn't know about the others, but it freaked *her* out. Not just the blood and whatever shit he said in another language, but the way he laughed. It reminded her of a guy she used to know who always laughed at his own off-color jokes, even when everyone else stood around him with puzzled expressions as if to ask, "Did you really just tell that?"

"I'm going up," Ladarius said.

"Same," Kiara said.

As everyone walked away, Richard said, "I'm going to hang down here for a bit."

Paul glared at him. "Whatever. Just try not to kill yourself."

Tanya took a cigarette from her pack on the table and lit it. "Well, what's he doing?"

"Looking around, I guess." Kenna couldn't think of anything better to say. Tanya was already uneasy enough about the house, the last thing she wanted to tell her was that there was a satanic altar right below them.

"Drink?" Kiara asked.

"I can use one," Dari said.

Hayden stood up as the others did so. "Count me in."

The seven of them passed through the bar room, pausing briefly to grab a glass for Tanya. As they entered the dining room, Hayden made an abrupt stop and looked at Tanya.

"Were you playing with the Ouija board while we were downstairs?"

"Really?" She looked at him like he was crazy.

"Someone was."

Kenna looked at the board on the table. Although it didn't look like the kind mass produced nowadays, it was recognizable. Above the two rows of letters was a pentagram with a goat head filling the spaces. Below that, in simple script, it said *Spirit Board*. The upper left-hand corner had an angry sun with the word *Yes* beneath it. The upper right-hand corner had a scowling moon and the word *No* below it.

The twenty-six letters of the alphabet were in an Old English engraver's style. Below them ran the numbers from one to zero.

In the bottom left corner was a small pentagram with *Hello* written across the middle. The opposite corner had the same image, but said *Goodbye*.

She wasn't sure why Hayden seemed so perturbed. It looked completely normal. The board was sitting there with the planchette in the middle, the hole at the top over the center of the goat's head.

Hayden looked at Tanya again and raised his eyebrows.

"I didn't touch it," she said.

"What's the big deal?" Paul asked.

Hayden had a grave expression on his face. "Because when we left this room, the planchette was *not* on the board." He glanced around. "Everyone who has ever used a Ouija board knows you *never* leave the planchette on the board."

Hayden rested his fingertips from both hands on the wooden pointer and said, "It's time to say 'goodbye.'"

Kenna studied the others. They all watched, gravid with expectation, except Paul, who appeared unamused.

"I said *go*," Hayden said. "*Goodbye*."

Slowly, the planchette glided across the board on an angle for the bottom right corner. As the hole moved over the word *Goodbye*, one of the three small legs of the pointer fell off the board.

Hayden picked it up and set it down on the table beside the board.

Dead Town

* * *

Richard waited for everyone to leave then crawled onto the altar and lay on his back. It was comfortable, all things considered. His arm burned where he had cut it. He held it away from his body, allowing it to bleed onto the stone slab without soaking his clothes. The cool stone against his back was oddly comforting.

He giggled to himself when he thought about their faces. Shock. Panic. Horror. It was like they expected a gigantic demon to rise from a puff of smoke.

He lay there staring at the joists in the ceiling. The wood showed stains from where blood had spattered up on it decades ago. This was the house. This was the place. Almost sixty years ago, his grandfather was in this very spot. Well, probably not laying on the altar like he was, but in this basement and house, taking out bodies. All that blood. All that carnage. All the unfinished business and spiritual trauma compacted into one small space. He had been looking for a place like this since he was an undergrad, studying religion and psychology. If ever a place might be haunted or a gateway to the other side, surely this was it.

Now, here it was just about midnight. The curtain between the living and dead was at its thinnest. He could feel the electrical charge of energy flowing through him like he was standing in a puddle of water and holding a live wire.

Countless times before, he tried summoning with great expectations, only to be let down. When he started working on his doctoral degree, he was still hopeful he would be the man Houdini wanted to be in death—the one who proved beyond a shadow of a doubt there was a way to cross over. By the time he completed his thesis, he had memorized and attempted numerous incantations to open the portal between life and death. Some claimed to create a gateway to hell—a place in which he didn't believe. He often argued Sheol or Hades was a more proper name. That Hell was a Catholic invention to scare people out of being human and into being good sheep-like parishioners with constant donations and an everlasting battle between their mind and body—their desires and their repressive natures.

Sheol, on the other hand, was where souls went after their journeys on earth had ended. It was neither a good nor a bad place. Just a type of limbo until the next phase of their existence. Whatever that might be.

Richard took a cigarette from his shirt pocket and lit it. He watched the smoke billow up as he exhaled.

Life was simpler when he was younger—before he was jaded by a formal and experimental education. Now, he recited the words at Halloween parties and open mic nights at clubs just to see the reaction of the people who—while running around violating almost every law of their Bibles—still managed to become disturbed or frightened by his *show*. That's all it was. He no longer expected anything to happen. Just like tonight.

Richard took another drag off his cigarette and began lazily reciting an ancient text he memorized long ago. He spoke the words in the original tongue, calling on the Dark Lord, the King of the Abyss, Master of the Netherworld to rise. He called the four winds to blow open the veil between hell and earth so men could bask in the brilliance of the Prince of Death. To open the mouth of Death and Hell so the living and dead could reunite. On and on for a few more verses, praising the god of the underworld for his mercy, wisdom and beneficence.

By the time he finished, he had smoked his cigarette down to the butt. He sat up and hopped off the table, then extinguished the cigarette in his blood which had found its way to the gutter. It went out with a loud sizzle.

Just as every time before, nothing happened.

Richard dipped his finger in his blood on the table and drew a small pentagram in the puddle. He sucked the tip of his finger clean then wiped it on his jeans. He was just about to turn around to head upstairs when it happened.

One by one, from left to right, the candles behind the altar went out. They didn't move or sputter as if someone or something blew them out. It was more like an invisible candle snuffer came down on each in rapid succession. Pff. Pff. Pff. All eighteen flames killed in about three seconds.

* * *

Dead Town

A cloud of smoke hung in the dining room. The candlelight tinted it an odd blue-gold.

Hayden watched as the cloud drifted, swirls twisting and curling as everyone sat at the table with cigarettes in hand or mouth. He couldn't resist the temptation of the power pulsing through his entire body. He concentrated on a thin wisp that was slowly circling clockwise, passing him from left to right. He started picturing it reversing course and twirling the other way. It came to a halt and obeyed his desire, slowly rolling right to left in counterclockwise fashion. He *knew* this energy he felt was real. For a split second he doubted, wondering if possibly someone exhaled just right to create a coincidence. So, he tried his experiment again. This time, though, he focused on a dissipating section and imagined it coming back together. The smoke congealed, forming a small sphere the size of a baseball, just as he wanted. Then it broke apart and drifted away when he turned his attention to a more urgent matter. He had to piss.

Hayden stood and turned on his cellphone's flashlight.

"What're you doing?" Paul asked.

"I have to take a leak," he said. "Just wasn't planning on announcing it."

Hayden headed across the hall to the bathroom and set his phone on the sink so the room was lit well enough that he could aim at the toilet. He realized he didn't close the door, but didn't think it mattered since no one would be coming. They all knew he was going to be in there and if someone else had to go, surely they would just wait until he returned.

Shortly after he started urinating, the door creaked and quickly closed. He jumped and twisted, his forceful stream spattering the rim and floor before he pinched it off. He looked at the closed door. Had he just done that by thinking about it? The door was heavier than smoke, but he had made the smoke move with little effort.

He aimed and began peeing again.

Click. The door locked. On its own accord. He *wasn't* thinking about that.

A twinge of fear trickled into him. He loved the feeling of the magickal energy, but he was uncomfortable with it having its own free will.

He tried to hurry. As he finished, his cellphone died and he had to tuck and zip in the dark.

Hayden fumbled around on the sink for his phone. Once he found it, he mashed the power button, but it didn't do anything. He didn't expect it would. So, he stuffed it in his back pocket.

Hayden pictured where the door was and cautiously stepped toward it. He reached out and waved his hand until he brushed the cool knob with his knuckles. He gripped it and turned. The door didn't open.

Lightning flashed and lit the room. Hayden jumped away from the door. It was only a second, but he'd have sworn he saw the silhouette of a man's head creeping across the door in front of him.

Had to be a tree's shadow, he told himself.

Hayden dug into his pocket and fished out his lighter. When he stroked the wheel and the flame popped up, another shadow race down the wall and under the door.

Hayden glanced at his reflection in the mirror. The dim light made him look distorted, grotesque. Worse were the shadows slithering across the wall behind him.

He spun around and they vanished in the flame's light.

This was no longer fun. His heart raced.

He lunged at the door and grabbed the knob again, shaking it. He found the lock and twisted it. As soon as it clicked, he yanked the door open.

Several shadows drifted over the hallway walls. He leaned out, holding his lighter, and looked both ways. Darkness engulfed both ends of the hall. Within the blackness to his right, something blacker stirred. It was a large mass that seemed to ripple and roil.

Hayden looked left, toward the front of the house. Something bigger and badder lurked there. He could feel it in his body. Panic set in. He thought he saw a set of pointy teeth several inches long opening, waiting for him to come that way.

Hayden looked to his right again. Something like the shape of a man appeared in the darkness. It was just an outline, like a void in the blackness. He was unnaturally tall—seven feet maybe—and slender. Hayden thought he saw an arm moving, reaching toward him. And though it had no corporeal body, it cast a lengthy, bony shadow on the wall in front of him. It was definitely an arm and hand that stretched toward him like a gnarly branch and twigs from a lifeless tree.

"Help," Hayden screamed, ducking back into the bathroom.

The darkness swelled around him, its cold touch running over his back.

He whipped around so fast his lighter went out.

He hurried to light it again. The hot wheel burned his thumb.

"Help!"

As he got the lighter lit again, the shadows retreated and reformed behind him. The darkness once more embraced him.

He spun back toward the door. A light approached. The darkness outside the room receded.

"What's wrong?" Paul asked with a concerned voice as he stepped into the doorway holding the candelabra.

"Oh my God," Hayden said, huffing.

There were some quick, heavy footsteps. Chase and Kiara crowded behind Paul.

"Are you okay?" Chase asked.

Kiara stepped into the bathroom. "What's wrong?"

Hayden looked around the room.

"The shadows," Hayden said.

Most of the shadows were gone, but a few still remained. They moved with the slow deliberateness of a cat stalking its prey.

"There's something in the shadows," Hayden said.

Kiara, Paul and Chase exchanged glances. He could tell they had no idea what he was talking about.

"Don't you see them moving?"

Again, his friends swapped puzzled expressions.

Kiara took his hand. "Come on," she said. "Let's go back to the other room."

She tugged, but he remained in place. He didn't want to go out there. To the left was the fanged shadow and to the right, the thin man. What if they were still there?

Kiara tugged again. This time, Hayden stepped forward.

* * *

Kiara sat at the dining room table with her feet up under her, whishing she had a cup of spiked hot cocoa or something sweet and chocolaty to munch on. She was drunk and stoned—high on liquor, weed, *and* magick.

She glanced at Tanya, sitting in the chair beside her. At least she no longer had that shell-shocked look on her face she had when they first woke her by running into the room.

As soon as Paul started rolling a joint and said, "This is for medicinal purposes only," Tanya settled down and regained some of her usual composure.

"I ain't gonna lie," Ladarius said. "That kind of scared me when he did that."

Paul laughed at him. "What did you think was going to happen?"

Ladarius shrugged his shoulders. "Fuck, I don't know. But come on, man. You *know* that was freaky."

"Weird, yeah." Paul crumbled and shredded a bud into the folded paper on the table. "*Scary*? No."

"Not even a little?"

Kiara looked over at Tanya again. The conversation clearly left her puzzled.

"Hell no." Paul shook his head. "I don't believe in any of this shit you fools do." He licked the gum strip on the paper and closed it up.

"Help!"

Everyone looked at the door as Hayden screamed.

"What *now*?" Paul said.

"Help!" Desperation and fear filled his voice.

Paul jumped up, grabbed the candelabra, and trotted toward the doorway just slow enough the flames bent on the wicks, but didn't blow out. Kiara and Chase followed.

She couldn't make sense out of what Hayden was babbling about. Something about shadows moving.

She took his hand and tried to lead him out of the bathroom, back to the dining room, but he wouldn't move. Finally, she coaxed him and they headed down the hall, led by Paul. Kiara watched Hayden. He had his eyes shut so tight they wrinkled around the edges.

"Did someone slip him something?" she asked.

"Like what?" Paul asked

"I don't know. *Look* at him."

"You really think we'd do that?" Paul said.

She didn't. But she had never seen him act like this, either.

As they walked into the dining room, she asked Hayden, "Did you drop acid or take something?"

He opened his eyes. "Nothing."

Hayden's eyes settled on the table and opened wide. "Why are y'all fucking with me?"

"What are you talking about?" Chase said.

Kiara's eyes followed Hayden's to the Ouija board. The planchette was on it again. This time, it rested over the word *Hello*.

* * *

No one moved or said a word as Paul repeated his question.

"Which one of you assholes did that?'

Kenna's voice was rife with contempt. "What part of *no one moved from their seat* do you *not* understand?"

Chase eyeballed the people at the table as he stood with Hayden, Paul and Kiara. He believed Kenna that she hadn't seen anyone move, but someone *had* to, because even leaning over, most of them weren't even within arm's length of the board and pointer. She would have been the closest person with Ladarius and Tanya coming second and third. In truth, he couldn't picture any of them fucking with Hayden like that. Chase might have done it as a joke to mess with Paul, but he wasn't in the room.

The four of them took their seats. As they did, Tanya said, "I *told* you something wasn't right with this place."

Paul pulled out a cigarette and lit it by poking it into the flame of one of the candles in front of him. "Yeah. Shit just up and moves on its own and no one notices." He exhaled and pushed the candelabra toward the center of the table. "Or maybe there's something wrong with *y'all* for not seeing it."

Hayden twisted in his seat. Looked over his right shoulder. Then his left. He leaned forward, grabbed the board and straightened it. Turned his attention to Kiara. "Help me?" he asked.

Hayden's eyes rocketed around the room for a couple seconds, not settling on anything. He looked like a paranoid schizophrenic in a room full of men dressed in black and carrying an assortment of weapons.

"We need to make it say goodbye," he told Kiara. *"For real* this time."

She nodded.

"Anyone else want to help?" Hayden asked.

Chase thought about volunteering, but he didn't believe in Ouija boards and such, so his disbelief might affect the board. Then he laughed at himself for not wanting his lack of belief to change the outcome of something in which he didn't believe. That was like a person saying they don't believe in Santa so they won't say Merry Christmas because it might make Santa come down his chimney later that night.

As Kiara and Hayden rested their fingers on the pointer, Chase stood and got closer. "What do I do?" he said, hoping at least one more person helping Hayden might set him at ease.

"Just barely touch it with your fingertips." Kiara said.

"Don't push down or in any direction," Hayden added. "Hello," He said to the board.

A small, bright light appeared in the front room, catching Chase's attention through the door. It moved closer as the pointer slowly glided toward the center of the board. It moved back to *Hello* as Richard entered the room.

"What the hell happened to you?" Tanya asked, pointing at his bloody left arm.

"You need to say goodbye," Hayden said.

The pointer started moving across the board to the goodbye symbol, then took a turn and headed for the center. Chase knew *he* wasn't pushing it. He was barely touching it, trying to maintain as little contact as possible to be certain he didn't subconsciously move it. He looked at Kiara's and Hayden's slightly arched, relaxed fingers. His gaze travelled up their hands to their wrists and forearms as the pointer began making a figure-8. At first it was slow and small, but then it grew in size and speed with each completion until it was almost running from the top to the bottom of the board. The movement was so swift, he could barely keep his fingers on the wooden pointer.

"We're done," Hayden said. "You need to say goodbye."

167

Dead Town

The pointer slowed and moved to the *J*.

"*Command* it to say goodbye," Richard said, walking over to them.

"Say goodbye *now*," Hayden said.

The pointer continued to slip around the board. *O-I*.

Then nothing for a couple seconds. It just sat on the *I*.

Richard turned off his phone's light and placed his hands on the pointer near Kiara's after she repositioned them to make room for him.

"Go," Hayden said. "*Now!*"

N-U-S.

"Joy noose?" Ladarius said with a grin. "Must be a damn redneck or something. Did David Duke die?"

Chase didn't know what to think. He didn't believe in ghosts. If there *were* such things, why would they need a stupid board to spell out stuff? If they could write, why not just pick up a pen and paper? Still, it didn't appear like any one of them was manipulating the thing. If it shot straight to *Goodbye*, he might be inclined to believe Hayden was pretending just to make himself look in control. Or Kiara did it to comfort Hayden. But that didn't happen.

Once more, the pointer took on a life of its own, circling the board in a figure-8.

"It's angry," Richard said.

"Leave, right now, dammit!" Hayden said.

Chase peeked up at Richard, wondering how he could possibly know this thing was *angry*.

The pointer rocketed down to the *Goodbye* and fell off the board.

Hayden grabbed it and tossed it on the floor near the kitchen door, far away from the table and board.

Everyone sat motionless and silent, save Hayden. His eyes darted around the room non-stop. He glanced over his shoulders, twisted in his seat, peered at the corners.

"I think it's gone," Kiara said.

"*We* should be gone," Tanya said. "The storm seems to have died down."

She was right. Water dripped from the roof into an unseen puddle outside the window, but it didn't sound like it was still beating down on the roof like it had been. Chase wasn't paying attention, but now that he thought about it, he didn't remember seeing lightning or hearing any thunder since they returned to the dining room.

Hayden stood. "I *can't* leave," he said as he gathered a couple boxes of utility candles.

"*What*?" Tanya said.

"What're you doing, sweetie?" Kiara asked, her voice gentle as a mother's trying to console a sick child.

"Going upstairs."

"*Why*?" Paul asked.

"Because I need to fucking rest." The way he snapped at Paul made it sound as if it were axiomatic and Paul should have known better than to ask such a stupid question.

Paul almost matched Hayden's tone. Almost, but not quite. "I meant why can't you leave?"

The abrasiveness fell from Hayden's voice. "You see how *dark* it is out there?"

Paul looked confused. "We have our phones. This is probably going to be our best chance to get out."

"I can't. Mine's dead. And it's dark."

"No one else's is," Paul said.

Tanya set her phone on the table. "Here. You can have mine."

Hayden looked at her then down at his feet like a scolded child. And like a child, his voice was weak. "I *can't*. That won't work. But y'all can go."

"I'm not leaving you here by yourself," Kiara said.

Chase heard the conversation. He understood the words. And yet he still found himself lost by it all.

"We'll have seven flashlights out there," Kenna said. "We'll stick together and to the road."

"That's not enough."

"Enough for *what*?" Paul asked. "We can easily see with that much light."

Hayden's eyes remained trained on the floor. "But it isn't enough to stop the shadow beasts."

* * *

Dead Town

"The *what*?" Ladarius asked, thinking he must have misheard Hayden.

"If you're still here, I'll see you in the morning," Hayden said to the group. He looked around the room as if expecting a lion to jump out of nowhere and pounce on him. His wild eyes reminded Ladarius of his oldest brother's friend Quintel, after he came back from his third or fourth tour in Afghanistan and shortly before he put a .45 in his mouth.

Hayden turned to leave, but turned back. His hands shook. His voice shook almost as much. "Will one or two of you walk with me?"

Ladarius scanned the faces of the others to see if they were as confused as he was. Hayden seemed like a pretty normal guy up until a few minutes ago. Now, he was like a whimpering child slowly walking to his dad's room where the old man had the belt ready for him.

"I'll go," Kiara said.

As she stood up, Paul stood, too. "Come on."

Paul grabbed the candelabra and Kiara pulled out her phone, turning on the light. They left the room with Paul leading and Hayden in the middle.

When they were out of earshot, Ladarius asked, "What the fuck is he talking about, shadow beasts?"

"Did one of you give him something?" Chase asked.

Everyone shook their head no or remained motionless.

"Do *you* know what's going on?" Ladarius asked Chase.

"He thinks there's someone or something in the shadows, shadow beasts, trying to kill him."

"Well, *that's* weird," Kenna said.

An uncomfortable silence descended on the room like a blanket snuffing out a small fire. Everyone just kind of sat there, smoking their cigarettes and sipping their drinks, but not speaking or even looking at one another.

A few minutes later, Paul returned. "Kiara's going to stay with him a while."

Ladarius knew this was a bad idea. He told them he didn't want to come. He wasn't scared—not like Hayden—but he didn't feel the party vibe anymore. That was for sure. He just wanted to leave. He may not know Hayden very well, but there was no way in hell he could leave the guy behind in this state. Especially not just him and Kiara.

Outside, the rain began again. It didn't have the same intensity as before and there was no lightning and thunder at the moment, but it was coming down hard.

"What now?" he asked.

"I'm not leaving them here alone," Chase said. "Y'all can leave if you want to. I'll go upstairs and crash in one of the rooms and bring him back in the morning."

"I'm staying," Kenna said, glancing at Chase.

Tanya's eyes wandered from face to face.

"There's three rooms up there," Paul started. "Four if you count the porn room. That means plenty of beds for everyone if we all double up."

Ladarius shook his head. "I'll sleep on the sofa. I ain't getting on that ratchet bed."

"We should all stick close," Kenna said.

"I'll sleep on the other sofa," Richard said.

Everyone, except Tanya, looked content with the plan to remain until morning and head out at first light.

CHAPTER 13

After Paul left, Kiara plopped down on the bed and Hayden settled on the floor.

"Don't turn off your light yet," he told her.

He opened the boxes of candles and poured them out before him. He lit one, let some wax drip on the hardwood floor and planted the candle in it. Then he repeated the step, over and over, slowly turning his body until he had made a large circle of candles around himself.

"What are you doing?" she asked.

"Making a circle of light the shadows can't penetrate."

"Oh. Okay," she said, as if that made perfect sense.

When he finished planting the last candle, he said, "You can save your battery now." She turned off her phone and he asked in a gentle voice, "Can I have a pillow?"

Kiara stood and passed him one above the flames that cast a golden glow over him.

The circle was about five-feet across. It wasn't large enough for him to stretch out in, but he had enough room to curl up in a ball and relax. The small flames kept him well-lit. He was right. There were no shadows touching him. A wall of light protected him from whatever he thought was after him.

Kiara gazed around the room at the bulky blocks and shapes the shadows made. The corners of the room, especially the one on the opposite side of the bed by her head, were near black. She watched the shadows dance with each flicker of the candles. For a moment, she understood what he was so afraid of. They looked almost alive. Scary. She wondered if he might be right. If something *did* live in the shadows. Something awful that had come for them.

* * *

Paul and Tanya took the first room on the right as Chase and Kenna continued back to Thornton's room. Paul had wanted that room, because the bed looked a little more comfortable and the photos and such made it feel more "lived-in," but Tanya insisted on being close to the stairs. She didn't even *want* to see the master bedroom or the porn room.

Paul rolled a quick joint then lit it.

As the two of them sat on the bed smoking, Tanya said, "I hope whatever it was is gone now."

He had no idea what she was talking about. And at the moment, he didn't care. Besides being drunk and stoned, all this stupidity wore him out. Richard, Hayden, her—like three little kids he had to babysit all damn night. This was supposed to be a fun hike in the woods. An adventure, like Huck Finn and Tom Sawyer looking for a cave full of treasure. But between the storm, which was spinning up again, and those three babies running from Injun Joe and his ghost all night, it was more like participating in a triathlon without training first.

Tanya tried again to spark a conversation. "Who do you think was here?"

The small flames from the candelabra on the dresser melded together and glinted off her blue eyes as a single pinpoint of light just outside her large pupils.

Not wanting to be drawn in, he said, "Us."

"Us, what?"

"*Us*. We're the only ones here."

"*Someone* was making the Ouija board move." Legs hanging off the bed, she lay back. "Or some*thing*."

"Yeah. Hayden. And the *things* are called hands. He was pushing it."

Paul lit a cigarette. He was okay with flicking the small bit of ash from the joint on the floor and crushing out the roach on the bottom of his shoe, but now he wished he had an ashtray. Somehow, it just seemed wrong to flick cigarette ashes everywhere. Even if it wasn't his or anyone else's house.

"I'll be back in a second," he told her.

"Where you going?"

Dead Town

He took a drag, cupped his hand and ashed in his palm. He rubbed it into his jeans on his thigh. "To get an ashtray," he said. "Then I'm going to check on them." He jerked his head toward the door, indicating Hayden and Kiara. "You good?"

"I'm stoned," she said. She scooted up the bed until her head was on the pillow then rolled onto her side to face him. "But I won't be *good* until we're out of here."

He stood up. "Back in a sec."

Paul walked out and closed the door behind him. He stood in the blackness for a second before pulling his cellphone out of his pocket for some light.

He crossed the hall and rapped gently on the closed door before cracking it open.

An eerie orange-gold glow flowed from the room.

"Hey," he whispered.

"Come on in," Kiara said in a quiet voice.

Paul stepped in and looked at the circle of candles on the floor. Hayden was curled in a fetal position in the middle of them. His eyes were closed.

"His fortress of light to keep the shadow beasts away," Kiara explained with an awkward smile.

The ivory skin of her arms seemed to shine as they reflected the candlelight. She was on her back with her legs crossed at the ankles, which made her luscious hips look more appealing. She had the pillow running longways behind her, so her head and shoulders were propped up against the headboard. Her long, silky brown hair cascaded down behind her back and flowed out from under her shoulders and arms. A couple wide strands streamed down over her collarbones and came together like two shiny rivers between her breasts. Her shirt clung tightly to her chest and rested against her flat stomach.

"I'm going downstairs to grab an ashtray. You need anything?"

When she opened her mouth to speak, he hoped she would say she was coming with him. "An ashtray would be nice," she said. "And a glass of bourbon." Kiara's inviting lips parted into a big, beautiful smile. "*On the rocks*, if you can swing it, Major Guns." She glanced at his arms, then back at him. "That's what I'm going to call you from

174

now on. *Major Guns*." She flexed her right biceps to explain the moniker.

"Okay, Captain Hotshit." He grinned.

With the middle finger of her right hand, Kiara pointed at her left shoulder and tapped it a couple times. "That's *Colonel* Hotshit. Don't you see the bird? I outrank you and always will."

"Yes, ma'am. My apologies."

They both giggled. It felt good to have a laugh tonight. It seemed like it had been so long since the last time.

"I'll be back," he said. He retreated from the room and closed the door gently behind him until he heard it click.

Paul made his way down the stairs, walking as quietly as possible so as not to disturb anyone. He glanced at the front door and wondered if the storm had shut it, before he wheeled around and headed down the hall, looking at the secret passage. He couldn't agree with Tanya that the place had bad mojo or Hayden that there were shadows trying to kill him, but it was definitely a strange place. Old Thornton could fly his freak flag with the best of them today.

He crushed out his cigarette in one of the pedestal ashtrays in the library, then picked up another one that was empty. It was heavier than he expected. He guessed the base was real bronze instead of some Chinese crap aluminum painted to look expensive. He wouldn't be able to carry two and a glass of bourbon for Kiara, so he just took the one and headed for the dining room. He could use a glass if he smoked again. He wasn't planning on staying up much later anyway.

"Fucking assholes," he said when he stepped up to the table. The pointer was back on the board and pointing at *Hello* again. He took it off and tossed it in the direction Hayden had earlier.

After filling a large glass with bourbon, he nestled it into another glass. He tucked his cellphone into the waistband of his jeans so the light looked like it shone from his belly, picked up the items, and headed for the stairs.

Paul decided to pass through the barroom and living room so he could check on the others. As he walked in, Ladarius was sacked out on one of the sofas but Richard wasn't there.

Dead Town

"Stupid fucker," he said in a whisper so quiet he almost couldn't hear himself. He knew exactly where the dumbass was. Back in the basement.

It's on him if he kills himself, he thought. *Would serve him right.*

Paul walked up the stairs with a little difficulty, trying to keep the phone from sliding down into his drawers. When he got to Kiara's door, he set the ashtray down and knocked then opened it. He maneuvered his way around Hayden's castle of light and placed the ashtray next to the bed.

"Your ashtray, Colonel Hotshit."

"Well done, Major Guns," she said with a smile as she patted the bed beside her. "I'll make sure you get a good reward for your meritorious service."

Paul grinned.

"*And* your drink."

She patted the bed again. "Sit. Smoke one with me."

He looked at the open door. It wasn't like anything was going to happen.

He sat beside her and pulled out a cigarette.

* * *

Tanya didn't know how long she had been asleep. It couldn't have been too long, because Paul had yet to return with an ashtray. She wished he was there with her. She had to pee something fierce, but she didn't want to go alone. She knew it was just one door over, because they had told her when they came up, but that still seemed like a long way to walk alone in this house.

She contemplated only taking a single candle from the candelabra so Paul had some light when he returned. That was silly. He had his phone. If he came back while she was peeing, he would know she had it. He'd see the glow emanating from the bathroom door she had already resolved to leave open. She didn't give a dang who saw her on the pot.

She grabbed the candelabra and opened the door. She poked her head out and looked both ways, hoping to see Paul coming back up the stairs. All she saw was darkness and the two closed doors across the hallway—Kiara's and Chase's.

Assured it was safe, she padded to the bathroom in short quick steps. She set the candles on the vanity, yanked her pants down and squatted. The stream made a loud tinkling sound as it hit the dry porcelain bowl. Above that, she heard something else. She tried to stop urinating, but couldn't. She had been holding it too long.

She leaned her ear toward the door. She couldn't make out any words, just the murmur of voices trying to remain quiet.

Finally, her stream slowed to a trickle. Then a few drops. She squeezed out the excess, raised up a little and snatched a hand towel that hung from a bar on the front of one of the vanity cabinet doors. She wiped and stood. Tanya tossed the towel in the sink, then pulled up her pants and fastened them. Someone giggled down the hall. A girl. A guy said something to her in a hushed tone and she giggled again.

Tanya peered down the hall to the right. The last door on that side was open. A yellow light poured out of the room and fell in a large bent rectangle across the floor and up the wall and door where Chase and Kenna were supposed to be sleeping.

Tanya left the candles on the vanity and tiptoed down to the door. If, for some reason Chase and Kenna had decided to sleep in there, she didn't want to disturb them. If Paul was in there with Kiara, she wanted to listen in and see what the hell was going on.

She paused just outside the door.

"Relax," Paul said quietly.

"Stop," Kiara said. Her voice, light and airy, lacked conviction.

"Come on."

"Quit." She giggled.

"She'll never find out."

Tanya's face and ears burned. She was suddenly very aware of herself. She was holding her breath. Her hands, clenched in tight fists, balled tighter when she heard them kissing.

"Hell yes, I'll find out," Tanya said, stomping into the room.

Paul whipped around, still holding Kiara in his arms. His eyes were wide. Panic painted his face.

Kiara looked down at the floor. "I'm sorry, sweetie," she said. "I told him not to."

Dead Town

Tanya tromped over without thinking and took a swing at Paul. He rocked back, narrowly escaping the blow. She swung again with the other hand and, missing, toppled over onto them.

Kiara jumped from the bed.

"Stop," Paul said. "Just quit."

"You fucking asshole. How could you do this to me?"

"We were just having some fun," he said. "Stop being such a bitch."

She balled her fist and kicked at him.

Paul grabbed her and flipped her onto her back. He straddled her waist and pinned her hands above her head.

"Get her pants off," Paul said.

She couldn't see Kiara, but felt her pants loosen as Kiara unbuttoned and unzipped them. As Tanya kicked, Kiara grabbed the hems near her ankles and tugged them, working them off her.

Tanya tried to scream, but Paul leaned down and buried his shoulder against her mouth. He transferred one of her hands to his other. While gripping both her hands in one hand, he snatched the pillow out from under her hand and placed it over her face.

He must have leaned down on it after separating her hands again, because it bore down on her, drowning out her voice, suffocating her.

"Stop! What are you doing?" she screamed.

Kiara grabbed her panties along each hip and ripped them down past her knees and over her feet.

Tanya kicked and bucked, but couldn't break free. She sucked at the pillow for air. Her cries for help died in the white cotton and down.

Paul shifted his weight and shimmied toward her hips. He let go of her left wrist and pressed down harder on the pillow. It felt like he was using his free hand to smother her. She swung and swatted at him. When she hit his neck, she did her best to claw at his flesh. She took another swipe, hoping to gouge his eyes out.

"The shirt," Paul said, laughing.

Oh my God, Tanya thought. *Why's he doing this?*

Kiara grabbed the hem of her T-shirt and pulled it up toward her face.

This has *to be a dream*, she thought. *Wake up. Wake up!*

Kiara fought with her until she managed to get Tanya's arm out of the shirt.

Wake up! Her eyes were open, but the pillow on her face blocked out all light.

"Get *off* me!"

"Shut the fuck up," Paul said. He punched the pillow. Stars filled the blackness. He punched her again. More bursts of silver light.

This was no dream. She was awake. She felt the pain. Terror ripped through her body. Her heart palpitated. She wondered if she would suffocate or have a heart attack first. There was no way she was surviving this.

Paul caught Tanya's loose wrist then set the other free. Kiara worked the shirt up and wrestled her arm out of it. Though she flailed and swatted at him, he quickly recaptured it and pinned it back down.

Something abrasive ran against her wrist. It wrapped and tightened. She tugged and jerked when Paul let go of that arm, but she couldn't move more than a couple inches. She was tied to the bed. Tanya fought, trying to pull her other arm free when she felt the rope encircle it, but Paul pressed down on her and held her forearm in both hands as the knot cinched.

Paul let go of her and rolled off.

Tanya screamed again. "Stop! Why are you doing this?"

Paul's strong hands grabbed her right ankle and extended her leg. Kiara quickly tied it to the bed.

Tanya shook her head back and forth until the pillow fell from her face. Paul grabbed her other leg and pulled.

"Don't!" Tanya pleaded.

Kiara gave her a lustful grin as she tied the rope.

Tanya lay there—spread eagle—with just a bra on and her T-shirt ringing her neck.

"Why are you doing this?"

Paul looked at her like he didn't understand the question. "Why? Because sometimes you are such an annoying little cunt. *That's* why."

Paul reached under the bed and pulled up a knife. It glistened in the light.

Tanya's breathing became labored. She huffed and gasped for air. He was going to kill her right here.

179

Dead Town

Paul drew a finger up to his lips. "Shh," he said. Then he walked over to the right side of the bed and cut her bra strap.

"Please."

He leaned over and cut the other. He slid the cold blade up between her sternum and bra, then jerked the knife. The thin fabric snapped, falling to the sides, off her breasts.

"Chase! Kenna! *Heeeelp!*"

"I told you to join us."

* * *

Chase and Kenna sat on the edge of the tub in the master bathroom smoking a cigarette and flicking their ashes in the dry toilet. The redneck candleholder they brought with them from downstairs and set on the vanity had three tapered red candles burning.

Chase studied Kenna in the warm light. She was beautiful. Everything about her from her long dark hair, to the way her olive skin glowed just then, to her white, white teeth flashing from beneath her wonderful lips as she spoke. For years, he wanted her. Now, he was alone with her and all he could think to say was, "What you gonna do tomorrow?"

He wanted to bitch slap himself. *Really?* That was the best he could come up with?

"Whatever you're doing."

Maybe it wasn't such a bad question after all.

"I promised my uncle I would come to his farm and help him pick up horse shit," he joked.

"Sounds like fun. What time are we going?"

He bumped her shoulder with his. "You flirting with me?"

He smiled. She smiled back.

She bumped his shoulder. "Would it make a difference if I was?"

Fuck it.

Chase leaned into her. She leaned. His lips touched her soft lips. Her mouth parted and his tongue slipped in.

The nerves in his stomach tingled.

He rested his hand on her knee.

She placed her hand on his. In the process, she crushed the cigarette he had protruding from between his fingers, sending a shower of hot embers down on the back of his knuckles.

"Shit!" Kenna said, jerking back not only her hand, but her head. "Sorry."

Chase brushed the embers off quickly. "No worries."

He crushed his cigarette out on the inside rim of the toilet and set the dead butt on the edge of the tub on the other side of him. He slipped Kiara's cigarette out from between her fingers and mashed it out, too.

"Come on," he said, bobbing his head toward the bedroom.

He stood and took her hand, helping her stand. After he grabbed the redneck candleholder, she walked out with her arm trailing behind her, still gripping his hand. Kenna crawled onto the bed as he set the candles down on the dresser. Then he lowered himself onto the bed, which was surprisingly comfortable.

Safe from any chance of more cigarette burns, he threw his arm over her and kissed her again. After a couple minutes, she came up for air.

"You know how long I've been wanting to do this?" she asked.

He shook his head and smiled. "Probably not as long as I have."

"Don't bet on it." She moved forward and kissed him again.

They had been making out a while—long enough for his hand to find its way over her shirt to her small breast. He cupped it. Caressed it. Felt her nipple grow hard against the fabrics of her bra and T-shirt.

Kenna moaned in his mouth. Her hand drew a slow line down his chest to his abs. Then lower.

"Chase! Kenna! *Heeeelp!*"

They broke apart and looked at each other.

"Tanya!" he said.

Chase leapt off the bed, yanked the door open and looked in the hallway.

* * *

Paul sat on the bed talking to Kiara about various inconsequential things—just trying to get to know her. She was a cool chick with a beautiful smile and a great body. She was the kind of girl he could take home. Not that Tanya wasn't. Tanya was more the type you took home and showed off, but you didn't marry. *Someone* would. But not him.

Kiara was the full package. She had that wholesome look about her that said she'd be a great mother when the kids were awake and a fucking devil in the bedroom after they went to sleep.

He was on his second cigarette and sipping her bourbon when he heard something. He looked at the door. It was closed. He furrowed his eyebrows.

"I'd swear that door was open a few minutes ago."

Kiara glanced over. "It was. Old houses and draughts."

Something bumped again down the hall. He looked at Kiara to see if she heard it. The expression on her face said she did.

Paul was about to stand up and check it out when it hit him. "Holy shit," he said. "I think Chase is finally bagging Kenna." He laughed and Kiara laughed with him.

Paul relaxed back onto the bed, thinking. *It's about time*.

"Chase! Kenna! *Heeeelp!*"

Paul jumped over Hayden and bolted out of the room.

* * *

As soon as he plopped down on the sofa, Ladarius started snoring.

Richard tried to sleep, but between the occasional thunder booms and the constant roar flowing from Ladarius's mouth, that was not going to happen. Instead, Richard lay there staring at the ceiling.

Richard contemplated the candles in the basement. He never felt a draught down there, yet those eighteen candles went out without so much as a sputter of drift. As he thought about this, he realized all the other candles were still burning. He doubted anything would become of it, but what if it did? What if, while they slept, those flames somehow set the house ablaze? Not only would the house be lost forever, but they could all burn up in the fire.

Richard felt the energy surging within him. Yes, ley lines intersected here, but it was more than that. It was as if Thornton's consecration of the land and home to Satan's care added to the natural power residing in this spot.

Thoughts of owning the house and using it as a place for study and work rekindled his youthful desire to tap into the unknown—to harness the ability to communicate with the dead and to work *real* magick— not the sleight-of-hand illusionist bullshit David Blaine and David Copperfield were known for.

Richard rose from the sofa, grabbed the candelabra and headed for the basement. Ladarius was asleep, he wouldn't miss the light.

He walked down the stairs and realized he wouldn't need the light he brought. The others were all still burning, save those behind the altar. The air down there bordered on cold—much cooler than he remembered. But he was also drunker at the time. He was still drunk, but sobering up a bit. His legs were definitely more stable now.

Richard sat on one of the front pews and stared at the altar. He wondered what it was like all those years ago when Thornton was here, leading their services. He conjured images in his mind of the man up front, offering sacrifices to the Lord of Light and Knowledge. His eyes drifted to the walls. He hadn't noticed before, but there were large stains on them. Many of the splotches so large and soaked in, they looked like they belonged. But there were patches of wall that showed the true color. It was a difference between cherry and garnet. Only with careful consideration would anyone perceive the various shades.

Richard got up and walked to the pentagram on the floor. He stood in the middle. It was like standing on one of those magic-fingers beds in hotels he stayed at as a kid with his parents while on vacation. Only he didn't have to drop in any quarters. He simply stood and felt the vibration of power seep into his body, rising from his soles to his scalp.

He stared at the floor for a moment, then at the candles behind the altar. Perhaps their extinguishment was a coincidence.

"Burn, damn it!" he said.

The candles obeyed and sprang to life with black flames that shed a cold, but brilliant silvery white light strong enough to illuminate the entire basement and drown out the other candles. Richard marveled as he slowly spun and took in the scene. There wasn't a shadow anywhere, not even in the spaces between the tresses overhead where they would naturally exist.

His heart pounded in his chest with both joy and fear. *This* was what he had been searching for all his life. His earlier incantation worked and opened the portal between life and death, between man and spirit. This was proof Azazel, the keeper of the black flame, had crossed at his command.

Richard stood in awe, basking in the light of the angel who fell for giving men knowledge and power.

He opened his mouth to speak then stopped himself. Did he dare command Azazel to stand before him and show his true form?

The thought excited and terrified him. The confluence of mixed emotions demanded he think twice about it. Maybe even three times. The house was here. He could always return. He knew what to say.

Richard walked back to the pews. Even beneath and behind them, there wasn't the slightest hint of a shadow. He lay down on the hard, wooden bench and closed his eyes.

As if in surround sound, he heard something release a deep breath.

He opened his eyes again. There was no one there but him.

Then came the noise again. It was so pervasive it was as if it were resounding inside his head.

Richard glanced around the room once more. His eyes settled on the altar.

The first black flame on the far left died. A few seconds later, the second went out without a sound or movement. Then the third. Every few seconds, the next one died, until finally, the last was gone. The room dimmed down to the glow it had before the black flames.

Richard sat up. He was about to command the black flames to rise again, but something unexpected happened. The flame closest to the altar on the left faded. Then the candle closest on the right went out. Alternating back and forth from left to right, every few seconds another flame died.

After a while, Richard was sitting on the pew in the shallow light of the candelabra he had brought. The first of its flames died. Then the next. Within a minute or so, Richard was sitting in the dark, his heart pounding against his chest, his body unwilling to move though every molecule of his being was screaming for it to get up and run.

The unseen thing breathed again—even closer if that was possible.

CHAPTER 14

Tanya had heard of night terrors, but never experienced one. Sure, she had nightmares like everyone else, but this one, this one went far beyond any of those. She *knew* she was dreaming when Paul said he told her to "join us." That was what the man with the piercing eyes said when she passed out earlier.

Wake up, Tanya Danielle Hicks. Wake up!

Her mind raced in a dozen different directions at the same time, most trying to figure out a way to rip herself from this wretched dream. Perhaps she could convince her hand to pinch herself. If she peed the bed she might wake up. But one path her mind took was completely out of left field.

Dari had said, "Joy noose."

She laughed with him when he made the quip about David Duke. But that *wasn't* what the board spelled. She saw all the letters again, together in her head. J-O-I-N-U-S. *Join us.*

Tanya peeked up at Paul. It wasn't him.

The man with the piercing near-white eyes stood beside the bed, towering over her, grinning down at her.

She cast a quick glance to the left side of the bed. Kiara was no longer there. Instead, there was a woman with a heavy layer of bright red lipstick and long, wavy black hair flowing down over her shoulders and ending at her bare breasts, which were neither large nor small. Her bright pink nipples stood erect, pointing at a slight upward angle. The woman ran one hand through a massive bush of dark pubic hair that would have rivaled any Seventies porn star. She wore only a pair of bright red heels that matched her mouth.

The man turned and grabbed a wooden rod from the wall behind him.

He wheeled back around and tapped the long stick against his left palm.

Dead Town

"A good servant does what she's told," he said with a stern look on his face.

He raised the stick over her abdomen and snapped it downward. She winced, anticipating the blow, but he stopped just shy of her flesh. With the top of the cool rod he lightly touched her belly then dragged it up toward her breasts.

The man traced the bottom curve of her right boob around to her side, lifted the stick and tapped her nipple with it several times. She gained no gratification from it, but felt her nipple stiffen from the touch.

"Say, 'yes, master,'" he told her.

Tanya glared at him.

Whack! He brought the stick down just above her belly button with a motion so quick she didn't have time to anticipate the blow and tighten her muscles.

Tanya yelped.

"Yes, master," he repeated.

Whack! Whack!

Even flexing her abs did nothing to lessen the sting.

Tanya's gaze shot to the naked woman who had spread her legs slightly and began fingering herself. Her eyes were half-shut, her mouth half-open. Lust covered her face. She moaned quietly.

Whack!

Tanya screamed.

She had never experienced such pain in a dream.

"Perhaps another instrument is required to teach you who your master is."

* * *

Chase ran into the room across the hall. He would swear that's where Tanya's screams had come from. The room was pitch black, but someone or something was on the bed breathing heavily.

He reached for his phone in his pocket, but he had left it on the dresser.

"Tanya?" he said.

No answer.

Kenna ran into the room, bumping into him and knocking him forward. A fraction of a second later, Paul came in. He flipped on his light.

"What the *fuck*?" Chase said, looking at Paul.

Paul shone the light on Tanya's naked body. "I didn't do it."

"What, she tied both hands herself?"

Paul panned the room with his light. Other than the four of them, there was no one there.

"I'm telling you, *I* didn't put her there."

Tanya screamed. A welt formed across her midsection. Then a couple more.

Kiara came into the room carrying the candelabra. She gasped when she saw Tanya.

Tanya's back arched. She screamed, "God, please!" Another large red ridge formed across her right thigh.

* * *

The man brought the stick down across the top of her thigh.

Tanya huffed for breath. Her stomach ached. Her heart pounded within her chest.

She jerked at the ropes holding her hands and feet to the bed.

Paul, Chase and Kenna were standing just inside the doorway looking at her. Why weren't they stopping the man with the stick?

"Paul, Please!"

The man hung the stick on the wall and grabbed a riding crop as the woman walked to the dresser at the foot of the bed. She bent over and her round naked ass bobbed in the air. She stood and turned. Within her hands she had a long object.

Snap! The riding crop came down across both breasts at once.

Her nipples burned.

"Owwww!" She looked at the man and begged, "Please, no."

Thwack! He hit her across her right hip, the end of the crop landing at the bottom of the thin line of trimmed pubic hair she had running up from between her legs.

"NOOO!" she screamed. "Oh, God!"

The woman jammed the object between her legs and penetrated her mercilessly.

Dead Town

Tanya felt the skin inside her ripping as it entered. Over and over the woman pulled and pushed, ramming it in deeper and deeper until it bottomed out.

Pain shot from her groin to her throat.

"I am your master and god," the man said. "Say it."

* * *

Kenna watched in horror. Stripes appeared across Tanya's midsection as if an unseen switch was whipping the hell out of her. Each time a new one appeared, Tanya let out an ear-busting squeal.

Tanya whimpered and begged and pleaded for help.

"Get her hand," Chase said as he rushed to her right side.

Paul hurried to the left.

Both boys worked furiously on the tightly knotted ropes.

Tanya's mouth bust open and blood spattered the boys' shirts and faces.

Kenna moved to Tanya's right foot. It was purple. Veins poked out everywhere. She tried to untie the first knot in the thick rope. She glanced up at Tanya's hands. Like her feet, the circulation had been cut off. They, too, were purple and getting darker.

Blood gushed from Tanya's vagina as if she was having the world's most horrible period ever, but the way the flesh of her lips puckered in and came out made it look more like the Invisible Man was on her vengeance-fucking her.

The lips relaxed. Kenna was glad for that until she saw Tanya's anus open wide, the upper edge ripping toward the bottom of her vagina.

Kenna had never heard a human or animal make a sound like Tanya did that instant.

* * *

Finally, they moved. Chase ran around to her right hand as Paul moved to the other.

The man leaned against the bed near her waist and peered down at her, a sadistic smile etched across his face.

"They can't save you," he said. "Now, say, 'yes, master.'"

He reared his arm back and swung it full-force like Serena Williams returning a serve. The leather tab at the end of the crop caught her cheek and the left corner of her mouth. Her lip split open. Blood coated tongue, leaving a metallic taste in her mouth.

The woman continued thrusting the object into her vagina. It was no longer dry down there. She couldn't see it, but she could feel the blood running down her ass and splatting against the insides of her thighs.

The woman stopped, thank God.

"YYYEEEOOOOWWWWWW!!!"

The object went straight up her ass, ripping the skin and crushing her guts.

"Yes, master! Yes, master!"

The woman yanked it all the way out and slammed it back in with tremendous force and speed.

Everything went black.

* * *

Kiara stood mortified, holding the candles and watching the others work as blood flowed from Tanya's mouth, crotch and ass.

"Yes, master. Yes, master," Tanya screamed.

More blood shot out her ass as it opened wide.

Then Tanya fell silent. Her body went limp.

Kiara panicked. A knot formed in her throat.

"Is she . . . *dead*?" she asked.

A red line appeared just under Tanya's breast. Her ass opened and puckered shut several times before another welt rose just below the last. Another another another. Tanya's body didn't react.

"Tanya!" Paul said.

"What the fuck, Paul?" Chase screamed, terror cracking his voice.

Paul didn't answer or even look up. He untied the last knot in the rope, slung her hand over her belly, and moved down to her foot.

Dead Town

Chase finally finished untying the knots on her right hand. He tossed the rope to the floor and laid her hand over the other.

Kiara had never felt so helpless in her life.

Pinpoints of blood seeped up through some of the marks on Tanya's skin.

"Move," Chase told Kenna as he yanked the rope from her hands and started undoing it.

Tanya's ass closed.

Kiara watched Tanya's body. Nothing happened. No new lines across her skin. No more movement between her legs. She was still and silent. Then her ribcage expanded a little. She was breathing. She was *alive*.

Paul finished with his rope and moved up by Tanya's head.

"Tanya . . . Tanya!" He patted the right side of her face lightly.

Her eyes slowly opened, confusion filling them as she looked around the room.

Kiara picked up Tanya's underwear and jeans while Paul and Chase tried to help her sit. Tanya grimaced.

"Let's get her out of here," Paul said, placing his arms under her back and knees.

Chase jerked his head toward the door. "Put her in our room. There's a stack of towels in the bathroom."

Paul carried Tanya out and the others followed.

* * *

Relief filled Tanya when Paul placed his arms under her. There was always something comforting about his embrace. And now, not only was she in his arms again, but she knew he wasn't the one who tied her to the bed. She had felt so betrayed at first—by both of them.

She leaned over and spit a mouthful of blood to the floor as Paul picked her up.

"Please tell me you killed him," she said.

"Who?"

Paul carried her through the door and across the hall to the master bedroom, which was dimly lit by a few candles on a plate.

"That psychotic asshole."

190

"*What* psychotic asshole?" He set her on the bed. "Don't move."

As Paul walked through another doorway, she panicked. She couldn't be left alone again. But then Kiara and Kenna came in and stood by her.

"I'll wait out here," Chase said from the hall as he turned his back to the room and stood like a sentry keeping watch.

Paul returned with two towels. He dabbed gently at her mouth.

"Let me have that one," Kiara said and he passed her the other.

Kiara walked around the foot of the bed and set the large candlestick holder on the dresser. She sat on the bed beside her thigh and lightly tugged her right leg near the knee. "Open up, sweetie."

Pain wracked her body as she used those abused muscles to comply. Still, she was glad Kiara was the one patting and wiping the blood and mess down there. Tanya didn't want Paul to see or ever remember her like that.

"What happened to them?" Tanya asked.

"Who, sweetie?"

She peered up at Paul then down at Kiara. They *had* to have seen the psycho couple.

Tanya thought her heart was about to explode when she saw it.

"*Him*!" she said, pointing at the man in the photo on the wall.

CHAPTER 15

Something cold and wet touched Richard's cheek. He sat, petrified. It touched him again, swiping upward. A *cold, wet* scaly tongue licked him.

Richard pawed at his shirt pocket, trying to get his lighter out.

A pervasive, deep and gruff voice, that sounded almost like a growl, said, "*You* do not command me. *I* command *you*."

He found his lighter, pulled it out and stroked the wheel several times. He couldn't get the flame lit, but each time, in the brief light of the spark, he saw it.

At first, there was only the wide-set flared nostrils of a flat nose and the ridges running up it. The second stroke showed large horns rising from the top of the head, rolling forward, doing a complete circle with about an eight-inch diameter and continuing until the tips were pointing forward and slightly upward in a wide rack that would be perfect for goring. The third time, he saw piranha-like teeth that were at least three inches long.

There wasn't a fourth time. He was too frightened by what he might see.

"Help!" Richard wanted to move, but fear paralyzed him.

The beast sniffed him. "There is no seasoning as good as fear," it said. Then licked him again.

"Help! Somebody!" He took a deep breath. "Heeeeelp!"

* * *

Chase stood outside the doorway with his back turned as the others attended to Tanya. He didn't know if it would bother her, him being in there, so he decided he would give her some semblance of privacy. He knew if it was him that had just been through something like that, he'd want as few people looking at him as possible.

But what *was* that? Welts and bruises and blood and tissue tears don't just happen. Something causes them. But there was nothing. They were the only ones in the room.

Paul came to the door and whispered in his ear. "Chase, man, what the fuck just happened?"

Chase shrugged his shoulders. He tried to keep his voice down. "I don't know, bro. You *saw* it. You tell *me*."

"The only *logical* explanations are the illogical ones. And I just ain't *that* illogical. Are you?"

Chase shook his head. "Psychosomatic, maybe? I know you can think yourself sick. We learned about it in Psych one-o-one. Maybe she thought herself wounded."

"That ma—"

"Shh." Chase held up his hand. He thought he heard something downstairs.

"You can come in now," Kenna called from behind.

Chase turned around. Tanya stood there, dressed, but with a blank look on her face. He forced a smile when she looked at him. Her eyes lowered to the floor. Chase looked down, too.

"Where are your shoes, sweetie?" Kiara asked.

"I must have taken them off in our room after I fell asleep," Tanya said.

Chase listened to their conversation, but tried to keep an ear open for something on the first floor.

"That's her," Tanya said as Kiara walked to the dresser. She pointed at the framed picture of Thornton and Layla beside the candelabra.

Chase heard it again. He held his breath, listening until it came again.

"Heeeeelp!"

"Fuck me," he said. "What now?"

Everyone froze and looked at each other. They had all heard Richard screaming.

"Stay with them," Chase told Paul just before he spun around and sprinted for the stairs.

* * *

"I don't give a fuck if there's a tornado outside the front door," Paul told Tanya. "We're getting you out now. Okay?"

She nodded.

"Can you walk?"

Her movements were understandably stiff. She walked slowly—her feet wider apart than usual. "I think so," she said, grimacing with each step.

Paul hated to leave her, but he had to. He looked Kiara in the eyes. "Y'all take her to get her shoes and come straight down. Understand?"

Kiara nodded. That wasn't good enough.

"Understand?"

"Yeah. Got it."

Paul ran after Chase. When he got to the stairs, he took them two or three at a time. Whatever he felt he could do with each stride without tripping in the darkness.

"Help!" Richard screamed again.

The stupid bastard was still in the basement.

* * *

Chase couldn't see shit in the darkness, but a fortunate strike of lightning lit his path when he got to the top of the stairs. Maintaining a mental image of their placement, he descended them as fast as he could, running his left hand along the wall for guidance all the way down. As he landed in the parlor, a high-pitched squeal rose from the basement.

* * *

"Hello," the demonic voice said and a vision of the Ouija board with the planchette on the greeting popped into Richard's head. *This* was the one manipulating the pointer.

As if reading his mind, the demon said, "Yes." Then said, "Fear not, meat-sack, I am not going to kill you."

Richard breathed heavily. His eyes scanned the blackness around him.

"No," the beast continued. "I'd rather keep you alive and eat you piece by piece."

The scaly tongue licked his neck.

Sharp teeth clamped down on Richard's left earlobe. He shrieked as the skin popped and a small stream of hot blood flowed onto his shoulder. Richard's hand shot to his ear in reflex and pawed at the missing lobe. His touch hurt worse than the bite. He withdrew fingers sticky with blood.

"Little by little."

* * *

Chase ran down into the dark basement. He should have brought his phone or something to see by, but in all the commotion, it never even crossed his mind. The third or fourth stair down splintered as his foot hit it.

"Where you at?" he asked.

No answer.

Chase stumbled slightly when he hit the platform, expecting another step to be there. He bumped the wall in front of him, turned and descended the remainder of the stairs.

"Richard?"

"Leave me alone." His voice was stern. It was also close.

"I thought you were screaming for help."

"I said go! Goodbye!"

Chase wasn't sure what to make of the situation. "Are you okay?"

"AAAAHHHHHHH!"

Richard's scream vibrated Chase's eardrums. It was a high, inhuman tone, a primal screech rising from his gut.

Chase followed the pain-filled shriek.

* * *

The darkness grew thicker and colder around Richard. It was as if it had a billion arms wrapping themselves around him from every angle and constricting. Azazel stood somewhere near him, breathing heavily, occasionally snorting.

195

"Go," Richard said with a weak voice.

"But you're supposed to command me to do your trivial, meaningless tricks." There was no mistaking the wicked sarcasm in his deep voice.

"Leave me alone," Richard said. There was a command for him.

A needle-sharp claw touched Richard on the top of his forehead at his hairline.

"I said go! Goodbye!"

With the ease of a laser burning through butter, Azazel pressed the nail through the skin, through the bone, into Richard's brain. Streaks of red, white, blue and gold light filled his vision, shooting in every direction.

"AAAAHHHHHHH!"

Azazel withdrew the long fingernail and blood trickled down Richard's forehead, over his brow, around the inside corner of his left eye and down alongside his nose.

* * *

Paul whipped around and headed for the secret passage.

The door was wide open and filled with the blackness of a dragon's hungry mouth.

What the fuck is he doing in the dark? Paul wondered.

Unable to see, he felt his way down the stairs, keeping one hand pressed against the wall and dipping each foot down until it tapped the next step. The wooden stairs creaked and groaned beneath his weight.

"Chase?" he whispered. "Richard?"

"Yeah," Chase said. "Over here."

Paul got to the landing and inched his way in a hundred-and-eighty degree circle then shuffled forward until one foot hung halfway off the edge.

"Turn on your phone or light your lighter for fuck's sake."

"Can't. Left them in the room."

"Same. Where's Richard?"

The blackness was as dark as anything he had ever seen. It reminded Paul of a cave he once explored with a friend in Jackson

County. At first, it wasn't so bad, but the deeper they got, the more blind he became until at last, the darkness was almost palpable.

"Here. With me."

"Well, bring your asses this way."

"I can't get him to move."

"You hurt, Richard?"

No answer.

"Can't get him to talk either."

"Fuck my life. Could this night get any worse?" Paul asked.

"I don't see how," Chase said as Paul made it to the basement floor. "Where are you?"

"On the pew. Follow my voice. One . . . two . . . three . . ."

Paul moved toward Chase until he bumped the pew. He reached out with both hands, waving his arms. He hit someone.

"That's me," Chase said.

Paul spoke into the near-suffocating dark. "Richard? What's the matter? Richard."

"He's here," Richard said with a drab voice.

Paul imagined him sitting there in shock like a person who just survived a tornado ripping through their house.

"Who?" Paul and Chase asked in unison.

"*He* is."

Paul reached out to where he thought Richard was sitting. He touched his damp shirt. A little more bumbling blindly and he found Richard's scrawny arm. His hand travelled down it until he had his wrist.

"Okay," Paul said. "He can stay here, but the three of us are leaving. *Now.*"

He reached out and grabbed Chase's shirt, yanking it and Richard's wrist at the same time. He managed to pull Richard to his feet. Chase stood on his own accord. Paul led them as fast as he could toward the stairs. When he hit the first one, he said, "Let's go!"

The three of them ran up the stairs, clomping up to the landing. Paul rounded the corner and could see a bit of light at the opening above.

He charged toward it. Halfway up, his foot crashed through one of the steps. The rough edges of the broken tread slashed his shin and calf.

Dead Town

There was a loud *crack!* Then the breaking of more boards. A quick yip from one of the guys and a deep thud.

Paul had made it to the top, but the others didn't.

Near the front door, Kiara stood with the candlestick holder.

"Bring that," he shouted.

Kiara hurried over. Paul grabbed the candelabra and thrust it into the doorway.

The third step down, was the one he broke. The couple stairs below that had broken as well. He couldn't see Chase or Richard.

"Chase?"

"I'm good," he said, his hand rising from the dark hole several steps down.

"Richard?"

"I'm okay."

There was no way they were coming back up that staircase. They might be able to run and jump over the missing steps, but that was too risky. It was a wide and high jump. Even if they didn't hit their heads on the slanted ceiling, there was a good chance the other steps might break. They were lucky neither of them was hurt already.

* * *

The ruckus woke Ladarius from an otherwise peaceful slumber. When he opened his eyes, he saw a couple of the girls in the parlor.

Unable to miss the urgency in Paul's voice when he told Kiara to bring the candles, Ladarius hopped off the comfortable sofa and dashed to the others.

"What's going on?" Ladarius asked. "Why are y'all shouting?"

Paul stepped aside, holding the candles inside the doorway. Ladarius leaned in and looked. "Oh, snap. That ain't good."

"Keep an eye on the girls," Paul said as he plucked one candle from the holder. "I'll be right back."

He ran up the stairs, shielding the flame with one hand.

Kiara and Kenna stood on either side of Tanya, each with an arm wrapped around her. Tanya stared at the floor, dread and anxiety stained her face. In the little light they had, she looked as if she had been crying.

"You okay, Tanya?" he asked. She didn't answer.

He looked at the other two girls. With solemn expressions, they both shook their heads side to side slightly, indicating he shouldn't press the issue.

By now, Chase and Richard were standing on the small landing.

"I think we can make it," Chase said.

Ladarius gazed into the stairwell and shook his head. He didn't see that turning out well.

"I wouldn't try. Wait for Paul to get back."

"*Back*?" Chase asked. "Where the fuck did he go?"

Ladarius wondered if he got down on his stomach and stretched out his arm if Chase and Richard would be able to grab it. No, there was no way. His arms weren't that long. Even if they were, he'd probably end up sliding forward and toppling through that hole headfirst.

* * *

Kenna had stood outside the doorway, looking in as the others tried to free Tanya. To say she was terrified by what she saw would be akin to saying the Atlantic Ocean is a small body of water. Then, as they were trying to clean Tanya up and tend to her bleeding, Chase took off. Paul followed. Now, here they all were, gathered in the parlor, two of the boys trapped in the basement.

Paul rushed down the stairs with a coiled rope in one hand and a flickering candle in the other.

"Tie this around your waist," he told Dari. "I need you to be anchor."

"*Anchor*? Bro, you weigh a hell of a lot more than me."

Paul wrapped the rope around Dari and started tying it. "I also *squat* a hell of a lot more than you."

Dari took the short end of the rope and started tying a couple more knots as Paul threw the other end down the stairs.

"Walk up the stairs as high as you can, Chase, but be careful." Paul said. "Pull the rope taut and hold on tight as fuck as you step off. You'll swing forward some, but we should be able to pull you up to this stair here."

Dead Town

* * *

For the first time since entering the basement, Chase could see Richard as they stood on the landing. The light from above wasn't enough to see great detail, but it was enough for him to see the blood running from his forehead to his chin.

Chase walked up the several stairs, trying to be light as a feather, but feeling stiff as a board.

"Hang on," he said. He was sure of his grip, but why chance it?

Chase began to tie the rope around his waist.

"Ready?" Paul asked.

Something caught Chase's attention. "Hang on."

Ten seconds ago, the basement was blacker than anything he had ever seen. Now, something glowed down there, as if one of the candles had been lit. But by who?

The light increased.

"Hurry," Paul said.

It got a little brighter. Chase turned to look back at Richard. He noticed it, too. The whites of his eyes showed, terror filling them. Richard stood rigid as a statue. His eyes cut to the left. Chase felt his own eyes stretch wide when he saw it. The bottom couple inches of Richard's shirt sleeve ripped as if a scalpel had gone through it. The skin on Richard's biceps started to open, splitting about an inch wide. The wound travelling slowly down to the top of his forearm.

* * *

They couldn't get out of there quick enough for Richard's tastes. It was cold and dark and Azazel was lurking somewhere, toying with him.

As Chase walked up a couple of stairs, Richard wondered if leaving the house would mean escaping Azazel. A candle lit somewhere below them. Then another. And another. Richard pictured them in his mind, lighting the same way they went out only a little while ago. Then came the snarling voice.

"Why would you want to leave when we have so many delicious tortures planned for you?"

200

Richard took a deep breath and went stiff as he cut his eyes to the left and saw the nearly seven-foot tall beast standing beside him, crouching slightly so as to look Richard eye to eye. Azazel's face was only inches from his own. His breath reminded Richard of a rancid piece of meat he once pulled from the back of his refrigerator. The un-clothed dull black body was well proportioned, but slightly wider and fuller than an average man. Leaner than any bodybuilder, the muscles and sinew rippled beneath the skin. His penis was like a horse's, thick and flaccid, hanging down his thigh about a foot. At the end of his hands were long claws—like eagle talons—only much larger.

Azazel barely touched Richard's arm with one of the hooked fin-gernails and dragged it slowly down.

"What the fuck are you doing?" Paul yelled.

* * *

Chase scurried down the stairs, taking the rope from around his waist. He didn't know what was going on with Richard, but he sensed it was more urgent that he get out first. He tied the rope around Richard and said, "Go!"

Richard stood motionless. Blood ran down his arm and dripped from his fingertips onto the floor.

"Take him first," Chase said as he got behind Richard and pushed him forward.

Several times, Chase hunkered down and buried his shoulder in Richard's back. Finally, he started to move on his own.

* * *

Paul sat on the floor with his bent legs spread and a foot planted on each side of the door frame. Richard stepped off the stair. His dead weight was more than Paul had anticipated. The horsehair rope slipped through his fingers a few inches, burning and leaving slivers. Finally, though, he stopped it before Richard hit the ground below.

As if on a row machine, Paul held the rope and pressed his bent legs, extending them and leaning back, drawing Richard up. He leaned forward, grabbing the rope further down, then bent his legs and pushed again until they were straight.

Richard bumped his head on the underside of the second step. His hands came up and gripped the stair as Paul pulled again.

"Got him?" Paul shouted to Dari.

"I think so."

Paul leaned forward and latched onto Richard's bloody wrist with one hand. Richard grabbed him back. Paul's other hand got a grip and he pulled for dear life.

A few minutes later, with Richard helping on the rope, they had Chase out of there, too. By then, the basement glowed with an unnerving light.

"Fuck this place. We're out," Paul said as he marched to the front door.

He twisted the knob and pulled, but it wouldn't open. He turned the oblong brass lock knob clockwise. When it clicked, he yanked the door again. His hand slipped from the knob.

"Why the hell did you close this door?" he asked Chase.

"We didn't. I thought *you* did."

"I told y'all to leave it open."

Everyone looked around mumbling or emphatically stating they had nothing to do with the closed door.

Paul shook his head and gave the only logical explanation he could think of. "Maybe a draught caught it. Doesn't matter. It's swole shut now."

He glanced at the window.

Dari ran out of the room and came back a few seconds later with one of the wooden stools from the bar room. He held it up by a couple of legs and said, "We're getting out."

Like Barry Bonds, Ladarius swung for the fences. There was a loud clatter as the stool shattered to pieces. Dari had a stupid, dumbstruck expression on his face as he looked at the two pieces of wood remaining in his hands.

"There's *no way* on God's green earth that's possible," Ladarius said.

"We're not *on* God's green earth anymore," Richard said. "We're on Satan's forsaken plot."

Chase bolted down the hall, disappearing into the library. He emerged carrying one of the bronze ashtray pedestals. As he entered the parlor—

BANG!

The black shutters outside slammed together. Before the group could react, the remainder of shutters closed with loud bangs.

After Chase took a few good swings at the window, the glass shattered and fell to the floor.

Bang! Bang! Bang! He beat against the black wooden shutters, but didn't even dent them.

"Oh my God," Kiara exclaimed. "We forgot Hayden!"

She ran up the dark stairs to get him.

* * *

Shouting and some ungodly racket downstairs woke Hayden. Several candles near his feet had toppled over and gone out. He must have stretched as he slept.

He flipped to his knees and picked one up, trying to light it off another.

It was too late.

The shadows on the wall moved. They had noticed his vulnerability and stalked forward across the floor.

He got the candle lit. Waited for the wax to drip and set it upright.

He reached outside the circle for the next fallen candle. A shadow passed dangerously close to his fingers. As he struggled to light it off the candle he had just put in place, that candle went out. Then the one beside it went out. Then the next.

With each diminishment of light, the shadows grew larger, bolder, more ferocious.

Hayden's heart jackhammered the inside of his breastbone.

When Kiara burst into the room, he thought, *Thank God.*

"Hayden!" she said.

Only one candle—the one behind him—remained lit.

A shadow grabbed a painfully tight hold of his right arm and flung him over the bed. He slammed into the dresser before falling to the floor.

Dead Town

"Oh my God," Kiara screamed.

A cold shadow shaped almost like a Rottweiler, but larger, leapt onto his chest. It opened its mouth.

* * *

Ladarius couldn't fathom how the glass didn't break when he bashed it with the stool. He figured Richard summed it up best when he said they were on Satan's turf. He *knew* he shouldn't have come out with these stupid mother fuckers. Sure, he loved them, but they were stupid as fuck for toying with this shit.

Once the shutters snapped over the windows and Chase was incapable of smashing his way through them, Ladarius knew things were about to get worse. He didn't have to wait long.

Something stirred to his left near the basement door, capturing his attention. A golden light glowed in the entranceway. Then it emerged. The snake's head was bigger than a pit bull's. Its tongue lapped the air a foot from its mouth.

Oh, hell no! he thought.

The wide head, followed by a thick body, slithered out, coming straight toward them.

* * *

Kiara gasped, paralyzed by awe, as Hayden's body left the ground. It seemed to happen in super-slow motion. He floated through the air until his back hit the dresser and he fell with a loud, "Oof!"

She ran around the foot of the bed. "Are you okay?"

Her mind was playing tricks on her. The house and the stress were getting to her. For a split second, as she rounded the corner, she thought she saw a large black—but transparent—dog sitting on Hayden's chest, its head turned to watch her, its eyes glowing like red LED lights, its lips curled back to expose the massive teeth in its open jowls.

Then it dissipated like fog in a hot morning sun, but faster than she could blink.

"Help!" Hayden said, terror raising his voice more than an octave.

Puncture wounds popped up on his right forearm. Then his arm straightened rapidly. His hand shot under the bed. Then his elbow. His shoulder. Some invisible force dragged him.

Kiara caught one of his flailing ankles as he screamed and writhed in pain. She pulled as hard as she could.

* * *

Exhausted from swinging so hard at the shutters, Chase dropped the ashtray base, and it hit the floor with a loud clang. He was out of ideas.

"What now?" he asked Richard. "You got us into this. How do we get out?"

"I didn't get you into this."

"You brought us here," Paul said.

"Last night," Richard said as if that was something completely un-related. "*You* invited *me* to come today."

"And you sacrificed yourself."

"You did *what*?" Tanya asked.

"Downstairs, at the altar," Paul said.

Tanya shook her head, her blonde hair bouncing. "Wait a minute," she said. "Altar? Sacrificed himself?"

"There's a devil worshipping altar downstairs," Chase said, trying to bring her up to speed quickly. "He cut his arm and said he was sac-rificing himself."

"Are you really that fucking crazy?" she asked.

"What else?" Kenna said.

Richard looked confused. The blood on his face had caked and dried.

Kenna took on the demanding tone of a perturbed mother. "What *else* did you do?"

"I didn't know it would work," Richard said.

Paul looked like he was about to coldcock Richard. "What?"

Richard raised his hands. His left arm still bleeding and spilling blood all over the floor and his clothes. He took a professorial stature and voice. "Know how I said the veil was thinnest between the living and dead at midnight?"

Dead Town

"What about it?" Chase said.

It had to be well-past twelve already.

"I said an incantation to tear the veil. To—"

"To *what?*" Kenna asked, placing her hands on her hips.

"To open a gateway . . . between here and the other side."

"Other side of what?" Tanya demanded.

"Life. But I didn't know it would actually work. It never did before. I guess the ley lines and history of this place—"

"Shut the fuck up before I knock your ass out," Paul said.

Chase agreed with Paul—in principle at least. He wanted to grab a hammer and pound the hell out of the lunatic.

* * *

The shadow beast sat on Hayden's abdomen, snarling and dripping hot saliva on his chest and neck. Despite its shadowy body, it had to weigh at least a hundred and twenty pounds. A growl came from under the bed. A giant dog-like head popped out and latched onto his arm. It yanked on him, pulling him into the darkness.

As the other dog hopped off him, Kiara grabbed his leg.

"Don't let them get me!" he said.

The first beast grabbed his other arm with its hot, wet mouth. Its powerful jaws clenched shut, snapping both bones like two pieces of raw spaghetti.

Kiara wasn't strong enough. She was losing ground. His head slid under the bed.

In the darkness, he peered into the glowing red eyes.

He pulled his arms and tried to roll away. It was the last mistake he would ever make.

One of the beasts grabbed a mouthful of throat and ripped.

Hot blood spurted up against his chin and face. It flowed down his throat.

Hayden gurgled for air as he drowned in his life.

* * *

Kiara kept pulling, fighting with whatever had ahold of Hayden. It was a tug-of-war and Hayden was the rope. She tightened her grip, planted her feet flat against the floor and leaned back as far as she could, trying to get some leverage.

Then his body went limp.

Whatever pulled him partway under the bed let go and she managed to drag him out by leaning and baby-stepping backwards.

Blood covered his face. His eyes stared off into the distance. The entire front half of his neck was missing.

She screamed.

* * *

Hayden's lungs, full of fluid, refused to draw in the slightest bit of air. Blackness filled his vision. Then, like a movie theater, the center of his view lit up with moving images. His mother bringing home George, a Welsh Corgi, for his fifth birthday. The Xbox 360 he received for Christmas when he was seven. The progress report from school he forged and returned at ten. A game of Truth-or-Dare with some male friends at twelve that left him with the knowledge he was definitely straight. Horseback riding in the mountains while on vacation in Colorado with his family at thirteen. Sex with MK—Melissa Katie—Shawna, and several other *favorite* exes. The day he met Kiara. Amber saying, "You shouldn't fuck around with things you don't understand" and "Nothing good exists there."

Hayden knew he was dead. Or *would be* in seconds if he wasn't already. He resigned himself to that fate and let go, ready to move on to that *better place* everyone always spoke of—the next phase of his existence.

When he got there, he realized it was *not* better.

It was a cold, dark endless space filled with hate . . . regret . . . sorrow. It was unnerving solitude, despite the millions of doleful wails resounding in the never-ending distance. It was pain—not only his, but *theirs*. And it was loneliness—especially when the seven-foot tall, horned black figure appeared and peeled back its leathery lips to reveal a mouth full of shark-like teeth.

Dead Town

Its voice was like a large, snarling dog. It said, "You've had your fun. Now *mine* begins."

CHAPTER 16

When Kiara's scream ripped through the house all voices stopped and all eyes shot to the darkness at the top of the stairs. Before Chase could move, he heard heavy footsteps. Kiara came into the candles' aura as she raced down the stairs.

"Holy shit," she said. "Holy mother fucking shit!"

"What?" several asked at the same time.

She hit the bottom of the stairs, bounded for the door and started tugging on the handle.

"Oh my God," she said.

"Where's Hayden?" Tanya asked.

The word stopped Kiara and she turned to face the group. The whites of her eyes fully outlined her irises. She blinked a few times in rapid succession. The pits of her T-shirt were wet with sweat. Her voice, slow and sober, was at odds with her panicked countenance. She said, "If we don't get out of here now, we're *all* going to die."

She blinked a few more times. Took a couple quick, deep breaths. Then she walked over to Paul and stared into his eyes.

"Hayden's dead—"

"*What?*" Paul and Kenna asked.

For some weird reason, Chase wasn't surprised. It was as if he almost expected it as soon as he heard her screaming upstairs.

"Dragged under the bed by something I couldn't fucking see. His throat ripped out."

Chase watched Paul for his reaction. He seemed to be taking it all in, but not comprehending it.

Kiara's eyes shrunk to slivers as she furrowed her brow and stuck her forefinger in his face. "Still believe just because you can't see it, it doesn't exist?"

Dead Town

Paul stared at her, his jaw muscles tightening. Chase had seen him in this position before, but with a guy, and Paul looked exactly the same right before he coldcocked him with a ferocious right hook.

"Maybe you imagined it," Paul finally said.

"What, like *she* imagined being tied to the bed?"

Chase glanced at Tanya. Her eyes dropped to the floor and she appeared as if she were trying to shrink inside herself so no one would see her.

"Calm down," Chase said. His eyes scanned the small area. "Where the hell is Dari?"

* * *

For a while, the serpent poked its head a few feet out the door and sort of hovered there a couple feet off the ground, swaying back and forth, bobbing up and down as if trying to acclimate itself to its surroundings.

Ladarius opened his mouth to warn everyone, but no sound came out. After trying to force it a couple times, he gave up. One thing was sure, he wasn't about to stick around to see what that fucking snake did.

Ladarius backed slowly into the front room. Everyone else stood, oblivious to the danger, as the snake slithered past them. It had to be at least thirteen feet long and two to three feet across. Its scales were as large as his hands and it gave off that oily, rancid smell he remembered from a school fieldtrip to the zoo when he was seven. The class had gone into the reptile house and he got his first look at snakes. One was eating a chicken—*whole*. The woman who worked there told them some snakes were large enough to eat children—so they better be good. After that, his chest seized up and his heart pounded whenever he saw or even *thought* he might encounter a snake.

Oh, mother fucker! he thought. *How can they* not *see it?*

The black, tan, and brown body swished back and forth as it slid over the floor like a figure skater across ice. It honed in on him, its head never turning left or right. From beneath the two-inch long nostrils always pointing straight for him, its bright red tongue darted in and out of its stiff, angry mouth.

Ladarius turned to run, tripping over a chair in the darkness.

* * *

"Where the hell is Dari?" Chase asked.

About the same time, there was a commotion in the front room, like a chair tumbling over.

Paul grabbed the candles and moved to the doorway to check it out.

Dari rolled off an upturned chair and scrambled to his feet.

"Don't you *see* it?" Dari asked.

Paul looked around. "I don't see anything but your drunk ass falling over shit."

"The snake!" He pointed at Paul's right foot.

Instinctively, Paul shifted left and looked down. There was nothing there.

* * *

Ladarius wondered if he was just tripping balls. If no one else saw what he saw, there had to be a reason. Maybe there was something in the weed or the booze. He had been on some bad acid trips before and been able to break out of them once or twice on his own by concentrating on good things and telling himself, "It's not real" over and over like a mantra.

His hands were sweaty. His heart *thump-thumped* against his chest.

The monstrous snake stopped a few feet shy of Ladarius.

Sssss! It hissed.

The gigantic tongue lapped at the space between them.

It's not real. It's not *real!*

"Come on, bro," Paul said. "Quit dicking around. We need to find a way out of here."

The large head moved back a foot or so, its powerful neck bending behind it.

It's not real! Think cute pit puppies. It's not real.

Ladarius tried to picture a newborn pit bull there instead.

It's not—

211

Dead Town

The movement was so fast, he never saw it. One second, he was staring at one of the massive goggle eyes on the head. Before that second ended, the snake lunged at him, it's jaw snapping shut with a *pop*.

The heavy body and force knocked him back and over the chair. It wrapped around him. Rolled him. Coiled around his legs and chest, pinning his right arm to his side.

It is *real!*

* * *

Kenna let out a short squeal and jumped when Dari flew back a couple feet as if an invisible rope behind him suddenly jerked him. It was so quick and unexpected Dari's facial expressions didn't even have time to change.

In the blink of an eye, he went from standing in one place to writhing on the ground a few feet away. His body straightened. Other than one hand flailing in the air, he looked rigid as a concrete statue standing at attention.

Kenna's stomach churned. She wanted to rush over and help him, but she couldn't speak or move. *Something* had a tight hold on him.

Chase leapt forward, throwing fists at nothing. Paul passed the candles to Kiara and charged toward Dari, who rolled on the floor and over the chair like he was having an epileptic seizure. But she knew it was impossible for one to roll *up* a piece of furniture.

* * *

Ladarius was at the mercy of the snake wrapped about him. It twisted and rolled its body, taking him with it. Ladarius's head banged against the hardwood floor with a loud *thud*, sending a shower of silver sparks across the spinning room.

Everything happened at incredible speed and yet somehow seemed to transpire slow enough for him to have time to think and react.

He swung at the snake's massive eye a couple times before landing a blow. It wasn't squishy like he expected. Instead, it was hard as any other part of the snake's body.

The snake flexed its muscles. The body tightened around him.

Ladarius tried to breathe, but couldn't because of the unearthly pressure constricting his chest walls. He thought for sure he was going to suffocate, even as Chase and Paul ran toward him to try to help. Then, in a matter of a few hellishly long microseconds, it happened.

His heart beat furiously—at least three or four times a second. A sharp pain rocked his chest like a dagger plunged deep into his breastbone. Between two beats came a painful *pop!* His heart exploded.

Damn, he thought.

Then everything went black.

* * *

As Paul and Chase charged forward, swatting at the empty air, both boys tripped over something unseen.

Kenna watched, petrified, as they scrambled to their feet.

Dari's body rose a few feet off the ground. Then he went limp.

Crunch! Snap! It was like a mega-amplified bowl of Rice Krispies. Dari's body imploded, his bones all breaking within a long second or two. *Crack!*

Bright red blood shot from his mouth. Blood and shit soiled his pants. His eyes bulged. Then popped out of the sockets and sat on the outside of his eyelids for a moment. His eyeballs shot off his face with ungodly force. One hit Chase in the chest. The other bounced and rolled, stopping near Kenna's foot, a short tangle of reddish-pink muscles attached like a tail.

Kenna turned and ran up the stairs, trying to get as far away as possible from whatever it was that just killed Dari.

* * *

There was a blinding white light flooding his vision, like he was staring into one of those massive searchlights at a carnival. Then it went out. Everything was blacker than before. People screamed in torment around him. For a brief moment, Ladarius thought he had completely lost his eyesight, but somehow managed to free himself from the snake's embrace. But then he saw a dark glow approaching him from afar. It was like a shiny, polished black object on a flat black background. It closed the distance with remarkable speed.

Before Ladarius could react, the massive beast towered over him. It stood taller than Kevin Durant, its rippling muscles visible with the slightest motion. A wide rack of horns protruded from its fearsome head.

A gigantic hand shot forward and seized him by the shoulder. Nails like a bear's claws dug into him with a burning pain. The powerful beast lifted him off the unseen ground and carried him, screaming, deeper into the blackness.

CHAPTER 17

Between the horrendous smell, the blood, and the surrealness of the situation, Chase lost it. When he realized it was an eyeball, *Dari's* eyeball that hit him, he leaned over and vomited. He had never felt so useless in his life. He tried. He couldn't get there in time. Even if he could have, what would he have done? He didn't even know what the fuck was happening. How could he stop it?

He coughed a couple times and spit out the last bitter remnants of puke from his mouth. With the back of his wrist, he wiped away the long strand of spittle that dangled from his lips.

A hand touched the center of his back.

Chase looked up. Paul looked as confused as he felt. Paul didn't speak. For the moment, that was okay by Chase, because he didn't think he'd be able to say a word without breaking down and bawling.

Behind him a couple of the girls sobbed. Chase looked under his arm at Kiara and Tanya.

He stood up and glanced around. They were the only four people there.

* * *

Kenna took off up the stairs. Richard followed her into the darkness. He didn't know where she was going and he didn't care. He just wanted to get away from the evil spectacle downstairs. Any place would be better than there.

The door to the first room on the left glowed with a warm, inviting light. Kenna ducked in and stopped so abruptly Richard almost ran her over.

One candle burned on the floor. Several others stood forming a semi-circle, but all extinguished.

Hayden's lifeless legs stuck out from behind the bed.

Dead Town

Kenna squatted down and picked up the single glowing candle.

"Wait," Richard said. He bent over and picked up one that had fallen on its side. "Here," he said, pushing the dead wick toward her flame.

Once it was lit, Kenna's eyes shot in the direction of Hayden's feet. "I can't stay in here," she said.

They walked out of the room. A Kelly Clarkson tune—*Because of You*—started playing quietly down the hall. They looked at each other.

Kenna said, "My phone!"

She hurried down the hall to the next room on the left with Richard right behind. The cellphone on the dresser lit the room a pale white. As she answered it, Richard pulled out his phone to see if he had signal, too.

He didn't.

* * *

Tears stained the faces of Kiara and Tanya. Black mascara ran down from their eyes making them look haggard.

"Where are the other two?" Chase asked.

Tanya didn't react. Kiara pointed up.

"Fuck!" Chase said. He looked at Paul. "Stay with them."

He pulled one of the short candles from the holder and slowly started up the stairs, dread filling him with each footfall. He couldn't believe they ran away. At the same time, he couldn't blame them, either. This was one fucked-up nightmare. Even still, there had to be some sort of safety in numbers. No. There wasn't. They were *all* present and witnesses of what just happened to Dari. They were all there and incapable of saving him.

He didn't want to go anywhere alone in this house, but he had to get to Kenna. He had to do whatever it took to keep her alive. If that meant dying, so be it. But he was determined he would breathe his last before he saw harm come to her.

* * *

As soon as the song started playing, Kiara felt a wave of relief crash over her. It was the warden's personalized ringtone. If someone asked her yesterday, she would have told them she could live to be a million years old and never be excited to hear the warden calling. Now, that was all different. Her *mama* was calling. She didn't give a flying fuck if her mother was just calling to ask for bail money again, at least there was contact with the outside world. She could tell her to send help.

Kiara picked up her phone and answered it. "Mama?"

"What," her mother sounded disappointed. "You aren't calling me the warden now?"

"We need help."

"Of course you do."

"I'm *serious*, mama. We need *help*."

"I *know* you do." Her voice had a sinister edge to it. "Because Matthew and me are here, and we are going to tear that tight little ass up." Kiara looked around, mortified. "Don't worry. Only the first couple inches hurt."

Something bumped in the bathroom.

"Now don't you worry, baby girl, we're coming for you."

Kiara tossed the phone down and bolted from the room.

* * *

Richard only heard one side of the conversation, but he knew it wasn't good.

Something stirred in the blackness of the bathroom. Kiara threw her phone at the floor and ran past him. He followed her across the hall to a room with a messy, bloodstained bed and instruments of pain hanging on the walls.

"Hide!" Kenna said.

She opened the closet door and stepped in.

Not only did her candle go out, *she vanished.*

"Kenna?" Richard peered into the small, empty closet. "Kenna."

He thrust his candle into the vacant space. It had to be at least fifty degrees cooler in there—definitely below freezing. The walls were lined with cedar, but it smelled of sulfur.

Dead Town

It took all he had not to piss his pants, especially when he heard footsteps clopping down the hall toward him. He couldn't run out into whatever danger was approaching in the hall. And he sure as hell wasn't getting in that closet.

Perhaps he could slip under the bed. It wasn't very high off the ground, but it was worth a shot.

Richard got near the side of the bed, blew out his candle then hunkered down. He was on his hands and knees with one foot under the bed when the room lit up.

Chase stood in the doorway with a single candle.

He glanced down at him. "What the fuck are you doing?" Before Richard could explain, he said, "Where's Kenna?"

Richard pushed himself to his feet, using the bed for leverage. He pointed at the closet.

Chase looked at it. "What about it?"

"There."

"There *what*? For fuck's sake, *Where's Kenna*?"

"She went in there."

Chase glanced at the closet again. "Where did she go *after* that, fuckhead?"

Richard shrugged his shoulders. "I don't know. The other side? Hell?" Chase opened his mouth to say something, but Richard said, "She ran in there and disappeared. I think it's the opened gateway."

Chase walked toward the closet, pausing at the threshold.

"Don't go in there," Richard said.

* * *

It was the first time she could remember since middle school she was happy her mother called, but it wasn't her mother. It was this fucked up house or whatever hellish things existed here. She didn't know what was going on, but she knew one thing. Whatever attacked them, only that person was able to see it. In that respect, she was glad when Richard heard the phone ring and seemed to hear the noise in the bathroom beside them.

Kenna-Grace felt like she was six again— filled with all the same hopelessness and angst that compelled her to hide whenever her mother came home at three, four, five o'clock in the morning from the bars or God only knew where. She could be a violent drunk at times. She'd stumble into Kenna's room and start fussing about toys or clothes in the wrong place. Then she'd rip her out of bed by the hair and make her clean it up after whooping the hell out of her. After a few times of that, Kenna slept with one ear open. As soon as she heard the car door slam, she would run and hide—usually in her closet or the pantry. She would pull her knees up to her chest, wrap her arms around them and try to get as small as possible.

It may not have been the best hiding place, but it always worked. Perhaps her mother was just too lazy to look for her, because she would stagger into the room fussing about something, see the empty bed, and totter out, still bitching.

The sex thing was new. At least for her mother. Only one of the boyfriends ever touched her and that was when she was nine. Her mother was passed out on the sofa from the drugs and alcohol. She was asleep in her own bed, wearing her Pokémon T-shirt and a pair of Hello Kitty panties. Suddenly, the mattress beside her sunk down. Mark had crawled into bed with her.

"Shh," he said. He wrapped his arm around her, the way her daddy did when she was four, and she felt safe. She was almost asleep again when he rolled onto his back and his rough fingers slipped between the waistband of her underwear and her skin. His hand slid down. The bed started jerking. The covers above him bounced. She lay there terrified as his nasty fingers touched her hooha.

A couple days later, he was replaced by Ben, a nice guy with a long Santa Claus beard that was brown rather than white.

"Hide!" she told Richard, fearing the house had the ability to make her mother and Matthew appear at any moment.

She ran to the next closest room, the one across the hall where Tanya was abused. She opened the closet door and jumped in, ready to hunker down, draw her knees up and shrink into oblivion, but she didn't get the chance.

Before she could turn and pull the door to behind her, the door and the house were gone and the candle she held went out, but she didn't need it. Her body emitted a dull golden glow that was just bright enough to light a space about three feet around her. She dropped the candle to the floor. When she didn't hear it hit, she looked down. It was like she was walking on a pane of glass. Below the glass was an overcrowded sea of agonized faces blending into the darkness. They were all black, but she could discern they were of every race and nation—male and female—young and old. They mourned and wailed. Black withered fingers and arms stretched up from the tangled mess and scratched at the space beneath her as if trying to claw her down.

The stench of death and rot was two fingers down her throat, wriggling and tapping her gag reflex.

In the distance something stood producing a shiny black aura. It growled and snorted as it approached her.

Kenna tried to run the opposite direction, but no matter which way she turned, the glowing black mass was in front of her, heading straight for her.

* * *

Kiara had to sit down. Her whole body was quivering. Her legs felt like they were filled with Jell-O instead of muscles and bones. She had only ever seen one dead person before. That was at her grandmother's viewing a few years ago. Now, she not only tripled that number, but she witnessed their horrific deaths.

She passed what remained of the candles to Tanya and backed over to the stairs, lowering herself onto the bottom step. Her gaze drifted around the room, never settling on anything for more than a second. The locked door. The closed shutters. Paul and Tanya in the flames' glow. The black hole of the front room behind them where Dari's mangled body lay. The rope on the floor. The open door to the basement. The high ceiling. Tanya and Paul embracing. The door. There was no time to let her eyes rest. She had to be on constant guard. The night wasn't over.

What next? . . . Who next?

She didn't know Paul that well, but she knew he was a natural leader and she trusted his instincts—at least more than she trusted her own at that moment. She had no fucking clue what to do. She just wanted to curl up in a warm, safe bed and cry That wouldn't happen here. A part of her wanted to die so she didn't have to see any more atrocities. Either of which was *very* likely to happen here.

Already, Hayden and Ladarius were dead and Tanya had been raped and tortured—*all* by an invisible entity.

Kiara finally found her voice. Even to her, it sounded feeble. It cracked when she spoke. "What now?"

Still holding Tanya, Paul glanced at her. "I don't know. Check the other windows?"

She doubted it would pan out. They had heard dozens of shutters slam together. Still, there was a possibility a shutter somewhere was broken over the years. If that was the case, she knew they could break the glass as Chase had done with the bronze ashtray base. Then they could get the hell out of there.

Something creaked on the stairs above her. She turned to see Richard descending with a candle in his hand.

"Where are Chase and Kenna?" Paul asked.

"Probably dead," he said when he was standing right behind her.

Paul released Tanya from his embrace. The shadows from the candlelight disfigured his face. He looked both confused and pissed. "*Probably*? Weren't you just with them? Don't you know?" He took a step forward.

* * *

Chase stood at the closet doorway and looked in. Sure, it stunk like rotten eggs, but other than that, it looked like any normal closet in any normal old house. The only odd thing, besides the smell, was that it was empty. Everywhere else in the house was just like it was decades ago. Hell, there was medicine in the cabinets, towels hanging in the bathrooms. Maybe there never was anything in this small space. After all, what kind of clothes would you hang in a bondage room closet? Leather panties?

If it was a gateway to somewhere else, Chase didn't give a shit where it led, as long as it took him to Kenna. If she went that way, that was the way he was going, too.

"Don't go in there," Richard said.

Dead Town

He looked over his shoulder at Richard standing there, holding a dead candle in one hand while fumbling at his bloody shirt pocket with the other for his cigarettes.

Even if Kenna did vanish as soon as she ran in there, Richard should have done something to try to help her. Reach in. Grab for her. Follow her. *Something.*

"Coward," Chase said.

He took a deep breath, held it, and stepped in, worried where it might take him, but even more worried it might not take him anywhere.

Chase's candle went out. The blackness engulfing him was painful, like a sinus headache or the time some asshole with a laser pointer at a party shone it directly into his eye. He couldn't quite place the discomfort because it was both sharp and dull at the same time.

The space itself went on forever and was Arctic cold but he wasn't freezing. It was weird. It was more like he *sensed* the cold than felt it—like it was a cerebral rather than physical chill.

Despite not having a candle, he could see a couple feet in front of himself. It was as if *he* was a candle, shining in the darkness.

All around him, women shrieked and men howled in agony—millions, maybe more. Despite the non-stop wails, it was—at the same time—incredibly quiet. Both the torment and the silence were the only thing he heard—as if he had two sets of ears and two brains and each could hear one or the other. Somehow, though, they both filtered through to the same central location so that he felt surrounded by pain and isolated from everything at the same time.

He breathed through his mouth, but the atrocious odor of rancid meat still inched its way up his nose and coated his tongue and taste buds.

Chase spun slowly to see if the door was still there. It wasn't. There was, however, far beyond him, a dim yellow-orange glow like his own with a deep black glow next to or attached to it. That *had* to be Kenna. At least he hoped it was as he began walking toward the light.

After his second step he wondered, *even if that's her, how the hell are we going to get out of here?*

* * *

Tanya's panties were soaked with blood from both places down there. She snuck a peek at the crotch of her jeans to see if it flowed through. It hadn't. She wanted to sit beside Kiara, but she didn't think she could. Standing hurt bad enough. She imagined sitting would just put pressure on all the wrong places.

Paul looked like he wanted to knock Richard out when he said Chase and Kenna were probably dead.

As Paul walked toward him, Richard backed up the stairs with his hands in front of his chest, palms exposed, as if someone had just pulled a gun on him.

"Look," Richard said, "I couldn't stop her . . . or him. As soon as her phone rang and she—"

"Her phone worked?"

Richard shook his head. "For like a minute. But then she—"

Paul's eyes flared with hope. "Maybe we can call someone for help."

Paul returned and grabbed Tanya by the wrist, tugging her into motion. Together, they all went upstairs. They stopped in the room they had been in to get their phones, then headed to the room across the hall from where she had been raped.

As each of them pulled out and unlocked their phones, Paul said, "Anything?"

No one had a signal.

Paul tried to make a call anyway. He flashed everyone the large screen that displayed CALL FAILED. After tucking it in his back pocket, he bent over and picked up Kenna's phone from the floor. "No signal."

Paul walked to the window and pulled back the curtain, exposing the window and closed shutters.

"Where did they disappear?" Paul asked.

Richard bobbed his head toward the door and said, "Over there."

Tanya felt like she just swallowed a heavy, jagged stone. Her throat hurt and stomach sank.

There was no way she was going back in that room. She'd rather die first. She looked at Paul, hoping he would pick up on her fear of returning.

"Show me."

Dead Town

Richard exited the room and Paul followed, pausing at the door. "I'm not going," Tanya said.

Before Paul could say anything, Kiara said, "I'll stay with her."

Tanya lay across the bed on her stomach thinking about her recent readings. They definitely hit the mark. Something awful happened. It was *still* happening. She wondered if what happened to her was the extent of her worries or if there was more to come.

* * *

Kiara's head hurt. She sat on the bed and reclined next to Tanya. Her gaze fixed on the ceiling.

In the room next to them, Hayden lay dead, a bloody mess with his throat ripped out by the shadow beasts. Downstairs, Ladarius's crushed and mangled body lay crumpled on the floor, destroyed by an invisible snake. Tanya, raped by invisible unseen people. Tears filled her eyes. She had a hard time believing the night had gotten so fucked up. How would they explain any of this if they made it out?

If . . . It didn't seem likely—especially with Chase and Kenna missing. They went from a group of eight happy, partying friends to four miserable souls in a matter of a couple hours.

A tear trickled from the corner of her eye, down over her left temple, and into her hair.

"I'm scared," Tanya said with a flat, calm voice as if she were describing something as mundane as a car color.

Kiara brushed the tear from her face and lied. "It's going to be okay."

"What if Paul and Richard disappear, too?"

Kiara hadn't thought about that. If one or both of them were stupid enough to step into whatever the gateway was, she and Tanya would be left to fend for themselves. She knew she wasn't up to the task. And Tanya could barely walk. How would she fight whatever they encountered? She wouldn't. They would both be severely screwed.

"Paul!" Kiara said.

No answer.

Something round and black—about the size of a small pancake—scurried in the dark corner of the ceiling. She swallowed hard. "Paul! Richard!"

CHAPTER 18

The demon held Kenna up by the throat, her feet off the ground as he stomped through the darkness. It wasn't a corridor down which they walked, because there were no walls and yet, somehow, there were walls on either side of her. It was like Moses parting the Red Sea, but this was a monster instead of a saint doing it. And rather than seeing walls of water on each side, there were black faces and bodies and limbs writhing in extreme torment. They reached for her as they had done earlier beneath her feet. She knew that had the beast turned right or left, she would see more of the same tortured souls. They were not walking a path, they were *forming* a path in the midst of them. Millions of them. She also knew, though she wasn't sure how, they were going downhill at a slight angle, deeper and deeper into the nightmare.

She tried punching the beast but she couldn't reach him. Hitting his forearms was like pounding on a granite boulder and about as effective. She looked down at his massive swinging dick and wondered if kicking him there would work. After two or three kicks to the thighs, she managed to hit the target, but he remained unaffected.

Kenna had no idea where he was taking her or what he had in store for her. He hadn't said a word. Perhaps he couldn't speak. She only knew wherever they were going was going to be much worse than the house. She found herself wishing she were back at Thornton's. Shit, she wished she was back at her house cornered by her mama and Matthew again.

Something over the beast's shoulder caught her eye. It was a dull glow, like hers, in the distance.

"Chase, you *idiot*," she whispered, closing her eyes. She hoped she was wrong, but it *had* to be him. Who else would it be? Who would she *rather* it be? There was no one else she could or would ever depend upon. He was always the one to pick her up after others let her down. He was the one who consoled her and made her laugh when she wept.

He was the one always trying to build her as the world tried to dismantle her. She had liked him. She had wanted him, especially when they kissed earlier, but now she knew she had loved him for a long time.

And now, they were both dead—despite not remembering how she died.

* * *

"That's it," Richard said, pointing at the open closet.

Paul moved forward to investigate.

"Don't go in!"

Paul turned to look at him, wondering if Richard actually thought he was that stupid. He didn't care if there was a billion dollars and his mother dying on top of it at the back of the closet, he wasn't about to set a foot in there.

Richard instructed him to just slip his hand in. "It's safe," he said.

After a few seconds of deliberation, Paul did as told and marveled at how cold it was. He wouldn't have been surprised if he pulled back a hand black with frostbite.

"So, where does it lead?"

Richard shrugged his shoulders. "No clue."

Paul studied him for a moment. With the dried blood in his hair and on his face and more stains on his shirt, he looked like a lunatic. "You mean to tell me you opened a portal or gateway to somewhere and you don't know *where*?"

Richard fiddled with his shirt pocket for his cigarettes. "Whatever's on the other side. Sheol, Hades . . ."

"*Hell?*"

"I don't believe in hell."

"Apparently, it believes in *you*." Paul suddenly felt like all the hypocritical Christians he had laughed at and mocked when they used the same line on him after he had told them he didn't believe in Jesus. *Well, he believes in you.* He didn't believe in hell either, but here he was pushing it.

He thought about grabbing Richard and throwing him into the closet to see what happened. Maybe if he held on to his arm tight enough, he could pull him back.

Dead Town

Paul untied one of the ropes from the bedpost.

"I have an idea," he said as he tied a slipknot in one end.

Richard squinted and looked at Paul from the corners of his eyes as he took a drag off his cigarette.

"Loop this around your waist and go in there. I'll pull—"

"Fuck you. I'm not going in there." All that snooty professorial air about him was gone and he was just like everyone else.

"I'll pull you out."

"Fuck you."

"You opened this shit. Go check it out." He shoved the rope into Richard's hands.

"Paul!" Kiara called from the other room.

Paul balled his fists and halved the distance between them. "Put it on or I'll throw your ass in there without it."

Richard's eyes shifted back and forth, left to right. He was clearly weighing his options and trying to size Paul up at the same time.

"You think I'm kidding?" Paul asked.

"Paul! Richard!" Panic filled Kiara's voice.

* * *

From out of the shadows a second one came. Kiara watched it creeping along the ceiling.

She reached over and tapped Tanya, then whispered, "Do you see that?"

She wasn't sure which answer would frighten her more. If Tanya didn't see it, it meant it was something straight from hell like the snake that got Ladarius or a shadow beast. If she did see it, it meant there were at least two gigantic spiders crawling on the ceiling.

Tanya rolled and looked up. "See what?"

A third came. Then a fourth. Then an army flooded toward the center of the ceiling from each corner.

One dropped, landing on her leg. She screamed. It was at least four or five inches long. It looked like a tarantula—all black and hairy with those creepy legs—but it wasn't a normal spider. It had a silver, glowing face that looked like a man with big goggle eyes and massive fangs for its size. Definitely large enough to bite her.

Kiara swatted at it. It flew off her leg and hit the floor, tumbling a couple of times before uprighting itself and coming back for her. Another one dropped. Then another.

She did her best to brush them off as they fell.

"What's wrong?" Tanya asked as she jumped up off the bed.

"Spiders!"

As she tried to flick one away, it sank its fangs into the side of her hand. It was like liquid fire injected into her flesh—a hundred times worse than any wasp sting she ever received as a kid. She screamed as she shook wildly, but the thing had a good hold on her and bit her a second time before it flew into the wall and dropped to the floor.

* * *

The rotting-flesh stench, the darkness, and the sea of howling faces disfigured by torment on either side of him left Chase scared shitless. A Bible verse from his youth kept running through his mind as he sprinted past them. *There will be weeping and gnashing of teeth.*

He had to get to Kenna. He sprinted toward the glow ahead, dread filling him with what he might find when he finally got there. What if it wasn't her? What if he was too late and something already happened to her? Even if nothing had happened, what was he going to do when he caught up to her? He didn't know how he got here, other than through a closet that disappeared as soon as he stepped in. How the hell were they going to find their way out?

Chase surprised himself with his stamina. He ran as hard as he could and had to have covered at least half a mile already and he was still going strong. He was quickly closing the gap between himself and the glow ahead.

Within a couple minutes, he should overtake her.

A black flash appeared in his periphery to his right, just before the huge mass crashed into him, tackling him like a linebacker blindsiding a quarterback on a blitz. Chase tumbled to the left, the beast on top of him. It was shorter and wider than he. It had the head and face of a baby, but its eye sockets were hollowed out. Two nubs protruded from its large round forehead. It opened its mouth exposing a double row of short triangular teeth like crosscut saw blades. The upper body was that of a muscular man, but the lower half was a pair of hairy goat legs and hooves.

The creature squealed, opened its mouth, and lunged toward his throat.

* * *

Richard wasn't a lover or a fighter. He was an intellect and his intellect told him even if he got one good shot in on Paul, he'd still end up getting his ass beat. He wasn't going in there willingly with or without a rope tied to him. There were too many unknown variables and one well-known variable—Azazel was present earlier. Whether he passed through that gateway or not was immaterial. He crossed over. There could be hordes of creatures on the other side not strong enough to cross the barrier, just waiting for them to enter. Either way, it was suicide and, as much as he hated himself at times, he still liked himself too much to kill himself right now.

After Kiara called their names, Paul turned toward the door. That was the opportunity he needed. Richard rushed past him. As he entered the hall, she screamed and he wondered if he wasn't jumping from the skillet into the fire. It was too late to change his mind, because at that instant Paul charged up behind him, forcing him through the doorway into the bedroom where the girls were.

Tanya stood, eyes wide, mouth agape, frozen as Kiara writhed on the bed, flailing at herself. She jumped to her feet and beat herself with wild hands.

"Get them off. Get them off!" she screamed.

Paul gazed at Tanya. "What the fuck?"

Richard didn't know what *they* were, but he hoped he could help. Kiara began stomping and writhing, still swinging at *them*. Little blood droplets formed on her exposed skin.

Richard dropped the rope, rushed over and began brushing her back and legs with both hands, hoping he knocked off whatever was on her. Something, like a scalding hot needle, seared into his finger, leaving two blood droplets.

He moved around to the front.

"What the *fuck* are you doing?" Paul asked when Richard's hands brushed over her breasts a couple times.

* * *

They were everywhere—dozens of hairy spiders with angry faces crawling all over her. Kiara felt the unnerving tickle of their multiple feet crawling on her arms, her neck, her head and back. One crept across her face, latching onto her brow with its fangs.

She danced around, stomping on them as they fell from her body and ceiling. They squished beneath her feet with a gooey pop and a shrill squeal, but more kept coming.

Someone began knocking them off her back. It was Richard. He came around front and wiped more off. Maybe he could see them. It didn't matter, as long as they were gone.

"What the *fuck* are you doing?" Paul asked.

"Help brush them off," Richard said.

"Brush *what* off?"

"Spiders," Tanya said.

Richard had moved to her backside again and Paul took up the front, running his hands down her in quick, long strokes.

They were winning the battle.

Then everything went dark.

* * *

The space around Kenna and the beast opened up into what might have been a room. With no walls, it was hard to say, but the thrashing bodies were no longer on either side of her. Instead, she clearly saw dozens of people in several rows and columns, men and women— black, Hispanic, Asian, white—all isolated beneath individual cones of black light that began as pinpoints far above them and came down over them in a circle about three feet across. She had never seen or imagined a complete blackness that could somehow illuminate something else in utter darkness.

All of them were naked and black like the faces in the sea of torment. Some stood with their hands together above them as if chained, others stood as if waiting on a bus. A fat old man was on all fours and the woman closest to him stood spread eagle with her feet and hands almost touching the dark light. Each one of them looked panicked and terrified.

Although they were all strangers, she knew all of them by name and deed. On all fours was Trevor Watson—fifty-six, white, stole money from his mother's purse when he was four, lied about thousands of things over his lifetime, molested seventeen girls under the age of eight and twin six-year-old boys. Martha Shuck, forty-four, white, shoplifter, drug addict, prostitute, set up several guys to be robbed after she had sex with them. One ended up dead when he tried to defend himself.

The list went on. The people and all their sins were laid bare for her to know intimately. Not just the murders and the rapes, but the lies and petty thefts, the adulteries and sundry vices.

A black flame with a fine line of blue-black trim shot up from the bottom of each cone like a massive flame from a stove eye. The people screamed and wriggled, howled and squirmed, trying to escape the searing heat.

Kenna almost peed her pants when another cone appeared vacant at the front. It had to be for her.

* * *

Chase wrestled with the beast, his eyes fixed on the snapping jaws trying to take a chunk out of him. A couple times, he managed to get a hand loose and hit the baby head, but it didn't seem to faze the creature.

He rolled and flipped the small devil onto its back, straddling the waist. Behind him, the goat legs flailed, trying—but unable—to kick him. Neither could they bend in such a way as to gain purchase on the ground and buck him. Chase wrapped both hands around its neck and began bashing its head against the floor. As he did, he saw all the souls trapped beneath them. They reached up, half-liquefied, as if out of a black pool. All of them melted together at the bottom. They scratched and batted at the invisible barrier separating him from them.

Chase continued to pound the head against the ground. There was a muted *crunch*. He banged the head a few more times, getting a few more crunches. The legs stopped kicking. A second later, there was a smokeless, black flash of flame and Chase was left kneeling over nothing, holding nothing.

Chase looked around trying to see where it went and to make sure nothing else was coming his way. He slowly stood, his side aching from the initial impact. Beneath him, the people still reached up as if trying to grab him, always falling a fraction of an inch short. He was alone again in both complete silence and the deafening shrieks of terror and agony.

With no walls or markers, it was impossible to discern which direction he had been travelling before his scuffle with the beast. Chase peered into the darkness, spinning on his feet in ninety-degree increments so he would know precisely when he completed a full circle, as he searched for the dim light he had been chasing. There was nothing but blackness. He felt as hopeless as those scratching at the walls around and beneath him.

* * *

Richard grabbed the black and white bedspread and tossed it over Kiara and Paul as she continued to squeal and curse in pain. He didn't know if it would work, but he hoped if they knocked all the invisible spiders from her, the cover would prevent any more from getting to her. He had no clue if they'd be able to seep through it, though.

He bunched it up around their feet as Paul said something, but Richard wasn't listening. He was focusing and thinking. He shot to his feet, opened his arms wide and knocked the noisy blob onto the bed.

"The fuck?" Paul shouted.

Their feet kicked out from beneath the bedspread. One end had fallen to the floor, the other came down over their calves.

Richard snatched the edge from the floor and held it up so nothing would be able to crawl up it.

"Hold this," he told Tanya.

Until that point, she had just been standing there with a dazed look upon her face. Now, she had something to do and sprang to life.

"Push them all down to your feet."

233

Dead Town

* * *

Kiara couldn't see the spiders in the darkness beneath the cover, but she still felt their fuzzy legs creeping over her flesh, some dragging their large, hairy abdomens across her. Their fiery bites pierced her clothing and skin, burning her like tiny briquettes of white-hot charcoal.

After they toppled onto the bed, Paul's hands started at her head and stroked down over her face and chest, down to just below her waist, knocking one from her ear just as it sunk its teeth into her and another from her neck.

"Yeow!" she screamed.

She rolled over with some difficulty and curled so he could take care of her back while she worked her front and legs.

She did what Richard told her to do, trying to get them down as far as possible. He, Tanya, or both whacked at her ankles and feet with their hands, shuffling them off.

"Let me know when they're all off," Richard said.

Paul kept clearing her head and back, down to just below her rump. Even when there were none left back there, his hands worked their way from the top down over and over.

"I think that's it," she said, breathing heavily.

Her entire body ached. Dozens of tiny flames burned beneath her skin where the spiders injected their venom.

Kiara wondered how toxic it was.

She rolled back to face Paul, even though she couldn't see him.

"I don't want to die," she whispered.

Paul wrapped his arms around her and pulled her close. There was an amazing comfort in his embrace, especially when he whispered back, "I'm not going to let you. I promise."

She relaxed, but wondered if that was a promise he would ever be able to keep.

* * *

A second and third cone of blackness appeared.

New faces and bodies filled them.

234

Xian Yi, Chinese, thirty-eight. He served in the Ministry of State Security where he tortured seventy-seven people and murdered fourteen, most of them Christians and other undesirable menaces to the socialist state.

Dula Gabra, a twenty-year-old Ethiopian who stole food from his starving neighbor Mengistu Masresha, even though he had plenty for he and his wife.

Natasha Nikolayevna, a beautiful house servant in Moscow, who hated her boss' husband and poisoned him one morning at breakfast because she thought it was the only way her friend would escape him.

Kenna was relieved for a moment when she realized none were for her.

The monster holding her spoke with a growling voice that startled her. "Watch."

From out of the darkness around her, hordes of goat-footed creatures with manly torsos and baby faces appeared. One had a long whip and began striping the spread-eagle woman, tearing chunks of flesh with each lash. Another had what looked like a vice. It placed it over Xian Yi's ears and began squeezing it until his black eyes popped out. One devil held a massive penis-shaped object covered with prickly thorns and rammed it up Trevor Watson's ass. Each one of them had an individualized torture. Each one screamed and cried in anguish.

"Soon, you will beg for this type of mercy."

* * *

As the two lay still, wrapped within the bedspread, Richard glanced at the rope and considered tying it around the hem to seal them off. After a few seconds, he decided it would be easier for the moment to just hold it all together.

Tanya sat on the bed by them. "You okay in there?"

"I think so," Kiara said, her voice calm. Then she groaned. "But I hurt all over."

Tanya gazed up at Richard. "What now?" she asked. "We can't leave them in there forever."

Richard shrugged his shoulders and shook his head. Without being able to see the spiders, he had no way of knowing if they had all retreated to wherever they came from or if they were creeping over the bed and floor, waiting for the opportunity to attack again.

"It's hot as shit in here," Paul said. "Let us out."

Richard glanced at Tanya then said, "Just give it a couple minutes."

After a minute, Richard had an idea.

"I'm going to open the bottom. Paul, you slide out as quickly as you can. Okay?"

"Yeah."

"One . . . two . . . three!"

As soon as Paul slithered out, Richard bagged Kiara back up. He scrunched the ends together as tight as he could, the excess opening near his knees like the mouth of a tied balloon.

"Kiara, carefully turn around so your head is where your feet are."

The lump on the bed began moving. After a few seconds it came to rest again.

"Now what?" she asked.

Richard loosened his hold on the spread, opening it a little. Barely able to see her face, she reminded him of a fox peeking out of its den.

"You see anything?" he asked.

She poked her head out a little and glanced around. The tight muscles of her blood-spotted and streaked face relaxed.

"Nothing."

Richard tossed the cover back, exposing her. She moved and sat on the foot of the bed.

"You got a cigarette?" she asked. "I don't know where mine are."

Richard retrieved his pack from his shirt pocket and offered her one. She took it with trembling fingers and placed it between her lips. Her eyes darted around the room pausing on the end of her cigarette as he lit it.

Although he couldn't see the spiders she saw, the evidence was clear. All over her face, ear, neck and arms, were raised red bumps with two puncture wounds and droplets of blood like the one on his finger.

Richard lit a cigarette for himself.

Paul sat on the corner of the bed between Tanya and Kiara. He pulled out his pack of American Spirits from his back pocket as Tanya stood and got a Newport off the dresser. She sat back down with a wince.

Richard sat on the other side of Kiara.

They smoked in silence. Richard didn't know why they were so quiet, he only knew he had no idea what to say. This was in part—if not fully—his fault.

Kiara placed a hot hand on Richard's knee. The dampness of her sweaty palm seeped through his jeans. She exhaled a cloud of blue smoke into the larger cloud hovering in the room.

"Thank you," she said, just above a whisper.

Richard contemplated placing a hand on her knee in return as a gesture of solidarity and understanding, but decided against it since he wasn't sure how she would take it. Instead, he just nodded with his cigarette dangling from his lips.

Kiara turned to Paul. "Thank you, too," she said in the same quiet voice.

"Bet," Paul said, wrapping his arm around her shoulder and pulling her near.

She dropped her head to his shoulder.

Whether Paul noticed the look Tanya was giving him or it was a natural motion, Richard wasn't sure, but Paul tucked his cigarette between his lips, wrapped his other arm around Tanya and pulled her closer. He took a draw off his smoke and exhaled.

"Are we going to die here?" Tanya asked, separating herself from him.

Kiara lingered a moment longer, then sat up.

"We'll figure this out," Paul said with amazing confidence.

Richard pulled his phone from his back pocket and looked at the screen. "I think I have good news . . . and bad news."

CHAPTER 19

A part of Kenna, deep inside, felt every pain those around her experienced. On some cerebral level, her head squished in the vice, the whips stung her skin, the cactus ripped her insides. Despite who they were and what they did, her heart ached for them when she shared their anguish and the utter hopelessness they felt. She looked at the beast with loathing as he relished in the hurt and suffering surrounding them.

After a few minutes, the tormentors scattered into the blackness and the afflicted stood motionless—just as they had been when she entered—waiting for the inevitable flames to come again.

He had called this "mercy." She couldn't imagine what might be worse, but as soon as he began moving again, she knew she was about to find out.

They moved between the people tortured by the black flames. As they reached the far side, the fires died out and she saw two cones stood empty, their occupants had vanished, but to where she didn't know. A couple fresh bodies filled the vacancies as the beast carried her out and the baby-headed demons reemerged.

This place seemed to go on forever. It was just darkness and suffering and more darkness and more suffering. Worse was the fact that neither she nor the demon carrying her seemed to tire. He still held her at arm's length as if she weighed nothing and she still had strength to kick and squirm, even though she had long resigned herself to the futility of it.

She had hoped she would choke to death in his grip or that he would set her down, neither of which happened. Her neck hurt from supporting the weight of her body so long. She wondered if she would be a couple inches taller when he finally turned her loose. *If* he ever turned her loose. Or perhaps her head would simply separate from her body.

They continued moving until they entered another open space about the size of a bedroom. Around the edges of the area, black flames rose chest-high. They offered no light, but intense heat. It had to be at least a hundred and twenty degrees in there.

From behind the flames, disfigured, monstrous faces peered at her with rabid anticipation. Like all the others she had seen, they were black, but their color, race, etcetera was still easily discernable—right down to the Irish woman who was fairer than the Englishman next to her, though they were the same shade of black. A tall thin man had skin that bubbled and boiled all over his naked body. Another's throat had been eaten away as if by acid. There was a black man with several large nails piercing his skull. And an emaciated woman who starved herself to death. Hundreds, maybe thousands, of burned, impaled, crushed, melted, despondent souls stared, waiting to see what happened to her.

A cone of dark light appeared out of nowhere in the center of the room.

"Living meat is a rare treat here," the demon said.

With the ease of one tossing a tennis ball, he threw Kenna at the beam. As she hit the outside edge, her clothes fell off and she passed into the dark light naked. Her body stopped before it hit the other edge of the beam, trapping her inside.

The flames around the room died down and the multitude of voracious beasts inched toward her, looking like a mob of hungry zombies.

Everything went blacker as even her body's light died.

* * *

Paul sat between Kiara and Tanya smoking in silence. He was amazed by how his mind managed to wander all over—from *how the hell do we get out of here?* To *what the fuck just happened?* To *damn, her body felt good.* At the time his hands were running up and down her, that thought didn't cross his mind, but now in retrospect, he replayed the sensations, the curves of her hips, the firmness of her breasts.

When she thanked him, he put his arm around her. She leaned into him, placing her head on his shoulder and he had the sudden realization that he truly adored her. A pang of guilt hit him, because Tanya was there beside him but, given his druthers, he would have preferred to be anywhere—other than here—alone with Kiara. But Tanya *was* there. They were *all* stuck there together—him doubly stuck.

With a mixture of guilt and concern, he reached over and wrapped an arm around Tanya. He adored her, too, but he never felt for her the way he did for Kiara. His relationship with Tanya was like the beginning of a long-distance race where runners started off standing up and settled into a steady pace. Kiara was like a Triple Crown contender bolting out of the gate at Churchill Downs. It was fast and thunderous and filled with excitement from start to finish.

Tanya sat up and asked if they were going to die.

"We'll figure this out," Paul told her, though he didn't have the slightest inkling how that was possible. He only knew there had to be a way to survive. At least he had to maintain that hope—if not for himself, then for the others.

As Kiara withdrew from him, Richard said, "I think I have good news . . . and bad news."

Every eye turned to him. Paul wasn't ready for any more bad news, but he certainly could use something good.

"It's after four-thirty," Richard said.

Paul shook his head, not understanding the significance, but suddenly understanding why he was so exhausted.

"I told you before, the veil between the living and dead was thinnest at midnight."

"And?" Paul asked.

"It's like a rubber band stretched to its fullest length. It gets really thin, but the closer we get to dawn, the less tension on the band and the thicker it gets."

"But you opened it completely," Kiara said.

Richard looked around. He crossed his left ankle over his knee and crushed out his cigarette, then pulled out his pack. He dumped the dead butt in and pulled out a fresh smoke. After he lit it, he continued.

"Not *fully* opened. More like stretched it thinner and opened a localized gateway between the two realms—the closet. Stronger entities can permeate the barrier while weaker ones, such as ourselves, can use the portal."

"How the fuck is that *good* news?" Paul asked, crushing out his cigarette in the same manner Richard did, but dropping the butt to the floor near the rope at his feet.

"It's good because if my hunch is correct, everything will reset itself at the first hint of light. The veil *should* go back to normal."

"Should," Paul repeated.

"And bad because . . ." Kiara's voice trailed off and Paul's picked up.

"There's no telling what else might come this way."

Richard nodded. "That . . . and if Chase and Kenna are still alive, they'll be trapped there forever if they don't make it out before the reset."

"So, what do we do?" Kiara asked.

Richard took a drag from his cigarette. "I don't know. Try to survive for the next hour or two?"

"Easier said than done," Tanya said.

"We just need a plan," Paul said, trying to think of a way they could all stay safe. "And we have to get Chase and Kenna back."

Tanya looked around. She pinched the end of her cigarette butt between her thumb and forefinger, with the cherry at the top, and asked Paul, "Will you put this out?"

As Paul picked up his foot to stub it out, Kiara dropped hers to the floor and crushed it with her boot. He tossed Tanya's filter to the floor by his and contemplated the situation. He considered locking themselves in the bathroom with as many candles as possible, but that didn't help Kenna and Chase. Nor did it prevent the invisible spiders or whatever other terrors awaited them from magically appearing in the tight room. Being that close together could help, but it might also be a hindrance.

Until tonight, Paul had never believed in heaven, hell, witchcraft or any of the other hoodoo shit Tanya did. Now, he was doing his best not to display how terrified he was of those unseen, unknown things. Up to this point, his greatest fear had always been failure. It led him to not assert himself at certain things for fear he might not excel. Other times, it demanded more from him than he knew he had. But now, he had two fears competing for dominance over his mind. Not only was he failing his friends and watching them die around him, but it looked like he would soon be dragged off to hell with them. He didn't know which was worse—being the last one standing before going to hell, or getting there before them and watching them arrive. One thing was for sure, hell wouldn't be the party he often joked it would be with rock stars, hot girls, and plenty of good drugs for all the cool people.

Tanya stood to get another cigarette from the dresser. As she did, the rope flew off the ground. In a lightning-fast, smooth motion, it slipped its untied end through the eye of the slip knot and landed around Tanya's neck. The rope pulled taut and yanked Tanya back. It jerked her over the bed and dragged her into the hall before anyone could get up.

* * *

Hopelessness filled Chase. It was as if all the desperation of the souls around him filtered into his body and being through every pore, devouring his soul like a cancer. The further he ran, the more he worried he would never see Kenna-Grace again. He tried to focus on her. He tried to picture her smiling as he found her. He had to believe if he could just center his attention on her—and her only—he would be guided to her. But with each second in this place, the cancerous oppression grew, consuming his hope.

Chase continued to run, constantly looking left and right, forward and over his shoulders to make sure he wasn't blindsided again. For the first time, he realized he was not running on level ground, but going downward, deeper and deeper.

The cries around him grew louder. So did the silence and feeling of isolation.

The blackness enveloping him opened up as he reached an area where a number of people stood frozen beneath cones of impossibly dark light.

Chase came to a dead stop, unsure what to expect. He worried they might attack, but none seemed to notice his presence.

Although he had never seen any of them before, he knew who they were and every bad thing about them. Murderers, rapists, child molesters, drug dealers. The one thing they all shared in common was the thing that terrified him most. They had all been dead and tortured in other chambers for years before being placed here for new torments.

Another wave of hopelessness rushed over him. Was he dead, too? If he was, when would he find himself in one of those?

Bursts of black flames shot up from beneath each soul, animating them with excruciating agony. As they burned, blistering and bubbling from the intense heat, Chase took off, running between them, trying to focus on the only thing that mattered—Kenna.

He weaved between the writhing souls, ignoring their screams. When he came out the other side, he had his first glimmer of hope—a dull glow in the distance.

* * *

Things had finally started to calm down, Tanya's heart included. The unseen spiders that attacked Kiara were gone and they were in a lull. Everything was back to normal, if that word could be used in a place like this. Normal meant her underwear were still wet and her insides still hurt from the abuse they took earlier, Kiara had bloody bumps like infected boils all over, and Richard had dried, scaling blood covering him. But nothing attacked them at the moment, so that was a good thing.

Paul suggested they come up with a plan. She had confidence in him. He would find a way to protect them until dawn came and—hopefully—things reset as Richard said. After that, who knew? Could anything ever be the same again?

She thought about the thousands of women raped each year and wondered if any of them ever went back to life as before. She wondered if it made a difference whether anyone else could see her attackers. *She* saw them. They were as real as anyone else in the room.

Tanya stood to get another cigarette.

As she fidgeted with the box, something thick and coarse looped around her throat and jerked. She flew backwards onto the bed, bounced, then slid off, her butt and ankles hitting the floor, but her head and shoulders suspended in the air as it pulled her out the door.

Dead Town

She tried to scream, but couldn't. She could barely breathe. Her hands clawed at her throat, trying to get some separation between the rope and her skin as she slid down the hallway.

Tanya kicked and thrashed. Paul ran out and grabbed one of her ankles, trying to pull her back. The rope tightened.

Blood pooled in her head. Her eyes watered. Her neck hurt. She couldn't breathe.

"Don't *pull* her," Kiara shouted.

* * *

Paul dashed out of the room and caught up with Tanya. At the same time, Richard or Kiara came out with a cellphone light on, illuminating the hall a cold blue-white.

He couldn't see what held the other end of the rope, but something had to because it was suspended high in the air, as if slung over a large man's shoulder.

Tanya gagged and choked, her hands clutching at her neck, her feet kicking.

By the time they were at the bathroom door, Paul caught her foot. He pulled on her, trying to wrestle her away from whatever had her. He didn't stop her motion, but he slowed it down. If one of the other idiots would help him, they might be able to snatch Tanya and the rope from the invisible hands.

"Don't pull her!" Kiara said.

"Fucking *help* me!"

"You're choking her!"

That was the dumbest thing he heard all night. He was *saving* her. No. He *wasn't*. Kiara was right. Him pulling on the rope only drew it tighter around her neck. He could see the skin cinching, the rope digging deeper into her throat as her face turned from red to plum purple. Her eyes were large and watery, protruding out like giant bug eyes. He had never seen a more terror-stricken face in his life—not even Dari's.

Paul felt helpless. He had only a couple seconds to save her and he had no idea how to do it. He couldn't hold her, that made it worse. If he let her go, she would be hauled off to God knows where.

Richard ran past him and grabbed ahold of the rope between the crook at the top and Tanya. He leaned back, tugging, his feet sputter-stepping as he tried like hell to keep them from passing the rooms at the top of the hall.

Paul let go of Tanya's ankle, resolved to run up front and help Richard. As he did, she was dragged faster. He was almost there when Richard flew back as if hit in the chest by a sledgehammer. Paul tripped over him.

Tanya slid past them, kicking and choking.

She flew into the air and over the bannister.

Snap!

The rope tied itself to the wooden rail.

Paul scrambled over Richard to the landing and looked down.

Tanya's head was cocked at an obscene angle as her body swung like a pendulum in an imperfect circle.

He failed again.

CHAPTER 20

Kenna-Grace opened her eyes and looked around. She was in her room, snug in her bed, the sheet pulled up to her chin. Sunlight pushed in through the thin drapes covering her window.

She closed her eyes and pressed the first few fingers of each hand into them, recalling the nightmare she had just had. She shuddered.

Her phone dinged, alerting her to a new message. She pulled it from beneath her pillow and looked at the text from Chase.

--WYD

--Just woke up

--Awful house?

That definitely sounded like a good idea. She was hungry as hell. At the same time, she just wanted to stay in bed and clear the dream from her mind. Maybe if she went back to sleep, she could dream something different, better.

--IDK

--Get your ass up. I'm coming to get you. I'm hangry af!!!

--K. Need to shower 1st

Kenna rolled out of bed. Outside, a mockingbird sang and a blue jay screeched.

She grabbed a fresh set of clothes and cracked her door, listening for signs of the warden. *Nothing.*

Kenna padded down the hall to the bathroom and entered, closing and locking the door behind her. She took off her clothes and turned the water on, waiting for it to get hot before she pulled up the knob and climbed into the shower.

The combination of heat and pressure was a soothing godsend. She imagined the steady stream washing away all the filth and grime left on her from last night's dream.

As she stood, eyes closed, letting the water beat down on her head, the shower curtain whipped open. The metal rings squealed against the shower rod.

In one single motion, Kenna jumped, opened her eyes and did her best to cover her chest with one arm and her crotch with the other.

"Hey, baby girl."

The warden's naked breasts sagged toward her paunchy stomach and exposed winter-bush. Matthew's blue and white basketball shorts, the only thing he had on, poked down and out several inches from his partial erection.

"Thought you'd get away that easy, bitch?" he said.

Matthew grabbed a fistful of hair and jerked her. Her legs hit the edge of the tub as her hip crashed to the floor. He dragged her out into the hallway, banging her shoulder against the doorframe on the way.

"You're about to get yours, baby girl," the warden said, following them out.

Kenna kicked and screamed as she clawed at the hand holding her hair.

"Shut the fuck up, bitch," Matthew said. He leaned over, hunkered down a tad, then dropped a heavy fist to her nose and mouth. Silvery streaks filled her field of vision like she was in the middle of an exploding skyrocket.

As she lay stunned, Matthew knelt over her hips. The warden walked up and, facing Matthew, straddled her head.

Kenna tried to buck Matthew off or roll, but couldn't. "Get the fuck off me!"

Pepe ran up, barking and growling, not understanding what was going on, but doing his best to help her. He nipped and jumped at Matthew's knee.

"Aw, so cute," Matthew said. He scooped Pepe up in one hand and stroked his back a couple times.

Pepe calmed down and looked at him as if to say, "Oh, okay. Everything's cool."

Then Matthew patted him on the head between the ears a couple times. His free hand grabbed the small head and twisted one direction while his other hand twisted the other way.

Dead Town

Crunch. Pepe went limp, but that wasn't enough for Matthew. He giggled as he continued twisting and pulling, until Pepe's head popped off. Hot blood spattered Kenna's abdomen just before Matthew tossed both pieces of Pepe down by her feet.

The warden cackled as she slowly lowered herself over Kenna's face. Kenna closed her eyes and turned her head. The warden ground her hairy, rotten-fish cooch up and down Kenna's cheek.

"Give mama a kiss," she said, pressing harder.

Kenna swung wildly, trying to knock the warden off her. She punched at the soft stomach a couple times, but knew she wasn't generating much force from her position. Then someone snatched one of her hands out of the air—then the other.

"You're a feisty little bitch, aren't you?" Matthew said.

The warden stood up a little. "Mama's all dry," she said. "Maybe this will help."

Just inches from Kenna's face, she began masturbating.

"Why are you doing this?" Kenna screamed.

The warden looked down between her legs at her. "Because you're an evil cunt, baby girl." Then she let loose a stream of piss that hit Kenna on the inside corner of her eye, stinging her. Hips gyrating, the warden sprayed Kenna's head and neck. Kenna held her breath and looked away.

The warden raised up a little higher and pissed on her breasts as Matthew grabbed them and squeezed like he was trying to juice a couple unripe limes.

"Show mama that face."

Kenna refused to open her eyes or turn her head back up.

"Bitch, you better listen to your mama!" Matthew said as he smooshed her breasts tighter in his hands and twisted until she screamed.

"That's better," the warden said as she squatted down and jammed her stinking crotch on Kenna's nose. She pushed down hard, covering her nose and mouth, squealing with delight as she rocked back and forth.

Kenna was sure she was about to suffocate in that rancid cooch.

BANG! BANG! There were two quick, deafening blasts.

The warden fell over backwards.

Kenna looked up. Chase held the gun he had taken from Matthew earlier. As Matthew whipped around and started to say something—*BANG!*

The bullet hit the right side of his head, and ripped through the other side, spraying her chest and face with blood, bone and brain matter.

Matthew slumped over. Chase grabbed him by the shoulder and knocked him off Kenna. She pulled up her legs as Chase pointed the gun down at Matthew's head and fired again.

Without saying a word, he stepped past her to where the warden lay, with two small bleeding holes—one in her cheek, the other in her neck. He pressed the muzzle up against the underside of her chin and pulled the trigger. Half her jaw vanished as the top of her head spattered against the wall, leaving gore, a patch of hair, and blood everywhere.

* * *

"Should we cut her down?" Kiara asked as she stood at the bannister with Richard and Paul, looking over at Tanya's swinging body.

"Why?" Richard asked.

Kiara scrunched up her face. She had expected them both to agree. "Do you really need to ask?"

Richard stood upright and began speaking with a more defensive and emotionless voice. "I'm not trying to be callous here, but let's be honest. There's nothing we can do for her. She's dead."

"She's my friend." The word stuck in her throat, cracking her voice.

"That's all good and well, but what good is pulling her up or cutting her down going to do? We need to be thinking of how *not* to end up like her."

Kiara wanted to beat the shit out of him or throw him over the railing for being so heartless.

"Every minute we stand here debating what to do with her or fiddling with her is a minute we can spend preparing for whatever else comes our way." He took a deep breath and nodded. "And it's coming. It *knows* its time is limited. It will take as many of us as it can before the veil thickens and the portal closes."

Dead Town

Kiara looked to Paul for support. That was his girlfriend he just watched get murdered.

He stood up and turned around. "He's right," he said, but he didn't sound happy about it.

"Then *what*? What do we do?" she asked, though she knew they were right. She didn't bother moving Hayden or Ladarius. No one even thought about it or mentioned it. But somehow this seemed different. Maybe because she was closer to Tanya than anyone else in the house. But just the image of Tanya swinging there, her head bent far to the right, was unsettling. It was almost as if it wasn't final. Tanya would never be able to find peace until she was on the ground.

"I guess we go to the gateway and try to figure out a way to get Chase and Kenna out," Paul said.

"Are you fucking nuts?" Kiara asked. "I'm not going in that room. Not after what happened to T—" She couldn't say her name. "*Her* in there."

Paul placed a hand on each of her shoulders and looked her in the eye as he spoke. His voice was calm and reassuring, despite the contrast of his words. "Do you really think *any* place is safer than another here?"

She shook her head.

"We need to be in there in case they scream or come back." He looked at Richard, then back at her. "And if they don't, we need to at least *try* to get them out."

He promised he wouldn't let her die, but he couldn't help Tanya or Ladarius. How would he keep her safe?

* * *

Chase gained on the dull light much faster than he closed the distance before. Perhaps she noticed him and paused for him to catch up or started walking back toward him. As he got closer, he realized a black cone shone down over the glow, muting it.

He moved closer, periodically glancing in various directions to make certain he didn't get ploughed into again. On either side were more and more faces and bodies along the barrier, pressing against it, trying in vain to get at him.

Then, when he was maybe eight feet from Kenna, the walls around him opened into another room. It was definitely her, frozen and naked, inside the conical prison while a mob of translucent hideous, black creatures crowded around her.

None of the other faces as he ran past them stood out to him. They were more like throngs of fans trying to get to a rock star or celebrity. They had individual, non-descript heads and faces, but their torsos and lower bodies all seemed to meld into one massive blob. These were different.

Those directly in front of him had their backs to him. They were men and women of different ages and backgrounds, heights and weights, but individuals. Chase glanced down to see if they had goat-feet. None did.

A short woman with ribbons of flesh hanging off her—or what might have been flesh if she were corporeal—tried squeezing her way between a woman with only the left side of her head and a taller man. The back of his head was opened and pushed out, resembling a lotus flower, as if he had taken a shotgun blast through the mouth.

He could see the faces of those on the other side of Kenna. Some looked almost normal, despite the mixture of hunger and delight in their darkened eyes as they pawed at the beam holding Kenna. Most, though, looked as if they had been the victim of intense physical trauma or torture.

Then the unthinkable happened.

First one, then another, then groups began to take notice of him. They disregarded Kenna and turned their attention and appetite toward him.

* * *

"If one place is as good as another," Kiara said, "then let's go in there." She pointed to the first door on the right.

Paul agreed. "Okay, you two go in and I'll get the candles."

With their cellphones on for light, Richard led Kiara into the bedroom as Paul walked down the hallway.

Once in the room, Richard sat on the comfortable bed.

"We're going to be okay," he said, trying to reassure himself as much as her as she stood at the door, her head poking out and staring in the direction Paul had gone. "We only have a little more to go."

Kiara remained in place until Paul returned with the candelabra.

"What're you doing?" she asked as he ducked back out of the room.

A few seconds later, he returned with an ashtray and set it next to the bed.

Kiara sat beside Richard and lit a cigarette while Paul remained by the door like a sentry, occasionally craning his neck and peeking out.

"Salt!" Richard said, breaking the uncomfortable silence and startling the others.

"What?" they asked.

Richard pushed himself off the bed.

"Salt," he said again. "It's a natural purifier and a supernatural one, too. Ghosts and demons can't stand it. They can't cross it, either."

Paul's voice dripped with sarcasm. "Cool. Got any in your shirt pocket there?"

"There's a kitchen downstairs."

"I can't . . ." Kiara said, trailing off and Richard immediately understood why.

"I'll go," he said. "Right after this."

Richard lit a cigarette and tried to mentally prepare to separate from the group—or what was left of it. From eight down to three. That was a lucky number, right? Maybe they would make it.

When he finished, he crushed out his cigarette, turned on his cellphone flashlight and left the room, saying, "Wish me luck."

He made his way down the stairs, constantly aware of the body hanging near him. When he got to the bottom, Richard shone his light up at Tanya. Her tongue stuck out as if mocking him. Her body slowly rotated toward him. A wet patch ran down the inside seams of her jeans from her crotch almost to her knees. Richard expected her eyes to pop open, but they didn't.

He stood and listened for a moment. Satisfied there was nothing but a quiet, high-pitched creak from the rope or bannister, he headed down the hallway for the kitchen. The hair on his body raised up and his skin goose-pimpled when he walked past the open door to the

252

basement. He couldn't decide, though, if a cold air was coming from it or it simply gave him the chills.

Every footstep filled him with anxiety, especially when his tennis shoes squeaked on the hardwood floor. For whatever reason, he felt like he was walking to his death, like a convict heading to the long-antici-pated electric chair. His steps became slower, measured, despite his instinct to run to the kitchen and back up the stairs.

Richard rambled through several cabinets finding countless place settings for every occasion, but no seasonings or salt cellars. He scanned the kitchen and noticed a couple doors. The first was a narrow staircase leading down, perhaps to a root cellar. The second was pre-cisely what he was looking for, a butler's pantry. He stepped in, held his phone up and began perusing the shelves until he found a couple cardboard canisters of salt. He grabbed them and walked out.

Cellar, he thought.

It was worth a shot. He shone his light down the stairs into the darkness. If there was a door up here, there might be a door leading out. He recalled the green double doors that opened up to his grandfather's cellar from the outside.

Richard walked with caution on the old stairs. Each one squeaked and groaned beneath his weight after having been neglected for so long. Halfway down he began testing them, slowly lowering himself onto the tread before fully committing, just in case it cracked like the other set.

At the bottom, he panned the room with his light. It was a small cellar with another staircase on his right leading up. He directed his light that way and saw a large wooden door on an angle. This could be their shot.

He approached the steps, wondering what he should do when he got the door open. His mind raced a million miles an hour allowing him to play the various scenarios through his head before he even made it to the possible exit. He could leave and try to get help, but by the time he was able to make a call or get someone, it would probably be first light and the others would be safe. Say, "Fuck it," and save himself? Maybe he could tear the shutters off the front window from the outside and then holler for them to come down. One thing was sure, once he was out, he did *not* want to come back in. No, if the door opened, he would run as fast as he could upstairs, shouting for them. They would meet around the parlor and head out together.

Richard set the salt on the top step and his phone next to it with the light shining on the door. He reached up with both hands and pushed. Nothing. It didn't budge half an inch. He grabbed his phone and tried to shine it through a small space between two boards, but he couldn't see anything. He set the phone back down and moved up a couple steps, bending over further with each stair until he was near the top. He raised up slowly. When his shoulder blades touched the wood, he tried to straighten his back and push with his legs. It still didn't move.

He hunkered down again and tried to push harder. This time the stair he stood on let out a quiet *crack*. Even with a lock, the door should move a little. There had to be a tree fallen on it or something.

Richard grabbed the salt and his phone, then walked back down the stairs. As he scanned the floor, a white bulbous object caught his attention. He got closer and crouched down. It appeared to be a bashed-in baby skull. A couple feet from it was another one with what looked like a hammer hole in it. Many of the small bones of that skeleton lay intact by it.

Richard stood and shook his head. Was it possible they had sacrificed babies and threw the corpses down here? Or maybe these were illegitimate children killed after birth. He didn't want to think about it. He had to get back upstairs.

As he reentered the kitchen, a glimmer on the center island snagged his eye. There, on the butcher block, was a large knife with about a ten-inch blade. He grabbed it and stuck it between his belt and jeans then headed back for the bedroom. He'd see what Paul thought about trying to escape through the cellar.

* * *

Paul remained at the door, watching and waiting.

"What's taking him so long?" Kiara asked.

He had his suspicions, but he didn't want to verbalize them. It was foolish, he knew, but it felt like if he said what he thought, he would end up speaking it into existence. As if Richard was more likely to return as long as he didn't say, "He probably died down there." But she was right. It was taking Richard far longer than it should have to run to the kitchen and back.

Kiara sniffled. When Paul turned, a tear glistened in the candle's glow on her cheek. She quickly wiped it away with the back of her hand.

God, she's beautiful, he thought. Almost immediately after, he pictured Tanya dangling over the parlor floor and a fresh burst of guilt exploded within him. He had to be the world's biggest douchebag.

Her next question shocked him. "You think you're the only one that hasn't been attacked because you're an atheist?"

That thought never even entered his mind. It was possible, but he doubted it.

"I've been attacked," he said.

"What? *When*?"

Paul walked over to the bed and sat beside her. "All night."

She gave him a confused look as her eyes travelled up and down his body.

He withdrew a cigarette from his pack and lit it.

"I can't tell you how many discussions and debates I got into with Christians." He took a drag and exhaled. "But at some point, they always ask, 'what if you're wrong?' In those heated moments, there was never a doubt, but I'd be lying if I said there weren't times when the question came back to haunt me—especially those instances where I thought I might have died." The expression on her face said Kiara wanted more detail. "Like when I had my wisdom teeth cut out and had an allergic reaction to the penicillin and Vicodin. I ended up in the emergency room that night. The next morning, I wondered what if I *did* die? I thought, in the grand scheme of things, on an earth over four billion years old, nineteen years is incredibly short. There *has* to be more to my existence. But then as quickly as it came, the thought perished."

Kiara grabbed her pack of Marlboro Menthols off the bed and fished one out. She lit it, then said, "True. But you're still the *only* one here that's been spared."

Paul shook his head emphatically, took a drag off his cigarette, and said, "But I haven't. Almost this whole night here has been like one constant attack against me. It sounds stupid in my head and will probably sound even dumber to you, but besides those rare doubts, my greatest fears have *always* been failing or being helpless. Like when I was a kid, I used to look up in the sky and see planes flying overhead. I thought the worst thing that could happen would be to see it coming down—crashing. Not because the people would die, but because I would be standing there, completely powerless to help. That's this night. One fucking plane crash after another. I couldn't help Dari. I couldn't save Tanya . . ."

Kiara placed a warm, comforting hand on his thigh. "You tried."

"And failed."

He didn't love Tanya. He didn't even want to date her anymore since meeting Kiara, but he sure as shit didn't want her to die. He'd rather walk out of the house with her unharmed and be trapped in a relationship with her for the next couple years than to have *this* happen to her. She called it. She *knew* bad shit was on the horizon and he pushed her forward anyway. Straight to her death.

Then something happened that hadn't happened since his grandmother died when he was fourteen. A tear spilled down his cheek.

CHAPTER 21

Chase panicked when the black souls noticed him. He understood what the old deer-in-headlights cliché meant, but it always pissed him off when he saw someone freeze in front of the psychotic killer or monster in a horror flick. He always knew *exactly* what he would do—grab this or that, run like hell, whatever—until now. *Now*, he understood that fear-freeze. But he wasn't a deer in a bright light, he was a package of ground meat on a shelf, waiting to get snatched up and eaten. He wanted to turn. He wanted to run. He wanted to get the fuck out of there as fast as possible, but his body wouldn't listen to what his brain shouted.

The first to reach him was a man in his mid-thirties with the top right quadrant of his head smashed in at about a forty-degree angle. That was how he landed after swan-diving from a three-story building. An eye and ear were missing. The other eye hung down on tendrils to his cheek, reminding him of Ladarius. The second, a woman, looked like a mummy covered in melted wax, but she had two smaller heads, torsos and sets of arms melted and attached to her ribcage. She had set her house on fire. With both her kids drugged and passed out in her bed, she lay down between them, waiting for the flames to consume them all.

She reached out and clawed at his forearm. Her fingers were even colder than the air around him. In her touch, he felt her desperation and sorrow. More than that, he felt like a piece of him died with her. A Bible verse came to mind, though he couldn't remember all of it. But Jesus was walking and a woman touched him and he said he knew it because virtue had gone out of him. Something like that. And that's how Chase felt—something like that. When he looked down and saw the red fingermarks she left on his flesh, his feet finally obeyed his brain. He turned and ran.

Dead Town

Chase went a few steps and cast a glance over his shoulder. They flew after him, running, but their feet not touching the ground. He wanted to try something, but he had to keep Kenna in sight, or at least her approximate location in relation to him. He made a quick left, running into the sea of screaming faces and bodies. As elsewhere, they parted for him, creating another corridor.

Several of the dark souls followed him, their movement hindered or halted as the darkness closed behind him. Whatever they were, they were not protected the way he was from the masses restrained by the invisible barrier.

After running a little further, he made another left. Kenna's glow radiated a short distance from him on his left. Once he had passed her, he made another left in the swarm of souls and, finally, another. He ran into the room from the opposite side and charged the cone of light, determined to dash through it and pull her from it as those originally in the room filtered back in from the other direction.

Like Mike Tyson once said, "Everybody has a plan until they get punched in the mouth."

Chase got his punch when he hit the dark cone and bounced off it, falling onto his ass, as if the beam of black light holding Kenna were made of steel. He took a second punch when those that had followed him into the screaming faces began emerging from the darkness into view.

He spun away from them and scrabbled backwards like a crab until he bumped against the icy cone. If he could just get to his feet, he might be able to lure them away again, this time further and deeper into the black sea to give himself more time to get her out.

But it was too late.

Groping hands and hungry, chomping jaws descended upon him.

* * *

Not twenty-four hours ago, Kiara was on Hayden's sofa, sleeping. He was alive. Tanya was alive. Her biggest concerns were trivial things like clothes and work. Even her guilt over immediately crushing on her friend's boyfriend seemed like an inconsequential matter. Now, she had *real* issues. Well, *one* issue. Living.

She sat beside Paul, listening as he confessed his fears. She hadn't known him long, but the way he carried and presented himself, she never would have guessed he struggled with those things. Even here, through this interminable night, he came off so confident and strong. But that's what leaders do. They push through the bullshit, hide their insecurities, and inspire others to march along with them. He was a natural leader and, though she wasn't a natural follower, she had faith in him for some reason.

Her ears perked up and her eyes shot to the doorway when she heard footsteps on the stairs. A second later, the aura of white light illuminated the hall floor.

"Got it," Richard said, stepping into the room.

He turned off his cellphone and stuck it in his back pocket. Tucked between his left forearm and ribs were two containers of Morton's salt. As he grabbed one with his right hand, she noticed the butcher knife he acquired from somewhere downstairs.

That could be useful, she thought, feeling a little satisfaction and relief at finally having a weapon.

Richard tossed the first can of salt to Paul. The front of his shirt, midway down his body, billowed out, fresh blood soaking it as he arched his back and screamed in pain. In one swift motion, his feet rose a couple feet off the floor and his body fell backwards, he flew upward then crashed down hard against the wooden floor with a *thud*!

* * *

Chase helped Kenna to her feet. She glanced down at the warden and Matthew's dead bodies. When she saw poor Pepe, she was glad they were dead. They deserved what happened to them.

Before Chase said a word, Kenna saw a figure standing behind him.

"Daddy!" she said.

"What have you done?" he asked with a voice as stiff as the Marine uniform he wore.

"They were . . . They . . ." She sputtered for the right words.

Chase moved over and her dad stepped up beside him.

Dead Town

"I joined the Marine Corps to keep you safe. I *died* because of you. I have to tell you, sugar bean, I've been watching you from above and it was *not* worth it. *You* weren't worth it."

Kenna's stomach dropped. Why would he say that?

"My heaven turned into a hell watching you. They were right. You're an evil little whore that should never have been born. I'd still be alive and happy if it weren't for you, you worthless cunt."

"But, daddy . . ."

His features began to change. His face and hands rotted in front of her, the flesh oozing and dripping from his bones. Thousands of maggots crawled over him and dropped from his sleeves to the floor. The stench gagged her, requiring all her will power to keep from vomiting on him.

Chase looked over at her dad then back at her. "He's right, you know," he said. "You are kind of a whore." He reached into his pocket and pulled out three brass bullets. After ejecting the spent cartridges from the cylinder, he loaded the fresh rounds.

"Look what you've done," her dad said, waving a semi-skeletal hand at the bodies on the floor. "We're all dead because of you."

Chase pressed the barrel against the side of her daddy's head and pulled the trigger. His body crumpled to the floor.

"He was a dick," Chase said. He pointed at the warden. "She was an asshole. And you're the piece of shit born from ass-fucking her."

Kenna's mind reeled. Between the thick odors of rot and piss and blood and gunpowder, her stomach churned. The one person she knew she could always count on just turned on her.

Chase surveyed the carnage. "He was right about you not being worth it. I ain't going to prison over your worthless ass."

He put the gun to his temple and pulled the trigger. Bone and brain splattered against the wall, but he didn't die. His eyes crossed and he dropped to the floor, writhing and wriggling uncontrollably, blood gushing from his nose. The pistol flew from his twitching hand.

Kenna stared, horror-struck.

Her breath hitched in her chest when Matthew grabbed her ankle.

* * *

He made it. He was back to the safety of the group. He kept expecting something hellish to happen the whole way up the stairs, but it didn't.

Richard put his phone away and tossed Paul some salt.

As he was about to tell him what to do with it, there was a loud snort behind him. A burning pain shot through his back and belly. Before he knew what was happening, his feet came up off the floor and he flew into the air like a slow runner in Pamplona. He smacked the floor, his left hand bending back at an unnatural angle with a snap.

Dazed, Richard looked up into Azazel's smoldering eyes. He had an evil grin that promised more to come. Blood and goo dripped from one horn.

Richard scrambled to his feet. Azazel reached out and clawed him down his chest, shredding the front of his shirt, barely penetrating his skin. The wounds bled and burned, but were superficial compared to what they would have been had Richard not staggered back.

Paul and Kiara remained on the bed, their eyes searching the room. They couldn't see the demon in front of them.

Azazel lowered his head and gored Richard again, the horn slicing through his gut and out his back. With one flick of his muscular neck, Azazel flung him into the ceiling. Before he hit the floor, the beast caught him with both horns. Burning pain riveted his body as one horn pierced his right thigh and the other ripped through the back of his left shoulder and out the front.

* * *

Richard flopped around like a sock monkey, getting tossed into the air, slammed down, tossed up again. After Richard's body crashed against the ceiling, leaving blood splotches that made it look like a modern art canvas to Paul, he came back down, but never hit the ground. Rather, his body was suspended at least six feet in the air like a magician's floating assistant. Two fresh, large wounds opened on his shoulder and leg. Blood quickly soaked through his shirt and jeans, blackening them then trickling off in thin streams.

Until that point, Paul sat on the bed trying to figure out where and what his attacker was and the best way to help. Once the blood flowed freely, it covered a wide set of horns and dripped down, partially painting a transparent face and shoulders. What hadn't been visible before, now was visible in part because of the blood.

"Here," Paul shoved the salt into Kiara's lap as Richard screamed in agony.

Lunging from the bed, Paul charged—shoulder first—at the unseen waist of the beast. It was like hitting a stone column.

Thwock! A powerful hand, hard as a brick, knocked Paul upside the head, sending him crashing into the dresser. Before Paul could regain his footing, the horns jerked and threw Richard into him. They toppled to the floor leaving Richard—groaning—on top.

Paul labored to push him off and get to his feet as the demon—for lack of a better term—approached.

Richard staggered to his feet a few inches in front of him, his right leg buckling a little, making him look almost drunk. He pulled the butcher knife from his belt and swung.

The bloody horn pitched forward and gored Richard again. His skin and organs ripped with an audible *guish!* He yelped like a kicked puppy and dropped the knife as his body doubled over and shot up into the air.

Blood spattered over the demon, bringing his chest and feet into view. Paul snatched up the knife, raised it over his head with both hands and brought it down as hard as he could against the blood-reddened breast.

Patang! The blade snapped off near the handle as his hands continued on and hit the hard skin.

* * *

Richard flew into Paul. His jaw snapped shut and shattered a couple teeth. There was no getting out of this alive—at least not for him. Even if Azazel tired of pitching him around and vanished, he would probably still end up bleeding to death.

Richard pushed himself to his feet, his thigh burning and unable to bear his weight. He withdrew the knife, determined to defend himself and the others. Perhaps, if he got a couple good blows in, Azazel would retreat temporarily.

He took a wild swing, the blade careening off the armor-like flesh of the demon.

He didn't have time to react when Azazel dropped his head forward and thrust the massive horn through his gut. All those symbols of protection on his torso did nothing to spare him. Pain, like he had never known, shot through him. Every finger and toe tingled and burned.

As Azazel lifted him into the air, he thought, *at least this will be over soon*.

Blood filling his eyes, Richard hung there as Paul tried to save him.

The blade flew past him with a *whiff!* For a fraction of a second, he thought there was hope for him, but that glimmer died when the blade broke and fell to the floor.

Azazel thrust out his foot and kicked Paul square in the chest. He flew backwards, slamming into the wall.

Azazel snorted, pitched his head forward and dumped Richard to the floor. The demon rose to his full stature and glared at him before plunging his hand down forcefully. There was a loud, painful *crunch* as the sharp claws ripped through the skin and destroyed his breastbone.

Fire ripped through Richard's body as Azazel gripped his heart and snatched it out.

Richard had just enough time to think, *it's all over now*, before everything went black.

But the blackness was brief, like a blink. He was still in the dimly lit room when Azazel pierced his body with both horns and lifted him up.

Richard hung in the air on Azazel's horns for a second. He looked down and saw his bloody corpse on the floor. That's when he knew this nightmare would *never* be over.

* * *

Kiara watched in horror from the bed as something brutalized Richard. Unsure what to do when it began, she opened the salt and poured a congruent circle around herself, making certain to fill in the wrinkles and low-lying places.

Dead Town

The more Richard bled, the more she could see what attacked him. The more she saw, the more her heart raced and the harder it became to breathe.

When Paul jumped into the fray, Kiara worried for both boys. Fear glued her to the bed. Whatever physical strength she might bring to the fight would be about as helpful as a plastic spoon was to someone trying to cut a tough steak. Then the knife broke.

Kiara skimmed through the catalogue of spells in her brain. The only book that might have useful information was the one she quickly read and shelved, keeping solely as a remembrance of Derek. She never imagined she would need *anything* from that book.

It all happened so fast, and yet it seemed to drag on forever.

Then it was over. Richard's heart flew out of his chest and dropped—still beating—to the floor beside him. Paul staggered toward the body and the blood-drenched demon dissolved into nothingness.

Kiara glanced at Paul. His eyes were wide, the whites glowing in the candlelight. Richard's blood covered Paul's face and body. He looked as frantic as she felt.

She shook her head and said, "We are so fucked."

CHAPTER 22

Matthew had a tight grip on her ankle. After a couple unsuccessful attempts to jerk her foot loose, Kenna stomped on his wrist with her free foot and pulled with the other at the same time. That worked.

It seemed impossible that Chase didn't kill Matthew, especially with all the blood and brain matter that spattered her, but there he was reaching for her again, blood and pinkish slime oozing from the large hole above his left ear. If she could just get to the gun by Chase's flopping body. There was one bullet left and one bullet in the right place was all it would take to finish the job.

Chase stopped twitching, but blood still seeped from both sides of his head.

Kenna grabbed the gun and spun toward Matthew. He was trying to push himself to his feet. Worse than that, the warden was moving, too. One bullet was not going to kill both of them.

"Sugar bean," her daddy said behind her, "it's a shame your mama didn't have an abortion. You know that?"

Kenna kicked Matthew's gory head, knocking him back enough that she could run past him and the warden for the safest place she knew. She charged into her room, closing and locking the door. Kenna leaned against the wood and listened. The amount of clunky commotion out there told her all she needed to know. At least three—if not all four—had gotten to their feet and were coming after her.

Someone rapped gently on her door. Kenna glanced at the window. Maybe she could dive out, hop in her car and take off. As if reading her mind, someone opened the front door. Her path would be cut off.

"Sugar bean, let daddy in." When she didn't respond, he said, "Come on, sugar bean. Let me in."

Still leaning against the door, Kenna closed her eyes. She didn't know when she started, but as a tear tickled her cheek, she realized she had been crying.

Dead Town

"Let us in, you worthless cunt!" the warden said.

Motion in her periphery caught her attention. Matthew stood outside her window. His fist smashed through the glass. He leaned in then pulled the curtains and rod down. At the same time, the door started shaking from someone trying to force it open.

"You know how much fun I'm going to have with you when we get in there?" Matthew asked. He extended both arms through the window and started pulling himself up, ignoring the large shards of glass cutting into his flesh. "After we take turns fucking every hole you got, I'm gonna make another one right above your belly button and fuck your guts out."

Kenna's heart *thump-thump-thumped* in her head as she started to cross the room, determined she wouldn't miss the one shot she had. Whatever was left of his brain was about to fly out the back of his skull. Once he was dead, she'd jump out the window and—

Boom!

The door flew open. Her daddy planted the foot he used to kick it in and smiled. Behind him, the warden and Chase stood, grinning like they knew something she didn't, hunger filling their eyes.

* * *

Kiara could almost taste the blood pooling over a large patch of the floor and spattering the walls and ceiling. The dresser, the bedspread, the clothes she wore—everything in the room had anywhere from a few drops to large smears of blood on it. Worse than the ferrous stench, though, was the odor of shit wafting up from Richard's exposed and broken intestines as his lifeless, mangled body lay crumpled between Paul and her.

Kiara dry-heaved a couple times. She had never smelled anything so wretched in her life.

"I didn't know *what* to do," she said, feeling like she owed Paul an explanation for not jumping in.

Still leaning back against the wall, he stroked the back of his head and neck a couple times. "You did what you should have."

She had no doubt he meant what he said, but it did little to assuage the guilt she felt. Maybe if she grabbed the ashtray and—

"You could have ended up like him." He declined his head toward Richard.

Kiara turned and stared at the darkened hall outside the open door. She had seen enough death for her entire lifetime in just a matter of hours. She couldn't look at Richard anymore. His body was like a barometer, a harbinger of things to come. It was just a matter of time before she and Paul ended up like that. She knew she would be the next to go. Not because she was any weaker or worse than Paul, but because he *promised* he would keep her alive and safe. Because the only thing more hellish than dying a brutal death was surviving and watching the slaughter of everyone around you. She wished she had been the first to go.

"Come on," Paul said, placing a hand on her shoulder as he slipped between the bed and Richard's body. Paul squatted down, picked up the container of salt Richard had dropped, and held it up. "Any left in that one?" he asked, pointing at the blue cylinder beside her.

"I think I used it all." She pulled it from the bed by her knee and shook it. A few grains rattled within.

Paul extended his hand and she took it. There was an unmistakable reassurance in his touch that compelled her to abandon the ring of salt. It was a fortress built on sand anyway. One slight tap or bounce on the bed and it would fall apart.

Paul led her out into the dark hallway and stopped. Her pulse skyrocketed when he let go of her hand and dipped back into the room. She spun on her heels to see what he was doing and caught another glimpse of Richard. She didn't have time to turn her head. Kiara doubled over as her stomach churned, tightened, forced all its contents up her throat and out her mouth. Vomit splattered against the floor, splashing on the door frame and her shoes. Just when she thought she was done, her stomach balled again and she puked until nothing else would come out.

Paul picked up the candelabra. Little stubs remained beneath the flickering flames. He tucked the salt between his forearm and body, then placed his free hand on her back as he stopped just shy of the puddle of vomit.

"It's all good," he said.

As she stood, he stepped over the puke and joined her in the hall. His hand gently stroked her hair a few times.

Dead Town

"Let's go," he said, jerking his head toward the back of the house.

The dark doorway ahead caused her heart to flutter.

There was an eerie silence. The only sounds were that of her breathing and the careful, light steps they took toward the back bedroom, as if they were both trying to sneak up on the room.

One of the candles sputtered out.

* * *

It was cold.

It was dark.

Black hands reached for him from a mob of tortured faces.

Chase sat with his back against the solid light, his knees drawn up. Each hand, each finger that touched him was like a block of frozen nitrogen—colder and darker than the air around him.

His skin burned as goose pimples covered his body.

With every touch, a morsel of virtue left him, devoured by the hopeless souls around him, replaced by an equal measure of their despair. It was inexplicable. Painful memories of children killed in car wrecks. Loves lost. Betrayals.

An icy hand touched his face like a mother stroking the child she hadn't seen in years. Chase remembered the baby's round face, her strawberry blonde hair pulled up and held by a pink plastic butterfly barrette. Her bright blue eyes stared up at him, her tongue protruding slightly from between her small mouth just before his hand brought the hammer down on her forehead. It went through easier than he had expected. The wooden handle crushed her nose and jaw. Blood flew up on his face as pink slime thwacked against the crib walls. It was easier this way. She would never know the pain of living—the heartache of abandonment—the torture of giving her love to someone who would tread on it like a zealous winemaker stomping grapes.

He recalled picking up the limp body and carrying her to the empty king-sized bed. He set her down on the pillow, covering her up to her chest so she wouldn't get cold, then walked to the other side of the bed where a full bottle of Oxycontin waited, already open, beside a liter of Absolut. He popped several pills at a time in his mouth, washing them down with the vodka until all ninety pills and more than half the

Absolut were gone. They he laid down beside her, pulled the sheet up to his breast and waited.

Another freezing hand latched onto his wrist. He remembered when the bitch left him, taking his son with her. As if that wasn't bad enough, the whore went to live with his best friend and business partner who had not only been fucking her for years, but ran the company into the ground, leaving him penniless. Despite how much he hated her, he still loved her. Sitting in what used to be her favorite chair, he pressed the shotgun muzzle into the soft skin beneath his jaw, slipped his big toe through the trigger guard, and pushed.

More and more hands lashed out at him. More and more memories filled his mind.

Mingled in with everyone else's despair was his own. Kenna was trapped, naked, behind him. He couldn't save her. Ladarius—dead. He couldn't help him. Hayden—dead. Paul, Tanya, Richard, Kiara. By now, they were all probably dead, too. He would never escape this. Even if he did, how would he ever forget it? Each one of these souls showed him, even if he could get out and somehow bleach the memories from his mind, life held nothing but misery for him and everyone else in the world. No one is ever truly happy. They are simply relieved in their small moments of reprieve from the long days of suffering.

Chase bawled. Tears streamed down his face. He couldn't take any more.

His break came when one of the souls near him dropped a 1911 he had used to end the pointless anguish of life.

Chase picked up the pistol and racked a round. He shoved the barrel in his mouth and placed his finger on the trigger.

It'll all be over soon, he thought.

He looked over his shoulder at Kenna's thigh and buttocks. Then up to her long dark hair flowing down her back. The only girl he ever really loved. Always this close and always miles away.

As his finger began to squeeze the trigger, eyes still on Kenna, he said, "I love you."

* * *

Dead Town

Paul looked at what remained of the candles as he set the holder on the dresser. They needed to get more, but he wasn't sure if he would be able to walk past Tanya without losing it. He already felt like he was going insane.

He glanced at the bloody sheets. He was reluctant—even scared—to sit on the bed.

Poor Tanya, he thought as he sat on the floor, leaning against the wall beneath the whips and bondage tools.

Kiara sat next to him. He guessed she was probably just as uncomfortable with the idea of getting on the bed. His gaze turned to the dark closet and he wondered if what raped Tanya was similar to the horned thing that got Richard or if something else crossed over from the other side. He'd never know now. Paul found himself wishing Richard were still alive if only so he could ask if everything that happened sprang from the closet or if it passed through that thinned veil to wherever it pleased.

What was it Richard said? Something about stronger spirits passing through the veil, but weaker beings using the portal. Then Paul wondered about the salt he had beside him. Would a ring around him and Kiara be like an infinite tube extending up and down? Or would airborne creatures be able to fly over it and spiders creep along the ceiling before dropping down? If that was the case, how useful was the damned salt anyways?

Paul pitched forward until he was on his knees.

"What're you doing?" Kiara asked.

It was worth a shot. He crawled over and poured a line of salt extending from door post to door post in front of the closet.

"Just in case," he said as he resumed his position beside her.

Another candle went out with a quiet *ffft*.

It was only a shade dimmer than before, but that lessening of light caused a dramatic increase in his heart rate—at least for a few seconds. It was just a matter of time before the other candles died and they would be forced to rely on their phones for light. Who knew how long they would last? His battery was already almost dead.

Paul glanced at the closet. It looked even darker in there now. He scooted over to the doorway, cupped his hands around his mouth and shouted into the small space.

"Chase! Kenna!"

"You really think they're going to hear you?" Kiara asked.

"Can it hurt to try?"

"It can if it brings something else out of there."

"Salt," he said, pointing at the floor. "Hopefully, that'll keep it in the closet."

Paul shouted a few more times. He had to look like a complete moron.

When he turned back to face Kiara, his eyes grazed over the bed and the three ropes at the top, each about six or seven feet long.

"I have an idea," he told Kiara as he pushed himself to his feet and made his way to the rope on the far side of the bed. After untying the knot that held it to the post, he tossed it on the pillow and walked back around. He grabbed one of the ends of the rope he just untied and the end of the other rope.

"Right over left. Left over right," he said. He held up the square knot he had just fastened. "Help me with the bed."

* * *

Time slowed in a way only the surreality of intense stress could bring about. Instead of seconds flying by, they melted, coagulated, and dripped off the clock like cool honey from the edge of a spoon.

Kenna looked right. Matthew was still struggling to pull himself up and through the window. Blood from his forearms smeared the windowsill and spilled to her carpet. She looked left. The warden, Chase and her daddy stood blocking the only door out of the room.

One second . . . two . . . three . . .

She had no idea how much time actually passed, but everything and everyone around her seemed to be wading through an invisible pool of tar in comparison to the lightning speed with which her mind raced.

Chase kicked off his shoes. He unbuttoned his pants, hooked his thumbs inside the waistband and pushed them and his drawers down around his ankles. "I'm riding that train, too," he said as he stepped out of them.

His actions and words were incongruent with the boy she thought she knew and crushed on since she was fourteen. For six years, he was

271

the rock and lighthouse she looked to and expected to keep her safe from the turbulent sea that was her life. Now, like everyone else, he betrayed her. His pretending to side with her and detest the warden was just an act. But it was a pointless façade. If all he wanted was to get in her pants, he could have asked. There was never anyone she adored more. Six years she waited for a sign from him he took a romantic interest in her. She would have gladly made the first move if he just *hinted* he wanted more than friendship. Hell, she would have done the whole friends-with-benefits thing just to know what it was like to kiss him and feel his warm naked body pressed against hers. Six long years—almost a third of her life—wasted waiting for Judas to reveal his true nature.

Contrary to what she had long thought, there wasn't a soul in this world she could depend upon.

"Everyone was right about you," Chase said as he pulled his T-shirt over his head. "You're nothing but a worthless cock tease."

"When did I *ever* do that to you?" she asked.

"Now, it's time to pay the piper, darlin'."

"Daddy has a little something for you, too." He unzipped his pants and pulled out his semi-erect penis.

"Ain't no one getting a piece of that ass before I do," Matthew said, finally dragging his torso through the window. He flopped to the floor. When he stood, blood covered his chest and stomach where the shattered glass gouged long lines through his flesh.

Kenna pointed the gun at Matthew. He stood motionless. She swung it around to the other three.

"You can't kill us all," the warden said.

By now, Matthew had lost his shorts. He pinched his limp dick between his thumb and first couple fingers. He jagged furiously, making it quickly stand on end. "You only got one bullet left."

"That's enough to at least take *one* of you out," she said, pointing the pistol at him.

Matthew wiped his abdomen with his right hand, smearing the blood. Using it as a lubricant, he stroked himself a few times, then went back for more blood and repeated the motions.

"You sure about that?" Matthew asked.

"One bullet, sugar bean." Her daddy shook his head from side to side.

"Who's it going to be?" the warden asked.

Kenna intended to use it on the first person who moved toward her, but the question made her wonder. Who did she *want* to come at her first? She couldn't decide who she hated more at that moment—the warden or Matthew. She only knew she hoped it wasn't Chase or her daddy. Despite everything transpiring, she wasn't sure she would ever be able to shoot either of them.

"Sugar bean, do you know who the last bullet is *always* for?" His bony fingers pawed at the exit wound on his skull. "Of course, you do."

He may not have actually meant it, but he was right. Four of them, one of her. Once she spent that round, the survivors would shred her to pieces.

The thought of being pinned down again and raped repeatedly sent a chill through her body. Her skin crawled. She understood—no matter what happened in the next few seconds—she wasn't getting out of here alive. Now, the only two questions that remained to be answered were how bad was it going to get and *who* would end up killing her?

She was standing there. She was breathing. Her heart was drumming out a quick, loud beat in her ears. A vein throbbed in her temple. And despite all that, she knew she was dead. It was just a matter of time before her body accepted that death and ceased to function.

Four of them. One of her. One bullet. Who was going to kill her when they got done with her? *No one.* One bullet was all it would take to rob *all* of them of the satisfaction.

Kenna cocked the hammer back with her thumb then shoved the barrel between her jaws until the cold metal pressed against the roof of her mouth.

One . . . she thought.

"You don't have the nerve, baby girl."

Two . . .

CHAPTER 23

Kiara grabbed the salt from where Paul left it and clutched it to her breast like a priest holding a crucifix. She thought his shouting at the closet was crazy, but now he looked even crazier untying and retying ropes.

"Help me with the bed," he said. She had no idea what he meant. "Come on."

She rose to her feet, still holding the salt in case something happened.

Paul took hold of the post at the top of the bed and pulled. The heavy feet scraped and scarred the hardwood floor as the bed moved.

He pointed at the post at the foot of the bed on the opposite side. "Get that one. Help me spin this."

The racket, amplified by the unnerving silence of the house, was awful. Eventually, though, they had it rotated about ninety degrees.

Paul got on her side of the bed, but closer to the top. "Now push."

They bumped and pressed the bed, scooting his post closer and closer to the closet door.

After a little more tweaking, they had it so the bed sat at an angle, the edge touching the dresser, with the pillow and rope near the closet's threshold.

Kiara looked at the setup and figured he was going to toss the rope into the closet. She imagined it coiled up and sitting on the floor, as useless as screaming into the darkness. But then he crawled onto the bed and began tying the rope around his waist.

"What the fuck are you doing?" she asked. Before he could answer, she said, "You are *not* going in there."

Once his knot was tied, Paul sat on the mattress, leaned back against the post and lit a cigarette.

"Someone has to."

"You're not leaving me here to die alone." The words felt like a golf ball in her throat.

"We're not both going," he said. He took a drag off his cigarette and exhaled. All that cool bravado he always wore abandoned him, leaving Paul with an air of uneasiness about him.

He puffed so hard and fast on his cigarette, he hotboxed it. The cherry had to be at least an inch long. When it was almost down to the filter, he tossed it over the edge of the bed near her and said, "Step on that, will you?"

She ground the butt between the floor and her boot.

"Please don't," she said.

"You're not going to die." He gave her a forced, synthetic smile. "I'll be right back. I just want to see what's there."

"And what if you can't get back? The other two didn't just jump in and out."

"The other two didn't have a rope to pull themselves out with, either."

Paul took out his cellphone and turned the flashlight on.

"It's going to be okay," he said. "You'll see."

Kiara wondered who he was trying to convince—her or *himself*. She hoped it worked on him, because she was not comforted in the slightest.

"See you in a sec," he said. Then he rolled off the bed into the closet, pulling the rope taut as he vanished.

* * *

It took a second to get his wits about him and figure out where he was and what happened.

Just before Chase pulled the trigger to slam a round through his brain, the hands and faces and shrieks of terror disappeared. As soon as he said, "I love you," Chase found himself standing in Kenna's living room. Multiple voices chattered down the hall.

Chase looked and saw a sliver of the warden's ass hanging out Kenna's bedroom door. He ran toward her.

"Kenna!" he said. "Are you okay?"

Dead Town

The warden poked her head out. By that time, he was already upon her. He barreled her over and rushed into the room, where Kenna stood naked with a gun in her mouth.

"Kenna!"

Although severely decomposed and bloody, he recognized her father immediately from the old photo in her room. Mr. Brooks wheeled around and grinned at him. Beside her father stood . . . *himself?* Chase scrutinized his disrobed mirror image. He, too, had a shit-eating grin on his face.

Chase looked past Kenna at Matthew, all cut-up and bloody, jerking on his pecker.

"Too late, bro," Matthew said.

"Kenna! Put the gun down."

Other Chase sucker punched him. His knees wobbled. Before he could regain his composure, Mr. Brooks walloped him alongside his head with an iron fist.

* * *

Paul landed in almost complete blackness, his phone screen and light having gone out immediately. He tried turning it back on, but the battery died. All around him, people shrieked and screamed in pain, but he couldn't see anything. His eyes still hadn't adjusted to the darkness. He glanced down at his hands. They had a dim golden glow to them.

He searched the icy space around him, seeing nothing save the rope he had fastened around his waist, extending up and up until it faded into the darkness, far beyond what was possible. There just wasn't that much rope when he tied it.

Paul wondered.

He took a few steps forward, testing the length and durability of the rope. It stayed with him, never tugging at his waist or loosening. It just seemed to move along with him as if he wasn't moving at all. It was like the rope was on a spool, lengthening as he needed it. When he stepped back two steps, it reeled back in, leaving no slack.

The noise of tortured people filling his ears was bad enough, but worse was the simultaneous silence and the isolation that a deaf-like quiet brought.

Paul looked at his feet to see if he could see the ground passing beneath him. There *was* no ground—only a thin sheet of glass or something. Beneath that were thousands of faces and hands reaching up for him. He jumped, before he realized they couldn't get to him.

He looked around some more. Now, with his eyes adjusted to the darkness, he saw masses of people on either side, in front of him, and behind—all pressing against an invisible wall that kept them from tearing him apart. For whatever reason, he was safe.

Out of nowhere, something bowled him over.

* * *

The rope was pulled tight from the bed to a little above the closet floor. It just ended in mid-air. Kiara sat on her knees on the bed, her eyes flitting from the rope to the dark closet to the itty-bitty candles to the door opening to the hallway and back again. She glanced down at a break in the salt extending across the threshold.

She picked up the salt canister and opened it. Before filling the gap, a thought occurred to her. What if they needed that space in the line to keep the rope attached to Paul or to get back out? She sat on her haunches, glimpsing the bloody sheets. Staying close to the closet made her feel as if she was still near Paul, but she couldn't remain on the bed—especially not after her gaze wandered to the instruments on the wall beside her.

She stood up—salt in hand—and took a step from the bed. That was far enough . . . And close enough. She crouched down and drew a ring around herself with the salt. Satisfied, she sat Indian-style on the floor within the circle. From here, she could still see the bed, the stretched rope, and the hallway.

Fear, hunger, fatigue all took their toll on her. Kiara closed her eyes for a moment, wishing she could fall asleep for a few minutes. She knew she couldn't, but oh how she would have loved to drift away in dream.

Something knocked near the closet. She opened her eyes, her heart leaping with excitement at seeing Paul again. But it wasn't Paul. A large beast with flat black, leathery skin and a wide set of horns stood

277

between her and the bed. His lips peeled back like a snarling dog's, revealing a row of jagged teeth. He looked down.

The salt!

He breathed heavily, like an asthmatic. Each expulsion of air reeked of death and decay.

Her heart pounded against the inside of her breastbone, threatening to explode at any minute as she absorbed his full countenance. He was muscular and sinewy with the thickest, longest penis she had ever seen. He raised one arm and reached for her. Long claws extended from the ends of his fingers.

Kiara's breath hitched in her throat. She was about to die—here, alone—despite Paul's promises. She closed her eyes anticipating the razor-sharp nails tearing through her flesh. But they never came.

When Kiara opened her eyes, she saw the monster's hand frozen in the air. He looked down again.

"Salt," he said, the word sounding more like a snarl. "How long do you think that will last, Kiara?"

Her stomach burned when he said her name.

She centered herself in the circle. Her eyes flicked to the wall with all the stuff hanging on it. He couldn't use those to get to her, could he?

"We have great plans for you," he said, thrusting his hand out for her.

It stopped as if hitting a brick wall.

"Just as we have some wonderful torments for Kenna and Chase—once they kill themselves."

He kicked at her. She flinched, even though his foot stopped just as sure as his hand had.

"When we peel your skin off inch by inch, should we start with your face or your feet?"

Kiara finally found her voice. "Go to hell!"

"I plan on it." He leaned closer and bared his teeth at her. "And I will take you back with me."

* * *

Kenna opened her eyes and pulled the gun from her mouth.
What the fuck? she thought.

How did Chase get his clothes back on so fast and why did they have him on the ground, kicking and punching him?

No. Chase was still naked.

She blinked a couple times then looked again.

Chase was definitely on the floor, curled in a fetal position. *And* he was standing there naked, kicking and raining fists on the one on the floor.

Like lightning illuminating a dark room, everything changed for a fraction of a second. Naked Chase wasn't Chase at all. It was a large-skulled, bald creature with black flesh that looked as if it had been melted on and stretched tight. It had no features on its face, save the tall suborbital ridge above hollowed out eye sockets that seemed to extend deep into eternity. Its jaw was narrow, long and pointy like a possum's, but with several rows of small, triangular teeth. Then it was Chase again.

Once more, time slowed for Kenna. She scrutinized the others. Like a strobe light flickering on and off, they flashed over and over. Warden beast warden beast warden. Daddy beast daddy.

Kenna knew exactly who she wanted to shoot most. She lunged forward, placed the muzzle of the gun against naked-Chase's head and pulled the trigger. As he toppled back, she dropped the gun and grabbed the real Chase's arm. She pulled as hard as she could. Despite the hands and fists hitting him, he managed to get to his feet.

She reached behind her, opened the closet door and dragged him in as the demons stopped the charade and dropped their masks. She jerked the door shut.

Chase's hands covered hers and she let go of the knob. As he held it, one of the devils on the other side tugged at the door. Light seeped in through the crack before Chase leaned back and slammed it closed again. The door rattled back and forth between them.

Then another demon beat on the wood.

Kenna knew they couldn't stay in there forever. They probably wouldn't last another couple minutes before Chase's strength evaporated and failed, leaving them completely exposed to the bald monsters.

"I thought that was really *you* out there," she whispered.

He sounded surprised. "Why would I be naked in your house with them around?"

Dead Town

"I don't know," she said, feeling foolish. "You were going to rape and torture me."

A flash of light leaped through the door just before he shut it again and she saw he was looking at her.

"I would *never* hurt you," he said. "Don't you know how much I'm in love with you?"

Kenna's heart throbbed. What a fucking load of shit life can sometimes be. *Now*, he tells her. Now that they're both about to die.

She wasn't going to hide it anymore. And she definitely wasn't going to die without telling him.

"I love you, too," she said with a bold voice.

Everything vanished—the door, the closet, the entire house and the demons within.

She found herself and Chase standing in the large room with the mob of disfigured black faces and bodies surrounding and approaching them. What did it matter whether she died in her closet or in this dark place? She heard and said the one thing she had been craving to say for years.

Kenna reached down and took Chase's glowing hand, giving it a loving squeeze.

Her glow—as well as his—multiplied exponentially—like going from two separate matches several feet apart to a bonfire. The dark souls around them receded from the light they generated. Within a moment, they were back where they were before the horned demon threw her into the prisonous cone. The wall of flame sprang back from the ground, blocking the desperate souls from the two of them.

* * *

Paul wrestled with something, but he didn't know *what*. It had the body of a man, but two heads. One was like a misshapen human man with a massive forehead and jaws, but narrow cheeks and large triangular teeth. The other head was dog-like with a long, hairless snout. Neither head had eyes, just oversized vacant sockets filled with a blackness that seemed to go on forever.

He had never seen anything like it, but he didn't doubt his eyes. He had seen a lot of fucked-up shit tonight. Shit he would have sworn twelve hours ago didn't exist.

The living horror rolled him over, both mouths snapping at him, the dog growling and barking.

Paul had one hand on the dog's neck pushing it away as the other hand punched the side of the human head a few times.

His punches did little to deter the abomination. It came at him, chomping its jaws. It moved in and latched onto the top of his shoulder. He didn't know if the thing injected some sort of acidic venom or what, but it burned like a blowtorch on his skin.

It thrashed its head a few times like a rabid pit bull with a squawking chicken in its mouth

Paul pulled his hand from the snarling dog and punched at the other head a couple times. Just as it let loose, the dog sank its fangs into his forearm. It was another dose of fiery venom. Paul felt woozy.

The dog growled and shook.

Paul stuffed a thumb in the man's icy cold eye socket. It gave him just enough leverage to push the head away. He knocked the heads together and the dog lost its grip.

Stiff-arming the human head, he held both heads at bay.

Saliva dripped from the snarling and snapping mouths. Each drop burned his skin.

Paul grabbed the rope from behind the thing's back and looped it around the exposed neck of the dog. He pulled with both hands as hard as he could. That head squealed, then fell silent, though still alive. The beast pummeled Paul's face, but he kept his grip on the rope and continued pulling it tighter. Then—

Snap.

Its trachea—if it had one—or something in its neck broke. It stopped fighting him for a second and Paul found inspiration in the turn of events. He flipped the monster off him then scramble to his feet. As the dog head flopped lifelessly, Paul wrapped the rope around the human neck and leveraged all his weight and force to draw the rope tight as the creature flailed. There was another *snap* as the rope cinched. With a small noiseless, black explosion, the monster vanished.

Paul's tether drew tight again.

CHAPTER 24

Chase looked at the wall of dark flames encircling them. He had no idea which way to go to get back. The only thing he was certain of was that if they went the wrong direction, they could wander around down there forever—at least until they died of starvation—if something else didn't kill them first.

Kenna's warm hand fit perfectly in his as if the two were custom-made for each other. He couldn't let her down.

He glanced at her. Her eyes roved the open space. It was amazing, almost miraculous, the way her bright eyes shone and glistened within their combined light.

King David popped into his head. For Sunday School one week he and the other kids in his class had to memorize all of Psalm 130. It was short, but he couldn't remember any of it now, except for something like "Out of the depths I cried to you, O Lord."

Please, he thought, feeling like a hypocrite, *if you can hear me down here, help us. At least get* her *out alive.*

"Which way?" Kenna asked.

"Through the fire," he said.

He took a step forward. She moved with him. He took a few more steps until they stood at the edge of the flames.

"Ready?" he asked, hoping the fire would be much like the rest of this place with fluid walls that parted for them.

Kenna pumped his hand a couple times, smiled, and said, "I'd walk through fire for you any day, Chase Parker."

He stepped through the flames, not knowing what to expect on the other side, and Kenna-Grace stayed with him, stride for stride.

Chase was relieved to find there were no more of the suicidal souls waiting for them. It was once again the sea of the damned dividing for them to pass, the hopeless souls pawing at the edge of their light. Other than that, there was nothing and no one to guide them safely home.

* * *

A couple more candles sputtered out, leaving large, grotesque shadows on the walls.

Kiara stood inside her circular fortress, feeling safe, yet scared shitless nonetheless.

The demon pressed against the rim and inhaled through his flat, wide-set nose as if sniffing her.

"You do well to be scared," he said. "Your heart would fail you now if you knew precisely what we have in store for you." Once more, he snarled and showed his teeth. "But if you just draw a line through the salt, I will show you some mercy."

"Like you showed Richard?"

He paced around her circle, his feet slamming against the floor as he looked down, presumably for chinks in her armor.

Kiara drew a second ring within the first about an inch from it. If he managed to breach the first one, he'd have another to get through. Besides, it seemed like the perfect way to tell him to fuck himself. She wasn't coming out or letting him in.

"Very well. We will devise something even worse for you. Sooner or later, though, you *will* step over that line and I will come for you."

With that, he disappeared through the floor.

Kiara's heart raced like a hummingbird's wings, tattooing a beat against the underside of her sternum.

What if he comes up from below? She wondered.

She stared at her feet, watching and waiting, but he never reappeared. Instead, spiders filtered into the room through the closet door. Thousands crept over and under the bed, most marching directly for her, others climbing the walls then crawling across the ceiling until they covered every inch of the room except the circles below her feet and above her head.

* * *

Paul stood alone in the darkness. He considered shouting for Chase and Kenna, but realized all the others voices would drown his out with ease. More than that, the last thing he wanted to do was draw attention to himself and attract a herd of monsters like the one he just killed. One was difficult enough. Two or more would be the end of him.

Paul pressed on through the countless faces, constantly searching for some glimmer of hope. Finally, he found it. Far in the distance was a golden glow like his. It was just a pinpoint of light, like a star at twilight.

He sprinted toward it, trusting it had to be at least *one* of them.

As he ran, a thought occurred to him. What happens to them if the portal closes before they escape? *Trapped forever.* That's what Richard said. The thought was like the sting of a whip on a thoroughbred's hind. Paul ran harder, faster than he ever had in his life. He probably could have beaten Usain Bolt, even if he gave him a head start.

The glow grew larger, brighter. He was gaining on it. With any luck—which didn't seem likely down here—they were heading his way.

* * *

Kenna tried to block out the cries and faces of the afflicted. Instead, she focused on the warmth of Chase's hand. She recalled the kiss on the bed and wondered how, while she was inside her house in that conical prison, she could have forgotten it. Then she thought of the souls trapped here. No doubt, they had been robbed of every good memory—loves, kisses, children. They were left with nothing but the memories of the valleys in their lives.

Her heart broke for them.

She wished she could give them just a morsel of joy, a piece of her light to brighten their dreary existence. She knew she couldn't, but if she could have . . .

"Look!" she said, pointing at a light in the distance. It was then she realized they had been walking upward at a shallow angle.

"What is it?" Chase said, then asked, "*Who* is it?"

"Does it matter? It's *light*."

Still holding onto one another, they ran forward, through the endless slough of faces until they entered a new room. They froze, not knowing what to expect.

Hundreds of people of every stripe and from several centuries hung in the air as if on meat hooks. Every head and eye slowly turned toward her and Chase.

Those that had just arrived to this part of hell still had most of their skin. Others were whittled down almost to the bone. Gobs and mounds of flesh lay piled beneath each victim. Kenna watched for a second as narrow ribbons of flesh were stripped from each person. It was as if an unseen potato peeler slowly worked its way down their bodies.

They were despicable humans, most of them, but she wondered if they truly deserved this type of punishment for eternity. No, it wasn't eternal. At some point, they would move on to new torments. Perhaps this was part of their penance before being cast into the outer edges of blackness where they would suffer their miseries forever. Despite their deeds, all of which she knew, she wished she could set them all free.

They weaved through the hanging bodies and exited out the other side, still on course for the growing light.

* * *

Kiara knelt down and looked at the hairy spiders. As she got closer, she heard them chattering with high-pitched voices. She got even closer. The tiny human faces attached to the large black abdomens looked angry as they squealed, "Kill! Kill! Kill!"

They all waited and watched her, like an army surrounding and laying siege to a castle.

There was almost zero space between their long front legs and the salt protecting her.

"Kill! Kill! Kill!"

Kiara stood up again, wishing she had a flame thrower or something to take the little fuckers out. She glanced at the closet, hoping Paul would return soon. Maybe he could stomp around the room, squishing out their guts. Then again, maybe they would attack him, too. They didn't earlier. Everyone seemed to be attacked as individuals. But maybe as dawn grew nearer, they would become less concerned with their targets and kill indiscriminately.

* * *

Dead Town

The faces blurred as Paul ran past them. He wished he knew what time the sun was supposed to rise. Then he realized he couldn't look at his phone to see what time it was now, anyway. He only knew twilight had to be close—a matter of minutes. Whether it was three or twenty, he had no clue.

They needed to get out of there. *He* needed to get out. Was he really prepared to be trapped in this hellhole for eternity?

His gait slowed.

Every second he ran *that* way was a second he had to run the *other* way to get back to the vanishing end of his rope.

The light grew brighter.

Visions of Chase and Kenna in the past popped into his head—swimming at the falls, the ridiculous looking fat snowman Kenna built and named Carter—his middle name—after him. She said while laughing, "A stupid snowman deserves a stupid name." Picking wild blackberries so Chase's mama could make them all a cobbler. Double and triple dates. Fast rides down dark side roads.

He picked up his step, running harder than before. Wherever they were, that's where he wanted to be—even if it meant staying in this shitty place.

* * *

Chase knew he could run faster if he wasn't holding Kenna's hand. She would probably be able to run faster, too. But he didn't want to let her go. There was something magical about her touch. Besides that, he felt he had a better chance of keeping her safe if he was holding her. He'd never leave her behind, but that didn't mean something couldn't snatch her away if she dropped back even a single step.

Her fate was his fate. That's all there was to it.

Wither thou goest, he thought as he glanced over at her—her long hair bouncing and blowing back behind her as she ran.

What was once a pinpoint of light was now much larger. It *had* to be running toward them.

A couple minutes later, Chase slowed and Kenna came to a stop with him.

"What the fuck are *you* doing here?" he asked Paul.

"I came to save you."

Dried blood covered almost every inch of Paul. "What happened to you?"

"We gotta go!"

"Go? *Where*?"

With an impish grin, Paul tugged at an impossibly long rope trailing behind him.

"Back to that fucked up house."

* * *

Paul's incredible sprint left him amazed. Maybe it was adrenaline. Maybe it was the nature of this place, but he felt like he could run ten times farther without even getting winded. The only issues he had were the burning wounds in his arm and shoulder.

"Follow me," he said.

Paul turned and looked at where the rope dissolved into the blackness. All he had to do was follow it. He began running, keeping his eye on the far end. Sooner or later it would be directly overhead. Then they could get out.

Every now and again, he cast a look over his shoulder to make sure Kenna and Chase were still with him. He knew they were, though, because the light they shed was much brighter than what he alone produced.

He wanted to run balls to the wall like before, but they couldn't keep up with him.

"Faster," he shouted a couple times and they managed to pick up the pace. But when he realized he was outrunning them, he slowed down.

It seemed to take forever, much longer than he remembered, but finally the rope went from being in front of him to behind him. They overshot their mark. They stopped running and walked back until the rope went straight up and down.

"Now what?" Kenna asked, looking up.

"Climb?" Chase said.

Dead Town

It sounded like a good idea . . . until Kenna jumped up, grabbed the rope, and went nowhere. Chase tried pushing her up from the soles of her shoes, but she didn't have the grip or the strength to get any higher than he could boost her.

* * *

Kiara wished she had brought her cigarettes with her, but she left them on the floor where she had been sitting. Now, spiders covered them. Even if she could walk over there and get them, she wasn't sure she'd be able to smoke one after knowing what had crawled all over them. She didn't even want to *touch* the pack.

She pulled out her phone and checked the time. It was almost 6:20. When was the sun going to rise and put an end to this night? She wished it would end right now. But she also wanted it to drag on at least until Paul made it back—hopefully, with the others.

CHAPTER 25

"Y'all go," Kenna said as she stood looking up the rope. She would never make it. There was no way she was going to be the reason the other two were stuck down here. She'd deal.

"I'm not fucking leaving you," Chase said. "I *can't*." He looked at Paul. "Go ahead, bro. It's all good."

"Fuck that. It's *not* all good."

Kenna took Chase's hands in hers. She looked him in the eyes. "Please," she said. "Just go."

"Dammit, Kenna-Grace Brooks, what part of I ain't leaving you here do you *not* understand?"

So much time, so many years wasted because they were both too afraid to say something.

She stood up on her toes and kissed him, wrapping her arms around his back and holding him tightly.

"We're getting out. Now." Paul said.

Chase shook his head. "You got the same hearing problem she does? She can't climb the rope and I'm not leaving her alone."

"She doesn't have to. I got an idea." Paul tugged on the rope with both hands. "It's tied to me. I'm scared if I untie it down here it will disappear completely. So, I'll climb up and throw it back down. You tie it around her waist and I'll hoist her up. Then it'll be *your* turn."

That sounded reasonable to Kenna.

Paul scampered up the rope like a monkey. The further up he went, the shorter the rope got until he was at the far end. Then he and the rope vanished.

* * *

Paul popped out of the icy netherworld into the warmer cold of the closet, his feet straddling an unseen hole.

Dead Town

He was overjoyed to see Kiara standing on the other side of the bed.

His relief was short-lived.

"What the hell?" he shouted.

Thousands of spiders crept along the walls, floor and bed.

"Salt!" she said. "Fix the line there."

He didn't understand what she meant. Then a few spiders crawled off the bed and scurried over the thin break in the salt he poured earlier.

As Paul bent over to close the gap, a spider dropped from the door-frame above him. It latched onto his hand and bit down, delivering a sting almost as painful as the bites received on the other side.

He grabbed it with his free hand and flung it over the bed, then adjusted the salt so it made a continuous line. By then, almost a dozen spiders crawled up his pant legs. He brushed them off as quick as he could and mashed them under foot, trying not to accidentally slip back through the invisible portal.

"Did you find them?" Kiara asked.

"Yeah." He began untying the rope from his waist.

"Well, where are they?"

"Down there."

"Are they . . . *dead*?"

"Not if I can help it."

He dropped the rope to the floor. It just sat there. He picked it up and dangled the end, bobbing it up and down on the floor. He felt like a blind man trying to thread a needle, but it never passed through the eye. He glanced at the third rope hanging from the bed. There was no way he could safely get to it.

Paul undid the square knot.

"What're you doing?" Kiara asked.

"Just let me think. Okay?" It came out sounding ruder than he meant it. "I'm not trying to be a dick. I'm just trying to concentrate. Give me a sec."

* * *

Chase stood holding Kenna. It had been a couple minutes and the rope never came down. He didn't believe Paul would have left them there. Something had to have happened. Maybe the portal closed. Maybe Paul died passing back through. Whatever it was, he wasn't about to mention it to Kenna. He'd stand here and hold her until she said something or until they died.

"You know I love you, right?" he said.

Kenna nodded. "You know how long I've been waiting to hear you say that?"

She kissed him. Despite the icy air around them, her lips were hot and soft.

Kenna pulled her head back and stared into his eyes. "What's taking him so long?"

* * *

Finally, it came to Paul—not just the what, but the how.

Paul wrapped the anchored rope around his waist again and tied it. He used a rolling hitch knot to secure the loose rope to the center of the other, so it created a Y.

Satisfied, he said, "Be right back . . . I hope." Then, holding the loose end of the second rope, he jumped at the center of the closet and found himself engulfed in the cold darkness once more.

Chase and Kenna stood right where he left them, hugging. A couple tears glistened on her cheeks.

"I told you we're getting out," he said.

"Why are you back here?" Chase asked.

Paul shook his head. "The rope wouldn't come through on its own. I guess something alive has to be attached to it."

He would wait before mentioning the spiders above.

"Okay, but . . ." Kenna's voice faded.

Paul tied the added rope around her waist. If his hunch was correct, he would be able to climb the magically extending rope. Because Kenna was tethered to the other rope, it would remain just as long as it currently was.

"Just wait here," he told her.

He scurried up the rope a few feet and looked down. Just as planned, she remained there.

Once he was out, he would pull that rope and drag her up.

291

Dead Town

* * *

Chase watched as Paul disappeared again. A few seconds later, Kenna's feet came up off the unseen ground. She floated up a foot or two at a time, leaving him in a diminished light.

"Don't forget me," he said, trying to sound casual and force a smile, but inside he worried what might happen if the portal closed or if something got them as soon as they stepped out of the closet.

"I love you," Kenna said. That was all the reassurance he needed. He smiled again. This time for real.

After she disappeared, the smile fell from his face and dread set in.

Less than a minute later, Paul stood in front of him again, with the same setup as before—only no Kenna.

They repeated the steps. But Chase didn't wait to get pulled up. Once Paul was a little more than a body length above him, Chase began to climb his own rope.

* * *

Kiara looked at her phone again. 6:25.

A scuffle in the closet startled her and she almost dropped the phone. She saw Kenna's back and hair. A moment later, Kenna peered at her through the doorway.

"Don't move," she told her.

Kenna gasped. Her eyes got big. She saw the spiders, too.

A minute later, Paul was back and Chase was with him.

There were no words or even thoughts she could use to express her elation at seeing them all.

Her joy turned to confusion when she noticed all the spiders crawling over one another, draining from the ceiling and walls like a dark ink spilling down and headed for the center of the room.

Pfft. Another candle went out, leaving only one.

* * *

292

Paul stood next to Kenna in the doorway, watching the spiders coalesce only a couple feet from Kiara. They piled onto one another, forming four large, thick black columns.

He didn't know what was going on, but he couldn't be bothered by that yet. He was more concerned with the fact the three of them were standing in a closet with an open gateway to hell behind them. The salt would keep the spiders out, but it would also trap anything that might come through the portal in the closet *with* them.

"Quick! Throw me the salt," he said.

Kiara squatted down and picked up the container.

You only have one shot, he thought, but didn't want to lump any additional pressure on her.

"You can do it. Just toss it underhand. Right here."

He cupped his hands together as if he were about to scoop water from a pond.

Kenna threw the salt. It went high in the air and landed on the bed, bouncing and settling against the pillow. Fortunately, most of the spiders had already abandoned the bed, but a few stragglers headed back.

Paul wondered if they would try to tote it away. He reached across the threshold and snatched it up before they got there.

"Stand here," he told Chase, grabbing him by the shoulders and swapping places with him.

Paul opened the container and drew three lines to create a box around them with the fourth side being the line already at the threshold.

He set the canister down and turned to peek between Chase and Kenna.

What had been four columns, came together several feet up, then continued upward as spiders crawled over one another, piling on. That column split into several more. Paul realized it wasn't columns. It was limbs. The ghoulish spiders came together to create a bristly demon that looked like a freaky cross between a man and a spider with four legs and four arms. Its black eyes, gigantic and perfectly round—about the size of plums—sat on long and wide protruding cheek bones. The mouth was vertical instead of horizontal with jaws extending down at least six inches. It opened its jaws wide—wide enough to encircle Paul's waist. Inside the mouth, several tongues thrashed.

Dead Town

The demon turned to Kiara and swung at her with all four arms. His hands stopped as if he slapped a wall. He swung again and again, batting at the unseen barrier. Each time, Kiara jumped and closed her eyes. But he never made contact with her.

"Hey," Paul said, hoping to distract the beast from her.

It worked. The hideous creature turned its attention to him.

"Let us out," it said.

* * *

The four legs arching and carefully stepping in an unnatural way toward her terrified Kenna. Its face frightened her more than the things inside the portal. Maybe that was because it was here, in *her* world.

"Let us out," it said.

She had no idea what it meant.

"Let us *out*!" With all four hands, it grabbed the bed and flung it back along the wall, narrowly missing Kiara's salt ring.

Still tied to it, Chase and Paul flew over the salt barrier into the room with it. They toppled over one another.

There was no way they would be able to fight that thing while tied to each other. Both boys fiddled with the knots at their waists as it approached them.

"Let us go back," it said, it's voice scratchy like an old man's, but full of vigor.

It raised a hand to take a swipe at one of them.

"Wait!" Kenna said, realizing what it wanted. "If I break the salt line, will you leave them alone?"

"No!" Chase and Paul shouted.

The monster stared at her with huge eyes.

"Yesss."

Kenna wondered how good a demon's word could ever be. She didn't trust him, but she had to take her chances. They both almost died trying to save her.

"Okay," she said.

It slowly approached her, scrutinizing her.

"Back up," she said. "I'll step out and break the salt line so you can pass."

The demon backed away from the boys and her.

Kenna stepped sideways over the salt, first her right foot then her left. All the while she remained ready to jump back in if it moved. But it didn't.

Still watching him, she dragged the toe of her left shoe through the salt, making a break.

The demon rushed forward. Kenna flinched, anticipating a blow, but it leapt past her.

As soon as it was in the closet, she squatted down and transferred the salt container she had hidden against her body in her left hand to her right. She poured out the rest, filling the gap.

The demon punched and kicked the invisible walls around him. Kenna watched, a sense of satisfaction filling her. It was payback for what they did to her down there. For what they tried to get her to believe and do. For what they did to all those other souls.

Chase slipped his arm around her waist and she smiled, knowing he literally—not figuratively—went through hell to be with her. Paul stepped up beside her and, together, they watched the thrashing and cursing demon.

The last candle went out, plunging them all in darkness. Then a light came from behind—Kiara's cellphone.

"Is it safe to come out?" Kiara asked.

"I think so," Paul said.

She stood on the other side of him and placed one arm around his waist as she rested her head against his chest.

Kenna liked her. She liked Tanya, too. But this one was more of a keeper. She could see them lasting a long time together if given the opportunity.

"Where's Tanya and everyone else?" Kenna asked.

Paul shot her a menacing look like she should know better than to ask a question like that.

"*What?*" she said.

He looked down at his feet.

"Tanya's dead." His voice was shaky and feeble. "So is everyone else."

Kenna reached over and placed her hand between his shoulder blades and rubbed gently.

Dead Town

She didn't know what to say. *Sorry* seemed as ineffective as trying to use one of those small round Band-Aids on someone who just got their leg chopped off. So, she said nothing.

Bang!

The shutters opened. *All* the shutters on the house opened. Through the space between the drapes, the distant sky faded from black to gray to orange. The silhouettes of treetops looked like kindling on fire.

The beast in the closet had sensed the hour. It stopped fighting and turned to face the window. It drew in a breath then said something in an unearthly language.

KaPOW! It exploded. Pieces of it splattered the invisible walls and slid down like black and blue pudding oozing down a window. And then it was gone—every trace of it—as if it never existed.

* * *

They filed out into the hallway with Paul leading. Pausing near the bathroom door, he turned and faced them in the cool white light of Kiara's cellphone, a grave expression on his face. After explaining how Tanya was hanged from the bannister ahead, he said, "Just keep your eyes on the wall or stairs and you won't have to see her."

The tone of Paul's voice and the glisten in his eye struck Chase. He had never seen or heard his friend like this. He wanted to say something to comfort him, but what? She's in a better place? He *knew* that wasn't necessarily true. He wanted to believe it, but he had seen too much in the last few hours. He saw the torments that awaited them all. But *maybe* she and the others weren't there. After all, he didn't *see* them. Maybe she wasn't as bad as anyone down there. Then again, some of those souls seemed like normal people, too. They all had their shortcomings . . . and their secrets.

They descended the stairs.

"It's open," Kenna said when they were almost down to the parlor.

Sure enough, the front door was cracked, exactly as they left it when they first entered the evil house.

Kiara pulled her necklace over her head and dropped it to the floor at the base of the steps.

As the others exited, Chase couldn't resist the urge to glance back. He felt like Lot's wife—freezing momentarily—when he saw Tanya's lifeless body dangling from the end of the rope. It was an image he would never scrub from his mind—as were so many others that night.

He stepped out onto the porch. One thing was certain, *nothing* the future held for him would ever be this bad again. Everything could only get better. He reached down and took Kenna's hand, lacing her fingers between his. It was better already.

EPILOGUE

Paul held flowers in one hand and Kiara's hand in his other as he stared down at the headstone marking the last place Tanya's body would ever go. It had been exactly a year since the last time he saw her alive.

Chase and Kenna were engaged and would be married in the spring. He would ask Kiara soon, but first he had something to do.

After lunch they returned to their apartment.

"I need to run to the Wal-Mart," Paul said. "Back in a bit."

Fortunately, no one volunteered to tag along.

He wasn't exactly lying. He did need to hit the store first. While there, he picked up a couple five-gallon red plastic gas cans. He filled them up at the gas pumps outside, then headed for Dead Town. Paul drove in silence, the radio off, the window cracked just a bit to release the smoke from his cigarette and the strong odor of gasoline.

After he parked on the side of the road, he got out and lugged both cans toward the house. No one would ever fall prey to that trap again.

The house looked exactly as it did a year ago, but scarier. His heart throbbed in his ears as he approached the front door. There was no way he was going back in, even though the door was open, almost encouraging him to enter. He assumed the coroner or police neglected to shut it on their way out after retrieving the bodies.

Paul sloshed gasoline all over the walls and windows. He slung as much as he could—as deep as he could—into the parlor. When the first gas can was a little less than half-full, he tossed it deep into the house, hoping it would feed the flames. He opened the second can and flung more all over the porch and columns. He poured a line down the stairs, then threw the can through the open door.

As he pulled out his lighter, he looked up.

"Burn, bitch!" he said.

He lit the gasoline on the bottom step and flames shot up, engulfing the porch.

Inside the doorway, stood two figures—James Thornton and Layla Vanderhoff.

Paul watched and grinned.

You're going to get yours now, he thought.

The door and all the shutters slammed shut.

Within a couple minutes, the gasoline had burned off. The house stood unmarred. Not even smoke from the flames tainted the white walls.

As the shutters and door reopened, the spectral couple stood motionless, grinning back at him . . .

Thank You

As a member of the Keller Falls Chamber of Corpses, I would like to thank you for visiting Keller Falls and Dead Town. I hope you enjoyed your stay.

Like most death traps, we can always use more victims. It would be greatly appreciated if you would take a moment to review your time here on mental travel sites like Amazon and Good Reads. Even if you want to complain there was too much or too little killing going on. Positive and negative reviews will all be read and considered so we can make sure your next trip back is even better.

Until we kill again, thanks,

-CN

About the Author

Cal lives in north Alabama with his wife, Rottweiler, Yorkie, two cats and several laying hens. He graduated from the University of Alabama having studied English, concentrating in Creative Writing, after deciding his original Physics major wasn't for him. He has lived all over the country, including Illinois, California, Arizona, Florida, and Georgia, but Alabama will always be *home*.

To learn more about him or other works in progress, check out his website at CalNoble.com. Feel free to e-mail him with questions, complaints, or compliments at Cal@calnoble.com.

www.ingramcontent.com/pod-product-compliance
Lightning Source LLC
Chambersburg PA
CBHW021503110726
47899CB00001BA/278